Jane Hennigan

TOXXIC

**ANGRY
ROBOT**

ANGRY ROBOT
An imprint of Watkins Media Ltd

Unit 11, Shepperton House
89 Shepperton Road
London N1 3DF
UK

angryrobotbooks.com
twitter.com/angryrobotbooks
Goodbye Matriarchy

An Angry Robot paperback original, 2024

Cover by Sarah O'Flaherty
Edited by Eleanor Teasdale and Alice Abrams
Set in Meridien

ISBN 978 1 91520 271 0
Ebook ISBN 978 1 91520 272 7

Printed and bound in the United Kingdom by TJ Books.

9 8 7 6 5 4 3 2 1

MIX
Paper from
responsible sources
FSC   FSC® C013056
www.fsc.org

To my husband, James, who loves me – despite the fact I spend my time creating worlds where all the men die or go insane.

RECAP

"Out they came, away from natural predators, nesting in damp corners and in the tops of trees, crossbreeding with common cousins and laying thousands upon thousands of eggs. Then… the eggs hatched and an army of hungry caterpillars spread their tiny toxic threads on every breath of wind."

Mary drifts in and out of a moth-induced coma, having succumbed to the huge amount of toxin produced by the moths in their annual mating eclipse. As she sleeps, she dreams of her sons: Ryan, who was a teenager in the first infestation, who she saved back then by swapping his wristband, condemning another boy to death in his stead. Ryan, whom she called Nicky and pretended was not a relation so she could visit him at the sanitorium where he was infected, addled, violent. She cries out in her sleep, reliving the horror as the sanitorium burns, and she watches on, paralysed, unable to save him from the flames.

She pictures her younger son, Nathan, so similar in looks and build to her late husband, unsure of himself in a room full of women, subject to their desires, lacking agency. She remembers fleeing with him and an ex-facility resident, Logan, trusting Sophia with the secret of the vaccine, the secret her friend Olivia died to protect.

She dreams of Tony, her favourite resident. Sweet, naïve, Tony, still locked inside the facility, with his nose pressed up to the glass in the viewing room, and wonders what he will say when he finds out that his love Logan is not dead.

She struggles to wake then – but her mind is muddled, and she cannot catch her thoughts; like minnows in a stream they dart from her grasp.

One thought remains as she slips further away, cocooning her mind in sticky threads. Is the world ready for a vaccine? One which allows men to once more walk free?

Did she do the right thing?

CHAPTER 1

XX104

One day, a long time from now, people might ask *why*.

Why did we choose the method we chose – why did I do these terrible things? But those people, those women, will ask such questions from a place of safety. Those *women* will be in command of their lives, free to live and look as they wish. Those women will not have to check their bodies against a list of standards nor feel the grasping fingers of a man's ego choke off their words. They will be central to their own lives.

The hard truth is that the men in the facilities are not men. Your generation doesn't know what a man is. You may have learned about them at school, maybe even had a visitation with one, sipping cheap wine and giggling about the strangeness of it all. But those mild-mannered boys with soft hands and shaved heads are not the real thing. They're a dormant version. When the moths came, they didn't just infect the men, they revealed their true and complete nature. They worked together to hunt us during those first days of the outbreak. Something glossed over in schools is the sexual violence. The infected, the Manics as they're known, violated women's bodies before slaughtering them.

But men are not like that now! I hear the liberals call as they wring their hands and offer up their daughters as sacrificial lambs. *We have a vaccine!*

Yes – we have a vaccine. We may never see another Manic again – *if it works.*

But it's not the Manics whom I fear. It's the men, the uninfected men. How long before we're back to where we were? Forcing ourselves and our daughters into grotesque shapes to please the greedy eyes of men, pretending that we have it all, when really we work twice as hard for half the reward. Oh, but you don't know what I'm talking about. You have only known this world – a hard existence, but a safe one. A *fair* one.

Perhaps, if I explain, I'll become a person to you, not the monster Union State radio would have you believe me to be. Or maybe you'll diagnose me – *the trauma of the infestation made her do it.* Then you can label me *damaged,* condemn me gently whilst offering excuses. All so *understandable…* It would have made a good TV show – if such a thing still existed.

All this conveniently overlooks the fact that you live in the freedom I protected. One I fought for – literally fought. Despite how unfashionable it is to talk about the time before, my story deserves to be told. And I know things about men – things that you, who've grown up without them, couldn't possibly know. I stand in the breach so you can live – because that and so much more is what this vaccination will take from you.

I've decided that, if I can make you understand what it was like before, and what happened that summer in London, at Waterloo, four decades ago, then you might not rush to condemn me. You may not agree, but at least you will understand why I have done the terrible things I have.

Tony

Dear Mary

They said you're sick, so I thought I'd cheer you up with a letter. Sorry about the paper – this crackly stuff is all they'd give us, thread-

proof they say. You remember it. My handwriting is getting better, at least.

So many things have happened around here, you wouldn't believe it. Yesterday, Artemis – from E-block – said loudly and in front of everyone that one carer – Lillian – had been familiar with him, without his permission, and not on a visitation day. That was the word he used: familiar. *Everyone was amazed. Lillian was furious. She replied that Artemis was mistaken and that she was just trying to be nice to him, and he was exaggerating. This argument happened over breakfast three days ago, and everyone is still talking about it. The thing is, Lillian has disappeared. She's not on the rota, no one has seen her on the rounds – we think she left. Artemis is being tight-lipped over the whole thing. He blushed and shook his head when I tried to get him talking during a gardening session last week.*

The other thing that everyone is talking about, of course, is these rumours of a vaccine. People have been saying – and by people, I mean the carer Isla – there's a way men can actually go outside, out into the air and the sun, that the moth threads won't affect us as long as we take some medicine every month. Isla says that it was you, Mary, that made sure we had a chance at the medicine. If that's true, I'm so proud. The other carers and ward-sisters won't say anything about the medicine and some of them get quite annoyed if I mention it, so I've let it go. But there's an odd fidgetiness with all the women who look after us, lots of shared looks and awkward pauses. When you're locked up your whole life, doing the same thing day in day out, you get a sense of when things are a bit off. Change has a vinegary smell.

Anyway, if it's true, and one day I can go outside, the first thing I'll do is come and see you. I've been practicing my guitar, and I think you'll love one song I've made – it's about Logan. Also, the drama club has been working on an adaptation of The Tempest *– maybe when you're better, you can come back and watch us? It's a crazy idea, but what if we could perform it outside! They offered me Prospero or even Mirando, but I chose Caliban. I like his style: "When I waked, I cried to dream again!"*

Get better soon.

Tony

Evie

Mary hasn't moved in two days. She used to wake up at about lunch time for a few sips of water, perhaps some soup – not anymore, it seems. I ought to get on with other stuff. I've three older women on my round, and one of them, Emma, likes to chat. She's from before and she wants to tell me about what it was like: the aeroplanes, the cities, her favourite sweet-and-sour chicken. I smile and nod. The thing is, when you work in geriatrics, you get this a lot. It's when they start talking about their sons and husbands that most of the girls here find it awkward, or they freak out completely. I was in the nurse's office yesterday, and one of our new girls burst through the door and could barely get her words out. Emma had told the poor girl a story about the first infestation, about how her father had killed her mother in front of her by tying her up with a skipping rope on the kitchen floor, before pouring lighter fluid over her clothes and setting her on fire. These stories can catch you out. I've been doing this for a while now and I sometimes think the dollies sneak these stories in just to see how you react. Anyway, apparently, Emma had gone into the gory details about the smell. No wonder the poor girl freaked out!

The problem is, they don't get taught about it at school these days. Twenty years ago, when I was at school, we learned all about the infestation, the reformation of the government, the fertility and contribution programmes. I remember one social history project, I was about fourteen, when we were taken to the records office in the nearest village, and each given the name of a victim or a family. We had to research them and find out what happened then present our findings to the class. I had the 'Sullivans' and their story was average. The mother survived the initial infestation but succumbed to suicide three years later. An Abidance Unit found her body in woodland on the South Downs way, wrists cut, a small, blood-soaked child's sweater in her arms. That's how they identified her. The sweater had *Marcus Sullivan* sewn into the label. The records officer explained to me that records in the first five years were sketchy. Mr Sullivan died overnight – a so-called 'Blue.' The son was seven years old, and he went manic. It's not known what happened to him, but they suspect it was exposure. That's what got most of the younger boys that didn't get picked up and taken to a sanatorium in time.

There was a picture of them as a family. The original records officers must have taken it from the house shortly after the infestation. It was a big picture, about the size of a book, with a crease at the edge where the frame had bitten into the paper. Melanie Sullivan was wearing a cream shirt and had long, mousy brown hair, parted in the middle, a moony freckled face and plump painted lips. Mr Sullivan had a lean face, very blue eyes, and stubble. Pictures of men are weird. I stared at that photo for ages. It was probably only the second or third time I'd seen the picture of a man's face and I marvelled at all that extra hair. I wanted to reach in and run my fingers over the dark shadow. Was it soft like the hair on my head or thicker like the hair on my legs?

The boy in the picture, Marcus, was a freckly faced kid. He was pretty, a bit babyish for seven years old, but not that different from the girls in the village. His chubby face was cute and moonish like his mother's, and his eyes were the same bright blue as his father's. He looked lost, like he wasn't used to having his picture taken like this, in some kind of studio. Smiling shyly, he had a mark on his top lip, a smudge of what looked like milk. Why hadn't the photographer got him to wipe his face?

I got permission from the office to take a copy of the picture – black and white, of course – so I could include it in my presentation. I snuck it home and stared and stared at Mr Sullivan's face. I still have it hidden in my dresser, and now and then I slip it out and just look at the young boy's cute half-smile and Mr Sullivan's stubble.

Sean was his name… Sean Sullivan.

My friend Bankie got an interesting family, the Couzins. I'll never forget the story. Mr Couzins went manic and tied up his wife and their sixteen year-old daughter. Then he drove them to a nearby cathedral. He made them climb all two hundred and fifty steps before pushing them off the top. An hour later, probably suffering from a moment of horrified lucidity, he jumped off himself. Bankie's presentation was by far the most interesting, but she didn't have any photos, so at least I won on that front. These are all horrible stories, of course, but that was so long ago. Even when I look at Sean's picture, I don't think it's real. Just a cold detail of history. But there's something that draws me back to the image hidden in my bottom drawer, some fascination with this strange old-fashioned family.

But since my school days, the syllabus has changed. I mean, it was always heavily skewed towards science, but now they study social engineering, civil logistics, agricultural and marine development, genetic research and so much more. There just isn't the space in the timetable for history. Which is all very well – until a young nurse turns up in the staff room hyperventilating because a patient has told them a story about a woman being cooked alive on the kitchen floor.

XX104

Last year I followed the Harting case on Union State radio.

I saw her once, about forty years ago. After Waterloo, they drafted me into the communication corps at a base near York, running comms for one hundred and fifty women as they went out to round up survivors of the first wave. She visited our barracks, spoke for an hour about her vision for the future, about how we needed to work together to create a new world. We hung on her every word, desperate to make any sense of the chaos outside. And now to find she'd created a vaccine, used it to create a personal harem and a club for powerful women to 'unwind'. I, like many others of my age, felt torn between the love we felt for our saviour and the shame of what she'd done. I don't think she should have been exiled, though. Not after everything she did for us before. We wouldn't have survived without her.

The existence of a vaccine was the worst part. Some retired carer had given the formula, along with proof, to the Council and now it was out there. It was something I'd been thinking about for years – like the sword of Damocles hanging over us all. As I watched society's ideas change from the embarrassment and indignity of the sire houses at the beginning – those women who volunteered to become pregnant when the only option was have sex with an infected at a sanatorium – to the insemination programmes that came after, followed by the hetero-recreation visits. I knew what was coming. Men went from being monsters, to a necessary evil, and eventually becoming a novelty, a rich woman's pastime. It seemed inevitable that one day some bright spark in a laboratory would come up with a cure, and what then? Cold anger gripped me at the idea – the men lost their right to freedom that hot summer at Waterloo station, over forty years ago.

The Women's Conservation Society seemed the obvious choice as allies to our cause. A network of women committed to protecting the way of life developed just after the infestation. They had a chapter in most regions of the Union, campaigning against hetero-recreational visits, decrying the large amounts of Council funding channelled into facility improvement, and objecting to boys' education in prep houses. They'd long spoken out about the purity of our society, some going as far as to suggest parthenogenesis – reproduction without sperm – was the future.

It wasn't hard to find a local chapter, and three months ago, I went to my first meeting in the backroom of an old flooring warehouse. To say I was disappointed was an understatement.

I had visions of a well-organised campaign headquarters, teams of enthusiastic young activists ready to take to the streets and win over the hearts and minds of communities and espouse the dangers of integration. What I found was three old women sitting at an old desk in a musty, cramped office, three little white heads like three stalks of cauliflower, shuffling a pile of dog-eared leaflets. All three peered at me with suspicion. Behind them in the grim brown room lay a confusion of files and papers, even a few rolls of ancient carpet stuffed in the corner. Beyond that, a kitchenette awash with tea-stained cups and dirty tea towels. The whole place smelt of damp and rotting rubber.

"Hi," I began tentatively, "Am I in the right place? I'm looking for the regional headquarters for the WCS."

The three women said nothing, just exchanged a few glances.

I tried again. "My name's –"

"No!" one woman sitting at the table snapped. "We don't use names anymore, only codes. 19" – she pointed to herself – "29" – she pointed to a woman on her right who was knitting – "and 62. Since the Council has come out as a bunch of *manfans*, the organisation has had to adapt. I'm sure you understand."

"Oh," I replied. "Yes, I do. I'd like to help if I can."

"Really?" number 19 raised her eyebrows. "Cos you look like one of those hand-wringing liberals. You can't have been that old when it all happened."

My eyes fell on the leaflets. "Where did they come from?" I asked. They were terrible – I could tell from three feet away, cheap looking with no headlines, no strong message, just black and white pages with huge blocks of blurry text.

"Head office," she replied. "They arrived yesterday. It's our job to get the message out there."

"Where is it? Head office?"

"I'm not telling you. I don't know you. You could be an Abidance agent, undercover. You could be sent from the Council."

I nearly said it then – *I'll tell you who I am, I'm one of the survivors of Waterloo, I watched women being torn apart. And when faced with the threat of a vaccine, I think your set up here is woefully inadequate.* But instead, I smiled my best smile. "I'm sorry. Of course, you need to get to know me. I believe men have their place in this world, just not anywhere near me or my family. I'm worried that by introducing men into society, we risk destabilising our culture."

My words had the desired effect and 19 visibly thawed. "Yes, so what we will need is for women to deliver the leaflets to a list of addresses that we think may be more receptive to the ideas of our movement. We're a bit long in the tooth for traipsing about, but you look strong enough. In the prime of your life, eh?" She winked. "I bet you could go out a few nights this week. Unless you have family commitments, of course."

I had no family commitments. My wife spent most of her time working. Neither of us wanted any children.

I smiled wider. "Oh, I'm sure my wife won't mind. By the way, does The Women's Conservation Society have a radio station?"

The women looked at each other, their faces stretching into blank expressions. "I guess it's something that head office might consider, if they knew someone who could set it up," said 19 dismissively, before pushing the pile of pamphlets towards me. "I'll get you a list of addresses. Do you have a bike?"

I nodded.

"Good. You should start right away."

"No problem," I replied, taking the smudged pamphlets. "Should I make you all some tea before I go?" I gestured to the small kitchenette. "You look like you've been working for a while."

All three women smiled.

Two weeks later, I visited the head office in the Citadel to tell them about my plans.

Tony

Dear Mary,

Don't worry about not replying, I'm sure you are busy getting better. I wanted to tell you some amazing news! Two men from our facility have been chosen to take the vaccine – just two – and I'm one of them! The day after tomorrow, I'm going to have an injection and then they say I can go outside. Apparently, after that, we can't stay at the facility (all this filtered air and anti-thread security would be wasted on us, and our rooms are needed for other men). We're not sure where we'll be taken, and I'm a bit nervous, I mean I've been in facilities since leaving the prep house at eighteen – ten years is a long time to go through the same routines every day. So, just the idea of going anywhere is worrisome. But it's exciting Mary, I really can't believe it.

Artemis has also been picked, which is a surprise. He's having a hard time at the moment. Some of the carers won't talk to him because of the things he said about Lilian, and the other men are avoiding him in case being seen with him suggests they believe him. The thing is that some of us do believe him. Sometimes, certain women want you to rub their arms and thighs. At the prep houses, one carer asked the teenage boys to kiss her on the mouth, like at visitation sessions. Some boys liked it, not me of course – you know how I feel about women's bodies – urgh. Anyway, we all know it happens, and, if you're friendly and cheerful about it, the women can make your life a lot easier. On the other hand, if, like Artemis, you shout out in the cafeteria that a woman has been too familiar, then they can make your life a lot harder. So, it's strange, isn't it Mary, that he's been picked for this honour?

But I'll not worry about that, Mary. I'm off, like Gulliver, like Prospero, out into the wide world – or will I be Mirando? Forever proclaiming in awe: O, wonder! – How many goodly creatures are there here!

I'll miss Isla. Of all the carers, she's my favourite (apart from you, of course!). I even saw her sneaking an extra piece of apple fritter to Artemis after his laundry shift, which I think was nice.

A really weird thing happened. When I told Old Nord about the vaccine, he begged me not to take it. Not because he wanted to go in my place – he's adamant that he will never take the vaccine – but because he thinks that it's not what they say it is. He says it's a trap, that me and the others are being experimented on and that we're going to die. Or worse, the vaccine simply doesn't work, and we were going to get infected by threads and end up raving and dribbling at a sanatorium. They were all muttering when we did our grooming before bed, talking about whether they were going to take the vaccine when they got called. I'm not even sure they have a choice.

Anyway, I don't know when I'll be able to write you another letter. I don't know where I'm going after I've had the vaccine. Anyway, I'll keep thinking of things to write to you, so I can send a nice long letter as soon as I get the chance.

Love,

Tony

CHAPTER 2

Evie

I usually avoid volunteering for things. Even at school, I'd blend into the background when they were looking for banner girls for Memorial Day or soloists for the midwinter choir, I stood at the back and mouthed along whilst wishing for the whole thing to be over.

So I surprised myself by deciding to attend an MWA integration and fostering meeting, to learn more about the upcoming arrivals. The MWA – the Men's Welfare Association – has come under attack recently. Its famous – now infamous – head, Jen Harting, has recently been sentenced to deportation for violence against men, human trafficking, medicinal treason, and a bewildering number of other crimes.

My comatose patient, Mary, had a hand in bringing her down. She talked about it before she lapsed into unconsciousness. That and her sons. Perhaps that's why I went this evening. Maybe Mary's words had had an effect.

It was thought Harting might get a reduced sentence, a rehabilitation centre, perhaps, due to how instrumental she was in the building of the Union. But the testimony offered, and the sheer scale of her transgressions, meant that deportation was inevitable.

Spain probably – it might as well be a death sentence.

There were a few dissenting voices when Harting was sentenced. The Women's Conservation Society had plenty to say – the ones who wanted to get rid of men even before the vaccine was discovered. They think Harting's a hero, a martyr to their cause. The rumour is that they've even started their own radio station – *XXFM*. Last market day I overheard a few women in Eastor whispering about it.

So there I stood on a damp autumn evening, just outside the Eastor village hall door, dithering about whether to go into the meeting or to abandon the whole enterprise, when from behind me, a voice said, "Evie! How wonderful to see you here!"

I jumped around like a kid caught stealing honeycomb to find the beaming smile of Molly Coombs.

Her smile was so enthusiastic that it was difficult to look directly into her gaze. "Hi Molly, I didn't realise this was your thing," I mumbled, although it was no surprise to see her here. Ever since we'd been at school, she'd joined everything and anything: school maths club, young engineering group, debating society. When we'd left school: PTA, Recycling Association, Law Abidance Volunteers, Remembrance Day Committee. Molly even sewed the costumes for the Eastor and Stevenage amateur dramatic society. That was all alongside raising four girls and running a successful smallholding. Sam, her partner, was an odd fish, older than me and Molly, born at least twenty years before the first wave. Sam had a hard time of it on all accounts. Something to do with the army rounding up certain groups of people and sending them to secret sites for their own protection. It was all very hush hush – like many things that happened at that time. It was also rumoured that Molly had contributed twice to gain the good arable land down by the stream, that two of her daughters had shared a womb with a twin brother. Two sons offered up to The Union – a noble sacrifice.

I was out of my depth, and I wanted to go home. The street

lighting wouldn't be turned on for another few weeks, and the September evening was cool and gloomy. Mae had brought me back a pile of books from her trip to the Citadel and I could have been at home, curled up by the fire, reading about the history of the Egyptian empire, or military tactics in the South Pacific. Being here was a mistake. I was about to make my excuses – *I was just taking a stroll, wondered what all the fuss was about. Not my cup of tea but you have a good evening…*

But then Molly's voice dipped to a conspiratorial whisper. "I'm surprised Mae signed off on this – what with her, you know, views on children…" She let the words trail off. Her smile dimmed and her eyes shifted down. Was it an expression of pity?

Damn village nosiness. Perhaps Mae was right. Maybe we should move to the Citadel, where no one gets up in your business. "Mae's fine with it – it was her idea, in fact." The lie rose into the cool evening air on a puff of ghostly breath. I don't know why I felt the need to lie to Molly. She might be on every committee in a three-mile radius and a terrible gossip, but she was harmless. And it wasn't like Mae needed protecting.

Molly raised her eyebrows a fraction, but then her smile returned. "Well, that's amazing, Evie. I'm so happy for you."

"I mean, I'm just looking into it. They won't place one with me, anyway. I haven't got any experience." I was backpedalling now as Molly led me through into the main hall. "I think they're looking for families with children already…"

The meeting had started, so nobody noticed a pair of latecomers. An overhead projector whirred at the front of the hall, casting words onto the white wall: *Integration – what it means to foster.* However, none of the fifty members of the audience were paying it any mind, nor, it seemed, listening as the amplified voice of a middle-aged woman with grey curly hair, dressed in a heavy woollen dress, was trying to regain the attention of the muttering crowd by waving her arms and crying *one at a time!* I recognised the woman as Anita Swift. A long-time resident of Eastor, she worked in a bicycle repair shop in the village and was married to Dr Rosya who worked at my hospital. Dr Rosya had mentioned that she was some kind of liaison officer in the local council.

The atmosphere was riotous. I sneaked a look at Molly, standing next to me at the back, but her face was unreadable as she scanned the chairs, all with their backs to us, and shuffled us towards the two nearest empty ones.

"I was afraid this might happen," she whispered as we sat. "The Citadel think they can make these decisions without fully consulting everyone involved."

What happens if the vaccine doesn't work? This, a shout from a gaunt-looking sandy-haired woman at the front, wrestling a fractious toddler on her lap.

Other shouts joined it – *Why here in Eastor? – Why not send them to Greenlake or Stevenage? – Will we be allocated extra energy rations? Will my daughters be safe?*

From the low stage at the front, Anita looked harried and completely unprepared. "The vaccine has been shown to be one hundred per cent effective when taken properly." Despite her microphone, her voice was almost drowned out by the crowd, some of them standing now – *What are the incentives? – Will the older ones work on the land? – Who will train them? – What if we don't want them here?*

I was just settling into my seat when the door behind us slammed, causing a shot of adrenaline to course through me. I was gratified to see that Molly, too, jumped a little. We all turned our heads to see which neighbour had caused such a disturbance. But it was a stranger, a very tall woman with severely short dark hair, peppered with grey. Dressed in a tailored suit, her leather brogues were buffed to a reflected gleam. As she walked up the gap between the two banks of chairs, silence descended upon the audience, punctuated only by the hard clicks as her soles struck the wooden floor.

"Ah," Anita was visibly relieved at her arrival. "This is Freya

Curtis, everyone. She will be living here in Eastor with us and overseeing the integration process."

The crowd fidgeted as they watched her walk to the front, but the chaotic demands from before did not resume.

The tall woman ascended three wooden steps to the raised area and turned to face the crowd. "Thank you, Anita." She took the hand-held microphone from the other woman.

Then the smartly dressed woman stepped forward, her eyes boring down from the dais into the unlucky faces of the women in the first few rows. "You have questions. That's understandable." Her tone had an edge to it, like cracking ice. Although she hadn't spoken any louder than Anita, her words seemed to echo round the draughty hall.

Another murmur rose from the crowd, muted this time.

"I will answer your questions." She paused, and the crowd stilled. "But before I do, I want you to know this…" The silence that settled was keen and absolute. "… I lived through the first infestation. I am fully aware of what men are capable of." A longer pause as her eyes scanned the women before her. "I survived Waterloo."

This last statement landed on the crowd, in the way it was intended, like a blacksmith's anvil dropped from above. I took in a quick breath and noticed that Molly's hand had crept up to her chest and she was clutching her pendant in a fist, her eyes wide with surprise.

Ms Curtis nodded, accepting the sound of awe that was her due. "So you can trust me when I say I would rather *die* than allow a member of this community to come to harm at the hands of a man."

No one argued. No one spoke. The last syllable resounded around the hall. I pondered the woman's words. She couldn't have been very old when she fought at Waterloo. Despite her greying hair and her severe suit, she couldn't be any more than what? In her fifties perhaps? which would make her, at the very most, a teenager forty-three years ago. Then I felt a small stab of shame. Who was I, a woman who lived only by the grace and strength of such women, to question her credentials? The MWA had obviously checked her and sent her here, it's not like you could lie about such things.

After Freya Curtis's speech, the meeting continued in a more orderly manner. Anita went through a bewildering number of slides on safety precautions, land incentives (woodland to the west and some derelict farmhouses, plus seven acres of pasture), educational incentives – a full scholarship for a member of each participating family at either engineering or agriculture technology school or a non-resident teaching course. These were valuable incentives indeed, and I noticed Molly sit a little straighter in her chair. Hardly surprising, four daughters, one of whom, Eloise, at nearly eighteen, was some kind of genius and won a national science prize last year. Molly had talked about it non-stop every time we met.

Anita talked about training for foster homes, the additional energy rations, clothing, and travel tokens. All listened keenly as it was explained that each chosen foster family would be allocated not one but two fosterlings – a boy from a prep house and a man from a facility. Some kind of buddy system. Any time a member of the audience asked a tough question, Anita deferred to Freya Curtis, who offered assurances on safety and protection protocols. By the end, most of the women were nodding. Only one or two still looked dubious, shaking their heads and muttering under their breath. But they didn't make their objections known.

Finally, it was time for the sign-ups. The clipboard came to me, its stubby pencil worn down to almost nothing, so it was difficult to hold on to. I nearly didn't sign it – there was no way Mae would go for it anyway, so what was the point? But Molly was watching, and I couldn't bring myself to prove her right.

So, I signed it, scribbling my name and ID number underneath a list of at least forty other names. I consoled myself with the thought that they only needed a handful of foster families – I mean, what were the chances they'd pick me?

XX104

By the time I visited the Women's Conservative Society head office, it had already become XX HQ.

The building, in a redeveloped chapel on the outskirts of the Citadel, was a far cry from the old carpet warehouse. Apparently, a rich donor with views sympathetic to those of the XX had been funding the movement and funding it well, by the looks of the sleek modern furniture and polished wooden floors. At least ten women were spread around the open-plan office, on phones, scribbling on pads of paper. There was even a reclaimed computer on one of the desks, its screen casting an eerie white glow onto the face of a young earnest-looking woman tapping on the keyboard. A fax machine was busy spitting out paper on a reel. There was a sign on the wall – Citadel Consultants and Ethical Advisory Service. A front, I suspected, for an organisation of which the Council would not approve. The idea gave me a fizz of excitement, and something else – a sense of rightness, the relief that finally someone was saying what needed to be said. Too long had I kept my thoughts to myself, when the visitation programs came along, even when the beginnings of the New Union had introduced the concepts of facilities and prep houses right back at the beginning. It would have been better if we just allowed the boys to become infected and kept them in sanatoriums, better still, sedated. And here, finally, women were making a stand.

They led me through a large, locked oak door into another smaller room. Women of all ages, from mid-twenties upwards were designing posters and tee shirts. *Manfans make bad plans! There's no Y in Future. Safety before Ideology! Nature knows best –*

this one with a picture of a moth in the O of knows. They were chatting as they painted, and no one looked up as I was led in.

A woman in her thirties, wearing an apron over a silky kaftan, put down her paintbrush and approached me. "Ahh, you must be the one who sent me the plans for the radio – fantastic idea. We can only go so far with pamphlets. Such a detailed plan. I was so impressed. Have you been assigned a number?"

I nodded, warmed to my core by her words. "104."

"Excellent, 104. Well, I'm Two. It's wonderful to meet you. Come." She untied the apron and led me through a set of glass doors and into a small office. As the doors closed the noise of the chatter from outside dimmed. She gestured to a leather chair and sat facing me on the other side of a wall desk.

"Will you be able to set it all up, do you think?" She poured a glass of something clear that smelt of lemons and handed it to me.

I wanted to ask what it was, but I felt my acceptance was a kind of test. I sipped the liquid; it reminded me of old-fashioned sherbet but with a hefty kick. I tried not to grimace. "Yes – I mean, I'll need equipment, people to help."

She waved at me, "Fine, fine, whatever you need. And will you be presenting on the radio?"

I nearly laughed out loud. "Goodness me, no! I am strictly technical – you'll need to get someone who likes that set of things. I'm more of a background person."

Two looked thoughtful. "I have someone in mind. A woman with similar views to our own, one who used to do a lot of stuff on the Internet before everything went crazy. An influencer if you remember such things." She knocked back the drink and poured another. I still sat nursing my first.

"Now," she said, folding her hands on the desk. "Tell me about this radio idea."

I was sixteen, almost seventeen, when the world changed. And, despite the horror, I consider myself lucky. The world before the infestation was worse for me than the one just after. I was afraid all the time back then. Afraid I'd say the wrong thing, or not say the right thing, afraid of sending out the wrong signals, of being the centre of attention, or worse, of being ignored; of being too much, or not enough – it was exhausting.

Teenage girls of today have little to fear, with their smooth earnest faces and their strength of purpose – they know their place and take up as much space as they wish. Girls are taught to change the world for the betterment of their sisters, develop new energy systems, science, technology, agriculture, marry a good woman, raise strong daughters. Contribute.

Sorority, maternity, and thrift – the mantra pledged in schools every day.

But that was not how it was for the daughters of the old world.

Back then, I navigated a thousand messages an hour. And most of them told me I was the one who had to change, that there was something fundamentally inadequate about me. But I took pains to understand the messages sent to me, to decode them. I wanted to work in media, TV, maybe, not news. Something to do with lifestyle or advertising. I was obsessed with click-bait, the drive to click on some things and not others.

It started on a Thursday – I know because Thursdays were the only days I had to be into college early. Despite this, I'd missed my usual bus and was standing at the stop, waiting for the next, scrolling on my mobile. I know you won't recognise some of the things I say – you may have to ask your grandmothers. But just this once: A mobile was a small wireless phone with many ways to communicate, not just talking. You could listen to music, play games, take photos.

In the immediate aftermath, when everything changed, everyone wanted their mobile phones back, wanted the Internet. But every drop of energy was precious, needed for immediate needs, heat, medical, repairs. We barely managed to get the power back in some areas after months of effort, and even then, it wasn't stable. Some engineers got a few local servers up and running, but without being connected to other servers, the information was pitiful, limited. The Internet is a tool of connection – there just weren't enough working computers to connect to make it worth it.

Finally, even if we'd somehow managed to get everything up and running, our phones would eventually stop working. The batteries wouldn't last forever, and we had no way of making new ones – no lithium. So, in the end we had to accept that bringing back the Internet wasn't possible.

It's hard to explain to those raised in the Union how important phones were to us before, so many other things were different. For example, how, as a teenage girl, waiting alone for the sixth form bus, you were exposed. It felt like just existing invited the wrong kind of attention. But having your nose ten centimetres from the mobile screen, wearing headphones, offered protection. Most of the time.

I looked up, suddenly aware of movement. Three boys about my age had arrived at the bus stop. Two sat on the pull-down seats, hunched over in black puffy jackets, hair short, trainers sitting like fat bricks at the end of their skinny jeans. The other leaned against the lamppost at the front of the stop, his arms folded. None of them looked at their phones. Three – not good. Most boys were okay on their own. In twos, they could be a bit annoying. In groups of three or more, sometimes they had an energy, like everything was a dare.

I fixed my eyes on my screen, whilst a song played through my earbuds, a new TikTok star my friend Kari had recommended. The news I was scrolling through was an almost continuous list of panic-inducing headlines, black on red: *BREAKING* – a story about a gang of men in Mexico going crazy – 76 women, raped and strangled and then dumped at a Mexican industrial estate, just across the Rio Bravo. I flicked to another site – *How to make the perfect Spanish omelette.* Flick – *How to protect your drink from being spiked and what to do if it happens…* flick… *Losing all that lockdown weight – 5 tips!* I clicked on one of my favourite YouTube channels, *Kuda Kottan* had just released a new video, and I settled to watch her demonstrate an easy smoky eye. She had a great voice – calm, soft, personal. If I were to ever work in front of the camera, that's the sort of voice I'd need. But I was nowhere near pretty enough to do what she did. No matter how much cleverly applied makeup I wore. Radio perhaps?

I felt a tug on my jacket. The boy pointed to his ears, silently asking for me to take out my buds. I didn't want to, but I did. I didn't want to seem rude.

"What's your name?" He was too close to me, and his breath smelled of chewing gum.

"Amber." I lied.

The boy grinned. "Well, Amber, my friend Nathan over there, wants to know if you'll wank him off." He jabbed his thumb over his shoulder at one of the other boys, who was laughing. The other boy made a pumping fist gesture.

I tried not to show my shock, but it must have shown on my face as all three boys laughed harder. I turned away, not sure whether I should put my earbuds back in (better to ignore them) or keep all my senses clear (better to know what's going on in case I need to run).

"Ahh, don't be like that," said the boy nearest to me. "We're just messing with you."

I stayed quiet, embarrassment smothering my anger.

"Can I have your number?"

I shook my head and crossed my arms over my chest. Just then, another boy came and stood at the bus stop who I recognised as a fellow regular passenger, although we'd never spoken. He looked at the four of us, then stood as far away from me and the boys as he could, searching through his bag, no doubt for his headphones.

"Are you frigid, then?" The boy on the seat at the bus stop called across.

That old trap. There was no right answer. I looked over to

the other boy, the one that had just arrived. I don't know what I was hoping for – a saviour? But in some ways, he was in as much danger as me, one lone skinny boy. I saw a flash of pity on his face as he caught my eye, but then he donned his earphones and stared down at his screen.

"She's ugly anyway," said Nathan coming over to us. "I wouldn't want her to wank me off with that face."

And you know what I felt at that moment? Beneath the rage and the shame? Failure. I know how that sounds and I know that any teenage girl of the New Union would have no idea why. But there it is. I was supposed to please men. I was never explicitly told this, that my self-worth depended on acceptance by a man – any man. But I remember clearly that I felt both disgust for these boys and a small spark of wanting them to like me. How insane. These boys! These assholes making me feel small and unworthy. I was explicitly told a hundred times a day, by teachers, by parents, by social media, to hold my head up high, that I could be anything I wanted, that the old gender divisions no longer mattered. But I was also told, implicitly, how I was supposed to look, act, feel as the "right type of girl". *At least they noticed you!* A voice whispered in my mind. It was exhausting holding these two imperatives in my mind all the time back then.

The bus arrived. I sat on my own at the front and put my earbuds back in, all the while feeling the hungry, mocking stare of the three boys on the back of my neck.

Later, at college, Kari, Oscar, and I were sitting in the canteen waiting for third period, sharing a portion of chips. I thought about telling them about the boys at the bus stop. But I didn't. What could I say? That I was hassled by some boys? I also knew that Kari would never have put up with it – she would have told them off, shouted them down, reported them. And she'd be disappointed in me for not doing the same. But reporting them, that would have been a whole big thing, and they didn't actually touch me – so was it that bad? Anyway, they wouldn't have hassled Kari, with her wildly dyed hair and assortment of nose rings. Oscar would have been more understanding. He always tried to understand, but what could he say?

"Have you heard about the attacks?" Kari asked, dipping a chip in a blob of ketchup. "In South America and Germany? They think it's some new drug that people are taking, men mostly. Makes them go insane."

"No," I replied, checking my phone. "Oh, I might have read something about a load of women murdered in Brazil or somewhere."

"That's all the world needs," added Oscar, hunching his shoulders and leaning his elbows on the table. "A drug that makes men even bigger assholes. Now if they could come up with a drug that made them less likely to jump you in a bathroom and chuck your sandwiches in the toilet..." Oscar had been bullied at his last school. Badly.

"It wouldn't matter," replied Kari. "Nobody would take it. Their perspective is ingrained, supported by our language, by the power of institutions, by –" Oscar and I shared a quick look, he rolled his eyes, and I suppressed a grin. We both loved Kari, but once she started, she could go on for ages.

My mind flicked back to the bus stop, to the other boy and that look of pity he'd given me. Then I looked at Oscar, dutifully nodding along to Kari's tirade. Not all boys, I thought. But I didn't say it. Kari was warming to her subject. Soon she'd move on to the environmental disaster and the consequences of consumerism. Oscar and I were saved by the bell.

"Double sociology," Kari said, getting up and grabbing her bag. "You coming to Oscar's house later?"

"I've got to go to my dad's for the weekend. Leaving after college tonight."

Oscar grimaced. "That sucks."

"I know."

"We'll see you on Monday though, yeah?" Kari finished the last chip and picked up the tray.

I nodded and grabbed my backpack, heading off to media studies. "Monday."

That was the last time anything in this world was normal, the last time I ever felt like I had any understanding of what the future might hold. It was the last time I felt young and protected and safe.

It was also the last time I ever saw Kari and Oscar.

Tony

Will this be the last time I ever see my friends? My dorm-brothers?

When I left the prep house to come to the facility nine years ago, I was eighteen years old. I was afraid, but as the carers told me, there wasn't much of a difference. Preps have more rules, but they're basically the same as facilities. I came up with a few boys from my house, so after a few weeks, it was like I'd always lived here. And I like it. I mean, there was the time I tried to jump out of the window, and the incident in the shower with the bedsheet, but for the most part, it's nice, safe, familiar. They don't make me take part in the visitations. They tried, but I just couldn't, you know, perform.

But now I'm faced with leaving, and I'm finding it hard.

I tried to talk to Artemis about it, but I shouldn't have bothered.

"You're locked up all day," was his reply. "The women get to go home, and you don't. You've no choice about when you go to bed, when to eat, what to eat. The women feel they can maul you whenever they want to – how can that be hard to leave?"

I didn't answer. He always seems angry. For example, yesterday at the carer's station, the little alcove in the corridor where the carers spend their shifts sipping tea and chatting, Isla tried to give him some advice. She called us over, especially as we are the only two from this block who will be leaving. I felt special to be singled out, special and excited and afraid. Anyway, she said that when we left, we would do well to listen to the women outside carefully, keep our voices calm and soft and smile as much as possible. We were ambassadors and our behaviour had implications for all men. I took this advice seriously, and I immediately began rehearsing my new role in my head, adding in a few deferential nods for good measure.

But you'd have thought she'd asked Artemis to paint himself green and parade around naked. "I will listen when I wish to listen, and smile when I choose to smile!" His voice was neither calm nor soft.

"Look out for him," Isla said to me, as Artemis stalked off to the recreation room, his silk robes swishing along the floor in angry whispers. I didn't know if she meant I should *look after him* or *beware of what he might do*. I was about to ask when Daisy bustled around the corner. Daisy hates me, and I do everything I can to ensure I am nowhere near her.

I slipped behind the carer's alcove and out of sight.

"Isla, I've been looking for you," the ward sister snapped. "You don't have time to be flirting with the residents, you're needed on B block. Harry's T levels are too high and he's starting fights."

Isla stood up so that Daisy's red face was level with her own. "I set Harry's T levels last week, and they were fine."

"You set them too high. He's jumping about like a kid on midwinter's eve." I knew from experience that there was nothing this ward-sister loved more than to bully someone she considered a *manfan*. That's why she hated Mary so much – Mary cared about us.

"If I set them lower, he gets depression." Isla wasn't backing down, and I loved her for it. Her voice was firm, and her entire posture faced down Daisy's petty puffing.

It was nearing lunchtime and everyone on first serving

would be settling down on the long benches of the refectory, readying for a good meal – a fact my stomach was pointing out with a rally of sharp nudges. But there was no way I was missing this. Anyway, if I made my presence known, as I would surely do by stepping a few paces forward, I would be in more trouble than I could handle. Daisy's voice upped a notch. "I'd rather he moped around in his dorm crying. He's disrupting the entire block. I've had to go and calm things down three times already today." Her voice became defensive and whiny.

"They've been locked up most of the day. No wonder they're a bit high-spirited." Isla's voice, in comparison, was low and unwavering. Then she played her trump card. "If I lower his T, he won't be able to take part in the upcoming visitations. He's a popular pick. I believe he has a session booked with someone high up in Law Abidance."

Daisy became very still. There was silence. I couldn't see her face from my vantage point, but I would have loved to see Daisy's expression. Oh, I couldn't wait to tell the others about this over lunch. I could already see the men's stunned faces begging me to tell them everything. My stomach growled loudly, and I thought for a terrifying moment that it would alert Daisy to my presence.

"I see," bit out Daisy. "I would have thought someone with your experience could time medications a little better, but this is very disappointing. Expect me to file a report on the matter."

"I apologise." Isla's voice lacked any emotion, especially contrition. She did not seem worried by Daisy's threat. Then I realised my foot was sticking out and I shuffled it back quickly. Isla's tone became conciliatory, friendly even. "Daisy, perhaps I could come with you to B block and have a word with Harry. You have a lot to do, and I don't wish to add to your already full plate."

"Yes – you girls have no idea how much is involved, especially now with all this vaccine fuss and the fallout from that trafficking scandal. And having to choose what men to

send away. You need to think more." The sting had left her
voice by the end. I heard footsteps in the corridor, going in
the opposite direction from my hiding place. I leaned out and
saw Isla leading Daisy away from where I was standing, her
palm pressed gently to the other women's back. With her other
hand, she seemed to gesture behind her back. Shooing me
away in the other direction.

I didn't need asking twice. I quietly jogged along the corridor,
putting as much distance as possible between me and Daisy.

I made it to the refectory just in time.

The night before leaving, I couldn't sleep. I lay still in my bunk
listening to the snores of my dorm mates. Where would I be
sleeping tomorrow night? My whole life I'd slept in a long
dorm like this one, first in the prep house and now here. Ten
beds, the head of each lined up against the wall and the foot
pointing to my storage shelves. I knew this place, its noises,
and its rules. I could take nothing with me except my clothes –
no mementoes. *The last thing your foster family needs is for you
to arrive laden with a lifetime of papier mâché models and silly toys.
These are working farms, not holiday camps.* Daisy's words were
still fresh from this afternoon's dressing down when she caught
me trying to sneak a collection of embroidered sock puppets
into my bag. I like to put on little plays in the recreation room,
using funny voices for each sock character. It makes the others
laugh, especially when I make the ugly purple sock sound like
Daisy. Also, I'm not sure what a holiday camp is, but Daisy's
tone made it sound like I was going to a terrible place. And
when I begged to be allowed to take my guitar, she laughed
at me. *You think you'll have time for that, Tony? For once, you'll
have to work for a living, rather than having everything done for you.
That'll be a rude awakening, eh?*

To be rudely awakened – I'd first need to be asleep.

Eventually, I admitted defeat and opened my eyes, only to

see the shape of Artemis sitting up in the bed three along from me and staring at the opposite wall. I leaned up on my elbow facing him, and was about to say something, ask if he, too, was feeling scared about the next day. But he slowly turned his head towards me and placed his finger to his lips in a sign of silence. His eyes were shadowy pits in the half-light, his skin impossibly pale. My words caught in my throat, and any thought of comfort I hoped to get from my dorm-brother drained away. He turned back to the wall and continued his morbid vigil.

I snuggled down low under the silky comforter and closed my eyes tight. Eventually, I must have dropped off, but it was a light sleep infected with images of Artemis's dark, formless eyes.

In the bright morning, after an excellent breakfast, I felt better. The men gathered around my table in the refectory and wished me luck, and I felt, if not excited, at least ready. Dimitri, who'd been with me right from prep school, had written a song and the men sang in wonderful harmony. Dimitri's tenor is beautiful, almost as good as Logan's. The singers rhymed 'Tony' with 'don't be lonely', 'you're the one and only', and, less obvious, but no less welcome, 'glad they had known me'.

Then there was lots of kissing and hugging and a few tears until Daisy strode over and scattered everyone to their allocated activities.

I will *not* miss Daisy.

Everything was going well until it came to actually leaving. The head Warden, Ms Danika, was leading me and Artemis. I'd not been under Ms Danika's care before she became facility warden, as she'd worked over on the other side of the complex. I felt shy in her presence, not something I'm used to feeling, so I just nodded as we walked.

She was talking about making a good impression, that we were ambassadors, that our actions and behaviour would reflect on the entire facility. That we were the vanguards of a new era and that what we did would pave the way for all men to follow in integrating into a strong new society. I was trying to listen, to take in the importance of what she was saying, but I couldn't stop thinking about the vastness awaiting us. Spending the last ten years gazing out of the window in the viewing hall, pressing my nose up to the glass and watching it fog up with my breath, was a long way from actually standing unprotected under a gaping blue sky.

The vaccine hadn't hurt, not much anyway. No more than the top-up hormone shot we were sometimes given just before the confinement in July, the month when all the moths come out to mate, and we have to stay in our rooms. When I got my jab, I felt tears well up in my eyes.

"So that's it," I asked, "the moths can't hurt me?"

"That's it," replied the duty nurse with a smile. "But you'll need a dose every month. Otherwise, the effect will wear off and you'll be in danger of infection."

"Why do they only give us a month's dose, why not a year, or a lifetime?" I asked, holding a wad of cotton to my arm.

The nurse cleared away the syringe and vial, before wiping down the table. She didn't look at me. "I'm not sure, something to do with the chemicals I guess." Her tone didn't invite any more questions.

Later that morning Artemis and I approached the decontamination area that marked the entrance of the main facility, then passed through the security door, past the boxy grey shower block and changing area. This was the first time I'd been outside the main body of the facility since I arrived from the prep houses a decade previously, but I was asleep in a transport pod then so that didn't count. A cleaner turned from her mopping to say, "Good luck," offering us a half-smile before carrying on with her work. I thought I noticed a stiffness in her posture, a hesitance. I guess it's hard seeing men going outside when you've spent your life being warned against it.

Artemis, Danika, and I stopped. Before us stood the thick

iron door to the outside. I'd dreamt of this moment – we all had. I imagined ripping it open and bursting through, claiming the freedom I'd always wanted. But I couldn't even will my feet to move. Artemis, it seemed was the same.

"Well, come on then," said Danika, striding towards the door. She realised that neither of us were following and stopped. "What is it?"

"I er…" I wanted to ask for just a few moments to gather myself, but I couldn't think of the words. I was afraid after a lifetime of being told that 'outside' meant inevitable death. It was that simple.

Artemis came to my rescue. "I need to use the toilet."

The head warden rolled her eyes and nodded to the shower block. "There's one in there. Be quick. The car's waiting."

Artemis headed for the shower block door.

"Do you need the bathroom, Tony? It'll be a twenty-minute drive, then I don't know if there will be a toilet at the drop-off point."

"No, I'm fine." The words came out mumbled. What was a drop-off point? What was I being dropped from? The door to the outside loomed large and forbidding. At that moment, I didn't think I could do it, and I wondered if I could just refuse. Perhaps I could beg to go back to the dorm and plead with them to pick someone else to go in my place. My palms sweated and my stomach turned. I couldn't do it.

"Tony!" A familiar voice called from behind, snapping me awake. Both Danika and I turned as Isla ran along the corridor, clutching a large, black bag in her arms. "You forgot your guitar."

She reached us, out of breath, and held the bag to me.

"I… I… didn't think I was allowed." I turned to Danika. "Daisy said I'd be sent to some kind of camp, and they didn't allow guitars…"

Danika and Isla shared a look, and the warden frowned. "You are allowed to take personal items, Tony. It's fine. As for a camp… I have no idea where she was suggesting you might go, but I've been assured that you are headed to a safe place. A nice place." She smiled. "I wouldn't let you go unless I was certain that you'd be looked after."

I'm good at reading voices. It comes with being a man, knowing how far you can bend the rules before the woman in charge gets angry, knowing when someone is pretending to be happy, knowing when you're being lied to. I caught something in her tone, a flicker of uncertainty.

Artemis returned standing a little straighter. When Danika said, "Ready then?" he nodded.

I clutched the guitar in its soft satin bag, fingering the familiar wooden neck and the frets and strings below the fabric. I didn't want to be shown up by Artemis.

"I'm ready, too," I said, walking towards the door and out into the cold, glaring light.

CHAPTER 3

Evie

"Where've you been?" Mae was sitting on the sofa, surrounded by a chaos of paperwork, her slim legs tucked under her. With her small round glasses perched on the bridge of her nose, she looked like an owl peering out of its paper nest. Her stare was hard, glinting in the light from the fire. I hesitated, deciding whether to tell her the truth. Before I spoke, she sighed and looked back down at the document in her hand. "I made some curry. It's in the kitchen."

I moved to the kitchen and pulled down a bowl. "I was in the village. At the fostering meeting," I called from the kitchen whilst ladling the claggy lentil and vegetable mixture. It smelled good.

Our cottage was full of beams, centuries-old rather than decades. It was large and rambling, although the rooms themselves were small, and it had been my house since I was a child. Mum had lived here before that, even. Since before the infestation. Few houses had been built since the infestation. There hadn't been much need. In the five years after the initial infestation, including the initial male violence, the suicides, disease, plummeting birth rate, the population in the Union fell to a fifth of what it was. In the next few decades, it recovered to an extent, with the insemination programmes, but even so, there'd been ample housing allocation for the population without building anything new. That was changing now. The Council had really upped the incentives for giving birth. Larger houses were becoming more and more in demand. The only buildings that have been built in the last ten years were the new style facilities for the men – what a waste of resources they'd turn out to be if the men all moved to the villages. I wondered for a moment if men would be allowed to visit the Citadel. Later, perhaps. After the Council had seen how they behaved in the villages.

"For goodness' sake!" came Mae's voice from the lounge. "Men – it's all anyone ever talks about these days."

I wandered back into the lounge, clutching the bowl of lukewarm curry and a slice of bread.

"Did you heat it up?" Mae was reading a document as she spoke. "It's probably cold by now, it's been sitting there for an hour."

"It's fine – it's good…" I mumbled through a mouthful of lentils. There were files and documents strewn over every surface, so I remained standing to eat my supper. "How's Mum?"

"She's fine. Asleep. She didn't eat but she had some warm milk and a couple of biscuits. I checked on her about half an hour ago."

My eyes flicked in the direction of my mother's room. It was at the top of the stairs. I considered putting my head in and checking on her myself. One day in the not-too-distant future, we'd need to move her bedroom downstairs, into the living room perhaps.

"So, what did they say – at this meeting?" She continued to examine the document as if she didn't care, but there was a note of interest in her tone. "Keep an eye on your daughters? Don't feed your allocated man too much protein?" Her face reflected her usual cynicism that this village was a hotbed of pettiness and stupidity.

When we were dating, eight years ago, I'd thought it was witty and cool.

"Apparently, you're allocated two – one man and one boy. The older man is supposed to help look after the boy, show him how to behave."

Mae snorted. "And who shows the man how to behave?"

"The foster family, I suppose." I wish I hadn't told her. I'd had a long day at the hospital, and I just wanted to sit down and eat my dinner.

"So, you not only have a man living with you, but you also have a child to deal with too. What a terrible proposition." As she spoke, she scribbled something in red on one of the documents and violently crossed out a section of typed text. "I bet Molly was there." She stopped what she was doing and looked at me. "Was she there?"

I nodded and swabbed the last of the curry up with my bread.

"That woman would sell her own grandmother for an extra acre of farmland. Just like all the smallholders around here. It makes me sick."

I felt like defending Molly, pointing out that she had four daughters – of course she wanted Union incentives. But after seven years of marriage, I could tell Mae's mood from the set of her shoulders and the edge in her voice. She wanted a fight. She was angry that I hadn't spoken to her about going to the town hall first, disappointed that I hadn't made supper as usual, even though we're supposed to share the cooking. But she couldn't point to any of these things as something to be rightfully pissed at. So, she attacked my village instead. *My* village. A place *I'd* wanted to stay instead of moving to the Citadel when we married. It was *my* ailing mother who lived with us, and *my* friends from school who'd become our neighbours. We'd gone through it all a hundred times.

"Great curry," I said, trying to defuse the situation. "Did you roast the garlic first?"

"What do you think it says about Eastor that the men are being sent here first?"

The curry ruse had not worked. I took my bowl into the kitchen and began filling the sink with water. "I dunno... that the Council trusts us to look after them?" I didn't speak loudly, worried about waking Mum. But it didn't matter. Mae had followed me through, standing in the doorway with her arms folded, her gaze slightly to my left as I ran the dishcloth over the dishes.

"It means that the Council thinks so little of this village that they are willing to put us at risk."

I rolled my eyes; I couldn't help it. "The vaccine is safe, Mae. I'm a nurse, trust me. Those XXs are just spreading rumours cos they don't want the men out at all."

Mae's face flushed, and she took a step towards me. She was a good six inches shorter than me, but my heart raced when she got up in my face like this. It made me feel dizzy and sick and flustered.

"Maybe that's true. But the men will bring nothing good here. Whether the vaccine fails, or the XXs come here and start making trouble, it's clear that the Council doesn't care. We're in the middle of an experiment, and not one I want to be part of. We should leave – before this village becomes a freak show."

It was still about moving to the Citadel.

I dried my hand on a towel, still facing away from Mae. "I can't leave Mum, Mae. We've been over this. She's ill." I lowered my voice. "She's not got long left. I won't leave whilst she's still here." This was something she'd agreed to when we married. Here, until Mum passes, then the Citadel.

The anger coming from my wife was palpable. I thought she was going to come at me, and a confusing mixture of fear and adrenaline fogged my mind. She'd never struck me before but there'd been a fair few objects thrown in my direction over the years. Bottles, pans, plates, a whole jar of pickled onions once. She was hot-tempered, sometimes jealous. I used to think it showed how much she loved me, but really, it was much simpler. If she didn't have her own way, she lost her shit.

But she didn't hit me or throw anything. Instead, she spun on her heel and disappeared back to the lounge, offering over her shoulder a bitter, "You'll see I'm right."

I thought again about the list I'd signed not two hours ago, the list volunteering to foster, and felt disappointment tinged with relief. Even if they picked us, Mae would never agree. And this was no place for a man or a boy. I wiped down the sink and trudged upstairs to bed.

XX104

I'd spent all of last month setting up the radio station, adapting an old transmitter, boosting the signal, connecting and soundproofing the top-secret studio. XX02 had been as good as her word. Anything I asked for was delivered within twenty-four hours. Whoever was funding this had deep pockets.

The radio had been running for only two weeks when I realised it was a success. The presenter was a great choice. She took an ideology that could have felt fanatical, a tirade of bitterness and ranting fear, but instead, she managed to infuse the messages with conciliatory rhetoric, a perfect down-to-earth tone and self-deprecating logic.

The station quickly gained a huge following, though most would never admit to listening. The Council tried to shut us down, but we always eluded them. My coordinator, XX02, had an informant that would warn us of a raid. That warning ensured we could stay on air. The presenter had a talent for saying the right things to crank the fear of men up just one more notch –especially for those who'd lived through the first wave.

Women were getting restless. Protests started to break out without the Women's Conservation Society having to do anything. The XX was created from our conviction, our determination to protect what we built. And then it began to replicate, spreading across the Union. XX – no Y required.

I returned to headquarters late last year to meet with XX02. I didn't know her real name, of course. Although she knew mine. I thought she'd be ecstatic with what we'd achieved, but when I entered her office, she was scowling down at a printout on her desk. She spoke without looking up. "The Council are going ahead with the vaccination programme. I thought perhaps with the protests they might reconsider, but…" She jabbed at the document. "The self-deluded idiots. What do we have to do to show them what a terrible idea this is?" I'd never seen XX02 like this. In the few times I'd met her she'd been composed, thoughtful, careful. The voice of calm. Her hair, usually sleek and neat, was scrunched up into an untidy bun, her skin showed dry patches and the skin under her eyes was puffy. As she pointed at the memo on her desk, I realised her nails were chewed to the quick.

"The radio station should make a difference," I said, quietly. "It's growing day by day." I'd thought we *were* making a difference. But it seemed the Council were more committed to the vaccination programme than we'd anticipated. Well, if we needed to up the stakes, so be it.

"It's vital the programme fails." I was surprised at the sharpness in her voice. And gladdened by it. She was younger than me. She hadn't even been born when men were last out in the world. Her commitment gave me strength.

"What can I do to help?"

She paused for a long time and stared down at her hands as if making up her mind on something. Then she gave a sigh. "You're my best agent. There is a mission, a difficult one."

I didn't hesitate. "What do you need me to do?"

"It involves being close to the fostering programme."

"So I'll be in contact with the men?" *Men*, in the flesh. A shudder passed down my spine. It had been decades since

I'd even seen a man. Could I really get close to them after everything? I took a deep breath. "What's the plan?"

XX02 shifted her gaze to the glass doors, but no one was within twenty yards of the office. She looked back at me but couldn't quite meet my eye. "It's controversial. It will take a huge commitment, so I understand if you say no. But the intelligence we've received from our informant suggests you are the best person for the job, especially with your background." She reached into a drawer and pulled out a file, handing it to me.

I took the file without looking at its contents. I didn't need to. Whatever it contained, I would do. The vaccination programme would fail, and men would stay where they were.

Tony

As I walked through the door of the facility, I was permitted to enjoy the wonderful bright blue expanse of open sky for about thirteen seconds before a gust of wind stung my eyes and I instinctively squinted, thus missing my maiden voyage into this brave new world. I'd prepared a few words in my head, imbued with weighty solemnity to mark the occasion, but instead, the fear of exiting the building made me hold my breath. The air felt so cold I thought it might freeze my insides and crystallise inside my lungs. Tears streamed from my stinging eyes and seemed to freeze on my cheeks.

Artemis and I were bundled into the back seat of a waiting car and when the door thudded shut, it was as if the outside stopped existing, like I'd been gobbled up. I clutched my guitar tightly and twisted my head around, watching the waving figures of Isla and the warden disappear. As the car got faster, I felt a strange sensation, like the air around me was pressing on my face. The view from the windows started to peel away, faster and faster. I held on to the door handle and noticed

Artemis doing the same. The facility became smaller as we approached the exit to the compound.

Inside the car, everything was neat and grey and mercifully warm. The smell of washing detergent seemed to be embedded in the fabric of the seats, and I leaned down, sniffing deeply, attracting a scathing look from Artemis. Such fabric was unthinkable in the facility – everything there was tile or plastic or polished wood. Our clothes and blankets were silk or satin, allowing no place for the moths' toxic threads to hide. I sniffed again, ignoring Artemis. It was almost as if the smell matched the colour of the car – the scent of sensible grey.

The woman driving offered no introduction. Even from my position in the back, I could see that she was strongly built, her short spiky hair brushing the ceiling of the car, her thick arms straining at the seams of her navy shirt as she clutched the wheel.

She caught my eye in a small rectangular mirror attached to the ceiling of the car. "There's trouble at the entrance to the compound. Keep your head down."

Artemis stiffened next to me. "What kind of trouble?"

She looked at me again in the mirror. "Try to sit as low in the seat as you can and don't worry, they can't get into the car."

I didn't find her words reassuring, but I dutifully burrowed down low in my seat.

As if pulled by unseen ropes, the large metal gates to the outside world rolled apart and we were greeted by a crowd of people holding banners and placards. They were being held back by a line of women in red and navy uniforms. I recognised the uniform from a woman who talked to us a few years back, a Law Abidance officer who'd visited us to explain how life and law worked outside the facility. How each village had its own LA department with professional officers and volunteers that reported to a special Council department in the Citadel – that they dealt with land disputes and the occasional teenage fight. But she'd said, with no small amount of pride, that the crime rate, especially of violent crime, was low. She'd not mentioned anything about riots.

The car moved past the crowd, not quickly, but not crawling either. I guessed by the twisted features and moving mouths of the crowd that, had the window been down, the noise would have been considerable.

"Why are they shouting?" I asked as I slipped further into my seat, clutching my guitar like a shield.

"Read the placards, dummy," Artemis hissed.

I smarted at Artemis's words but did as he suggested.

Some contained words and phrases: MEN STAY AWAY! Untested is Unsafe… Integration = INVASION!!… ReMeMbEr WaTeRlOo!

But some held signs that just had the symbol "XX" in red paint. The paint had run, and the signs looked like they were bleeding.

"What does 'XX' mean?" I asked, preparing myself for more of Artemis's scorn, but he didn't answer.

I could see the driver frown in the little mirror as she navigated around a woman, wearing an 'XX' painted shirt, who'd broken through the LA ranks and was now standing in front of the car with her arms outstretched. She was shouting so violently that I could see spittle flying from her lips. As she pointed to the car, right at me, her eyes widened, and I could see pure fury on her face.

"Fuck this," muttered the driver. The car moved towards the woman at a jogging pace and, had not an LA officer pushed the woman aside, I believe we would have mown her down. I hugged my guitar tighter and turned to Artemis, who was pale, sitting up straight in his seat. I thought of grabbing his hand – what I wanted more than anything in that moment was a connection. But his stare scared me more than the crowd outside. His eyes were cold, similar to the look I'd seen on him the night before in the dorm.

I consoled myself with the soft silk of my guitar case, rubbing the fabric between my fingers, until, finally, we were free of the baying women.

"I told you to keep your head down back there!" As my head was almost flat on the seat, I could only imagine the driver was talking to Artemis.

A few moments later she spoke again. "Okay, you can sit up now. They're gone."

Shuffling back upright and still holding my guitar, I looked out of the window and gawped at the sheer expanse of grass, hedges, and trees speeding past on either side of the winding road. It made me feel sick, like the scenery was rolling away in two great columns on either side as the sky remained fixed above.

"I'm not afraid of them," said Artemis. But his voice wobbled a little despite his words. "Why should I hide? I've every right to be here."

The driver snorted, "Well, they're afraid of you." She looked at Artemis in the little mirror. "You're gonna have a hard time in the villages if you can't keep your head down when you're told. Your friend there will do better, I reckon." She gave me a quick flash of a smile before turning her attention back to the road.

Artemis didn't answer and he didn't look at me. He raised his chin a little higher and stared straight out of the front of the car towards the oncoming road.

I felt a small burst of pride in my chest. Yes! I would make this work. I could keep my head down and I could prove that men and women could live together just fine. Warden Danika was right – I was to be an ambassador for all men, and I would be so kind and funny and helpful that the woman back there would realise there was nothing to be afraid of.

Evie

"Evie! What a brave, kind thing to do. If you ever need any help, or even just someone to talk to, just come and find me, okay? Don't listen to those old dollies muttering on about manfans and Waterloo. I think it's great. Well done."

I was at work when Dr Pearl Rosya caught my arm, outside the geriatrics ward. She was a tall slender woman with curly black hair in tight close braids, brisk in manner and quick to criticise the junior staff. I couldn't recall her ever addressing me using my first name before. It was always Nurse Brighton. Or more often, just Nurse!

"I... err... what?" I said, looking at her hand on my arm and up into her flinty brown eyes.

She smiled as if we were long-lost sisters. "I heard about the foster placement. You must be so excited. I did my undergraduate thesis on the role of testosterone in stress situations. I mean, our subjects were male hamsters, but I think that given the circumstances..."

I couldn't focus on what she was saying. Foster placement? No... Surely not. "Dr Rosya, I mean, where did you hear that I... that we'd been selected? I mean, am I being considered or...?"

"Oh! I'm so sorry. I thought you'd have received the letter days ago. Maybe it was delayed in the post. It's all decided. You're one of the hallowed few, so to speak." Her grin widened as she leaned in and lowered her voice. "It's all a bit hush-hush. You know my wife, Anita, is part of the foster committee, right? You would have seen her at the community hall meeting. I recognised your name on the list and asked her about it. I shouldn't have, but I'm so excited about the entire project. You'll need to pass the home assessment of course, but that'll just be a formality since you've been background checked – unless it turns out you're a secret member of the XXs of course!" she laughed. Then her smile dropped. "Oh – you really didn't know?"

I shook my head. I'd left before the post arrived this morning. But Mae had still been there. Shit. Had Mae opened it? "I... I guess I'll get it when I get home." I needed to get home now, see if the letter was still there.

"Good. Anita's been working so hard, poor dear, over the last few weeks, trying to sift out those who want to help from those who are just in it for the incentives. I think it went in your favour as you didn't fill anything in the incentive list. If you know what I mean." She gave a half grimace, which could have meant many things. "You'll have to keep me posted. Let me know how it goes."

I thought back to the list I'd signed a couple of weeks ago at the village hall. Was there a section on incentives? I'd been flustered with Molly looking over my shoulder and the thought of Mae's looming disapproval. Mae would be livid at the idea that I'd volunteered without telling her – she'd be even angrier if it turned out I hadn't even signed up for more land, or a better job, or even a few extra transport tokens. If I could get to the letter before Mae, I'd phone them retracting my application. My wife wouldn't be any the wiser.

There was a part of me then that felt a flicker of loss at the thought. I'd gone to the hall that night for a reason. I had a romantic notion that I could give a boy a home, a cute little boy like Marcus Sullivan in the picture in my drawer at home. Mae hadn't wanted a daughter – but a son, perhaps? I inwardly groaned. What a stupid idea! Mae didn't want children at all, and she definitely didn't want a boy child, with alien genitalia and unpredictable moods. My daydreams lay before me in an embarrassing heap.

"Thank you for telling me – yes, I'll let you know how it goes." I left Dr Rosya standing in the corridor and immediately found the hospital administrator in her office. "I'm not well." I almost barked the words. "I have to go."

The administrator frowned in concern. "Do you want to see one of the doctors, Evie? What's wrong?"

"It's just… just a migraine. I just need to go home and lie down. Can you get Isobel to cover the rest of my shift? It's only an hour." I touched my head and lowered my eyes for effect.

The administrator stood up and came over to me. Holding

her palm tenderly against my brow, she steered me to the door. "Don't worry, Sweetheart. I'll sort it out. Go. Take a hospital cab and bill the department. Do you want me to come with you?"

I felt like a horrible person lying. I'd rarely called in sick, and never on a ruse. "It's okay," I mumbled, "I can manage." Then I half walked, half ran, off to the hospital cab rank.

CHAPTER 4

Tony

Artemis and I were the second group to arrive at the stone building. Since then, more had come, each in a pebble grey car, until there were about twenty men, standing about in nervous little knots of twos and threes. We stood in a chilly, cavernous hall, struggling to take in all the newness. I'd assumed that the women lived in tiny versions of facilities, but this place was more like a castle from a story. It felt ancient and sombre, and the stone walls echoed with our whispers. We hadn't been told to keep our voices down, but the air felt heavy, as if we were being watched, and it wouldn't have seemed right to speak above a murmur. The ceilings were high, higher even than those of the viewing room back home, with dark beams curving towards the highest point at the end like a vast ribcage. And the windows were extraordinary. Small sections of coloured glass lay in such a way as to create pictures – scenes of people on their knees, of faces of men and women crying and reaching up towards the sky. Some windows had been covered with wooden boards, but one enormous window, showing some kind of procession, stretched above me. It was as if the joy on the people's faces was something I could reach out and touch. What made them so joyful? I thought as I gazed up into that radiance of colours. It was an overcast day, but if the sun broke through, would the whole vision light up? Would coloured light come streaming through the windows in a chorus of blues, reds, golds? Such a thing would be beautiful. The genius who'd designed these windows must have had that in mind, and I found myself desperately willing the sun to appear so I could bathe in the light, become part of it, join the happy procession of people and animals, and follow the white glinting star at the top.

The men's whispers became louder. I could see my own breath – a pale coiling plume, and I thought of a dragon breathing fire. It was fascinating, this weird smoky phenomenon. Everyone was wearing our facility smocks and sandals – perfect for the facilities, but woefully inadequate for wherever this was. I'd never really been cold. The air conditioning at the facility and at the prep house maintained a constant temperature. Some of the senior men, the ones who had lived in the older style facilities, had told us stories of being cold, of using a type of crinkly metal blanket to keep warm, and needing to pair up in bed. But I'd never experienced anything like it. It felt awful, like the moment after coming out of a shower, when the warmth of the water faded and before you were fully dry, only many times worse. I felt myself tremble and wondered if this was from cold or nerves. Some men clutched what looked like pillowcases stuffed with belongings. I still held my guitar. Its weight and bulk comforted me.

Two men began jumping about and slapping themselves. "It helps keep you warm," one of them said, a handsome blonde man in his early twenties, smiling at my obviously bewildered stare. "Our heating went down about two years ago, and this is what we had to do – this and snuggle up close in bed." He winked at me, and I felt my cheeks heat up. But I smiled back.

"Evan," he said.

"Tony," I replied and clutched my guitar tighter. "Nice to meet you."

"And who's your friend?" He nodded to Artemis.

Artemis offered his usual scowl. "What's it to you?" he snapped.

Evan's smile dropped and a flash of hurt crossed his fine features. I cringed inside. I wanted to say that this guy wasn't my friend; he was just someone I'd arrived with. I wanted to edge away from Artemis and join the little group of men to our left who were now huddling together and rubbing their hands over each other's arms. Instead, I sighed and said, "Don't worry about Artemis. He didn't sleep well last night."

Evan's smile returned, and he addressed Artemis. "Don't worry, brother. I don't think any of us got much sleep. What a crazy time to be alive, eh?"

Artemis didn't answer, but at least he didn't say anything rude.

Our awkward pause was interrupted then when a woman made her way into the chamber. All eyes turned to her as she walked past us and up to front of the hall.

"Welcome... gentlemen."

We all stopped our shuffling and turned attentively to the lady. She was not as old as Mary, but oldish. Her grey hair was fixed into a pile on her head and some curls had escaped, bouncing down onto her shoulders. Her thick green coat swung as she walked and her scarf was made of some fluffy material that, when she stood by me, I only just stopped myself from reaching out and running my fingers over.

"Gentlemen. I hope you had a pleasant journey here. You are part of the southern fostering initiative. My name is Anita Swift, I live in Eastor, and I am a volunteer working for the Men's Welfare Authority."

There was a muttering from those around me. Artemis narrowed his eyes and Evan looked at the floor. Obviously, it hadn't just been our facility rife with rumours about the MWA.

Anita nodded and raised her hands, palms up. "I know that you may have heard some bad things recently." She spoke in a soft voice. "You may even hear more when you reach your foster families. But let me reassure you that the MWA is committed to men's protection, welfare, and social integration."

I heard a soft derisive snort come from Artemis, but Anita didn't seem to notice.

"Before we start your integration training, are there any questions?" It was such a surprising thing for a woman to say that all the men stared at Anita with blank faces. Men were rarely invited to ask questions. By the time you reached the facilities at eighteen, the instinct to keep quiet was pretty much baked in.

I thought for a moment that Artemis was going to ask something – he inhaled as if to speak and I flinched, wondering in what way he was about to offend this nice lady with the soft scarf, but one of the other men beat him to it.

"Why is it so cold?"

Anita blinked twice and then her eyes widened as if remembering something. "Sorry, yes... sorry." Then she turned and began walking towards the gloomy depths of the chamber. She stopped and turned back when she realised that no one was following. "Um... this way, gentlemen," she said, beckoning us with her hand. Dutifully, we followed her in a line, along a walkway flanked on either side by long, hard-looking benches. At the foot of the last bench on our right sat four fat sacks, each twice as big as a pillowcase, and tied at the top with a cord. Anita grabbed the heavy-looking bags and hoisted them, one by one, into the walkway as we all stood and watched. Then she untied the cord of the first bag before carefully lifting out piles of folded fabric items and placing them in lines on the benches. No one moved.

"Some of it is reclaimed. Most of it was made by volunteers, using offcuts or donated wool. Obviously, your facility robes are made in a factory in Devon, but everything else made in factories is not quite sized for your... you know?" She moved on to the next sack and began laying out more neat piles on the benches. I hadn't known that my robe was made in a factory. Although, I knew what a factory was. I also had no idea about the location of Devon – it could have been a mile away or a thousand.

"You." I thought she was pointing at me, but it was Artemis. "You lay out the clothes from the next sack and be careful. All clothes are valuable and are to be treated with care." Artemis stiffened and made no move to do what he was told. I panicked. Should I push him to do it? Volunteer myself? This woman probably knew we arrived together – what if she thought everyone from my facility was this rude? What if she sent us back?

Evan stepped forward. He smiled, untying the sack and helping the woman, laying out fabric shapes in all colours, so many colours. One item I recognised as trousers – trousers! Like the ones I wanted to wear to play Romeo in the facility production of Romeo and Julian. They didn't look very comfortable – restrictive in the groin area – but they were so exotic. Another man tipped out a cascade of shoes, all used and scuffed and made from the same brown shiny material. Tufts of muddy grass still clung to the soles of some.

"Find your sizes, come on." Anita was frowning. "What's wrong with you all? Why are you just standing there?"

Evan answered. "We're not sure what goes where." He gestured to his chest and legs.

"Oh." Anita blushed as she mumbled, "I guess that makes sense." Then she started holding items up to herself. "Jumpers on top, arms through here. Skirts or trousers on the bottom… see?" She held up a fluffy skirt, made from the same material as her scarf, and I made a point of remembering where she put it. "Coats…" she held up a long-knitted cloak. "Over everything else. Start trying things on, perhaps?"

There was a pause, then an excited rush towards the benches as every man went for the items they'd been coveting since the bags opened.

"Slow down, treat them carefully. More care, less repair!" But Anita's words were ignored as the men began rifling through the clothes. A lifetime in grey and suddenly we were faced with such strange and vibrant riches. I grabbed my skirt, a gentle blue in soft wool, and looked around for a jumper in a similar colour. I found a thick yellow one, with a knitted pattern down the sleeves, and hugged it to me. It smelt a bit fusty, like well-boiled soup, but I didn't care. I noticed Artemis and Evan both clutching the same pair of dark-grey trousers and caught Evan's words, "I had them first."

"No, I did! They're the only ones my size." Artemis snatched them away and Evan let go. Why they were fighting over something grey, I couldn't fathom.

We all removed our silken robes to try on our prizes but stopped at a sharp cry which echoed around the walls.

"You're not wearing any underwear!" It was Anita, her eyes wide and her face a fiery red.

"We don't wear anything underneath," replied Evan, replacing his robe. "It's not hygienic." Most of the men were nodding, me included. Hygiene was an important part of life in both the preps and the facilities.

"Well, err." The woman looked flustered and turned away from the naked men, standing in just their sandals surrounding her.

"Put your clothes on over the top of your shift. That way you'll be warmer," she said, although her voice was shaking a little. "Out here we put on as many layers as we can, especially in the colder months."

I could see her point. It was colder outside, even than in here. But despite being silk, the shifts were bulky. They pushed out the fabric of my skirt in an annoying way, making my hips look lumpy.

Artemis was wearing his hard-won grey trousers paired with a plain black sweater. I could see no evidence of his robe bunching up his waistband. Then I spied it stuffed in a dark corner by his left foot. I sidled over. "You need to put it back on," I whispered. "She told you to leave it on!"

"I don't want to. I'm sick of it."

"Put it on." My voice contained an edge of hysteria. "Please!"

"Or what?"

"I don't know. She'll make you put it on, I guess."

He turned to me with a thoughtful look on his face. "I don't think she will. Did you see how she looked at us when we were undressed?"

I shrugged. "She was just worried that we'd get cold."

"No," Artemis looked back at Anita, who was kneeling to help one man try on a pair of shoes. "She was scared – scared of us."

XX104

"Hey Beans! We're going to Dad's!"

Bella threw herself at me – a ball of eight year-old energy with a round chubby face and hair that always seemed a mess, despite the effort Mum put into taming it. It defied all attempts to arrange into pigtails, plaits and buns, wriggling out of its confines into a wild halo.

She snaked her skinny arm around my waist and squeezed before I had time to drop my bag on the hallway floor.

"Hey, Bells." I dropped a kiss on her head and then tried to manoeuvre further into the house. Bella was having none of it and held on even tighter. I had to tickle her under the arms to make her let go. Then, as she collapsed in giggles onto the floor, it seemed a wasted opportunity to just leave her there, so I tickled her for another couple of minutes just to make sure she stayed down.

"*Stop it*" – giggle-giggle-giggle – "*Stop!* Gonna wet myself!"

When she'd recovered, I dumped my bag and jacket and slumped on the sofa. She climbed on top of me, ensuring that her bony knees and elbows pushed into every tender area of flesh.

"Ow! Be careful."

Bells wedged herself next to me and, for the next half an hour, we played some game on my phone, something with farm animals that Bella loved.

News alerts kept flashing up on the screen.

Breaking – Violent attacks up 24%!

Breaking – WHO to make an announcement about new sleeping sickness.

Bella's little finger swept them away, and she continued to feed her animated goats.

We had soup and toast for dinner. I let Bella drink the dregs straight from the bowl. "Don't tell Mum," I said sternly, as I wiped her top lip clean with a tea towel. Kari texted me a video of a Reclaim the Night protestor and added *There's a march in London tomorrow. You should go!*

Maybe! I texted back, even though I knew there was no way Dad would let me. Also, it wasn't exactly my idea of a perfect long weekend. Then again, nor was spending "quality time" with Dad and Miranda and my new baby brother. Left to my own devices, I'd have probably spent Thursday evening with Kari and Oscar, and Friday through to Sunday hanging around here in my pyjamas, binge-watching TV series – anything with Vikings or hobbits or dragons.

"Have you had dinner?" Mum appeared in the doorway bleary-eyed in a nightie. She'd had a long shift on the maternity ward the night before and hadn't arrived home until morning.

"Soup," replied Bella. "And I didn't drink from the bowl."

Mum gave me a half-smile. "I should think not. You need to pack. I'll have a quick shower, then take you to the station."

"Do I have to go?"

Bella dragged her eyes away from her farmyard and frowned at me. There was a note of betrayal in her stare. "If we don't go, Dad'll be sad."

I didn't think he'd be that sad. He'd almost certainly work most of the weekend and Miranda would be busy with Jorge. It would be up to me to entertain Bella in a small flat with no garden and none of her toys. Worse still, Jorge was a fractious nine month-old, teething, grumpy and, if you asked me, a bit of a tyrant.

"We've agreed you'll go." Mum spoke gently, her tone suggesting that she knew it was going to be hard work for me. "I don't think it's right that you pull out at the last minute. The train tickets are booked."

I wanted to say that none of this was right and that it was his decision to leave, and we didn't really owe him anything – at least, not some stupid train tickets. But then I looked from Mum's exhausted face to Bella's look of misery and rolled my eyes. "Fine. I'll go pack."

"Yay!" shouted Bella, jumping up and giving me a wet kiss on the temple.

Just as I was leaving the room, I turned to Mum and spoke in a low voice. "Have you seen the Internet?"

She shook her head. "Just woke up. Why?"

"The WHO is suggesting there might be another pandemic on its way – some kind of sleeping sickness."

She sighed. "We could do without a lockdown. Remember to pack masks and sanitizer."

I nodded.

"And thanks, baby. I know this isn't ideal. It's just Bella... she misses him."

"I know, Mum. Are you working tonight?"

"Yep. Extra shift. The maternity ward's understaffed, and people will keep having babies. Now pack."

I went upstairs and did what I was told. Headphones, charger, PJs, spare jeans and hoodie, wash bag. The same routine I'd been doing for the past year. At first, it had been fun navigating the underground, feeling grown-up and capable. Now, the novelty had worn off and it was just too many people breathing, pushing, hunting out spaces and darting in front of each other.

My phone beeped. It was a selfie of Kari and Oscar, sticking out their tongues. It was taken in Oscar's garden. I recognised the steps they were sitting on, leading up to the pool house. The same steps that he and I had kissed on at his fourteenth birthday party. My first kiss, his third. By embarrassing mutual consent, the next day it was decided that it would be our last kiss with each other. YA novels will have you believe that kissing your closest friend inevitably leads to a whirlwind romance. This, it turns out, is not always the case. We carried on being best friends, despite the lack of fireworks. And then Kari came along and our platonic two became three.

Her message attached to the photo read: *sad-face emoji – Missing you! – heart emoji.*

"C'mon Beans! Mum's waiting in the car."

I chucked my phone in my bag, scraped my hair back into a ponytail and went downstairs.

Evie

I fumbled with my keys, my fingers shaking. Mae usually took the bus into the village. Her team worked out of the labour exchange building. Unless she was called into the Citadel, then she might stay overnight. As far as I understood it, it was her job to organise the power infrastructure needs of Eastor and its surrounding villages – overseeing the construction of turbines, connecting power to the localised grids. She also allocated the power so that those who needed it got enough, schools for example, or the men's facilities. According to Mae, it consumed vast amounts of power.

I opened the door, nearly falling over the threshold. No post on the rug. Not a good sign.

"Hello!" I called. "Anyone home? Mum?" No reply.

Then I looked up and saw Mae's purple knitted coat still on its peg. It would have been too cold this morning to go without it. My heart sank. I made my way through the tiny hallway and into the sitting room. Mae was sitting by the fire, her cardigan wrapped around her knees. She was prodding at the blaze with a poker. The scraping of it on the hearth sounded rusty and raw. Although it was only lunchtime, the room was dark and very warm, the curtains, still drawn from last night. Light from the fire reflected from the side of her face nearest to me, and the other side of her face was in shadows.

"No work today?" I tried to keep my voice light, but it came out as a croak.

She didn't turn and face me. I wondered how she could sit so close to such heat – I could feel it from the doorway.

She dropped the poker on the stone hearth with a clank. "When were you going to tell me?"

I knew Mae. She'd been sitting here, stoking herself up, rehearsing this ever since she'd read the letter. The way she sat, the fire, the letter, which I could see now, on the floor next to her, pinned under her splayed fingers – this was the scene. Now, it was my job to pick up on the cues and play the part I'd been assigned. If I failed to play the part correctly, the anger and the silences could go on for days, weeks. This whole situation would be resurrected every time she needed to win a point. Who was I kidding? That would happen anyway. This would be filed away in the same place as not-moving-to-the-citadel and not-trying-for-a-promotion-at-work to be retrieved and pushed in my face, loudly and with unremitting resentment.

Then she did something I didn't expect – she laughed. "Were you going to wait until they arrived, until a fully grown male and a boy-child turned up on the doorstep and demanded to be fed?" She moved round to face me.

I took a step into the baking hot room. "Look, Mae, things got out of hand... I'll call them and tell them I changed my mind. They haven't even done the home assessment yet, so it's not too late."

"They called in this morning."

"What?" Despite the heat of the room, I felt a shiver run down my shoulders and back.

"The assessment, a woman from the MWA came round, looked in a few cupboards, poked her head in the spare room."

This was worse than I'd expected. I could just imagine Mae reading the letter, then answering the door to a delegate from the MWA. No warning. "I'm sorry, Mae. I know you didn't sign up for this. Did you tell her it was a mistake? That's fine. It was a stupid idea. I don't know what came over me." I gave a shaky exhale. At least now this entire episode was over with.

There was a long silence. "I didn't, actually." She stood up, her small heart-shaped face flushed pink from the heat of the fire. For a moment, she reminded me of when we'd first got together seven years ago, flushed with homemade wine at a party, and trying to explain to me how you could get electricity from genetically modified algae. She smiled and her eyes glinted in the half-light. It was a different smile from the one she'd had back then. But at least it was a smile.

"What do you mean?" I was wary. There was something in her posture as she rose from the sofa, a tilt to her head. "What did you say to her?"

She came towards me and took my wrists gently. Her hands were warm and clammy, and her words came out quickly as if she was working up to something. "I said that we couldn't wait to do our civic duty. That we'd always wanted a child, but that work had made it difficult, and that now we were honoured to help in this very exciting part of the Union's future."

I frowned. "What? Why would you?"

"Things have been tough for us for a while, Evie. I know you want children, and I've been working. Your mother's illness. Obviously, it would have been better if you'd talked to me about it first, but now it's done…" She looked up at me, and for a moment I thought I could see my Mae, the Mae who used to turn up at the hospital with sandwiches for me, sit behind me in the bath and wash my hair.

"Are you sure?" I asked, unable to keep the caution from my voice.

She ran her hands up my arms. "It might be nice. A fresh start, a project for you. It's only for a few months. You never know. I might get to like children."

I wrapped her up in my arms, "Mae – this means so much to me... thank you."

Mae burrowed into my embrace, and I allowed a small hope to flicker to life. It was good between us once; it could be again.

"Also," Mae spoke softly, her breath brushing my neck, "the woman who came round agreed that this would look excellent on our transfer application. She even pointed out that a move to the Citadel was one of the incentives on the list and it wasn't too late for us to apply. So, I added it to our application."

I went still. I could feel her waiting for a response. I'd fought this battle so many times, Mum going into a nursing home, leaving everything I knew. But she now had an extra card to play. The irony was that I didn't even know if this was what I wanted. A little boy rolling around the place, a man, learning how to live in the world. It was all too much. I felt my arms go slack. "Okay," I said. "After the placement, we'll look at moving."

Mae's arms pulled me in closer. "We'll make it work. You and me. We always do."

"I bet Mae went nuts." My mother's soft croaking voice echoed my own thoughts as I perched on the edge of her bed and tried to get her to eat a little more vegetable lasagne.

"Actually, she was okay with it." I felt bad lying by omission.

My mother shooed my hand and the spoon away, making me spill some pasta sauce on the crochet blanket – I took a hankie from the side table and sponged off the stain. My mother had always been a tidy person, fastidious about her surroundings and her appearance before she became sick. Before the cancer, she'd always looked well groomed, her clothes ironed and spotless. She would wear a full face of make up too, much to Mae's amusement. "It's such a dolly thing to do, slap all that mush on your face," she'd say with a snort.

Mum dabbed her mouth with a napkin, signalling that lunchtime was over. "That doesn't sound like Mae."

"I guess she knew I wanted a child... and she didn't want one, so this is the next best thing." Mae didn't like children. She became awkward around them; said they were too chaotic and difficult to reason with. But she might have come round to the idea if I could have carried a child. But I was turned down by the department of Artificial Insemination. Nor, they pointed out in the letter, was I eligible to apply for a hetero-visitation. Mum's cancer was genetic. Her mother and her aunt both had it. The Union had strict rules about such things.

"Mae doesn't do anything that isn't directly in the interests of Mae," said my mother, pulling her wrinkled mouth into a grim line.

I looked at the closed door. "Keep your voice down, Mum."

She sniffed. "I don't know why you put up with it."

"Mum! Enough." I tucked her in, checking she had enough water. "I put up with it, because I'm committed to Mae. I love her." The words sounded hollow in my ears. If Mae's job stopped being so stressful, or if I could stop mooning over having a baby, then we'd be back to how we were, snuggling up on the sofa, talking. Maybe going to the Citadel would be the right thing for us. "Do you need the bedpan?" I said, sharper than I intended.

She shook her head. "When are they arriving – the... men?"

I noted the apprehension in the pause. Mum was a woman from the time before, commonly referred to as a 'dolly.' She'd been twenty-two when the first wave had hit. She didn't talk about it much, but women of this age had many reasons to be wary of men. However, my mother had never seemed particularly worried about men. She was a supporter of the vaccine programme when we'd heard about it on Union radio, and when an XX leaflet had been anonymously put through our letterbox a couple of weeks ago, she'd torn it into little pieces and dropped the in the fire muttering, *Bloody, fearful idiots.*

"Are you worried?" I asked. I placed my hand on hers on the bed, noting how cold it was. "The vaccine is one hundred per cent effective. They've tested it. But if you're scared, I'll call it off. I don't care what the MWA put on my record, I'll just cancel the whole thing."

"No… not scared. I want them here. It's been a long time since… well, I think it's a good thing. It's the right thing to do. And having a child around will be nice."

I patted her hand, and then went and collected another blanket from the cupboard. "Here."

She sighed as if I was fussing too much. "I'm fine." But she took the blanket and smoothed it down with her palms, running her fingertips over its woollen surface and straightening the edge before wriggling down further under the covers.

I picked up the book that was by her bed. It was Shakespeare's Romeo and Juliet, an original copy from before the infestation, unaltered. "Haven't you read this a thousand times?" I smiled and flicked through the well-worn pages, seeing my mother's notes in pencil. She'd wanted to be an actress once, even went to drama school, when the world was different. "Would you like me to read it with you now?"

My mother smiled, although as she did, a small wince of pain flashed across her features. "I'm tired now, love. Later?"

"No problem." I replaced the book and checked the bottle of painkillers on the side. Half full.

"Did you take your pain meds this morning, Mum?"

"Honestly, stop fussing. I know where they are if I need them. I've got water, yes?"

"All in place."

"Then leave me be."

I sighed. "It's not like the infestation days, Mum. You don't have to hoard medicine. I'm a nurse. I can get you whatever you need. If you're in pain, just take a tablet."

Mum settled back under the covers and closed her eyes. "I'm fine. Now off you go. You've got some preparing to do, I should think."

Tony

Dressed in our new clothes and looking like a flock of exotic birds, we were led by Anita away from the big building with the pointy roof, and down a pathway which cut through a small field. Ancient slabs of stone sprouted from the grass every few meters, covered in mouldy-looking growths. We slowed our pace to huddle around one of the cleaner stones, trying to make out what was engraved on the ravaged surface.

"Is that a number?" asked Evan behind me, resplendent in a colourfully woven dress.

I peered closer, noting how the musty yellow growths bled into the stone in circular patterns. "It's a date, I think, or a set of dates. 1938 to... 2016. I think that's a name." I rubbed at the stone to remove some of the muck, careful not to get any on my new sweater.

"I don't read that well," replied Evan, a little embarrassment creeping into his tone. "I'm better at recognising numbers."

"Me neither," said someone on my left as we all bent down, a shorter, dark-skinned man dressed in a loose blue frock and a long cardigan. He spelt out the letters. "H... e... r... e L... i... e... s"

Feeling a little superior and grateful towards Mary for how well she'd taught me, I read it aloud. "Here lies Jonathan P...

Pewsey. 1938 – 2016..." and below in slanting letters, "*He will wipe every tear from their eyes. There will be no more death or mourning or crying or pain, for the old order of things has passed away.*"

"Where?" asked Evan, looking around on the ground. "Where is Jonathan Pewsey lying?"

I was more interested in the rest of the strange message. There was a beautiful rhythm to it – like poetry. And the words seemed so strong, so certain.

"Come on everyone," Anita had hurried back to find us and was now trying to herd us all together. The group of men had become stretched out as each had found other wonders to explore in the field. "Please, let's stick together. Your mentors are waiting for us at the village hall, and we were due there ten minutes ago." The men stopped what they were doing and regrouped around our stone.

"Anita?" I asked. "What does it mean? Here lies Jonathan Pewsey?"

She was only half-listening, tugging at one man who was bending down, fascinated by some prickly looking plants. "It's from before the infestation when people used to bury their dead instead of cremating them. Now, come on, quicker, please."

"In the ground?" Evan replied, unable to keep the horror out of his voice. "Does that mean..." He looked around at the field, at all the other stone slabs. "That under everyone is a... a... dead person!"

Mumbling began amongst the men, me included, as the realisation dawned upon us. The mumbling grew louder, then gave way to panic.

Bodies! We scattered in every direction, desperate to get away from the stones. Dead people! Under our very feet! Even Artemis, usually so stoic and self-composed, was running. Not knowing what else to do, I followed him.

I could hear Anita shouting for us to come back, something like *They can't hurt you, for goodness' sake!* But no one was listening, intent on putting as much space as possible between them and the death stones. We ran for a minute or so, and I was feeling it in my lungs, wishing I'd used the treadmill more at the facility. I stopped, leaning over, trying to catch my breath. I assumed Artemis had continued running, so I was surprised when I looked up and he was staring down at me. "You alright?"

I shrugged and straightened as my breathing came under control. "I think so... you?"

He didn't answer, didn't even nod. He was looking around. "What now?"

"I guess we go back and find Anita. Wait outside the field for her to come and collect us."

He frowned. "Maybe. Or we could just keep going." He was looking at the surrounding fields away from where we'd just come.

Near the pointy stone building behind us, there were other buildings – the village, I assumed. In the opposite direction, there were smaller buildings dotted about and the vast openness of fields. Brown stubbled square spaces, with the occasional tree here and there. So much space made me dizzy. And afraid. "I don't want to," I said. "You can go, but I don't think it's safe."

He gave me a narrow-eyed look. "And you think it's safe back there?" He nodded to the village. "With Anita, and whatever women we end up being placed with?"

I did think it was safe. At least I wanted to think so. Anita reminded me of the carers at the facility, not the ones like Daisy, but rather like Isla.

"What on earth are you doing out here without a chaperone!" The voice commanded attention, and I spun in terror to face a woman coming towards us along a path around the field. "I can't believe this! Where the hell is Anita?"

The woman was very tall, taller than me, and almost as tall as Artemis. Oldish, although I find it hard to tell women's ages. Her hair was dark, almost black, and cropped and peppered with grey, her face lean. She came over to Artemis and shouted directly into his face. "Why did you leave your chaperone?" She held her hand over a plastic lumpy object at the side of her trousers. I'd only seen a benzo gun once in my life – when there was a riot at the facility and some nurses medicated the residents using the small needle-tipped devices. But I recognised it.

"I SAID, why have you left Anita? If you don't give me an appropriate answer in the next five seconds, I will treat this as an escape attempt. I will assume you are hostile. FIVE… FOUR."

Artemis didn't move, didn't speak. He just stared the woman directly in the eye, with a look of pure defiance.

My words came out in a rush. "I was running away, and Artemis came after me. I got scared when Anita told us we were in a field of dead people. I ran, and then Artemis stopped me, and we were about to go back and find Anita when you… you found us."

"Is this true?" The woman hadn't, for a moment, moved her attention away from Artemis. "Well, is it?"

Artemis pursed his lips. Looking down, I could see his fists clenched into two pale, shaking balls.

"TONY! ARTEMIS!"

From a hundred meters or so away came Anita, lurching towards us. Behind her, the rest of the men held hands crocodile style, weaving their way over the mud and grass.

"I'm so sorry, Freya. They got spooked in the graveyard." When Anita caught up, she was panting. "I've been rounding them up. These are my last two lost sheep." She smiled at me, and I returned her smile with gratitude.

The tall dark-haired women broke her gaze from Artemis and gave Anita a withering stare. "Men are not children, Anita. They need a much greater level of control." Then she spoke to the arriving man-crocodile. "This is a privilege, not a right. You men are extremely lucky, and you must not forget that this is new for everyone. NEVER run away from your chaperone or your foster carer. If you are in public and you are seen running, it will be assumed that you are a hostile, infected, and you will be dealt with accordingly. Do you understand?"

There were some mumbled sorrys and some nods. Artemis remained stock still, his fists still clenched. The woman turned back to face him and spoke directly to him, keeping her hand over the lump on her belt. Her voice was low, and she spoke through clenched teeth. "Do you understand?"

A pause stretched out for an eternity of seconds. Finally, Artemis gave a quick nod.

"Good." Then she turned to Anita. "Get them to the village hall right now. The boys are already there, and the foster mothers will be arriving soon. Oh, and if any of them run off again, use cuffs."

CHAPTER 5

Jonah

Twelve little boys, aged between seven and nine, sit in a line on the wooden floor of the village hall, their eyes as wide and round as dinner plates. Three prep nurses sit beside them on chairs, chatting but also keeping close watch as the boys crane their necks, trying to take in their surroundings. Jonah sits in the line and looks up, up into the high wooden ceiling of the hall. Soon he will meet his foster brother and his foster family. Will they be nice? Will he have his own room? Jonah doesn't want to be on his own in the dark.

Three of the boys sitting with him are from the prep house. Graham has white-blonde hair and pale skin. He's quiet, like Jonah, and will give you his custard if you're sitting with him at lunch. Graham hates custard. Sanjit is very good at running. He can beat anyone in a race, even the older boys and it's always good to be picked to be on a team with him. Then there's Conrad. Jonah leans closer to Conrad, and his friend gently pushes back. His friend's warm flank offers Jonah all the reassurance he needs. He would like Conrad to groom him, to have his friend run his small fingers over his scalp and neck and check for moth hairs, as he's done every night since they graduated the nurseries. But now, he doesn't need to be groomed. The moth hairs can't hurt him since the injection.

The injection hurt. It kept hurting as the nurse pushed on the needle gun, and Jonah hadn't known if it would just keep on getting worse and worse until his arm exploded. He'd been about to wrench his arm away when the nurse pulled out and the pain went away. He was given a boiled sweet and sent to lie down in the dorm. He was told how lucky he was.

That was a week ago.

The wood on the floor is a shiny deep brown and the whole place smells dusty. He catches Conrad's eye.

Conrad smiles. "You okay, Jo-Jo?"

Jonah wishes he wasn't so scared, but he can't help it. He has bad dreams. Moths fluttering and landing on him, but he can't move, can't escape – monsters waiting for him in the darkness, ready to burn him with their fiery breath. But he must grow up. He must be brave. "Yeah… I guess. I wish Daniel was with us." Daniel is Conrad and Jonah's other best friend, their prep-brother. He was sent to a different bus, and Jonah has no idea if he will see Daniel again.

"He'll be fine," says Conrad, quiet but firm. "Daniel's kind. That's why his foster family will love him."

Conrad's right, thinks Jonah. *Daniel is kind.* Then another thought right after – *I must remember to be kind. And quiet.*

"Look, they're coming in." Jonah looks to where Conrad is pointing. A gaggle of older men are entering, dressed in colourful clothes. Jonah's never seen older men before and marvels at how tall and strong they look. Jonah hadn't expected them to be so big, their arms so thick. Would he get that strong one day? He rubs the top of his own spidery arms. The other boys fidget, squirming with excitement. The men smile at the boys and give them small waves as they are ushered to a small seating area nearby.

Finally, the doors open again, and a group of women come in. They look like nurses and carers but without uniforms. Some women smile and wave at the young boys. Some don't. They, too, come into the hall and sit on a group of chairs to the right.

"Which is mine? Which is mine?" murmurs Jonah, without realising he was speaking out loud.

A soft sweaty hand covers his on the shiny wooden floor. Conrad's hand. "Jo-Jo. Try to smile."

A lady with long blonde hair stands in the centre of the hall and speaks. But all the boys, including Jonah, find it hard to listen. They are all turning to look at the woman and the men. Some men pull funny faces at the boys. One very tall man points at Jonah, smiles and gives a thumbs up gesture. Jonah smiles back, shyly.

"… All men and boys must only leave their foster homes in the presence of a member of the family. Vaccine medications will be the responsibility of the primary carer and any failure to take medications will result in the immediate withdrawal of freedom. Remember, gentlemen, the vaccine is a privilege, not a right. In a moment –"

The door bursts open once more, and a lone woman stands in the doorway draped in a heavy coat. She is older than the rest of the women, plump with long greying hair. On her back, she carries a heavy-looking bag.

"Come in, come in. We've just started," says the blonde speaker in the middle of the hall. "Foster families are over there." She waves the newcomer in the direction of the other women, but the woman in the heavy coat doesn't move in their direction. Instead, she moves towards the blonde woman in the middle of the room.

"No, madam – I said over there."

Jonah looks to Conrad, who is frowning. "Who is she?"

Conrad holds Jonah's hand a little tighter. "I don't know."

The grey-haired woman in the middle of the room opens her coat to reveal a tee shirt emblazoned with two Xs in a circle. "For the Union," she cries, her face contorted into a mask of hatred and fear. "In the name of the women killed in the infestation. For the sanctity and purity of our new world. I give my life so the women of future generations will be safe and FREE!"

The woman reaches around into her pack and fumbles with something. Women begin running towards the door.

"Conrad, what's happening?" Jonah grabs his best friend's hand and holds on.

There's a flash of light and the roar of a thousand monsters. The unanswered question drifts like ash onto the ruined floor.

Outside, it begins to rain.

Evie

I'd been awake all night, fretting about the day. The room was ready for the men. Mae, although not particularly helpful over the last week, had at least kept out of the way. She'd been quiet about the whole thing, in fact.

The MWA had allocated us extra household rations, and I'd splurged on jars of honey, jams, extra rich cream, hard cheese. I'd even managed to get hold of a few oranges, Mum's favourite. We also doubled our usual fare of potatoes, vegetables, eggs, beans, nuts, and flour. Apparently, boys eat a lot.

Both Mae and I had been granted six weeks off work to run sequentially so that for at least the next three months one of us would be home with the boys. I don't know how Mae felt about this. When the message came through the post, I thought she'd refuse immediately. Instead, she gave me a nervous look over the top of her owlish glasses and shrugged. "Fine," she'd said. "I'll babysit the boys. How hard can it be?"

The boys. That's what they'd become. A unit, a project, a concept. A few nights ago, after fidgeting and wriggling, I'd snuck out of bed to the spare room to find the picture of the Sullivans, which I'd stowed at the back of the wardrobe. I ran my finger over Marcus's top lip to try and remove his milk moustache and then over Mr Sullivan's cheek, imagining I could feel the stubble. Mae had come looking for me, and I'd only just been able to stuff the picture back in the cupboard and shut the door in time.

"What are you doing?" she'd asked, finding me standing in the spare room, looking like a rat caught by torchlight.

"I… er… Just checking everything's in place," I replied, gesturing to the two neatly made-up beds.

She gave me a scathing look. "Come back to bed."

Pick-up day finally arrived. To nobody's surprise, Molly had also been selected, so she and I had spent the previous evening at our house pondering on how it would go, chatting over tea, trying to get our heads around what we'd signed up for, what to expect.

Mae came down after checking on Mum. "You've had four kids, Molly, four! This should be a breeze for you."

"Four *girls*, Mae. I don't have the faintest idea what to do with a boy. I mean, shaving for a start! No, we are in the same boat on this one."

As Mae and I left the house, I picked up two extra coats. I'd no idea how warmly the boys would be dressed. The morning air was chilly.

We reached the village hall and joined several other women huddled around outside the door. Molly was there, clutching a couple of shawls, as were a few others I recognised from the village. Others may have come from farmsteads further out or nearby villages. The babble of voices was excited and restless.

Are we given a benzo gun do you think?

Geraldine thought we needed a whole different type of toilet system – can you imagine?

It's a pity we don't get to pick.

I need one to help Jemima in the field. Can they ride a horse?

Do they know how to read, do you think?

They can use a bathroom unaided, right?

The babble of questions and comments was then aimed at Anita, Dr Rosya's wife who was replying with admirable speed and patience. "Yes, they can use a bathroom, no they can't ride a horse... but I'm sure they can learn. The men are quite strong, but they tire easily. Some can read, but usually not very well." She stood and waved her hands at the twittering mob. "Now listen, you will be given lots of information in the hall and sent home with a pamphlet outlining everything you need to know. Either Freya or I will be on call 24/7 based right here in Eastor, in case there is something you need to ask, or you get into difficulties. Both the foster men and the boys have been settled down in the hall. I recommend that when you go in, give them a smile and keep calm. I imagine they are feeling a little nervous, this is a lot of change for them, especially the little ones."

The little ones. The words gave me an excited flutter in my stomach. I was about to have a child!

As the doors opened, I looked sideways at Mae. She wasn't smiling. Then she caught my look and gave a half-hearted grin. "Here we go," she said. She was trying, at least.

In the hall, the men were sitting to one side on a set of chairs, and the boys sat cross-legged in the centre. A few nurses sat on chairs near the little boys, keeping watch over their wards. We were ushered into another seating area. It felt very organised, almost like a ceremony. The smell of beeswax suggested that the floors had recently been polished and woodland flowers sat in vases around the room. The men were dressed in an assortment of what looked like donated clothing, sitting quietly, most with their heads down, sneaking shy looks at us now and then. The little boys were still in their prep house uniform grey shifts. They were less bashful, offering gappy smiles and small waves. I raised my hand and half waved in return at one freckled boy with ginger hair.

The Waterloo survivor from the initial meeting, Freya Curtis, strode to the centre of the room. She wore another tailored suit, this time in navy, her dark hair slicked back.

"Ladies," she addressed us with a small bow then turned to the men and boys. "Gentlemen." A titter rose from the women at the oddness of it all. "Allow me to welcome you to Eastor and its surrounding hamlets. In a moment, Anita will take you all through the things you need to know about this mentoring programme." Her voice was clipped and rough like granite. "But first I wanted to impress upon our gentleman visitors one vital piece of information. Something that you should have been told before arriving."

I had the impression that the men were listening intently, although most of them had their heads bowed and were looking at their hands in their laps. All except one. One man was looking directly at Curtis, unblinking, and it seemed as if it was to that one man, she was directing this little speech. "Men and boys MUST NOT leave their foster house without a female chaperone."

Her eyes lingered for a few more moments on the single man who still sat and stared boldly ahead, before her stare fell on the little boys. "Am I clear?" Her voice dropped a fraction as she addressed the children, but even so, twelve frightened little faces gave frantic nods. "Good." She went on "I also want to extend a huge thank you to all of you women who have taken on such a noble task. The Union called for brave pioneers, and you have heeded that call. You should all consider yourselves patriots of the Union and, despite the challenges ahead, you have shown kindness, fortitude and sacrifice for the betterment of the Union." There were a few blushes and smiles at this. Mae's face, however, reflected a tinge of panic at Freya's words.

"Now I shall hand over to –" But just then, the doors opened again and in burst a woman I'd never seen before. The woman made a beeline for Anita and Freya, clutching her coat around her thick frame.

She spoke in an urgent whisper. Gesticulating and shooting glances back at the doors.

Anita went pale. She ran and stood by the door, opening

it and peeking out. Freya spoke again, ignoring the men and speaking directly to us. Her voice was cool, unemotional. "It seems there has been an incident at the village hall in Chesterford. Considering this, we will need you to collect your wards, and a pamphlet, and take your men and boys home immediately. You will be contacted by an MWA case worker in the next few days. Anita has a list of your allotted fosterlings."

There was chattering around me. And then movement. Whatever this was, I suspected it wasn't the nice, organised handover the MWA had hoped for.

I looked at Molly and she frowned. "This doesn't feel right."

I nodded.

Mae looked from side to side. "None of this feels right."

We stood in line as numbers were called out and small boys and men came over nervously, to be escorted away by ones and twos of women. It was all happening quickly. Molly was allocated a grinning little boy with dark skin and sparkling dark eyes and a gently smiling man in a knitted skirt and jersey. As she led them away, one in each hand, she mouthed to me: *It'll be fine!*

Then it was our turn. Two numbers were called out and a delicate and very serious-looking young boy approached. "What's your name?" I asked, smiling a little too widely.

"Daniel," he replied, his little face freckled and anxious.

"I'm Artemis," said a tall man approaching us by the door. It was the same man I'd noticed when Freya was speaking. The one with the bold stare.

"Great," said Mae, not sounding at all enthusiastic. "I'm Mae, this is Evie. Now, let's get back to the house. It's raining."

XX104

We didn't know what she was going to do, the red-haired woman I'd only known as XX62. Or rather I didn't know. I'd seen her at headquarters a few times, painting banners, in the art hall, once in XX02's office. She scampered out as I went in, flicking quick looks in my direction. She reminded me of a squirrel, with her greyish-red hair and her quick movements. There was a brightness to her eyes that made me shiver.

When the news broke of the incident in Chesterford, I was horrified. Children? Boy-children, yes. But still – *children*. I spoke to the co-ordinator XX02 that night on the phone, holding the receiver close and checking over my shoulder to make sure no one was in earshot.

"None of us knew," she said over the crackling line. "She went rogue. It wasn't sanctioned by the movement."

"But she was one of us."

"She was acting alone – I didn't know anything about it. Now, tell me about the mission. Is everything in place at the facility?" There was something in her voice that gave me pause, a tautness that suggested there was more to it, but I let it lie.

We talked about the mission. I reported that I'd managed to recruit some facility workers to the cause and that the plan was on track. Her last words to me: *Good work. After this the Council will have no option but to reconsider.* I replaced the handset and stood in the hallway for a few moments, listening to the sound of the radio coming from the living room. Doubts crept through me like damp. How did XX62 get explosives? It wasn't like there was a black market for such things these days. What if she'd chosen another handover? The one at Eastor for example? I shuddered at the thought.

Terrorism. Is that what I was? A terrorist? I felt queasy and all the bravado of the last few months began to drain from me. But then I thought of Bella, of my mother, of Miranda and a long-buried memory of a woman on an underground station in a yellow dress. Well so be it, I thought, as I slammed down rising guilt and shame. The Council brought this on themselves by not thinking this through. They started a war, and in a war, people get hurt.

But children?

I swallowed hard and took a deep breath. Worse things would happen if the Council went down this road. Not just the deaths of a few boy-children but widespread violence against women, young girls' rape, subjugation. No, I was no terrorist – I was a soldier, and my fight was life or death.

At first, I thought he must have been a terrorist.

In London at that time, it wasn't unheard of for some lone person to go crazy and start stabbing people or blowing themselves up. It wasn't common, but it happened. Maybe that's why the New Union discouraged religions after the infestation. When the girls learn about religions at school, these days, they are all portrayed as savage. Most weren't – it was just some oddball extremists taking their beliefs in weird directions. But it's true that we've had no mass killings or bombings in the name of any religious figures for the last forty years.

We'd negotiated Waterloo and ridden the long escalator down to the tube, squashing ourselves to the right as much busier people, laden with bags, marched down on the left. I held onto Bella's hand as we weaved our way through the crowds. Her bag was heavy, so she'd whined until I'd agreed to carry it for her. I had the arms of our two backpacks awkwardly threaded on my shoulder and her sticky hand in mine while the platform crowd pressed on us as we waited for the tube. It was unbearably hot. Whooshing superheated wind, like mini Saharan storms, blew over us every time a tube went past on another line. I nudged forward on the edge of the platform.

"MIND the gap!" said Bella, mimicking the announcer as she tugged me back from the edge. Another woman, one in a yellow maxi dress and doc martin boots, stepped eagerly into the prime spot Bella had just forced me to vacate.

I rolled my eyes. "We're miles away from the edge."

"It's what the voice says," she replied without apology.

My phone started ringing in my pack. It had to be Mum or Dad. No one else used the phone to ring. I tried to flip around and get to my pack, but Bella's got in the way. I'd have to dump both bags and let go of Bella's hand to dig my phone out, and I wasn't about to do that. Not with the tube due imminently. They'd leave a message. A voicemail probably, like we were living in the dark ages.

The train was almost there. I could hear the grinding wheels and feel the warm wind from up the tracks. It was then that someone started jostling nearby, a man with tanned skin and straight black hair making a weird noise, a groan, like he'd been punched in the stomach. Then he turned to the woman in front of us, the one in the yellow dress, and curled his hands around her shoulders. I could see his fingers digging into her skin, making fat dimples with his nails.

"Who the hell are you? What are you doing?" She tried to back off, but she backed into us, stepping on my feet, and I couldn't step out of her way – there were too many people crowding the platform.

I looked back to see if I could find a space to reverse into, maybe say something to the person behind. I didn't like the way his hands gripped her or the noise he was making. Perhaps someone else – someone older – could see what was going on, help out, take charge. Then there was a scream, barely audible over the screech of the arriving tube, and the crowd suddenly surged backwards. I nearly fell over, but gripped Bella's hand. She was pallid in the artificial station light, her eyes unblinking and her lips moving slightly as if reciting a silent prayer. I looked in the direction of her gaze. The black-haired man and the woman were no longer on the platform. A few people peered over the edge, and one pointed. My eyes followed and I saw a flash of yellow fabric. "Oh," I murmured, sucking a short breath in… "Oh, no."

I pulled Bella back. What had she seen whilst I'd been distracted?

People panicked and started pushing from all directions. We were perilously close to the edge, and I clung to my sister's hand as I tried to force my way back through the crowd.

Voices cut through the stifling air. *What happened? Did she jump? Were they together?* People raised their phones, recording the chaos, sending the images around the world in moments. Broken limbs, flesh, horror. There were places on the internet where these images would be celebrated, devoured.

I needed to get us as far away as possible. I swallowed the shock and almost ran from the platform, up the stairs and towards the main exit to Waterloo, dragging poor Bella behind me.

When we got outside into the sunshine, we were both breathing hard.

"Are you okay?" I asked, dumping our bags on the ground, crouching down, running my hand over her cheek.

Her big brown eyes were still a little unfocussed. There was sweat beading on her top lip. "I want to get to Dad's." Her voice came out as a croak.

I got my phone out and checked the messages. One from Dad.

Hey, baby. I've had to go out for a meeting, and I won't be back till late. Be a love and bring something home for dinner. Miranda's got her hands full with Jorge. Pizza? Love you.

Irritation surged through me. Bella needed to talk to a grownup about what just happened. I didn't know what she saw, how this sort of thing affected the mind of an eight year-old. I was out of my depth. If we'd stayed at home, watching Netflix, none of this would have happened. *If Dad hadn't left us, none of this would have happened!*

I picked up the bags and turned to Bella. "How do you fancy a taxi ride? And some pizza?"

She shrugged and didn't look up. "And ice-cream," I added.

"The expensive kind with the chunks in?" Still nothing. I gently took her hand and led her towards the rank thinking about all the things I was going to say to Dad when I saw him next.

Tony

Molly, Sam, Martha, Eloise, Melanie, Tess and Layton! Molly, Sam, Martha –

I repeated the names over and over. This is my new family, at least for the next few months. Molly, one of my new mothers – although I was to call her by her first name – collected me from Eastor village hall. As we were leaving, I got my bad feeling. Logan used to tease me about my bad feeling, used to say it was too much lemon-curd pie. But I had it the day Logan became infected at the facility all those years ago. I had it when poor Cole disappeared a few months ago. And I had it again today. But it wasn't Molly who was giving me the jitters. There was something about the looks on the faces of the women in charge as they hustled us out of the hall – the sharp whispers and the nervous looks. I asked Molly about it, but she said it was nothing to worry about. Then, as we got outside, she smiled and pulled a long soft fluffy scarf out of her bag, leaned up and tucked it round my neck.

"It's chilly today. Let's not catch a cold before we even get home."

She took out a matching one and did the same for Layton, my new little brother, who grinned, immediately unwound it and began using it as a skipping rope. In horror, I leapt towards the little boy, trying to stop him from dragging his new gift through the mud. But Molly just chuckled and gently plucked the now grubby scarf from Layton's small fingers. "I'll get you a proper jump rope when we get back, sweetheart. This one is to keep you warm."

Any residual bad feeling from the hall dimmed, and a tide

of gratitude washed over me. I liked Molly. She took us, one in each hand, and led us along the path towards our awaiting transportation.

I'd never seen such an animal before, and with mounting terror I realised Molly was leading us straight towards it. It was taller than me at its shoulder, producing a spluttering noise that sat somewhere between a growl and a sneeze. I wondered briefly if it was dangerous, if I should run away from its snapping jaws, but as it just stood placidly, allowing Layton to stroke its comically long face and its softly quivering nostrils, I realised that it was not about to tear me to pieces.

Molly led me and Layton to a small open wooden box with wheels and a low seat, just big enough for two. The boy had to clamber onto my lap. I held him tightly as Molly picked up the ropes attached to bindings on the creature, and the wheeled box jigged along. *Get me some ink and paper and hire some horses to ride!* Of course – this was a horse! And we were riding. "It's a horse," I said to Layton as he held on to my arms. I pointed a finger at the creature.

"I know," replied the boy. "We were shown pictures of them at the prep house. And this is a trap." He pointed down to the wheeled box.

"Very good, Layton. This is indeed a trap." Molly gave the boy one of her magical smiles.

Molly's praise annoyed me, as did Layton's casual dismissal of my comment. In my mind I'd imagined the boy clinging to my every word, fascinated and awed by his elder brother in equal measure, looking to me for reassurance. But he showed no fear at all. Instead, he jumped about on my lap, trying to look in every direction at once. Then he started naming things we passed. "Tree! House! COW!"

"Very good, Layton," replied Molly. "And what do we get from cows?"

Layton looked confused. "Eggs?"

"Milk," I replied, trying to keep the smugness out of my tone.

"Good, Tony. What else?" It was the first time she'd used my name, and I felt myself inflate with joy. But then I realised she'd asked a question. "Umm, cheese?"

She smiled. "Yes, but not just cheese. Leather and sometimes meat for dinner."

I frowned. "What do you mean, leather? How can leather come from cows? And what's meat?" Whatever it was, we weren't given it in the facility. Unless it was a kind of lentil.

Molly kept her eyes on the road and steered us expertly around a pothole. "Not usually girl cows. They're too valuable for making the milk. But boy cows, they don't produce the milk so..."

Layton wasn't listening. "Stream! Field! CAR!"

"So..." I replied. "What happens to the boy cows, Molly?" I tried to keep my voice even, but the bad feeling had returned, and, along with the jogging of the trap, was making me feel sick.

Molly glanced my way, and I couldn't read her expression. "Never mind. We'll talk about it later."

"TONY! TONY! It's a CAR! See, over there. A new car!"

I wanted to carry on talking about the boy cows, but Layton was making it difficult to concentrate, pointing so hard to the left that he nearly fell out of the trap. I caught him and tucked him firmly under my arm as I followed his gaze. We passed a new-looking grey car parked outside a large, red-bricked house with ivy growing around the windows. A car just like the one Artemis and I travelled in. I wondered for a moment how Artemis was getting on in his new family.

"So that's where that Freya Curtis woman is staying," murmured Molly. "It's a bit out in the sticks." Then she shot me a glance. "Nearly home," she said sharply. "Get yourself ready to meet the tribe."

"What's a tribe?" asked Layton, and I was relieved because I didn't know either.

"It's a large family. And we have a very large family."

I didn't know how to prepare myself for meeting a larger family, so I asked, "what are their names?"

"Your other foster carer is called Sam. Then your foster sisters are Martha, Eloise, Melanie and the youngest one is Tess. Martha, the oldest, is away, working on a road repair crew near Birmingham, so you won't meet her yet. Tess, she's about the same age as you, Layton."

Layton grinned. "That's not a big family, he replied. There were twelve of us in my dorm room and I remembered everyone's name and all the carers and prep nurses in our wing. I can remember a hundred names!"

Molly laughed. "I'm sure you can, my handsome little gentleman."

I was less certain of my name-remembering ability.

Molly, Sam, Martha, Eloise, Melanie, Tess and Layton!

I ran through the names again and again in my mind.

CHAPTER 6

Evie

SECTION 5
SEXUAL RELATIONSHIPS AND THE MEN IN YOUR CARE

SEX AND THE LAW:
The Social Welfare Law Abidance Act of 2039 set the legal age of consent at sixteen. This is for all acts of penetrative and oral sex, and mutual masturbation. The Act, however, did not cover men, as at the time, the MWA reasoned infected men were incapable of offering up consent. Decades later, with the introduction of the hetero-recreation programme, it was decided that the age of consent for men should be set at eighteen.

Half of the male fosterlings are children, well below the age of consent, and so this section of the leaflet does not apply in these cases. All men under the age of eighteen are, in the eyes of the law, incapable of consent, and to engage in a sexual relationship with a child, of any sex, is, of course, a serious crime.

MALES AND SEXUALITY:
The men from the facilities are all over the age of consent, and most will have been active participants

in the recreation programmes run at facilities all over the Union. Sex with men is not prohibited, however, there are some things to consider if embarking on a heterosexual relationship that may not have occurred to you before.

1. Pregnancy.

Without precautions, you may become pregnant. If this happened without the input of the insemination gene screening procedure, you could not choose the sex of your child and you may conceive a male child. Rules on this are changing all the time in light of the vaccine, and the MWA have decided that male children born after 2073 will not automatically be eligible for contribution. Unless circumstances dictate otherwise, they will be the responsibility of the birthmother and, if applicable, her wife, rather than the responsibility of the state. Also, without screening, the unborn foetus, whatever sex, may carry genes which could lead to diseases and disabilities later in life. Termination of a non-engineered foetus will be available. However, it is best to prevent this from happening in the first place. Before arrival, the men will have been provided with contraceptive medicines and instructions on how to use them, (most will be familiar with this process due to being participants in the hetero-recreation visitations), but you must check that the correct medication has been administered.

2. Emotional considerations

The men in your care have grown up in a protected environment. Research carried out in the facilities has shown that men may become invested in relationships very quickly. If guided, they are generally affectionate, obliging, and intuitive. However, the researchers observed that, occasionally, men can become territorial or depressed. If this happens, especially if the man under your guidance displays any anti-social behaviour, it is important that you let your foster coordinator know immediately, so that the man in question can be prescribed hormone modification therapy and counselling.

3. The risk of coercion

Men are usually keen to form physical relationships. However, as their primary guide in this new environment, and as facilitators of their wellbeing, you are held in a position of trust. Be mindful of this dynamic and ensure that all sexual activities are consensual. Do not, for example, suggest either implicitly or explicitly that their continued care and support is in any way dependent on their engagement in a physical relationship.

Mae flung the pamphlet across the cramped sitting room. It skittered over the floor and landed in a crumpled heap perilously close to the fire. "Coercion. Seriously?"

She held her glass of wine aloft from her vantage on the sofa and her voice grew louder. "This makes us sound like a bunch of, of... what's the word, rapists!"

"Shhhh. They'll hear you." I bent down and picked up the booklet, smoothed out some pages, placing it on an old pine coffee table. It had been a long day. We arrived home at lunch, which had been a strained affair, me asking questions and the boys giving one-word answers and Mae not speaking at all. Then I'd showed the boys the house, which had taken about ten whole minutes. Mum had been feeling ill, so I'd left her room out of the tour. Mae had disappeared after lunch, mumbling about important errands. I'd tried to interest the boys in a game of Snakes and Ladders, one of my old favourites.

Artemis, the older one, had declined and gone to sit alone in the garden. Daniel had tried to play, but his luck was atrocious and he barely made it off the first row before I landed home. He sat, head bowed with a why-is-this-fun look in his eyes but carried on for my benefit, I think.

After a quiet dinner they both went to bed and Mae had arrived home, a little drunk, clutching a bottle of blackberry wine.

"So, I can't even speak in my own house now?" Her voice swayed. "It's not like I was planning to jump into bed with a man. All those extra bits. It's unnatural if you ask me."

I thought of pointing out that I hadn't asked, but held my tongue. What was the point? Might as well try to halt a bloated river. But it pained me to keep quiet. We'd been doing so well these last few days. Not completely back to normal, but better. Why did she have to spoil everything, on this day of all days?

She was still talking. "And anyway, I wouldn't want Artemis. He's as miserable as a February breeze. Hardly spoke a word on the way here, looking around him as if it's all beneath him, as if he deserves better. One thing's for sure – he needn't worry about being coerced." She gave a mean bark of laughter and I stared at the living room door, silently begging it to keep her words inside the room.

It was true, Artemis had said little on the short walk from the village hall. He hadn't smiled either. The only time he'd paid any attention was when the little boy, Daniel, asked him in a small polite voice if he liked his new trousers. "Yes," he'd replied. And then after a pause, "Thank you, young man." Also, when he'd reached the house, his height and heft had made the small rooms feel tiny. I lost count of the number of times he'd bumped his head on a low beam, each time giving the offending beam a resentful stare. "I'll have to walk about bent over, like I'm bowing," he mumbled, before going outside.

"I think they're both adjusting, Mae. They'll be more with it tomorrow."

Mae made a face like she'd just caught a whiff of overripe cheese. "The boy's too quiet. I thought he'd be like a bouncy little girl, you know, cheeky, into everything – like the boy Molly took home. But he's as grumpy as his foster brother."

"I think he's just shy. Would you like another pasty? There's one left."

But Mae was warming to her cause. "What have you lumbered us with, Evie, what with your mother upstairs and now two more mouths to feed? I honestly don't know why I agreed."

I kept quiet and didn't remind my wife that she agreed as a way of forcing me to move to the Citadel, away from everything I knew and loved, including my mother and my home. A wave of irritation prickled my skin.

Mae was still talking, her wine sloshing around in its glass. "Perhaps the XXs have a point, eh? Maybe this whole thing has been rushed. Not thought through. What if –"

"Mae!" I couldn't help myself. I could feel rage pulsing through me. Still mindful that the boys were asleep upstairs, I kept my voice low. "How could you say such a terrible thing? People died today in Chesterford. Four little boys died! The XXs are a bunch of lunatics."

Mae rolled her eyes and didn't keep her voice down. "Of course, I don't condone blowing up kids! But that doesn't mean we can't consider the message. Those boys… that man we brought home today will not integrate into our world. I saw it on his face – he could barely look at us. Don't tell me you didn't notice."

I gave a weary sigh. "It will take some time. If we just –"

"We? This is *you* now, Evie. There's no *we*. You made sure of that when you went behind my back and applied in the first place. And if you think –"

Mae's bitter crescendo was cut short by a firm tap. We both looked at each other in surprise before I stepped back and opened the door. There in the doorway stood Artemis, his too-short nightgown and robe riding high on his pale thighs. He gave both me and Mae a cool stare. "Daniel has had a little... accident," he said. "He's crying about it. I've tried to console him, but he will need more bedding." And with that, he spun on his heel and went back upstairs.

I didn't even look to see if Mae had reacted. I shot upstairs and into the boys' bedroom. Artemis had got back into bed but was sitting up, offering me a guarded stare. Daniel sat on a rumpled bed, his knees up to his chin, a sheet bunched up in his small fist. The tell-tale splodge of damper material trailed out at one end.

"I'm so... so sorry," the little boy managed, thrusting the soiled sheet towards me, before dissolving into mumbling sobs.

I took the sheet and dumped it in the corner of the room. Before I knew what I was doing, I'd scooped his little body in my arms and begun making nonsensical noises. "Heyayaya, chchch, shhhh." After a few moments of rocking his bony collection of limbs, I cleared my throat. "It's okay. I'll make up the bed for you, good as new."

"I'm... sorry," he said again through a bout of hiccups. "I... don't usually..."

"I know. It's all very new." I sat him on my lap facing me and wiped the tears from his face with the palm of my hand. His hiccups became deep shuddering breaths which eventually returned to normal.

He rubbed his hands over his eyes and yawned. Then in a small voice he mumbled, "You smell nice, Evie. Like sunshine."

"Maybe it's my soap," I said, bringing him in for another hug and marvelling at the softness of his cheek. "It's got lavender in it." Over Daniel's shoulder, my eyes rested on Artemis. I thought I caught something in his expression shift, a flash of something warmer, before his features settled back into cool indifference.

I dragged my attention back to the boy. "Shall we get you out of these wet things, Daniel?"

The boy nodded and climbed from my lap, meekly allowing

me to change him from his wet nightdress, raising his arms as I pulled it over his head.

A few minutes later, Daniel was tucked up, warm and dry and breathing deeply. I sat on the edge of the bed, not sure whether to leave. He'd worn such a worried expression all day, it was nice to watch his little face relax in sleep.

"I'll make sure he's okay." Artemis's voice jolted me from my thoughts. "If he gets upset, I'll come and find you."

There was something loaded about the way he said *you* that made me pause, something suggesting that he knew not to go to Mae. I nodded. "Thank you Artemis. That's very kind." I gave one last look at the sleeping Daniel and left the room.

On my way past, I popped my head around Mum's door, even though it was late. Her eyes were open in the low light. "Everything alright?" she croaked.

"Yeah – nothing I can't handle. I'll tell you all about it tomorrow."

"I was thinking I might try to come downstairs tomorrow, meet the boys."

I was surprised. Mum hadn't been downstairs in weeks. "Okay, I'll give you a hand down the stairs before breakfast."

Then, as I was about to go, she added, "You're doing the right thing, fostering. For the Union."

"Thanks, Mum," I said, and shut the door quietly.

Was she right? I thought, as I made my way down to the basement with an armful of dirty bedclothes. *Am I doing the right thing?* But I couldn't shake a creeping doubt filling my heart. *I'm woefully out of my depth.*

XX104

The house was a state.

Miranda met us at the door in jogging pants and a stained tee shirt, her coppery hair pulled up into a messy top knot. She was clutching a squirming Jorge. "Oh hi, did you get Simon's message?"

It annoyed me that she called Dad 'Simon,' especially when Bella was there. It was like she was gently tugging him further away from being our dad. Would she refer to him as 'Simon' to Jorge when he grew up? I doubted it.

"Yeah, here," I said, offering her a bag of frozen pizzas.

She jerked her chin to the kitchen as Jorge tried to launch himself into a full backflip. "Put them in there. I've got my hands full." She said it lightly, but there was an edge. There was always an edge with Miranda. I'd known her forever – she'd been a neighbour, the daughter of our neighbour, to be more precise. She'd even babysat me before Bella was born. When she'd returned from university, she'd moved back in with her parents and joined the same running club as Dad. One minute she was knocking on the door dressed in Sweaty Betty Lycra as Dad slid past us in the hall fumbling with his laces, the next, Dad was starting a new job, moving to London, and leaving us.

Mum was tight-lipped, refusing to be mean about him in front of me and Bella. But I was fourteen. I gave Mum a hard time, blaming her. "I can't keep him here if he doesn't want to stay," she said to me one evening when I'd shouted at her for letting him go. Then she burst into tears. I've never felt like such a dickhead as I did then.

I dumped the pizzas on the side of their tiny kitchen as Jorge wailed. Miranda looked tired and I was glad. I was glad Jorge was a difficult baby. I was glad they lived in this small, untidy space that smelled like spoiled milk, and I was glad that Miranda looked puffy and miserable and Dad had to work all the time. Served them both right.

Jorge stopped wailing, and I put my head around the doorway. Bella sat on the sofa, next to a pile of laundry, and held Jorge under his arms as his little legs pushed at her thighs. Miranda, it seemed, had left the two of them and had gone to shower.

"Look at his tiny fists," she said, as I shifted the laundry and sat down next to her. "And his little nubby teeth."

"I remember when you were this small." I threaded my finger into Jorge's grip, marvelling at how strong he was.

"Was I this cute?"

"Cuter. So much cuter."

"I don't think so."

"It's true." Jorge then treated us to an owlish yawn, which added to his cuteness, and we both laughed.

"Bells… today on the platform. Do you want to talk about what happened? About what you saw?"

"Nah, I was looking at you." She smiled at the baby as she spoke, and Jorge gave a small half-smile back. I wondered then if she was lying to me. Or if her mind was protecting itself, lying to itself.

Later, after the infestation, there was an initiative by the New Union called the Unburdening. Women talked themselves raw of the horror, the violence. A few, though, just pretended it didn't happen. They built their new lives on the graves of husbands, fathers, sons, and the hordes of murdered women, but never looked down. Eyes fixed ahead, day after day, hour after hour.

Miranda came in wearing slightly cleaner sweatpants and a tee shirt, her hair wrapped in a towel. "Hey, look at you guys getting along." She looked at me. "Could I have a quick word?"

I got up.

Miranda turned to Bella. "If he kicks off, give me a shout."

We went into the main bedroom, unmade bed, clothes everywhere. I wondered how Dad could choose to live like this over us and Mum. When I'd asked him why he left, he'd shrugged. "Miranda needs me, and… I don't have to try as hard with her. Your mum and me… I dunno, it was hard. This is easier. But I still love you and Bells. Never forget it." But at the end of the day, he didn't love us enough to stay. I mean, it's an undeniable fact. If he loved us more, he would have stayed.

"Have you heard about the weird stuff happening in Europe? The murders and the deaths?" Miranda picked a pile of baby onesies off the unmade bed and dumped them on an already loaded chair, then sat down in the space she'd made.

"I thought it was just in Germany," I replied, looking round for a space to sit and not finding one.

"No, it's all over the place. They say some of it's in France." She waved her phone at me. "And I can't get through to your dad. I've been calling and texting, but nothing."

I repressed an eye roll. "Dad'll be working, you know what he's been like since…" I nearly said since he moved out, but the words felt bitter on my tongue.

"Yes, but he usually texts back – even if it's just an emoji."

So, Dad was using emojis now. Miranda had dark crescents under her eyes, and as she held her mobile in her hand, I noted her short nails, bitten right down to the quick. My mood softened. "Did you get any sleep? You look knackered."

She shook her head, still staring at the screen. "No – Jorge won't settle if I'm not holding him. And this stuff in the news, it's freaking me out."

I had planned on telling her about Bella's encounter on the underground earlier. I wanted to ask whether I should get Bella talking about it. But one look at Miranda's bloodshot eyes told me she was right on the edge of what she could cope with. "You stay in here for a bit and have a nap. I'll watch Jorge and Bells, okay?"

Her face changed to one of abject gratitude, and she reached towards me. I thought she was going to hug me, and I took a tiny step back.

She patted me on the arm instead. "That would be great – just an hour or so. Okay? There's some expressed milk in the fridge in a bottle. And a puree apple pot."

"Sure." I left her on her bed, clasping her phone, texting Dad again.

I walked into the sitting room and Bella was holding a smiling Jorge out at arm's length. "He smells bad, Beans. I think he's done a poo."

I groaned. "Great. Hand him over."

Tony

I didn't meet the whole tribe at once – which was a relief. Sam was still working in the fields. Martha was away working. We were greeted by Eloise, a neatly dressed older teenager, with smooth copper braids, pale skin, and almond eyes; Melanie, a stout, dark-eyed girl of about fifteen who wore a scowl – an expression I was to discover in time that rarely left her features; and little Tess. Tess was scruffy with frizzy hair. She had a wide gappy grin to match Layton's.

"I'm Tess," she shouted, as soon as we entered the large warm kitchen. "And I've been waiting for you to get here all morning."

"Hello," replied Layton, sidling behind Molly in a somewhat rare moment of shyness.

"Tess, take Layton upstairs and show him his room," said Molly, unbuttoning her coat.

"You're it!" Tess lunged at Layton and started a spirited game of tag with the boy who dropped any coy pretence in an instant and began tearing after the little girl, both of them clattering up a wide flight of wooden stairs, laughing.

Molly turned to me. "You'll be sharing a room. Just you and Layton."

"Which means me and Tess have to bunk in with Eloise. And Eloise fidgets and talks in her sleep." The scowling Melanie delivered her grievance in a low, clipped whine.

"Melanie!" snapped Eloise. "Don't be rude."

"Make Tony a cup of tea. I'm going to take Sam some lunch," said Molly, unmoved, it seemed, by Melanie's complaints. She took a package from the sideboard and left through the door from which we'd come.

I'd never seen girls before. The carers at the facility join in their early twenties, post university, so I'd no idea what to expect. What struck me was how confident they seemed, how they owned the space in which they stood, despite being so small and young. Also, they seemed oddly unfinished, like the original sketch upon which the older women I'd known were based. I thought about Mary. How she must have looked like these girls at one point, and even more strange, that these girls would look like her in many years' time. I tried to age them up in my mind, but I couldn't do it.

"Say something," said Eloise with a smile. "I want to hear your voice."

The two girls stared at me, waiting, and I felt a hot blush creep up my neck. "I don't know what to say," I mumbled back. I looked at my guitar where Molly had left it by the door. I wished I had it in my arms.

Eloise gave a chuckle, and Melanie snorted.

"I don't know what to say," repeated Melanie in a comically deep voice. "He sounds like Sam."

Eloise laughed again, and I blushed a deeper red. Eloise's attitude changed immediately. "Oh, I'm sorry Tony. I didn't mean to make you uncomfortable. We've never heard a young man speak. We've seen pictures in school, but not… I mean, pictures don't speak, do they, eh?"

"No, I'm fine. It's fine." I stumbled over my words, not wanting to offend anyone on my first day. "Your voices are very high. Which is… nice."

Both girls dissolved into giggles, but they didn't seem offended. Even Melanie's scowl softened slightly. "I'll put the kettle on," she said, and started puttering about the kitchen.

"Come and see, Tony! Come and see our room!" The cry came from the top of the stairs.

I looked at Eloise as if seeking permission. She gave a nod. "Go see."

At the top of the stairs was a cramped, dark corridor with several doors leading from it. Layton was hanging out of one door and beckoning me with theatrical hand gestures. I had to duck my head to enter the low doorway. Inside, the room was set into the eaves of the house. The room was tiny and had space for two small beds and nothing else. I looked down at both beds dubiously, not sure that either one would allow me to stretch out fully. "Isn't it great!" said Layton, jumping on the other bed, Tess jumping alongside him.

"This used to be my bed, but now it's Layton's. And I don't mind one bit. I'm just glad he's here, and he likes to play games. And…" Then she stopped bouncing, turned, and grabbed Layton's arm, her small eyes wide with excitement. "Have you met Snow?"

Layton nodded. "The horse? He's quite big."

"He's the best horse in the whole world! Come on. I'll show you how to groom him." Then she dragged the boy out of the room and down the stairs.

I needed space and some quiet. Everything was too new. I sat on my bed for a few minutes with my head buried in my hands and tried to block out the world. This is what I wanted, what I dreamed about. But what if I just wanted a holiday from the facility rather than leaving it behind completely? I longed for just a drop of the routine I'd left behind, the smell of mushroom pies, the sound of the clattering canteen, even the soft snores of my dorm-mates after lights out.

"Tea's ready." It was Eloise, leaning in the doorway. She gave me a soft look, then came and sat down beside me. "Are you okay? It's got to be a lot, yes? Don't worry about Melanie. She's always snippy. She's –"

"No, it's not her." I really didn't want to suggest that I'd been offended. "You're right, though. It's a lot."

Eloise patted my knee. "You'll get used to it. And I'm here

if you want to talk about stuff." There was a commotion downstairs and the sound of a deep booming voice. "Ah, sounds like Sam came back from the fields early." She let her hand rest on my knee, and I could feel it there through my skirt. "Now don't let Sam scare you."

Which, of course, made me immediately terrified of this unknown person. I was about to ask why Sam might scare me, but Eloise rose from the bed, and I followed, feeling it was expected of me, my mind whirling with questions.

Downstairs, sitting at the kitchen table, was Molly, and next to Molly, towering over the table, despite being seated, was the tallest person I'd ever seen, even taller than Artemis. Head shaved, wearing a flannel shirt and dungarees, and biting down into a sandwich held in one large hand, whilst fending off Tess, who was making a game of trying to steal the sandwich. Layton stood in the corner, obviously in awe of the new arrival, and it sounded like the entire room was trying to speak at once.

"Ah, and here he is, Sam," said Molly, only just audible over the din.

"Hello," I replied, feeling the blush return to my neck.

The newcomer at the table put down the sandwich and gave me an appraising look. Then nodded. "Come an ave ya tea." Sam's voice was deep and gravelly.

I did what I was told and sat at the table.

As I sipped my tea, I couldn't escape the feeling that Sam was, for want of a better word, *manly*.

CHAPTER 7

Evie

The morning after the bedwetting incident, I was up early and had started some porridge for breakfast when Dr Rosya called from the hospital to tell me that my patient, Mary, had died. It was sad news. But the poor woman had been in a coma for many weeks and exposure to such high levels of moth toxin had damaged pretty much every one of her organs. I thought back to our late-night chats, about televisions and mobile phones and going on holidays to other countries, warm countries. She was careful when talking about the men from before. Many old women don't mention men for fear of being labelled dollies. But I didn't mind. I enjoyed hearing about her son. Sons, she had two. Mae would call me out as a dolly if she knew, tease me for it. But the idea of men wandering around outside, having jobs even, I think it's nice – wholesome. She spoke about her sons a little, Ryan and Nathan. How she'd found Nathan at a retreat run by Jen Harting, and how Harting had tried to blackmail her and, when that didn't work, had given the order for Ryan's sanatorium to be burned to the ground. She'd managed to free Nathan and the other man, Logan, but she hadn't heard anything from either of them since. She talked about how much she missed both of her sons, her husband, her old life. I ignored the tide of strangeness that swept over me at her words – her mirrored world, but one bevelled and warped. She needed me to listen, and so I did. I think that helped towards the end.

I thought it was odd that Dr Rosya called me personally. "You and she were close," she said in a low, almost conspiratorial tone. But then she continued, "How are the boys settling in?" and I realised that the call was not about Mary at all.

"Fine, I think." I looked out of the small window at the bedding, which was now washed and hanging on a line in the garden. "I mean, it will take time for them to settle in, but so far, so good."

"Hmmm." There was a pause, and I felt the pull of her interest urging me to say more.

And when I didn't, she continued, "I could pop over and help. I think I mentioned that my research is based on the study of males, especially biological perspectives on masculine behaviour. I mean, it would be useful to get some real-world experience. I asked my wife, Anita, if it was okay to ask, and she said if it was okay with you..." she offered a strange high laugh.

The way she spoke seemed unnaturally offhand. It was obvious that Dr Rosya was unaccustomed to asking for anything, being more used to giving orders on the wards. The very last thing I wanted was another person poking around in our house, passing judgement, offering advice. Not to mention how Mae would react to more upheaval. But I also knew who she was – and to whom she was married. I didn't want to get on the wrong side of the MWA, and although Anita didn't seem the type to pull rank, it was best to keep them both on my side.

"Sure. That would be great." I tried to include the requisite enthusiasm. Not that it mattered. I'd hardly finished the sentence before Dr Rosya spoke over me, her usual bossiness restored. "Excellent, I'll be over on Tuesday to meet everyone and take some measurements, bloods, that sort of thing. If you could hold back on feeding them that day, I'd like to get a fasting count."

I looked at the porridge now bubbling on the stove. "Err, no, I've got to feed them. It's in the MWA contract. And I'm planning to keep to a routine with meals and such."

There was a heavy sigh from down the phone. "Fine. It was only for the glucose. The hormone tests won't be affected, I guess. Also, can you have to hand their hormone inhibitor prescriptions?"

I could hear movement upstairs and I was desperate to get off the phone. "The MWA nurse has their prescriptions. She's due Wednesday evening to check their levels and the vaccine's immune response."

"Hmm, right, well, in that case, I'll come at the same time as the nurse. I'm fascinated by the mechanisms of the vaccine. I'll be there after work, about six?"

"Sure, see you then. Bye."

I replaced the handset and groaned. Turning to the doorway, I found a young boy and a much larger man looming behind him, both still in their night dresses. We all looked at each other in silence for a moment.

"How did you sleep?" I spoke a little louder than I had intended, and I suspected my smile was overly wide. Daniel at least returned my smile, if only tentatively. Artemis kept his expression neutral.

"Okay," replied the young boy.

I nodded to the kitchen table, which was already laid for four. "Sit down and I'll finish making the porridge. It won't be long."

Both did as I asked, and the small kitchen felt smaller than ever. I added some more milk, adjusting the heat on the small electric ring. With my back to the table, I carried on in the same cheery tone. "I got some honey in specially. Did you have honey in the facility? It's my favourite with porridge. And I chopped up a bit of dried apple too, so it'll be nice and sweet."

Daniel grinned. "I *love* honey."

There was a commotion behind me on the stairs. Mum had been trying to make her way down, unaided, but had slipped and was clinging on to the banister. I shot towards her to help, but Artemis was ahead of me, holding her firmly by the waist and helping her to right herself.

He led her to the table, as I fluttered around them, trying to see if she was hurt.

"Thank you," she said to Artemis as he helped lower her into the nearest seat at the table. "My old legs just don't do what I ask of them sometimes."

"Are you hurt, Mum?" I tried to run my hands over her shoulders, her arms. "Is anything broken?"

"Stop fussing Evie, I'm fine. This fine young man came to my aid, and all is well."

"You're welcome, old woman," replied Artemis, formally.

"Call me Lois," replied Mum, and Artemis gave a half nod.

I leaned into Artemis. "She's a bit blind, so she can't see you very well."

His eyes widened. "Sorry. Yes, Lois. I will."

"Ah, I can still see a bit. Don't worry about it. Something smells good," she said and turned her head towards the pot on the stove.

Mum had shown no interest in food for a long while, so the small look of hope on her wrinkly face as she faced the porridge was a good sign.

"It has honey and apple in it!" Daniel said it with enthusiasm, but then a pained shyness clouded his face. "Sorry." Although for what he was apologising, I don't think even he knew. Speaking perhaps?

"Has it, indeed? Honey and apple! Well, that's marvellous. And what should I call you, young man?"

"Daniel." His voice was quiet, but the pained look on his face softened.

"Daniel – a fine name. And you, my stairwell saviour?"

It looked for a moment that Artemis was going to smile. Instead, he cleared his throat. "Artemis... ma'am... Lois."

"Daniel, Artemis. No Mae this morning, Evie?"

"No. She had errands." I didn't want to say what actually happened, that when I woke up, she was gone. No note, no word, just an empty space on her side of the bed. None of her stuff was missing, so she can't have gone far. Maybe she did have errands, at six o'clock on a Saturday morning in November? Maybe.

I carried the heavy pan over to the table and slopped out the porridge into four bowls, before replacing the pan and giving everyone their helping, placing Mum's hand gently on her spoon by her side. "Careful, it's hot."

"Stop fussing, Evelyn."

Daniel gave Artemis a quick look, and the older man offered the boy a tiny nod. Daniel picked up his spoon and began attacking his breakfast, as I sat down and realised once more that this kitchen was a bit too small for the number of people in it. But there was something nice about it, about the clink of spoons and the warmth of the air.

"Who was on the phone?" asked Mum, blowing on the porridge on her spoon.

"My colleague called to tell me that one of my patients had died."

"Oh, I'm sorry, pet."

"She was very sick. Mary Langham – you might have heard of her. She was the one who uncovered the MWA vaccine corruption."

Mum nodded. "I remember hearing about her on the radio. She was a carer, wasn't she? At the facility over near Ashwood common?"

"Yes, that's her."

"Terrible business," Lois dabbed at her mouth with a napkin. "There was a couple of murders too, I believe. A young man and another carer. And that awful incident with the fire.

Banishment was too good for that woman. I know she did a lot at the beginning, but it just shows how people think that the laws don't apply to them – even if they were the ones who made them. I mean –"

"Mum!" Artemis had gone very still, his breakfast lying untouched before him. "Is everything alright, Artemis?" I asked. I realised that the Jen Harting case probably hadn't filtered through to the facilities, that this was all new to him.

Artemis looked up at me, tears in his eyes. "Mary? From our facility?"

Realisation dawned. "Oh, I'm sorry Artemis. Did you know her well?"

"No, I…" He fell silent, his expression was no longer a scowl. Suddenly he looked younger and a little lost. "We need to tell Tony. Poor Tony will be devastated."

Tony

My first day at the farm was exhausting. They didn't ease me in, that's for sure. Up at seven for breakfast, given some shabby patchwork overalls to wear, which apparently had belonged to Sam. Then out on the farm. Molly had been up two hours earlier to milk the cows. It was to my enormous relief that Eloise, Melanie, and I were not on milking duty. As the three of us left the farmhouse, I eyed the cows in the opposite field with mistrust. I felt they were eying me right back. Eight brutish-looking animals lumbering around with heavy hooves and flaring nostrils grinding their huge teeth. I asked Eloise what to do if I was ever attacked by a cow.

Both she and Melanie started laughing.

Melanie replied. "Sing to it, Tony. That usually calms them down."

"What should I sing?" This made them both dissolve into laughter, so much so that we had to stop. But they didn't answer, which I felt was unfair, as my life could very much depend upon their answer.

First, we fed the chickens. I liked this – the chickens were small and although their beaks were sharp, they seemed far more interested in the feed we were scattering than in attacking me. I liked the funny way they walked, bobbing and jerking across the yard. What I didn't like was the smell or the mess. And when I was rummaging around for the eggs in the coop, I got something sticky on my hand.

Melanie rolled her eyes when I brought my sticky hand to her attention. "Just wipe it on your trousers, Tony. Stop being such a baby."

Eloise was, as expected, nicer. She produced a piece of cloth, something she called a hankie, and using some water from a flask, wiped the splodge from my fingers. "It's fine, just a bit of manure. All gone now."

I didn't know for sure what manure was, but I had a pretty good idea and spent the rest of the day rubbing my hand on my trousers. *Out damned spot!* I could hear the line on repeat in my mind.

Eloise sat me down on a bucket and lifted one of the chickens. "Put your arms out, Tony."

I did as I was told, not because I wanted to hold a chicken, but because Eloise had been so nice, and I didn't want to disappoint her.

Melanie stood by and sighed. "Come on, Elly. Stop fannying about. Mum'll flip if we don't bring in the leeks soon. They're due for market."

But Eloise hushed her. "Just a second." Then she put the chicken into my outstretched arms.

I expected it to flap, and I readied myself. But it just sat, calm as anything. It was so soft. I've never felt anything like it, and its small warm body felt wonderful nestled in my arms – like it trusted me. One shiny black eye looked up at me as I sank my hands deeper into its silky feathers. "What's his name?" I whispered, the feeling of the little heartbeat next to my chest filling me with a kind of wonder.

Melanie started to speak, to say something mean by her tone, but Eloise spoke over her. "What would you like her name to be?"

So, it was a she. "Mary," I said without hesitation. "I want her to be called Mary."

Eloise smiled then, and she suddenly looked like a child. "Mary she is then."

"Leeks!" said Melanie. "Come on!"

I replaced Mary as gently as I could on the ground and watched as she joined her chicken friends. "Are they all girls?"

"These are, yes. Only the girl chickens lay eggs." We started walking towards some raised beds a short way off.

"Where are the boy chickens?"

"There are a few about – cockerels. They're bigger and they've got a kind of wobbly bit on their head so you can tell them apart from the chickens."

Melanie, it seemed, had got sick of waiting for us and was walking a fair way ahead of us.

"Thanks," I said to Eloise. "Thanks for giving me one to hold, and thanks for letting me name her."

She smiled. "Is Mary someone you know? A woman from the visitation programme, perhaps?" Her voice had changed; it was higher.

"I didn't really take part in the visitations." I didn't want to go into the details. About how I'd tried it once when I was younger, with a woman from outside who'd signed up for a hetero-recreation visit. About how it had been a disaster, how I hadn't known what to do, or where everything went. How it felt weird and wrong and not at all like when me and Logan had sex. How I'd pressed the emergency button, and the woman had been angry. "Mary is my best friend. She is a – was a carer at the facility. She helped me when my friend –"

"Honestly! If you two don't get a fork and start digging up

some leeks, I'm gonna tell Mum and Sam that you spent all day nattering and flirting." Melanie's scowl had grown, and her face was pink. She flung a large wooden pole at me with a metal fork on the end. I picked it up and examined the muddy prongs.

Eloise rounded on Melanie. "You mind your own business," she snapped.

I didn't know what to do. They were staring at each other and there was a hot energy in the air. Should I say something? Break the tension?

Then Eloise turned away from her sister and picked up another fork. "Like this Tony." She began thrusting the fork into the ground. The energy disappeared as quickly as it had arrived. She pushed the fork downwards and levered up a long and green vegetable. She reached down and grabbed it before ripping it from the soil. I recognised the vegetable from cooking class although these were a lot bigger and covered in mud. She placed the dug-up leek in a nearby crate and started on the next.

"Are you going to stand and watch us do all the work, Tony?" Melanie wiped her hand over her forehead, leaving a smudge of dirt.

"Sorry," I mumbled back, and copied what they did, digging up a leek then pulling it free before placing it in the crate.

It was hard work.

XX104

Years ago, these stories about the days when the first infestation hit used to be a kind of currency. There would be a moment, not long into the conversation with someone you'd just met, a quietness, a cue. Not everyone took up the cue. Some, as I mentioned, pretended that this was always the way it had been, that the world hadn't been yanked by its throat into a new reality. But then, twenty years ago, perhaps, the stories became old-fashioned, embarrassing. It was then I first heard the term 'dolly', a person who couldn't let go of before, someone who wanted it to go back to being as it was. I don't know if it was engineered by the Council or just an organic reaction to what had happened. Perhaps we were all tired of grieving. Or perhaps the next generation were bored by our grief, desperate to move on.

My story still had high currency. I was right 'there', so to speak, when it all went to shit. But I was relieved when I didn't have to tell anymore. Some of those who survived Waterloo still go round on the 'circuit' as it's known. Schools, village halls, even talks in the Citadel. I declined. I don't like the way it's become a form of entertainment.

Anyway, the way I tell it is not the way people want to hear about it. They want inspirational nuggets and dramatic pauses; they want sacrifice and glory. I can only give them blood and fear and screaming.

And that's the problem, right there. Everyone has bought into the positives. They've bought into a sanitized version. And after the death and the bereavement and the despair, now it seems it's swung the other way. Those wanting the men to get their vaccines don't remember it. They weren't there, either, in the infestation, when men ran rampant, murdering and raping and hating. Or before that – when the same things happened just on a stretched out sporadic scale.

'Not all men', they used to say – usually, the men that is. Like that was supposed to make us feel better. But it was most men – not doing the raping and the murdering, but the implicit victim-blaming, the toxic banter, the damning double standards. They were half the population, after all – if they'd all turned round and agreed one day to do it differently, things might have improved.

The manfans, it's them that need reminding. I'm not just fighting against the risks of letting men out without properly testing the vaccine, I'm fighting about what happens in two, five, or twenty years. When men decide that women have had their day in the sun and reclaim their old seat at the head of the table.

Jorge woke up after his feed at about seven pm in a monstrous mood. He let out scream after scream as if I was torturing him in some unimaginably terrible way.

Bella took out her earphones and looked up from her iPad. "Is he okay?"

Miranda had been asleep for a while. She padded through to the living room, dozy-eyed and sleep-crumpled. "What's wrong little fella?" She picked him up from the travel cot. He arched his back, red-faced, and screamed some more. "Whoa, how long's he been like this?"

I didn't like the insinuation in her voice, like I'd done something wrong. "He only woke up a few seconds ago." No thank-you-for-looking-after-a-baby-and-an-eight-year-old.

"Did he take his bottle?"

"Some." I nodded to the half-finished bottle of milk on the coffee table.

Miranda sighed. She brought him, wriggling and screaming, to her chest to feed, putting him under her baggy tee shirt. "Go on then," she cooed at him. "You know what to d – OW! Jeezus. Fuck!" She ripped him away and thrust him on the sofa, then placed her hand up her tee shirt and over her right breast. When she brought out her hand, it was bloody. "What the hell?"

Miranda and I both looked at the baby. He was working himself up in a fury, balling and spreading his hands and screaming almost without pausing to breathe. Lining his lips lay the faintest trace of blood. Miranda picked him up and held him, despite the fact he seemed to be doing everything he could to push her away. His fingers caught in her hair and came away with a small fistful of copper strands.

Miranda winced.

"What's wrong with Jorgey?" Bella came over to us. "Hey, little Jorgey... Jorgey Porgey." She made a face and spoke in a singsong voice. But the baby continued to scream.

"Stop it," snapped Miranda. "You're making him worse."

Bella backed off. I could see she was hurt.

I was about to snap back at Miranda when a voice sounded from the doorway. "Hey, my lovely ladies!" Dad wandered into the living room, shirt untucked, tie undone. "Wow, Jorge is giving it his all." It was hard to hear what he said over the screaming.

"Take him." Miranda handed the baby to Dad and disappeared into the bedroom.

We looked at each other as Jorge's cries filled the small apartment. Dad jiggled him on his shoulder, to no avail. "Have you eaten yet?"

Bella shook her head. "We bought pizza. It's in the freezer."

Dad looked around. "Let's go out for a bit. Eh? Get some chips to go with the pizza and take Jorge here for a walk. Might calm him down."

"Great idea!" I said. I would have agreed to anything to get out of that apartment right then. Even if Jorge carried on screaming, at least we'd be outside.

Ten minutes later, we'd bundled the baby into a stroller and were heading down in the lift. He was still crying, but his cries were quieter, more because he'd exhausted himself. I didn't feel that he was any happier but at least I could hear myself think. By the time the four of us, me, Dad, Bella and Jorge were making our way through the park towards the shops, Jorge was mercifully asleep.

"So, how was the tube on the way over? Busy?" asked Dad.

I waited a moment to see if Bella said anything about the man pushing the woman off the platform, but she kept her eyes on the ground. "The tube was cancelled," I replied. "We had to get a cab."

"How much was it?" the words came out too quickly. An edge to his voice.

"Twenty-eight pounds."

There was a brief silence. I thought perhaps he might tell me off for spending so much. Then I could point out that the only reason I spent the money was that he'd left his family and moved here. I almost wanted him to say it so we could have the fight.

But he just sighed. "Fair enough. Okay, who wants chips?"

"Me! I do!" Bella opened the door to the chip shop and Dad wheeled in Jorge's pram. "And curry sauce please."

My phone buzzed in my pocket. It was a text message from Oscar:

I think I've killed Kari.

CHAPTER 8

Tony

"Slow down," said Molly, as she pushed another egg onto my plate from a heaped tray. "You'll make yourself ill."

I'd never been that hungry in my whole life. I fell on lunch like a crazy man and ate everything that was set in front of me. Nothing was ever going to fill the space in my stomach.

Sam sat at the other end of the table, shovelling fried mushrooms with a spoon held in a meaty fist. "We'll build him up. Turn some of that puppy fat into muscle."

I slowed my eating and ran my hand over my thigh and stomach under the table. I didn't think Sam's words were meant to make me to feel self-conscious, but as I looked at the women around the table, Molly, Sam, Melanie and Eloise, I realised that there wasn't a handful of fat between them. Melanie and Sam were broad, but it was a muscular thickness. Hardly surprising as they spent their days digging and feeding and walking, so much walking between pens and fields and stables. I must have walked more in this morning than I did in a week back at the facility. But it had felt good. The wind on the back of my neck and the tiny amount of sun that had appeared between the clouds and shone on my face, so instead of feeling tired, the work had made me feel more awake. I wasn't looking forward to going out this afternoon and doing it all again, though. It was comfortable in the kitchen and the food was settling like a warm stone in my stomach. The thought of working was a grim one. What I really wanted was a nap. In the facility, we were encouraged to nap after lunch and in the prep houses, we were given special milk to help us sleep. Just the thought of that slightly sweet milk made me profoundly tired.

"It's hardly puppy fat, Sam. He's over thirty, I reckon. It's just regular fat." This from Melanie, of course.

"I'm twenty-seven," I replied, and replaced my spoon on the plate to signal I'd had enough as Molly hovered over me, offering me more buttery toast.

"Well, you look older."

"Melanie!" Eloise's fork clattered onto her plate. "Why are you being so mean?"

Melanie shrugged. "I'm just saying what's true," she mumbled.

"Girls, stop your wittering." Sam got up and towered over everyone. "I've got to bring in three crates of chard and three of tats before the light fades. I don't need my kids blathering on and giving me a headache. Now, who's gonna come and help?"

"I promised Mum I'd help with filling up the cart for market," said Melanie, immediately.

"I've got research to do," Eloise answered equally quickly.

Sam sniffed. "Me an' you it is then, Tony."

I really, really didn't want to go. My shoulders, back and legs were aching. They hadn't when I'd been working, but it was like some kind of delayed injury. Bringing in chard and tats, whatever they were, was the last thing I wanted to do. "I… er, perhaps I should stay and help Eloise with her research. I don't want to overdo it on my first day," I asked hopefully.

Everyone looked at each other, and then Molly, Sam, and Melanie burst out laughing.

Eloise didn't laugh, she looked embarrassed. She whispered as the other three continued to laugh, "My field is advanced biology, Tony. Phylogenetics and genomics. I don't think they teach it in the facilities."

It was true – I'd never heard such strange words. "Oh," I said, wishing I didn't blush so much. "Sorry. But it sounds interesting. Perhaps you can teach me sometime."

Sam's voice boomed from the end of the table. "You have a long way to go before you can study the sciences. If, in fact, you can learn that sort of thing. Now come on Tony, that chard won't pick itself. Where's the young lad, Layton? He could help too."

Molly was washing up some dishes at the sink and didn't turn to answer. "He's upstairs in his room. He's upset because Tess went to school today and he wasn't allowed to go."

I frowned. "Why wasn't he allowed to go?" I'd assumed he was out playing with Tess. The two had seemed inseparable yesterday.

There was a silence in the room, and I realised I'd said something stupid, but not something funny-stupid – not like my comment about Shakespeare. Awkward-stupid.

Molly turned around, her hands dripping with soapy water. She shared a quick look with Sam and then looked back at me. "Um, the school... isn't equipped for boys. Not yet anyway. That's what they said when we asked."

It sounded fair. We were the first few men, and these things take time – isn't that what they told us at the facility? We were the ambassadors, the chosen few, and it was our job to show that men could be trusted out in the world. But I was sad for Layton. It wasn't that little boy's fault that the world was only just getting ready to accept us. Also, I wasn't sure what equipment they needed to put in place. Boys would use the same books, the same... pens? Wouldn't they? I looked at my hands and then at Eloise's. Hers were a bit smaller, I guess. Did that mean I needed special bigger pens? Surely not – Sam's hands were bigger than mine.

I was about to ask when Layton arrived at the bottom of the stairs. His red eyes suggested he'd been crying. "I'll come and help. Pick the chards."

I wondered if he'd get into trouble for listening from upstairs. Instead, Molly smiled and paced over to him. "Good boy," she said, patting him on the shoulder.

Sam stood up. "We'll get you nice and strong. By the spring I'll have you riding a horse. Would you like that?"

The boy's eyes widened. He looked tiny standing next to the bulk of Sam. "Yes. I think so."

So, off the three of us went for another long, *long* walk to another distant field, Layton munching on a jam sandwich and chattering as we walked, and me trying not to think about the increasing pain that was dragging down every part of my body.

XX104

"Do you want salt and vinegar?"

Someone was talking to me.

"Beans! The lady just asked about vinegar." Bella tugged on my arm. Dad was outside the shop with the pram, having given me ten pounds to pay. A slim, hair-netted woman with tattoos shovelled chips into a Styrofoam tray.

I shook my head, then looked down at the unblinking screen. "Er, no thanks."

From Oscar: *I think I've killed Kari.*

It was a joke. A weird joke that Oscar and Kari had thought was funny for some reason. But how was this funny? I took the chips and stepped out into the cooling evening. It was still light, and a couple of women joggers sped past, their ponytails swinging in unison. They both glanced down into the pram as they passed.

Jorge was screaming again, red-faced and dribbling with fury. Dad put his hand on his son's forehead. "He's a bit warm. He might be coming down with something." As he spoke, two ambulances went past in quick succession, blaring their sirens into the evening air.

We made our way back to the apartment through the park. People were lying about, scattered across the grass, enjoying the last of the day's sunshine. A few weeks and it'd be the summer holidays. Nothing to do but lounge about and eat ice cream. I'd probably be on Bella babysitting duty, but that was okay. Also, I was going camping in August with Kari and Oscar in Torquay. My first solo trip.

We weaved our group around a group of shirtless young men, and I kept my gaze on the phone.

"Everything alright?" said Dad, jiggling the pram, attempting to calm Jorge.

I nearly showed him the weird message, but his attention was on Jorge.

"Yeah, fine," I said as I texted back – *Why? Did she spend more than her allotted twenty minutes talking about trans rights?*

A pause, then…

Oscar: *I'm not joking. She won't wake up.*

I wrote back – *Stop it. It's not funny.*

Then nothing. This was not like Oscar – or Kari. We weren't the kind of friends who played mean jokes on each other. I shivered and got into the lift. Jorge's screams echoed around the small metal box.

"Jesus, Jorge! Give it a rest, will you!" Dad's voice was strained. I think he meant it to come out as mock annoyance, but the lift created an echo and he sounded angry. Bella nuzzled a little closer to my side.

We opened the door to the smell of burning pizza. The news was on TV and Miranda was perched on the edge of the sofa watching a Cambridge professor talk about plausible reasons for the recent increase in violence sweeping South America. She jumped up when we entered and switched off the TV. "Shit, shit, sorry." She raced over to the oven and slid out some bubbling pizzas, not black but darker than the pictures on the box suggested. "It's fine, they're fine. Did you bring chips? Oh, Jorge! What a fuss."

We put the chips on the table, and Miranda picked up the squalling baby. "Oh dear, little man, is it milk you'll be wanting? Well, I can help – Oh Christ!" Jorge was convulsing in Maranda's grasp like a salmon out of water. It was terrifying to watch. He jerked back and forth so that Miranda could hardly hold on to him. "Simon! Simon! Help me – something's really wrong!"

Dad was by her side in two strides. "He's having a seizure. We need to get him to a hospital. I'll drive, you bring Jorge." He swiped the keys from the table. "You girls stay here. I'll call when we know what's going on."

I nodded. I just wanted to go home to be with Mum. First the thing at the station, then Oscar's weird text, and now this. Fear ran its greasy fingers down my back. Then the door slammed shut and there was silence, a jarring change from Jorge's screams.

"Is he going to be okay?" asked Bella in a small voice.

"Yeah, he's going to be fine. The doctors will sort him out. Now, eat some pizza and chips, then we can watch a film, something animated, preferably with talking animals." I handed her the least charred piece of pizza.

I tried to eat myself but wasn't that hungry. The chips were cold and had lost their crunch. When Bella finished and I'd settled her in front of the TV, I tried calling Kari. But no answer. What the hell were they playing at? Had they raided Oscar's parents' wine cellar?

Then Oscar called. I took the call in the spare bedroom, the one me and Bella slept in.

"Hi, Oscar. What's that text message about?"

His voice was hoarse. "I don't know why I did it. We were just playing around, and I then I felt this weird anger, and I put my hands on her neck. I don't remember how it happened. She won't wake up."

The words drifted around me, but the idea was so preposterous. Oscar, the nicest, most gentle man I'd ever met. Not a macho bone in his body. "Don't be ridiculous. Oscar. Stop it. Put Kari on."

"Something is wrong with me. Something is really wrong." His voice was quiet and lost.

"Oscar! Are you serious right now?" I still couldn't face the possibility that this was real, but there was definitely something wrong. "Oh god, you need to call an ambulance. Oscar! Do you understand? I don't know what you've done but call 999."

"I've got to go. I'm sorry. I'm so sorry."

The line went dead.

Tony

My second trip to the field, the one with Sam and Layton, was, surprisingly, easier than my first. No Melanie, carping and sighing at me for one thing. Sam was so strong she hardly needed my help at all. I packed one crate to every three of hers.

After we'd picked twenty crates of chard and stacked them on Snow's cart, the sun was setting. We sat on the sheltered side of a wood pile at the end of the field, and Sam pulled out a bag of dried berries and handed it to me. "Share them with the boy," she said, and nodded to Layton.

We sat on the wood and stared into distance, me and Layton munching on sweet tart berries. The sunset bled in yellow and pink, with the shapes of trees and bushes, dark as ink, lining the horizon. The trees nearest shivered in the breeze, a few leaves clinging to their bony forms. It reminded me of the view from the viewing room at the facility, although when I stared at that, I was always in a constantly maintained temperature. No breeze, no sun, just silk robes and the smell of disinfectant. Being outside had so many dimensions – not just smell, but the combination of smell and sight. The harsh feel of the frost in your lungs along with the sight of the setting sun, the ache in your arms after a day lugging crates, and the sweet taste of dried berries. There was a completeness to it, a recipe, which was denied me in my old home. Sam then added another dimension. She'd rolled a white paper cylinder, about the length of my index finger, and set fire to one end. I watched in amazement as she sucked on it and then blew out a plumb of pungent smoke. The smell fitted the view perfectly.

"Are you on fire?" asked Layton in awe.

Sam chuckled. "No lad, it's a cigarette. And I'll thank you not to tell Molly. She doesn't approve."

I didn't know about keeping things from Molly. It didn't seem right. But then I didn't want to get Sam in trouble. It wouldn't hurt, I thought, not to mention it.

Instead, I changed the subject and said what I'd been thinking moments before. "I always thought it was cruel, that trees were forced to be naked in the coldest months of the year." I looked at Sam wondering if she was going to laugh at me again.

But instead, she looked thoughtful. "It's true, Tony. It does seem wrong."

The wind blew again and the tree closest to us gave up a few of its remaining brown leaves.

"Sam, are you a man?"

I choked on the dried berry I was eating. "Layton!"

"Sorry!" Layton gave me and Sam a wide-eyed look. "Was that the wrong thing to say?"

I looked at Sam expecting her to be furious, but she looked just as thoughtful as before. "Don't worry about it, Layton. It's a fair question. One I thought about a lot when I was younger. As it happens, I am. But you shouldn't say that to anyone else, mind. People, out there," she... he... nodded in the direction of the village, just visible in the distance, "get funny about that sort of thing."

Layton nodded. Then whispered, "How did you escape the moths? Were you vaccinated?"

Sam took a long drag on the cigarette. "Let's just say I was born with a woman's natural ability to fight off the toxin."

Layton's eyes were as wide as dinner plates. "Were there other men born like that?"

A darkness clouded Sam's features. "Aye. And they were rounded up, like me, in the first infestation and given a choice. Go into a sanatorium for the rest of their lives, or go back to pretending to be women." There was a bitterness in his voice that was sharper than the scent of smoke on the cold air.

"Does Molly know?" I blurted the question out. The forbidden cigarette was one thing, but this was so much bigger. I didn't think I could keep a secret of such importance.

Sam paused, looking at my stricken face, then laughed. "Yes Tony, Molly knows. And the girls." He crushed the cigarette into the cold mud with his boot. "C'mon. It'll be dark soon. We need to get this stuff ready for the upcoming market. He hitched the cart to the ever-patient Snow and picked up Layton, putting him on top of a crate. I climbed in up front.

"Let's go and see what Moll's got us for supper shall we?" said Sam, climbing up next to me.

"Hope there's an apple pie. That's my favourite pie," Layton cried out enthusiastically from the back.

We were about to move off when Sam handed me Snow's reins. "Be firm, let him know you won't stand for any nonsense."

I looked down at the leather straps in my palm. "Oh no. I don't think I should. I mean, perhaps tomorrow. It's been a long day –" Snow was so big. The idea that I could control him seemed ridiculous.

Sam grinned. "You can, Tony. He's nout but a big pussy cat. Tap the reins. Off ye go."

I tapped them, convinced that Snow would ignore me and go off at a deadly pelt into the near darkness, dragging all of us to our deaths. But the horse just gently lurched into action. "He's doing it," I said in wonder, as we made our way across the field.

"It's you that's doing it lad," said Sam.

My heart nearly burst with pride.

Evie

Of course, Tony would be heartbroken. I'd read his letters to Mary – I knew how much she'd meant to him. We headed off to Molly's house just after dinner. I called ahead and left a message with one of the girls that we'd be coming. Mum had gone to bed early, exhausted and pale, but as Artemis helped her up the stairs, her steps seemed a fraction stronger than of late. I wrapped Daniel in a thick knitted kaftan, taking him with me, mainly because I didn't want to leave him with Mae, who was already halfway through her second bottle of homemade wine. She'd returned earlier in a jumpy mood and wouldn't tell me where she'd been.

"I don't have to answer to you," she'd snapped, clattering around the kitchen, looking for the wine. I was glad to get out of the house. Artemis surprised me by wanting to come too.

"I could do with the walk," was all he said.

It was cold, and we only had one rechargeable torch, so we walked in a huddle to Molly's place. It was about two miles, first through the village, then past the church and over a couple of fields.

"How much further?" Daniel was panting with the exertion of the walk, and I realised he was struggling.

"Sorry, Daniel." I slowed down and held his small hand, soft as a plum, in mine as we made our way towards Molly's.

"Why is Mae always angry?" Artemis was a few steps behind us.

The question caught me off guard. I was about to answer when Daniel spoke. "Is she angry because I wet the bed?" His voice was small. "Or because I had three spoonfuls of honey on my toast for breakfast. They warned us at the prep houses, not to eat too much."

I stopped, crouched down and faced the little boy. "No, Daniel. Of course not. You can have three spoons of honey. It's fine. "Mae has a lot to do at work and it makes her tired. But she's not angry."

Artemis and Daniel shared a look.

"You're welcome here, and safe. I promise."

Another sceptical look passed between them.

I sighed, stood up and we set off again towards the farmhouse on the hill.

The earth on the field was hard, almost frozen, and our breath was steaming. It was because the ground was so hard that I heard something behind us. I thought at first I imagined it. With our three pairs of boots shuffling along the path at the edge of the field, it was easy to dismiss any extra footsteps. As we were nearing the farmhouse, we stopped again to readjust Daniel's kaftan, which was trailing on the ground, and that was when I heard a couple of extra footsteps come to an abrupt halt. I turned and flashed the light behind me.

"Hello?" I called. "Who is it? Are you okay?" It didn't occur to me to be afraid.

The light fell on a figure about ten meters behind us. A scarf wrapped around their face prevented me from seeing who it was. In their hand, they held something I couldn't quite make out. "Hello?" I said again. "Are you going to Molly's?"

The figure stood unmoving, backdropped against a bramble hedge, so it was hard to get a sense of their size. They raised the thing in their hand so that it was pointing towards, us their fingers curled around the handle. Then I recognised what it was, something I'd only ever seen in a museum. Like a mini version of the rifles farmers used to cull rabbits. But this one wasn't meant for rabbits. It was a handgun, and it was trained on us.

The gun in the stranger's hand was shaking and the stranger's breath was coming fast.

"Run," I said through a surge of adrenaline. I grabbed Daniel's hand, letting his kaftan fall to the floor, and pulled him, scrambling up the path and through a gap in the hedge. From behind me came an almighty crack that seemed to bounce off the very sky. Artemis grabbed Daniel's other hand and all three of us dragged each other up the final hundred metres to Molly's house. At some point, I must have dropped the torch, but our focus was fixed on reaching the building on the top of the hill. Any moment, I expected the loud crack to sound again. I didn't want to think about what would happen if the gun found its mark. Exploding flesh and bone? Fire and poison? What happened in the time before when people got shot? My mind was spinning with a million bloody images. I drove onward. But there were no more loud cracks into the night – the cold air forcing its way into my gasping lungs was the only noise I could hear. As we got to the doorway, and I bundled Daniel inside, Artemis following on behind. I turned to see if the stranger had followed. I expected to see their masked face lurching from the dark, bearing down on me, holding the gun to my head.

The field was dark. A muted light cast by a clouded moon gave no clues to the stranger's whereabouts. There was a light in the field, a few hundred meters back, but I realised it must have been my torch. I followed the boys into the house.

Everyone in the large kitchen looked up at our abrupt entrance in surprise. We burst into the homely scene like the sudden appearance of a wolf pack. Two older girls were doing the dishes, Molly knitting and Sam sipping some tea as a young boy sat playing cards with little Tess on the floor. It was so far removed from our moment of terror that I wondered if I'd imagined the whole thing. Artemis was catching his breath as Daniel began to sob.

"There's a woman out there." My voice was ragged with effort and my hand trembled as I pointed to the door. "She has a gun. She pointed it at us… and fired it."

Sam was standing in a second, and peering out of the window, trying to see anyone out there. "Lock the doors. Molly. Now!" The room descended into chaos. Daniel's crying mixed with the women's voices as they all started speaking at once.

"Who was it? Did you get a look?"

"Who owns a gun in the village?"

"What about your shotgun, Sam? Should you go and get it?"

"Are you hit, Evelyn? Are you hurt?"

"No, Molly." I replied. "No one's hurt." I nearly said that I thought the stranger didn't want to shoot us, that her hand was shaking like she was afraid. But I didn't because I couldn't be sure it was the truth. I pulled Daniel into me and stroked his hair.

Glancing up, I saw Artemis was wearing a look of anger. "It was us," he said, almost as a whisper. "They aimed at us."

It took a long time for us to calm down, but eventually, warm drinks were provided and extra blankets. Sam had to be talked out of going out to look for the stranger, pacing the kitchen.

"She's probably long gone now – the last thing we need is you getting shot. Let Law Abidance deal with it," said Molly.

"When they eventually get here," replied Sam, still at the window. "They have to come all the way from Heron's Wood."

"They said on the phone they'd be here soon. Sit down, Sammy."

Sam sat at the large kitchen table and muttered. "Law abidance, bloody biddies, about as useful as tits on a bull."

"Sammy!" Molly turned to Sam with a look of horror on her face, as the girls caught each other's eye and swallowed down giggles.

"Did you get any sense of her?" Sam directed this question to me. "Tall? Stocky? Blonde? Anything?"

"I... no. Sorry. It was dark, and it all happened so quickly. I –"

"Medium height." Everyone stopped speaking when Artemis spoke. Probably because he'd said so little since we'd been there. "And they held the... the..." he made a shooting gesture.

"The gun?" replied Sam.

"Yes, the gun. They held the gun in their left hand."

"Good, good observation young man, well done." Sam nodded in approval.

Artemis's face was blank, unreadable at Sam's praise.

Molly spoke. "Tell the LA that when they arrive." Then she turned to me. "They can give you a lift back when they're done. You don't want to be wandering about with some crazed gunwoman roaming the –"

"Why do you assume it's a woman?" Artemis cut in.

Everyone looked at him. There was an awkward pause before Sam said. "A Manic couldn't work a gun, not if he'd never seen one before. An infected would just charge you down, not steal a gun."

"Not one of the infected... a man like me."

Sam frowned. "But why would an uninfected man do that?"

"They're being kept indoors, aren't they?" This from the daughter, Melanie.

Artemis shrugged and stayed quiet.

Molly was rubbing her hands together. "This after all that trouble down at Chesterford. Those poor, poor boys. And to think that could have been –"

"Molly!" I gave a small nod towards Daniel, who was looking at her with wide eyes.

"Jonah went to Chesterford, I think. What happened?"

No one spoke or moved.

Instead of answering him, I changed the subject. "Where's Tony? I need to talk to him about something."

"Oh, the poor boy," said Molly, when I explained what we'd come for. "He went to bed just after dinner. He was exhausted. I'll let him know in the morning about Mary."

"I think he might want to go to the funeral." I said, "I'm going. It's on Saturday – at the crematorium over in Stevenage. I could take him – if he wants."

Then there was the sound of tyres on gravel and a light at the window. The Law Abidance had arrived.

CHAPTER 9

Tony

I wriggled out of bed, trying not to wake Layton. He'd crept into my bed sometime in the night complaining of a nightmare, so I'd spent the next few dark-filled hours being jabbed, kicked and generally squished by his small sweaty form. How I was supposed to do a full day's work on so little sleep I could only guess.

Molly was sitting at the table. It was odd to see her so, not bustling around the kitchen, juggling pans and dishes, shouting at people to lay the table and picking her way over boots and wrestling children into coats. Or at the very least, knitting. But this morning she was quiet.

"No Tony," Molly said, when I went to leave with the others. "You're with me this morning."

I was surprised, and a little relieved. Yesterday, Sam had said that today I was to go out with Eloise and Melanie – harvesting cabbages for the afternoon's market. I didn't know what harvesting cabbages entailed, but it seemed that harvesting, in general, was tiring. Also, I could see an icy white cover on the ground through the window. Sparklingly beautiful, but I didn't relish the idea of walking about in it. I'd spent my life wanting to be out, nose rested up against the viewing room window, watching the seasons change, and now that I could go out into the yard whenever I wanted, I found outside uncomfortably cold and open. Spending the morning in a warm kitchen, in the vicinity of a batch of freshly baked muffins, would suit me fine.

"Why does he get let off?" replied Melanie, through the muffin she was eating. "What makes him so special? With just the two of us, it's gonna take all morning."

"Don't be mean, Mel," replied Eloise. "Remember what happened last night." She waggled her eyebrows and nodded in my direction.

I was about to ask what had happened after I'd gone to bed, when Sam appeared in the doorway. "Stop mithering your mother and come now. I'll give you a hand with the greens." This didn't seem to appease Mel, who left the kitchen with sighs and huffs and eyerolls. Eloise gave me a pitying look.

"Sit down, Tony. Do you want another muffin?" Molly pushed the plate towards me.

I did, indeed, and happily accepted my second treat of the morning, as large as a fist and stuffed with dried apple. Today was shaping up well. The kitchen was dim and steamy. The small windows didn't let in much light. But this just added to the cosiness.

"Something happened last night after you went to bed."

"Mmmm?" I chewed as I listened.

"One of my friends, Evie... and one of your friends, Artemis, came to the house."

I stopped chewing. "Artemis was here? Oh, it would have been nice to see him." I made my voice sound more disappointed than I actually felt. Of all the men in the vaccination programme, Artemis's gruff presence would be the least welcome. I was hoping I might bump into Evan, at some point, the nice man from the drop off point, with the blonde hair and the soft smile.

"On the way here, they were chased by someone with a handgun. Do you know what a handgun is, Tony?"

I shook my head as I finished my muffin. "Is it like a benzo gun?" Benzo guns are what the nurses wore on their belts in the facility although they were only used in the worst of circumstances – if a man was infected. They were small and plastic and had little needles which delivered a drug that made the man sleep until he could be taken away to a sanatorium. The fact that Artemis had been chased by someone didn't surprise me one bit. He'd probably said the wrong thing and upset someone. I nearly said this to Molly.

"No, it's not like a benzo gun. It's... well... it's more dangerous. You can shoot it from much further away. And it doesn't make you sleep."

"Is it the same as the gun that Sam uses to shoot deer?" I recognised deer. They were one of the few animals that wandered into the field below the viewing room at the facility. When they appeared, we would all squeeze around the window to catch a glimpse. So beautiful with their reddish fur and their big dark eyes. Always on guard, haunted even. I was horrified when Sam explained about culling and even more so at the thought of venison. "It's the natural order of things," Sam had replied, patting me on the shoulder and giving Molly a wide-eyed what-should-I-do look as I cried.

"No, handguns are really just for killing people. We got rid of most of them ages ago."

"Did someone want to kill Artemis?" I asked Molly. This was far more serious. Artemis upset people, sure, but wanting to actually kill him? "Why?"

"We don't know. We don't even know if they were after Artemis, or Evie, or even Evie's fosterling Daniel."

I remembered Daniel from the village hall. A pale freckled boy who didn't smile. "What kind of monster would kill a little innocent boy?"

I felt a strange anger surge through me, hot and fierce. What if it had been Layton? Sweet cheeky Layton? I looked out of the window. The icy field looks a little less magical now, and I started to see things in the trees at the end, faces leering from the shadows.

"The Law Abidance, that's the people who make sure no one hurts us, they're out looking for the stranger with the gun. Until then, I want you and Layton to take extra care. Keep your eyes peeled for anyone you don't know, is that clear?"

I nodded and took another bite of muffin. I considered pointing out that I hardly knew anyone, so everyone was a potential threat, but instead I just carried on chewing thoughtfully, my mind swirling with images of deer and guns and hidden faces. One thing was certain: I was going to be on the lookout the next time I went out. And I would not go out after dark, that was a fact. I swallowed down my mouthful. "Okay, should we warn Layton? Make sure he doesn't go too far away with Tess?"

"When he comes down, I'll have a chat with him. Tony, there's one other thing." Her voice was lower, and she clutched her tea tightly. "Mary, your friend Mary from the facility. She passed away yesterday."

I frowned. I'd never heard the phrase 'passed away' before. "You mean she left the hospital? Could I go and see her? I really would like to. I think of things to tell her all the time, but I would really like to see her if she would –"

"No, Tony. She died. Last night. She was very poorly."

It took a few seconds for Molly's words to sink in. Mary – kind Mary, who'd taught me Shakespeare, who'd recited poetry and made-up stories, and sat with me when I lost Logan. Mary, who'd saved my life one night in the viewing room, when I'd thought I'd come to the end of what I could bear. I felt all the energy drain from me. My sight went blurry as tears filled my eyes. "Are you sure?" It was all I managed to croak out.

"Yes, I'm sure." Then, after a few moments of us sitting quietly at the table: "Do you want to go to the funeral? It's in a few days." And when I didn't answer: "It's a way to say goodbye to the people we love."

I didn't want to say goodbye! I wanted to sit and talk to her.

I thought she'd get better – at the facility they'd told me she was 'doing very well'. How come then she was gone?

I couldn't help it. I took in a shuddering breath, and the tears raced down my face. So much death, so much loss. Why did it have to be like this? Logan, my friend Cole, and now Mary. It was unbearable, and I sobbed into Molly's arms as she held me tightly, the last half of my muffin lying abandoned on the kitchen table.

Evie

I was so scared after the evening's events, I barely slept. Instead, I lay awake, listening to Mae sleep, staring up at the ceiling and thinking about what would have happened if one of us had been shot. Earlier, Law Abidance took our statements, then drove us home. I'd put Daniel to bed and come downstairs. The fire was low, and it was dark. Mae was lying on the sofa. "You're late getting home," she said, sitting up and rubbing her eyes. "Discussing good parenting tips into the small hours?"

I ignored her sarcastic tone and gave a quick rundown of the night's events. I don't know if I was expecting her to be worried, or angry at the stranger, or to make light of the whole thing. But what I didn't expect was for her to turn it round on me. "Oh, Evie. This is exactly the sort of thing you should have thought about. Look at what happened at Chesterford. And now we're a target it seems."

I was so tired, I couldn't summon the energy to defend myself. "Nevertheless, Mae. I don't want to leave the boys alone. I have to go to the market tomorrow afternoon for groceries. Could you work from here rather than go into the office?" I knew from her grimace as soon as I said the words, it was a mistake. I backtracked. "Or perhaps you can go to the market, and I'll stay here?"

Mae slurred a bit as she spoke. "What do you think I do all day, Evie? Do you think I can just drop it all and babysit at a moment's notice?"

I didn't really know what she did. Had meetings with other engineers? Called people on the telephone and talked about new projects? What I did know – she could have taken time off. The Union was invested in the integration programme and had written to our employers explaining about the fostering. No one would say no. But it wasn't that she couldn't, it was that she didn't want to.

"Leave them with your mother. She seems to get on with them – with Artemis especially."

It was true that my mother had taken a shine to the boys and perked up when they were around. She'd have been in her early twenties in the first infestation, so I guess she found boys, men, far less strange. That said, I would not leave Artemis and Daniel with a vulnerable old woman. Not if there was a gun toting nutcase on the loose.

"I'll take them with me," I replied quietly, swallowing down my disappointment that Mae wouldn't even do this one thing. "I'm going to bed."

In the morning, she went to work early. She'd done this all week, I suspect, to avoid running into the boys at breakfast. I thought perhaps that when she got to know them, talked with them, that she might realise that they were not aliens from a distant planet. But it seemed there was little chance of that.

Mum was again downstairs for breakfast, pouring out the tea and pushing an extra helping of honey on both of them.

"Steady on," I said, as she scooped a large dollop onto an eager Daniel's toast.

"You're going to the market this afternoon. You can get some more."

"I'm more worried about tooth decay."

"Pah – you only live once. Isn't that right, Daniel?"

"Yes, Lois," he mumbled through a mouthful of toast, as butter and honey dribbled down his chin.

I smiled. When Mum tried to foist more honey on Artemis, he politely declined. "I'm full, Lois. But thank you."

"Why, Artemis, are you watching your weight?" she gave a grin and a wink. It was an odd thing to say, not something she'd ever said to me, or something I'd ever heard anyone say, for that matter. And I'd never seen my mother wink.

Artemis laughed, something I hadn't heard him do before either. "No, but I've already had two slices."

As I sat down and began my own breakfast, I nearly pointed out that it was me providing the food, vast quantities of it, three times a day. But held back. Both boys would have already been taught at the prep house to be ashamed of their appetites, so I remained silent and enjoyed the scene at the table, Artemis's laugh, Daniel licking his sticky fingers and the morning sun steaming in from the backyard, my mum downstairs, dressed, eating. I wished for a moment that Mae was sitting with us, laughing and chatting. But in my heart, I knew that if she were here, this happy little scene would be something quite different. She'd taint everything with sarcasm and derision. I don't know when I first noticed this about her sense of humour. Had it always been the case that her jokes relied on someone else's misfortune or stupidity? Or had she changed? Was it me? Had I changed her? The arrival of the boys had only highlighted what was already happening. I ignored the mounting hopelessness I felt when I thought of me and Mae. Instead, I just stayed in the moment, bathed in sunlight and with the sound of Mum explaining how the toaster worked, and allowed myself an oasis of calm.

There was a silence at the kitchen table. I realised I'd missed something. "What?" I asked, trying to catch up with the conversation.

"I said, I would love to hear about what it was like before," Artemis sipped his tea. "Before the moths came. And what happened when they came."

I stifled a gasp. "Artemis! We don't ask those things; we should never ask those things. Surely, they taught you that at the facility."

Artemis frowned, and he put his tea on the table. "I... I thought that was only in the facilities. I just assumed that people could talk about what they want out here."

"No, sorry. It's the same out here." I could hear my voice getting higher. "Never ask an older woman –"

"It's okay, Evie. It's okay."

"But Mum!"

She turned to face Artemis. "I'll tell you whatever you want to know. But later. Some of those things are not for little ears." Then she gave a small nod to Daniel.

Daniel looked from Artemis to Mum and then back again. Then he rolled his eyes. "I don't even want to know about before. I want to know more about how toasters work."

Mum smiled. "If you're good, I'll show you how to take it apart and put it together again. Although you'll have to describe to me what you're seeing."

Daniel's honey smeared lips spread into a very wide smile. "I'll be good."

Tony

I didn't want to go to the market. I didn't want to go anywhere or do anything except play my guitar and think about Mary. Beautiful, sweet Mary and her stories about talking animals and wizards and sea monsters. I argued against going, even though Sam said I was being rude. Eloise then pointed out that at the market there would be a lending library of books and I could choose some to take with me. At the facility, we'd had a handful of laminated books. Laminated, as it was thought the moth hairs could too easily wedge themselves down between the pages of normal books. Also, few of the residents could read very well. The idea of an entire room of books swayed me. I thought Mary would approve of such a thing. In fact, I knew what she would say as if she was sitting in my ear. *Come on, Tony, stop moping around. Go get some books and use that brain of yours.*

I came out just as everyone was piling up the cart with crates of muddy vegetables. We set off with poor old Snow having to pull the whole thing. I would have liked to wear my nice clothes, the blouse and skirt I got when I first arrived at the church, but Sam insisted I wear my overalls and an old jumper, saying, "Market's a messy business."

There was no room on the cart for Melanie and Eloise and me, so the three of us walked behind. Snow couldn't go very fast anyway, so it wasn't hard to keep up. Before we left, Molly had warned us to keep a lookout for anyone we didn't recognise and to point them out to her if we saw them, no doubt because of the person with the gun. I didn't recognise anyone, of course. But I still kept my eyes peeled for anyone holding what might look like a weapon. We didn't see very many people on the road. Apparently, we were getting there early to 'set up'. But those women whom we passed stared long and hard at me and Layton. There were giggles and a few frowns, and one woman, clutching a bag of coloured cloth, called out in a coarse voice, "Hope you're puttin' the older one to work, Sam." Then offered up a throaty laugh.

"You mind your peace, Gloria Puddiefort," replied Sam, and hurried Snow so that we had to pick up the pace. I marched close to Eloise, afraid of straying too far.

Melanie gave Eloise a sideways glance and lowered her voice. "A few people have been looking for you. Penny Glib told me that her sister wanted some, you know…"

"Shh" Eloise gave a pointed look towards Molly who was fussily wiping Layton's mouth clean of apple juice. "Later."

I wanted to ask what they were talking about but one look

at Eloise's grim expression and I changed my mind. Whatever it was, I wanted no part in it.

Instead, I tried to take in the multitude of new sights and sounds. Although I was getting used to being outside now, I was still in awe at how vast everything was. Every direction was space. And although the colours were muted, mostly browns and greens and greys, it had a misty beauty. Everyone, with their rough clothes and sun-touched faces, seemed to blend in like the scenery was painted just for them. Even Layton, in the cart with Molly and Sam, matched the scene, munching on an apple, his eyes bright in the watery sun and a faint darkness on his crown suggesting his hair needed shaving. But it didn't need shaving. No more danger from the moths' tiny toxic threads meant my hair could be long. I imagined having long hair, as long as Eloise's, perhaps down past my shoulders. I liked the thought and then ran my hand over my head, feeling the prickly stubble catch my palm.

"You're starting to grow whiskers," said Eloise, turning to me as we walked. She'd lost the serious look of moments before. "It means your hormone medication has started wearing off."

I rubbed my chin and sure enough, my hand was met by the same stubbly brush. In the facility, I was shaved all over by one of the carers regularly to prevent any risk of threads hiding on my skin. I didn't like the feel of my face. How long would it grow? "Can you shave it for me? When we get home?"

Eloise gave a shy smile. "Okay." Then, after a pause, "But I don't mind if you grow it. I think you might suit some chin hair."

I didn't answer. I didn't want any chin hair – whether or not it suited me. There was also something in Eloise's tone, something that made me uneasy.

The sides of the roads now had more buildings, old ones by the looks of them, with wooden beams and pokey-out windows on the front. We passed one large building that had a sign hanging outside showing a picture of a horse like Snow and the words *The Old Dray*. The cart slowed, so I was almost alongside. Sam's head turned towards the building, and I caught Molly's words, "Later. After we're done."

"I could pick up some info on the stranger. See if anyone else has seen anything." Sam replied hopefully.

I missed Molly's retort as I looked in wonder along the road which widened into a stone square, easily four times the size of the refectory at the facility. It was filling up with carts and horses, bicycles and even a couple of brightly painted reclaimed vehicles, bigger than the car Artemis and I had travelled in. And so many women, weaving in and out, clutching baskets of bread and fruit and cloth and carved objects. Here and there stood knots of women chatting and laughing and girls running around and screaming. And the smell! Frying onions, yeasty bread and something warm and sweet like apple pie but spicier. My stomach lurched, and I looked around for the source of the sweet smell.

"Can I go and look?" Layton's voice rose over the chaos, and he stood on the bench of the cart to get a better view. Sam dragged him from his vantage point – but not before a ripple went through the crowd and people looked our way. Whispers drifted towards us on the damp air.

It's one of the boys –

And a man! Look –

Molly and Sam's fosterlings…

One by one, heads turned towards us and the noise in the square, which had been raucous a moment ago, softened to a muted murmur.

"We shouldn't have brought them. They're not ready," said Molly under her breath, as she helped Layton down from the cart. I suspected Layton and I were the "they" Molly was referring to.

"This is the point of the programme, Moll. Integration." Sam's voice was low. I felt myself being grabbed by the shoulder and marched further into the square. Layton was being led by

Molly, his eyes wide in wonder. She brought him round the front of her but placed her arms in a protective vee around his neck and chest.

"Morning everyone," Sam's voice boomed around the courtyard and my ears rang with it. Everyone was looking at us, and I wanted to disappear, to be dragged down into the earth, or better still, suddenly develop the ability to fly and escape from all the staring eyes. Some expressions on the faces were curious. One or two were smiling, but some looked annoyed. "As you know," Sam's voice continued to echo, "We have some special visitors. The MWA and the Union have handpicked our village to show the country how we can adapt – be forward thinking. And I trust you will show how welcoming Eastor can be." Most people were paying attention, a few nodded. There were some who turned away and a few heavy looks were passed between neighbours. "Be mindful. We have a member of the MWA, a survivor of Waterloo, staying in the village and reporting back to the Council on how this goes. I hope you will all do your best to help it go smoothly."

Molly squeezed Layton closer and gave me a quick smile.

"Those who wish to hear a bit more about it, maybe even meet this lad" – Sam nodded to me – "Come to the Dray after market's done and buy me a drink! I'll tell you everything you need to know." Some laughs and a few jeers went up. The tension in the square disappeared like spent breath, and everyone went back to talking loudly. Some of the women came over to us and started fussing over Layton, who looked like he was enjoying the attention, and the sugar covered apple he was given by a young woman with smiling eyes and a puckered scar across one cheek looked good.

A muscular teenage girl, with long honey-coloured hair approached me as I was picking up a crate of chard. "Are you okay there? Can I give you a hand?" she asked. I was about to say yes, that some help would be good when Eloise stepped between us. "He's fine. He's quite strong."

"You are strong." The girl replied. "Good arms. And you have a pleasant face."

"Don't you need to get back to the fish, Marigold?" snapped Eloise. "They won't sell themselves." I hadn't heard Eloise be quite so sharp before. Even when Melanie was being truly horrible, she stayed calm rather than rising to the bait. She took my arm and led me to the other side of the cart and away from Marigold. "Come on Tony, the others can finish the unpacking. We'll go find someone who sells toffee apples."

I allowed her to take my hand and lead me. It was a strange feeling having the crowd part before you, to have loud voices fall to a whisper as you pass. Eloise didn't seem to mind. She kept her head up, smiling at everyone as we dredged a path through the throng. That sugary smell wafted towards me, stronger now.

In front of us, hidden by the crowd, a commotion started up – people backed away and someone was shouting.

"That's not fair! It's just not *right!*"

It was a man's voice, high, arrogant, complaining. I knew without having to look, which man's voice it was.

Artemis. What now?

XX104

I tried calling Oscar and Kari repeatedly. Both phones just rang through to voice mail. I considered calling an ambulance and sending it to Oscar's house, but in the end, I didn't. What if it was a mistake? What if they'd just got really drunk, and this was a joke?

Bells fell asleep at about nine. I tried to call Mum, but she was at work and if she was attending a 'tricky birth', she might not get back to me for a few hours. I paced around, tried Dad, but his phone was switched off. I stared out of the glass-paned door and towards central London. This high up I could see the beginnings of the city of London looming in the distance, taller buildings like fangs set against a hazy sky. The door led out onto a narrow balcony, and beyond that, seven floors down, a scrubby patch of grass bordered the road.

Oscar couldn't have killed Kari. They'd taken something – mushrooms, maybe. Out of character, but not beyond possibility. He was tripping. It would be fine tomorrow. She'd call again tomorrow, and they'd tell her about their night and laugh about how freaked out Oscar had become.

A bang at the window startled me. I sprung back, my heart pounding, peering out as a black object fell on the balcony floor. It was a crow, in a mess of feathers, beak open, spindly legs thrust upwards with small curling talons. Then another hit the window, and another. Three birds, all large and black, all a crumpled mass of feathers.

I rubbed my arms and backed away from the window. I'd read about it, hadn't I? Electrical storms, power cables, messing with the bird's internal navigation? But even as I tried to rationalise what was happening, the beat of the birds hitting the glass continued, discordant and loud.

My phone buzzed, and I jumped. I was afraid it was Oscar again. "Mum!"

"Are you and Bella safe? Is Dad with you?" Her voice was urgent.

"We're here, but there's something wrong with Jorge." My voice came out in a rush. "Miranda and Dad have driven him to the hospital. And Oscar called, Mum, and he was acting weird, and then there's these birds that are just, I dunno, just smashing into the window and dying. And there was this thing that happened at the station today, and I think Bella saw –"

"Honey, you have to stay there. You can't leave the apartment. No matter what. Do you understand?" This was as serious as I'd ever heard her.

"What? Yeah. What's going on? Mum?"

"Don't let anyone in. I'm going to drive to you right now. I shouldn't be longer than a couple of hours."

"Okay," I was relieved that Mum was coming, but the intensity in her tone was not making me feel any calmer.

"I mean it. No one." There was a pause. "Not even Dad."

I gripped the receiver tightly, whispering as if frightened of being overheard. "What? I can't –"

"Listen to me. We've had... incidents here and one of the specialists thinks it's an infection. Something affecting the brain, specifically men's brains. It's making them do horrible things... I don't know how infectious it is, but men are, well they're hurting people, women mostly." I couldn't believe what she was saying. "I want you to lock the door. Is there a chain?"

I didn't answer.

"Is there a chain on the door?!" She was shouting now and running by the sounds of her breathing.

I went to the door. "Yeah, there's a chain."

"Latch it, and don't unlatch it until I get there. I'll be there soon. Okay? I love you, baby."

"Okay." My voice was small, the voice of a six year-old afraid of the dark. "Mum?"

But the line was dead.

I stood in the hallway in bewildered shock, staring at the door. I grabbed the latch, fumbling with it, dropping it twice, terrified that there was a monster on the other side at this very moment. I should check it by opening the door and looking out into the hallway, but I was too afraid of what I might see. So, I backed away into the living room and switched on the news. The top story was about a civil war breaking out in South America. The second story was how the WHO were investigating several reports of mass deaths from the sleeping sickness Kari mentioned earlier.

Kari!

If men were becoming violent, then Oscar... He could have

really hurt her. The drone of a siren rose and fell outside. I dialled 999. I could just report what he said, and they could check it out.

We are experiencing high volumes of calls at this time. Please wait on the line and an agent will be available to take your call.

I hung up. I wanted the line clear in case Mum called back.

The news was now explaining a new system of emergency alert text messages. How the government or local police could blanket text any phone in the area directly from the mast, not needing contact details. This would be used when there was a direct threat to life, red weather warnings, gas leaks, that sort of thing. Then the news switched to a report on unexplained deaths of bats in the last few days. The hypothesis was something about toxins in the riverways making their way into the food chain. The news, as bad as it was, soothed me. A female newsreader, with well-styled hair, smartly dressed, and a clipped accent, sat on the screen and swapped light-hearted banter with the weather presenter. *More of this beautiful sunshine please, Thomas!*

I checked the door again. The chain was on; it was locked.

Don't open it until I get there.

It was a ridiculous notion. Dad would never hurt us. No matter what he was infected with. Yes, he was a selfish annoying idiot who'd abandoned his family for a girl only slightly older than his daughter. But he loved us.

"Beans?" Bella came in, rubbing her eyes. "I had a bad dream, that someone was trying to get in through the window. They kept knocking. Can I sleep out here with you?"

I picked her up, using my body to block any glimpse she might have caught of the dead birds outside, and allowed her to wrap her skinny legs around my waist. "Sure thing, Bells. But first, we're gonna get you dressed."

"Why?" She gave a small pink yawn.

"Mum's coming to collect us. Dad and Miranda are still at the hospital."

"Oh, alright." It didn't occur to her to ask why Mum would pick us up so late.

An hour later, we were packed, dressed, and watching a cartoon on Netflix.

Bella was drowsy, and I thought she might fall back to sleep. That would be fine. I'd just carry her down to the car.

There was a bang as the door opened, but only as far as the chain.

"Is that Mum?" Bella's voice was sleepy.

"No, she doesn't have a key." The hairs on my arms stood straight up.

"Hey," came a deep voice from the crack in the door. "It's Dad. Let me in."

CHAPTER 10

Evie

"Artemis?" I called out, although I couldn't see him. "Artemis? Daniel?" He'd slipped on ahead as I was beset by people wanting to know how the programme was going.

"Do they eat much?"

"Are they well behaved?"

"Can they use the bathroom unaided?"

"Oh, Evie – well done!"

So much for a quick trip to market. Now I could hear raised voices, and at least one of them was an adult male.

I struggled through a gathering crowd and at the centre stood Artemis holding a terrified-looking Daniel. Artemis was waving his hands at an angry-looking toffee apple vendor.

"You shouldn't say that." I could tell that was Artemis was near tears. "He's just a little boy who wants a sugary apple." The woman scowling at Artemis from behind a pile of toffee apples was in her late fifties, frizzy copper hair and sunburned forearms, crisscrossed with sugar burns. I'd seen her around the market before.

"What's going on?" I asked, stepping in and clutching Daniel, who looked like he was about to faint. "Is everything okay?"

She pursed her lips. "He was trying to buy apples without

tokens." she replied, addressing the banks of nosy faces crowding in rather than looking at me.

"Oh... Is that all?" I said, exhaling deeply. "I've got some tokens. Hang on." I rummaged about in my bag for my purse.

"That's not what she said." Artemis had got a hold of himself and was speaking calmly now. "She said... that she wouldn't sell a toffee apple to the likes of us. That I should go back to the facility and stop putting... good people in danger."

I stopped rummaging and looked up at the woman, who was rearranging a mound of sugared doughnuts. "Are you sure?" I said, and then to the toffee-apple seller, "did Artemis misunderstand?"

But nobody was misunderstanding anything. I could see in the set of her stare and the way she planted those forearms on the counter.

"They're my apples. I can sell them to whoever I want."

A murmur rose from the crowd, and I caught at least a few mumbles, *"She's right. She gets to decide."*

"SHAME ON YOU!" A call came from my left and we all turned to see one of Molly's girls, Eloise, red with rage and dragging a mortified Tony along behind. "Carol! Shame on you!"

The vendor folded her arms tightly across her broad frame, as Eloise approached her counter. "It's our duty, to the Union – to ensure the men in our care are treated eq –"

"Oh, stop your young lips flappin' there, Eloise Coombs. You don't know what a man even is." The woman gave the girl a look of disgust. "You don't know what it was like back then."

"I know that men had rights and –"

"Oh yes, they had rights! Did they have the right to attack women, to hurt them, to pounce on them whilst they were walking home, whilst they were out running, to rape and kill? No, but they did it, anyway. That was even before the moths came. You have no idea what you're bringing back into the world, cos you weren't there – I was!" There was a mumble from the crowd, especially from some of the older women. "When the moths came, every woman had to face their worst nightmare. The men we loved, sons, husbands, fathers, running at us, screaming, threatening. Men who'd never lifted a finger against us, rearing up with murder in their eyes. Aye some of them died right away, but some of them didn't, and the things they did were beyond wicked." The crowd was silent. "But the worst is, Eloise..." She leaned over the counter then, so her face was close to the girl's, her arms still clutched tightly around her, and I noticed she was shaking. "The worst is that they were like it before the moths. Not all men, no. But some, enough so that I couldn't go out at night alone or go for a walk somewhere quiet without thinking about what I'd do if someone jumped me. And what was done about it? Nothing, that's what. Them in charge just shrugged. And you know who was in charge back then?"

Eloise's eyes narrowed. Her face had gone from pink to red. She still clung to Tony's hand. Tony looked like he wanted the floor to open up and eat him.

"It was men, of course. It didn't matter to me much back then cos that was how it had always been. But now, I wouldn't have that back for anything. I'll say it one more time." She looked from Eloise to me to Tony before her eyes settled on Artemis. "I'll sell my apples to anyone I want to."

Artemis opened his mouth as if to say something, but I put my hand on his arm and he closed it again.

"Come on, Tony," replied Eloise with a sniff. "You don't want to buy from this... this *dolly*, anyway. Let's go to the library." She led him away towards the other side of the market.

I realised my hand was still clutching Artemis's arm, so hard I'd left a red mark. "Sorry." I said releasing him from my grasp. He didn't answer, his mouth set in a grim line.

The mood of those around had shifted a little, and I felt a brooding unrest press in from all sides. Just as I turned, I saw a woman I recognised standing a little way back behind the crowd and watching me and Artemis intently. Freya Curtis, the woman in charge of the vaccination program, stood with her hands by her sides, wearing a thoughtful frown. With her, stood her helper, Anita, fidgeting and looking in every direction except ours. Freya saw me looking but made no acknowledgement of the fact. After a moment, she turned on her heel and walked away, Anita following along behind.

"Did we do something wrong?" Daniel clutched my hand so tightly it hurt.

"No sweetheart, of course not. It's just some women…" I honestly couldn't finish the sentence. It had always been complicated, those from before and those born after, but now even more so. I couldn't imagine a boy like Daniel being a danger to me, even Artemis, as taciturn as he was, had never shown any aggression. But I wasn't there. Could I even imagine such a time?

I bent down so my face was level with Daniel's. There was a faint smear of something on his cheek, food or mud, I couldn't tell. But I found myself licking my finger and gently rubbing the mark away.

The boy stood passively, allowing me to clean him. "I don't really want a sugar apple, anyway," he said, in a quiet voice. "I want to go back to your house and see Lois."

I plastered a wide grin on my face. "Soon, but have you ever tried a jammy doughnut, Daniel?"

He shook his head. "I've had nuts a few times. Is that the same?"

"No. Doughnuts are much nicer than nuts – nicer than sugar apples too. And I happen to know a woman who makes the best doughnuts in the whole world, and she's just over there." I pointed to a tea shop near the village square. Lilly's prices were high, and this was an indulgence I wouldn't normally contemplate, but looking into Daniel's little crestfallen face, I felt like I would have done anything to make him smile. "Do you want to try one?"

"Yes."

"Will she sell to people like us?" Artemis mumbled, as I led them through the market and towards the tea shop.

"Of course." I replied, lightly. "But it's a small shop, so you wait outside with Daniel."

Artemis raised his eyebrows but kept silent.

Tony

The library was closed by the time we reached it. It was a huge stone building with a flight of stone steps leading to a glass door. From the top step I could see the books lined up on shelves along the walls inside. So many, a patchwork of stories and interesting facts, just out of reach. I pushed my nose up to the glass, desperate to be allowed past the invisible barrier. There was a sign on the glass, just below a poster advertising a jumble sale and a number to call if you were worried that someone you knew was spreading anti-Union sentiment.

NO UNACCOMPANIED MEN.
All Men in Eastor's recent foster programme will only be admitted if in the company of a female member of the Eastor community. Many thanks.

"Sorry Tony," said Eloise from the bottom step. "I forgot the library shut early on market days. But it'll be open in the week. I've got some research papers on order that I'll need to collect – I'll take you in then. I promise."

Slowly I plodded back down the steps and allowed Eloise to lead me towards the Old Dray pub on the other side of the street.

The pub was well named, as it smelled like horses. This was perhaps because all the women inside smelled of horses.

I secretly tried to catch a smell of my own skin and yes, it, too, smelled of horses. Of horses and muddy onions. Sam looked happy, sitting holding a large glass of something pale brown. I was given a drink of what can only be described as sour apple juice, and when I winced at the taste, Sam and the group of women sitting with us laughed at me. "Get it down ya," said one woman. "Won't kill ya." Most of those sitting with us were older, like Sam.

Despite the encouragement, it sat untouched on the small wooden table by my knees. I could only imagine that this place was like a version of the facility's rec-room – but one with a roaring fire, which reflected off shining wooden surfaces, and a couple of dogs sprawled out across the carpet. Every nerve in my body was aware of the dogs, they, on the other hand, didn't seem to notice me at all. Dogs were known to be lethal to men, their coats were usually loaded with the poisonous hairs produced by the moths and caterpillars. I had to keep reminding myself that I wasn't at any risk after the vaccine. But knowing and believing are two different things. Also, these dogs had sharp yellowing teeth that appeared every time they yawned. I understood that they were supposed to be tame, but what if one day they decided not to be? What if that was today? Snow was one thing, with his heavy feet and dopey eyes, but these animals had a wolfish look that I really didn't like.

Eloise left to go and run some errands, leaving me with the group of women. I gave her a panicked look as she was leaving but it didn't stop her abandoning me. "I'll be back in a few minutes, Tony. Have a drink. Relax."

"Did you take part in the visitations, Tony?" Another of the women, clutching a glass of something clear that smelled faintly of vinegar, asked me this as she leaned in and tapped me on the knee. She was the third woman to ask me this. They'd all been very nice to me, these women, but I was beginning to feel uncomfortable. They touched me a lot, not obviously, but when they spoke, they brushed my knee and held the top of my arm, complimenting me about my muscles. I didn't want to tell them it was making me feel uncomfortable, not after the toffee apple woman's outburst. It was obvious that not everyone wanted us here, and I didn't want to say the wrong thing. At least these women were not telling me I should go back to the facility. Also, the attention was nice – in that they meant well. I didn't want to explain that I had opted out of the visitation programme, and that I found sex with women bewildering and strange. I thought it might hurt their feelings, which was the last thing I wanted to do. I was an ambassador, after all.

About twenty minutes later, Eloise came back and saved me from having to answer at all.

"It's just shandy for you, Ellie," said Sam with a grin. "You're too young for the hard stuff."

Ellie rolled her eyes. "Mum wants you back in an hour. She asked me to take Tony home now. She said it's getting dark, and he'll be needing his tea."

"Aye, okay, I'll be back in an hour." Sam gave a big wink to the women at the table, who burst out laughing.

I stood up, massively relieved to be called home, but all the women complained. "Sit now, stay, finish your cider."

I didn't know what to do, torn between an escape with Eloise and appearing rude. Then I was hit by an idea of pure genius. "I, err… could someone show me where the bathroom is?

"Follow me." Eloise led me through the pub before the women had another chance to complain. We stood in front of two doors, both with the words LAVATORY written on them. "Which one should I use?" I asked.

Eloise shrugged. "Either."

"What if there's someone in there?"

"So?"

I pushed the door open and walked in. As I did so, a woman exited one of the stalls. The look of horror on her face as she saw me was unreserved.

"Are you okay, Tony?" Eloise from the outside.

It was the apple seller from earlier. I flinched back from her.

"Don't get too comfortable. You'll not be staying long," the woman hissed, before brushing past me and out of the door.

"Did she say something to you?" Eloise said, glaring in the direction the women had left.

I shook my head. "No, but… go out and keep an eye on the door, perhaps? Get anyone who comes to use the other toilet?"

Eloise nodded. "Ignore people like her, Tony. Most women don't think like that. Most want the integration programme to work." Then she left and closed the door behind her.

As we were leaving the Old Dray a slim woman with a nasty scab on the bottom of her nose approached Eloise and whispered something to her. A pained look flashed across Eloise's face then she nodded. "Not here. Round the back."

The three of us then left the pub and squeezed along a narrow passageway between the buildings until we emerged behind the pub into a yard of unhealthy dry-looking grass.

"What about him?" said the women pointing to me. She was one of the untidiest women I'd seen that day, which was saying a lot. Her hair hung in clumps around her unwashed face and her torn jumper seemed matted with all manner of unidentified matter.

"He's fine," replied Eloise. "He's no idea." Then Eloise handed the woman a small bottle of silvery liquid and the woman gave Eloise three slips of printed paper.

"I'll give you three more for a go with the boy, she said grinning and revealing a gap where her front teeth should have been.

"He's not part of the deal." Then she nodded at the bottle in the woman's grubby hand. "It's strong – you mind yourself. Inhale for a few seconds, no more. And if you tell anyone where you got it, Sam'll come and skin you like a summer hare."

The woman gave Eloise a scathing look. "I know how to take

Drift. And I'm no snitch." She put the bottle in her pocket. Then all three of us made our way back through the passageway, waiting a few moments for the woman to go ahead.

"Thanks," I said, as we made our way towards the edge of the village.

"What for?"

"Not selling me to the woman with missing teeth."

Eloise laughed. "I need money, Tony. But not that badly."

"Why do you need money?"

She sighed. "If I want to continue my research I need proper labs, funds. I need to be accepted by Winchester."

"Who's Winchester?"

"It's not a person, it's a place. A university." And then at my blank expression. "A place where people go to study and learn."

"And you have to pay to go and learn?"

It had begun to rain, and she took an umbrella from her bag, opening it as we both huddled under. "The Council pays for some of it, but they expect your family to give you tokens for food and board. My family doesn't have many tokens to spare."

"And what will you do with the learning, once you've researched all the things?" It all sounded like a lot of hard work for little reward.

She stopped on the path, turning to look up at me. "I want to change the world, Tony. I want to make a difference."

The look of earnestness in her face and the force of her words had an effect on me. Oh, to be so confident in something, rather than just surviving each day as it came.

"Tony, I've been meaning to talk to you about something." She caught my hand in hers and stared up at me in the dying light, moving closer. Her look changed and my heart sank. I knew that look. When she spoke, her voice was unsteady. "I wanted to try a hetero-recreation visit, um... with you." She cleared her throat, and her voice became firmer. "As a kind of scientific experiment."

I thought desperately of what to say, "Aren't you a bit

young?" I managed to croak. On the one disastrous occasion that I'd taken part, I remember the women being mostly over thirty.

She blushed hard. "I'm eighteen in a couple of weeks."

In this whole place, Eloise was the closest person I had to a friend. Molly and Sam looked after me and were very good to me, but I got the impression that there were incentives involved, and that they weren't acting completely out of kindness. Layton was a bundle of energy, like a small animal, inseparable from his idol, Tess, except when Tess was at school and he was forced to stay home and study at the kitchen table. Melanie disliked me, or rather she disliked everyone, including me. That left Artemis, and he was as much a liability as he was a friend. I didn't want to lose Eloise. But teenagers' hearts are easily dented. I chose my words with care. "Eloise. I don't feel that way about... girls."

Eloise gave me a wide-eyed look. "Oh... I didn't realise... I mean of course, I err..."

"It's not you," I continued hurriedly. "It's just I don't like..." I let the words drift off, realising too late that I was making a mess of this whole thing.

"No don't worry. I err... pretend I didn't ask, in fact." Her face was flame red and her gaze fell on the floor, then over my shoulder, anywhere but at me. "Let's get home, Molly will be worried."

The journey back to the farmhouse was as silent as it was awkward.

Evie

"Fascinating!"

The nurse from the MWA was explaining to Dr Rosya how the vaccine worked. She, Daniel and Artemis sat in our cramped kitchen holding cups of tea, as the nurse bustled round preparing to take blood from the boys.

"So, I guess it's like an antihistamine? Protecting the men's own physiology from the toxin. How marvellous! I'd like to speak to the ones who designed it."

"It's all hush, hush. Comes from a lab in Wiltshire is all I know. It's where they manufacture it, too."

I stood by Daniel, who was eyeing the needles with suspicion. "It's okay," I whispered, and picked up his hand from his lap, giving it a squeeze. "I've seen nurses take blood many times. This one knows what she's doing."

The nurse smiled and leaned in to draw from Daniel. He gripped my hand so that his entire arm trembled. "Steady. It's just a quick prick, see?"

Artemis spoke up. "In the facilities, we're usually given our shots after some milk."

"I have some milk," I said, still sitting and holding the frightened boy's hand. "Artemis, would you mind grabbing it from the icebox?"

"Sure, but I don't think you have the same kind of milk."

"They would have laced it with a mild sedative." Dr Rosya seemed pleased to be involved in the discussion. "A derivative of the same benzodiazepine they used to use in the benzo guns. I wrote a paper on dosage protocols for my undergraduate degree." She turned back to the nurse. "What markers are you looking for in the bloodwork? Is it hormonal? IgE antibodies?"

I went to hand Daniel a toffee, but his hands were busy holding a small wad of cloth to his bleeding arm, so I unwrapped it and popped it into his mouth. He grinned. "Didn't hurt," he said through a mouthful of glistening goo.

"Above my pay grade, I'm afraid," replied the nurse, screwing the top on the little vial and writing a note on it and putting it with the one she collected from Artemis a few moments earlier. "I just take the bloods and deliver them to the lab." She turned to me. "If there's a problem with any of the readings, someone will be in touch."

Dr Rosya sighed. "Anita doesn't tell me anything either. The MWA can be a close-lipped bunch sometimes."

I thought back to the things Mary had told me in the hospital before she died, about how some members of the MWA, including its head, Jen Harting, had hidden the vaccine from the country and used it to set up their own private members' club. Those involved had been exposed, sent to rehabilitation centres, or banished to Europe. But even so, the reputation of the MWA had suffered a huge blow. Some even blamed them for sowing the seeds of the XX movement. Much of what Mary told me had been on the radio, of course. But not all, not about the club or the murder of her eldest son or the fate of the men at the club. None of that had been made public.

The nurse shuffled to the door, clutching her bag. "Same time next week?"

I nodded.

"How do I get to Molly's farm? I need to look in on her two before I go."

"Take the South Road about a mile then take a turning on the left. Big house on the hill," I replied. "You'll see the barn before the house but keep going."

Then she looked back at Daniel, chewing toffee with his mouth open, and Artemis flicking through the pages of an old cookbook. "I didn't know how it would work. But they look at home here. You're doing well."

"Thanks," I said, a pleasant warmth from her words reaching my face.

"Although mind you don't give them too much sugar – it's not good for them, they'll get cavities."

"Yes, I mean the toffee is just a one off." I thought about the warm sugary donuts earlier and made a mental note to slow down on the treats.

"Let's get started!" said Dr Rosya as soon as the door had closed. She was grinning and rummaging around in her knapsack. "I have a list of questions for the boys, if you could –"

"I don't want to." Artemis looked from me to the doctor and back. Then he stood up. "I've been prodded enough today. Lois said she'd tell me about the time before the infestation this evening, and I haven't seen her at all today." He stood up.

"If Artemis isn't doing it, then I'm not doing it." Daniel stood. I had a mutiny on my hands.

Dr Rosya's smile soured. She ignored the boys and addressed me directly. "I came all the way out here. I think the least you could do is get them to participate."

I turned to the boys. "It's important we answer Dr Rosya's questions. I tried to impress upon them quite how important it was by giving them a pained stare.

Artemis caught on. Rolling his eyes, he turned in his seat to Dr Rosya. "Fine. What do you want to know?"

"Can I go and play?" asked Daniel, squirming in his chair.

Dr Rosya nodded. "I don't need them both this time. The older one will be enough."

"Stay out of Mae's things," I told him. "She gets upset if you touch her papers."

Earlier, Mae had marched into our bedroom clutching a file. "Look!" She'd hissed between clenched teeth, waving it in my face. The grey official looking document had been decorated with smiling faces scribbled in green crayon. "The boy did it on purpose, just to annoy me. He needs discipline, Evie!"

I heard his soft footsteps on the stairs. I suspected the drawings were Daniel's way of trying to connect with Mae, his childish tentative offering. Whereas all my wife saw was a transgression.

Dr Rosya, sitting at the table, pulled out a pad of paper and shuffled through several pages covered in tight, scruffy script. "Right. Name?"

"Artemis.

"Age?"

"Twenty-two."

"Height?"

"181cm"

"Weight?"

"I... I don't know."

"Never mind. Artemis, I am going to ask you some questions about your mood so we can establish a baseline. Does that sound okay?"

Artemis shot me a quick I'm-doing-this-for-you look. I gave him a grateful smile in return.

"Okay, let's do it," he said with an almost smile.

"What would you say your level of happiness has been today? With 'one' being terribly unhappy and 'ten' being the happiest you've ever been?"

"Um..." He gave a small shrug. "Six?"

This pleased me. Artemis usually looked so miserable.

"When was the last time you considered yourself to be angry?"

Artemis hardly paused. "Today at the market. A woman wouldn't sell us some apples."

Dr Rosya's pen hovered over the paper as he said this. Then she looked up. "What woman?"

Artemis looked at me. "It was Carol, the candy vendor."

The doctor scribbled it down and continued.

"What was the last time you considered yourself to be relaxed, Artemis?"

"Last night. In bed after Daniel fell asleep." More scribbling.

"Do you feel that your happiness has increased or decreased since leaving the facility?"

I couldn't help leaning in for this one. He thought for a while. "Increased... I think."

The doctor nodded and scribbled for a longer while than before.

"And when was the last time you were attracted to someone sexually?"

The question took me by surprise. "Wow. Is that necessary?"

The doctor scratched her forehead. "It is part of the standard questionnaire which is given to assess mood at the facilities. I didn't think the subject, I mean Artemis, would mind."

"I think we're all quite tired," I cut in. "Perhaps we can try to do this again another –"

He was staring at me and there was something in his look I'd never seen from him before. A hardness, and something else. A look I hadn't seen in a long time from anyone, and it made me blush. His eyes never left mine as he spoke. "About ten minutes ago."

CHAPTER 11

XX104

We used to play the dinosaur game, Dad and me. In a small copse of trees behind our old house. I call it small now, but at the time we called it 'the forest.'

"Let's go to the forest," he would say, "and hunt dinosaurs."

Overjoyed, I would stuff my small feet into a pair of wellington boots, and he'd help me pull on my coat before setting off into the wilderness.

I would close my eyes as he hid behind a tree. I would then wander around the forest – a brave dinosaur hunter tracking her prey. When I reached him, he would jump out with a roar, and I would raise my sword. Then he would cease to be the dinosaur and we would both turn and fight our imaginary, ferocious foe.

"It's got me!" he would shout, collapsing to his knees on the muddy ground. "Save me!"

And I would, vanquishing the monster with nimble parries and savage thrusts.

Then he'd pick me up and carry me home on his back, both of us victorious, ravenous, and muddy.

"It's Dad. Let me in."

"It's Dad!" Bella was off the sofa and halfway to the door before I could move.

"Wait!" I grabbed her arm. "Just wait a minute." I whispered.

She looked up at me, confused. "Why? It's just Dad."

"I know, but –"

"What the hell, why's the chain across?" His voice sounded angry, tired. But he still sounded like Dad.

"Dad?" I called over to the door. "Are you feeling alright?"

He leaned in so I could just see his face in the small space the chain allowed. His voice became calm, overly patient as if I was being silly. "Baby, I'm tired and hungry, and for some unknown reason my eldest daughter is not letting me into my own home. Apart from that, I'm fine. Now, let me in, please, Beans. It's been a really long night."

He sounded rational – normal even. I went over to where his face was. "It's just, Mum said that there was this infection going around, and it affected men's minds, and that I shouldn't let you in. I know it sounds crazy, but she seemed serious…"

He rolled his eyes. "Yeah, well, your mother would say that. She thinks we're all evil sons-of-bitches."

My hand paused on its way to the door. Dad had never said a bad word about Mum to us, not even after the divorce. It was like an unwritten rule, a united front of parenting. No matter what was going on behind the scenes, they only ever said things about how the other one loved us and wanted us to feel safe and loved.

Safe.

Did I feel safe? "How's Jorge and Miranda?" I asked, stalling for time.

There was a pause, just a fraction longer than I would have expected. His eyes seemed to glaze over in the strip of space he'd squashed his face into. A breeze drifted over the back of my neck, like the broken threads of a spider's web.

"They're fine. They're still at the hospital," he replied.

I shivered – it felt like a lie. "Why did you leave them?"

"They were asleep, and I was worried about you and Bella. Look, sweetheart. Let me in." He looked behind him into the stone hallway, dimly lit by municipal low-watt bulbs. "There are some bad people about, bad and drunk. I don't want to mess around out here too long."

"C'mon, Beans. It's just Dad." Bella stood beside me. "Let him in."

I might have then. Bella's voice was so sad, and all I wanted was for Dad to come in, give me a hug, help me slay the horror that had been building in my gut since this afternoon at the station. Then he curled his hand around the edge of the door. As I reached for the chain I noticed it, there on the back of his hand, a scratch, almost brown in the muted light, a trail of crusted blood. It didn't have to be anything sinister. It could have been dirt, or chocolate. Or he could have got it from a branch or a door handle.

He smiled. "I hope there's some pizza left and you greedy guts didn't eat it all."

"Dad." I spoke carefully, trying to hide the rising panic in my voice. "I'm going to wait till Mum gets here before letting you in." I pushed Bella away from the door, putting my fingers to my lips.

Immediately, the door slammed open, hitting the chain at full stretch. "What the Fuck!" Dad's voice was screeching now. "Open the fucking door, you little bitch! This is my flat and I won't be kept out. OPEN IT!"

"What's wrong, Beans? Why's he shouting?" Her voice was not much more than a wavering whisper steeped in confusion.

"I think he's sick, Bells." I wished my voice didn't sound so scared.

"Then shouldn't we look after him, make him better?"

"He needs medicine, and we don't have any. Mum will sort it out when she gets here."

Her face crumpled into tears. "This is just because you h–hate him. This is because you think he l–left us, and you're still a–a–angry. He's angry because of you." Bella sobbed as the relentless banging of the door continued. Dad carried on shouting mean things, cruel words – about how worthless I was, about how I deserved to be taught a lesson. Things he would never say unless he was sick.

I tried to take Bella into the other room and away from the things Dad was shouting. "We just need to wait for Mum. She'll calm him down," I said, as I tried to gently manoeuvre her away from the door. Bella ignored me, slipping from my hand and going back to the door. "Dad! It's Bella! Don't be angry. It's gonna be okay."

The banging stopped and Dad's voice changed, becoming calm again. "BabyBells, open the door for me. I'm fine. I just need one of your extra special hugs to make me feel better."

"NO!" I ripped her hand from the lock, harder than I intended, and dragged her away.

"Get… off… me!" she wriggled in my arms. "Dad!"

I got her to the bedroom and threw her on the bed. "We need to wait for Mum," I gasped.

"This is all your fault!" she cried out. "This is because you didn't want to come."

Suddenly, there was an almighty crash in the other room. I left Bella on the bed and moved into the living room, my nerves on high alert. Another crash. He was hitting the door with something heavy, trying to smash the chain from the doorframe.

SMASH! The door thrust open again, making the bolts holding the chain in place jiggle.

It was going to break free.

I looked around for another way out, but we were on the seventh floor.

Trapped.

Tony

That evening after dinner, Molly sent Eloise and Melanie to milk the cows but kept me back.

Melanie grumbled as she went. "It'll take me ages on my own. Why can't Tony help."

"You won't be on your own. You'll have Eloise," replied Molly. "Sam will be back soon too."

"Sure, I'll have Eloise to help." A look passed between Eloise and Melanie,

When they'd stomped off into the dark, wrapped up in cloaks and boots, Molly turned to me. "I want you to keep an eye on Layton and Tess, Tony. Keep them out from under my feet for a while.

I was relieved. Although I'd discovered that cows were not aggressive, their bulkiness and their big muddy feet still made me nervous. And the smell. In the facility I'd longed for smells less familiar, desperate to get rid of the smell of disinfectant which lingered on every surface. That was before I smelt the inside of the milking sheds.

I tried to keep Layton and Tess occupied with reading, but neither was interested. Tess, because the lesson was too easy, and Layton because it was too hard.

"What's the point in all this reading?" Layton pushed his copy of *Wind in the Willows* away. "We never had to do so much at the prep house."

"You're not at the prep house, now," I replied. "Out in the world, you're going to need it."

"What for?" The 'for' was stretched out into one long whine.

"Learning new things," I replied.

"He doesn't need to read," offered Tess, hoping for a way to get them both free of this unplanned extra lesson. "I can tell him anything he needs to know."

Layton held up his bony arms, his hands poking out from the sleeves of an old blouse. "See. The women can tell me things. I don't have to read. It's only cos you were friends with that old carer that you read so well. No one expects me to read."

At the mention of Mary, I felt a sharp dig in my chest. I would go for hours without thinking about her, and then suddenly remember she was dead and that I would never see her again. The thought of never seemed too big for my mind. Even when Logan was taken away, I believed in my heart that I would see him again one day. That was the frightening thing about being outside. Everything was huge – even the ideas.

Sam came back from the pub, bobbing and laughing too easily.

"I knew I should have come and fetched you," scolded Molly. "Look at you. Like a cart with three wheels."

"Why's this one not out helping with the milking? That's what we got him for, ain't it?" Sam sat down and gave me a deep wink to show it was a joke.

Molly slopped down a bowl of root stew and a plate of bread. "It's cold. The girls can manage. It'll just take them a bit longer, is all."

Sam shrugged. "If you say so." Then to Layton, "You doin' some reading, lad?"

Tess answered as Layton always got quiet in front of Sam. "He doesn't like it, and he's no good at it."

Sam laughed; a soft woofing sound that made the table shake. "Me neither lad, me neither. I hated that school stuff. Better using all that book paper for kindling if you ask me."

I was horrified at the notion. Tess and Layton laughed.

Molly washed the dishes with a large amount of annoyed splashing.

Over the next few days, things carried on in the same way as before, milking, digging, eating, sleeping. The only difference was I didn't see much of Eloise. And when I did see her, she looked unhappy. She spent a lot of time out on the farm, or 'doing research,' and when she came in for tea, she would eat fast and then excuse herself, go out for a walk despite the cold and the dark. I wondered if she'd said something to Sam and Molly about the hetero-recreation visit. It would be a lot easier if I could just do it.

And then, a few days after the market, something happened

that changed everything. I was in the kitchen with Layton, Molly and Tess, making bread. It was my favourite chore, not least because it was warm, but also because the smell of yeast and baking made me think of the time I'd spent in the facility kitchen. Every second Wednesday before I left, I was on the kitchen rota. And now I missed it. I missed the men and the jokes and sneaking pinches of sugar when the carers weren't looking.

We'd got one batch in the oven, and another was just being put aside to prove when Melanie burst in, panting.

"Boots, Melanie," said Molly, lifting the heavy kettle to the stove. "You know the rules."

"It's Snow. Something's wrong."

Tess jumped up and scrambled outside bootless before anyone could stop her. The rest of us shoved on our boots and followed Eloise out into the barns. There were three stalls and the last one housed the big white horse, Snow. The poor animal lay on the straw-strewn floor on his side, trembling. His solid neck gulped as if trying to swallow and a thick foam dripped from the side of his mouth. Tess was kneeling by his head and stroking his soft cheek.

Molly turned to Melanie. "Run and find Sam, now!"

Melanie nodded and was gone.

Then to Tess, "Come away, love. We don't know what's wrong. If he fits, you'll get hurt."

Snow gave a whine. The most pitiful noise I had ever heard. Then his legs began to bend and straighten, digging into the straw.

"Easy, boy," said Tess, ignoring Molly and kneeling down next to Snow.

Layton moved behind Tess and curled his arm around her. "He'll be okay," he said, although the tremble in his voice betrayed how scared he was.

I didn't know what to do and just stood by the door of the stall watching the poor animal jerk and writhe on the floor, his eyes so wide I could see a rim of pinkish white around the brown orb. I wanted to run away, go back to a place I understood, where animals did not get sick. I wanted to go back to the kitchen and mind the bread and have nothing to do with this.

Then Sam bumped past me, kneeling down by Snow and leaning over the shuddering horse.

"What is it?" said Molly, moving closer.

"I dunno, foxglove maybe? Ragwort wouldn't make him retch like this."

"Where would it come from? We check the feed. There's nothing near the pasture. What do we do, Sam?"

"I don't know, Moll. I don't think there's anything to do. If it's foxglove… take the kids inside. I'll stay with him."

Misery etched itself into Molly's face, but she turned to the door and ushered out Melanie, Layton and me.

Tess didn't move. "I'm staying. I don't want to leave."

Molly seemed about to argue, but Sam spoke first. "She can stay."

Layton moved towards Tess. "I'll stay too."

But Molly took his arm. "Give them space. You can see her when she comes in."

The little girl knelt in the straw next to Sam and held out her hand to the trembling horse. The four of us left the stall and walked the short way back to the house. As we approached, we could see something on the door, a knife pinning a folded piece of paper, which fluttered in the breeze like a trapped bird. It hadn't been there when we left. Layton ran over and plucked it from the wood, tearing the corner of the paper where it had been pinned. He opened it and frowned, handing it to Molly. I read it over her shoulder:

A poison for a poison. Send them back!
XX

Evie

I finally got rid of Dr Rosya. I don't think she noticed the way Artemis looked at me, or if she did, she made no mention of it. She asked him some more about his mood, about how he felt about the outdoors, about his life at the facility, and about his views towards women in general. Artemis answered politely enough but kept sliding glances in my direction. He'd crossed a line, and we both knew it.

It had been months since my wife had wanted me. The picture of Mr Sullivan still sat in the drawer. Artemis didn't have his facial hair and his eyes were dark green rather than the brown of Mr Sullivan's. But there was a similarity in the shape of his face, a leanness to his jaw. I dismissed the thought. I was not one of those women who went to the facilities for visitations. Mae and I mocked them, in fact, as dollies trying to re-create the old times. Or women with too many tokens and nothing better to do with them. Sex with Artemis would cause complications, especially with things with Mae as they were. Also, what had the pamphlet said? Something about strong affections?

After Rosya left, it was still early. I started making dinner. Mae rang and said she'd been called to some meeting in the Citadel, and she was catching a lift with a colleague – back in the morning. Did I believe her? I don't know. Perhaps she was having an affair, or maybe she was just hiding out at the office, uncomfortable around Daniel and Artemis. If I was honest, I didn't care either way. Her absence, I realised, was a relief.

Artemis sat at the table and watched me rinse lentils. I knew he wanted to say something, but I mentally begged him not to. I wanted to pretend that everything was as before.

"Evie… are you –"

"Go ask Mum if she's coming down for dinner or if she wants a tray. And call Daniel down."

"I'm here." It was Mum on the stairs. Artemis jumped up to help her come down. "Daniel's asleep."

That was annoying – if I woke him, he'd be grumpy and sleepy throughout dinner, and if I didn't, he'd wake up in the middle of the night hungry. I hovered at the bottom of the stairs, not knowing what to do.

"Make him a sandwich and a glass of milk and leave it by his bed. He can eat it in the night if he wakes up." Artemis poured a glass of juice for Mum and placed it on the table. His shoulder brushed mine as he passed me, and the kitchen suddenly seemed impossibly small and warm.

"Yes – thanks. Good idea." I stepped away and busied myself making the lentils for us, and a sandwich for Daniel.

I could still feel Artemis watching me, though. And I desperately needed him to stop. I wanted some space to untangle the feelings whirling around in me. "Mum, weren't you going to tell Artemis about the time before?"

Artemis sat up straight. "I'd like to hear about it, Lois."

Mum took a sip of juice and then winced. "Artemis, if you give me a glass of Mae's wine, a large one, I'll tell you anything you want to know."

Artemis looked over at me and I nodded, not meeting his eye. "Under the sink," I replied.

I'd not seen my mother drink anything other than a small glass at midwinter, so I was mildly shocked when she gulped down most of the glass at once and then tapped it for a refill. Clutching her second glass, she leaned back in the chair. "What you have to remember, Artemis, is that we were not prepared at all."

CHAPTER 12

Lois

We thought we were – that Coronavirus had made us ready for anything. But Covid, as it turned out, was only the warm-up act. Also, much of what I say won't make sense – I know you've never heard of energy drinks or Airbnb's. But let me finish before you ask questions, okay?

I was twenty-four and had just returned from travelling around Europe. Yes, Evie, I know the idea of your mother packing her bag and wandering off to a different country is shocking. But at the time, despite politicians and the legacy of Covid making it difficult, it was not uncommon to take a year out after university, scrape some money together and head for the sunshine. There were plenty of jobs, paid-in-cash, for bar staff and cleaners in hostels. I'd worked in hotels, in kitchens, even in a Spanish building supplies warehouse just outside Alicante. My job was to fix labels on items for shipping. I know very little Spanish, but I learned the words for pipe, ceramic tile, and double faucet. It was so hot that one day, when I left work for lunch on that big industrial estate, the rubber soles of my shoes melted on the pavement, leaving footprints down the street. I never admitted to anyone it was my cheap English shoes that had left the marks. Soon after, I got a job as a bartender in a town nearer to the beach.

I met some good friends. When I think of those first few weeks, so filled with violence and terror, I think of the French man I met in a club in Santa Pola, *Mama's*. We'd danced all night and drank and kissed as the sun rose on the beach. Or I think about the girls I shared a room with in a hostel in Paphos, and how we'd share one hairdryer between the three of us and borrow each other's clothes. I wonder how their stories, away from the swift response of the UK, would have been much worse.

You could go anywhere in those days, Artemis. You just got an aeroplane, and a few hours later you were in a different country. It would hit you, the heat, when you got off the plane, like a physical thing. Even at night.

I'd run out of money and come back to the UK to work in a call centre as an emergency operator. Like the exchange centre we have now, but much bigger. Mobile phones were everywhere, but all emergency calls were routed through the same switchboards. If you were in trouble, if you needed an ambulance or the… the Law Abidance, as they're now called, you would call 999 and an operator would put you through. It was well paid, relatively, back when you weren't just paid by the government. Also, I would flirt with the security guards – ha, don't look so scandalised Evie. I was young once, in a world very different from this one.

I had half a mind to get together some more money and continue travelling. I hadn't been to Australia, Thailand, Japan. I didn't want to settle down, not then. I was living with my mum, rent-free.

I think about what might have happened if everything changed when I was in another country. When we finally got the power grids up and running, those in charge at the time, Jen Harting and the like, said they'd send out envoys to see what state the rest of the world was in, but it never happened – or at least they never told us what they found. But that all came after.

I was at work when the first infestation hit, and to a certain extent, that helped me realise what was going on before most. I'd taken the night shift, although it was July, so the sun was coming up at about five am. Anyone who's done a night shift knows you feel like you've made it when the sun rises, no matter how early. There were about eight of us on the floor that night, all huddled around one island of monitors, surrounded by an ocean of chocolate wrappers and half-drunk energy drinks to help us stay awake. Of the group on that shift, I remember my boss, Joel, sniffling in one corner – allergies, he'd said. The conversation had mostly been about the mystery virus in Germany and whether there would be a lockdown here. If there was, would we still have to come to work?

It had been a busy night for a weekday, but not unusually so. Thinking back, there may have been a few more 999 calls than you'd expect. I'd been looking forward to a weekend off; I was considering going to the coast with a group of friends and getting a cheap Airbnb – as long as there weren't any new restrictions, of course. Suddenly, the bank of monitors lit up with calls. Usually at this time, at most, one or two would be online. All around I heard the *ding-ding* that accompanied the call, our screens edged in red. So, everyone began their call, everyone except Joel. He was ignoring his screen and instead stared out of the window into the distance.

My call was a young woman, gasping into her receiver.

I began my script. "Emergency. Which service? Fire, Police or Ambulance?" The caller needed to request a service. If they couldn't, it was my job to connect to the police and stay on the line.

"I… he's… I don't know. He's blue. Ambulance. My little boy – AMBULANCE!"

My heart raced as I connected the call. This was a bad one. Most of the calls we received involve falls, sprains, drunk teenagers, muggings, or it was someone coming home to find that their house had been broken into. Serious, but not life-threatening. A child turning blue? The panic was thick in the mother's voice. She tried to speak over me when the ambulance service answered, but I had to complete my script – "Aldershot connecting 01276 997088. Go ahead, caller."

As soon as the woman began speaking, through breathless, shuddering sobs, I dropped out of my call. Sometimes, we stayed on the line and listened. Occasionally, the ambulance would need a repeat of the address to which we had access. But I had three more calls in a queue. I picked up the next one. I could hear those around me connecting calls to the police, the ambulance service. There must have been an incident, some kind of massive pile up or a terrorist attack, maybe?

"Emergency, which service –"

"Help me, please." It was a little girl, whispering.

I lowered my voice. "Can you tell me which service you want? Is there a grown up with you?" We had training in what to do when speaking to minors. This time I was going to need to stay on the line.

"My daddy. But there's something the matter with him."

"Does he need an ambulance?" I prepared to connect the call.

"He has a knife."

The blood in my veins turned icy and slow. "I'm going to connect you with the police. Stay there?"

But I couldn't. I tried and tried. Usually, if your regional service was busy, it would reroute to a major hub, Southampton or London. This time it just rang on. I looked around at my manager, waving to get his attention, but he continued to sit, staring out of the window as if he couldn't look away. His own monitor flashed red as the calls built up.

The little girl began to cry.

"It's okay," I said, trying to make my voice sound as reassuring as possible. "I'm going to get through. What's your name?"

"Charlotte."

"Okay, Charlotte. Can you hide somewhere?"

"I'm inside my wardrobe."

"Good. Good girl. Stay there." I checked her address – Maidstone! Why were calls from Maidstone being routed towards us?

The girls on either side of me were also struggling to connect. "What the hell's going on?" said the operator to my right, a neat, efficient woman named Jean. She'd been working in the exchange for over ten years, and in the four months I'd known her, she'd never once raised her voice, never allowed a call to ruffle her, not even heavy breathers or the prank calls. But as she turned to me, she was pale in the artificial light, her tone shrill and frantic. "I've got a call from a man who says he's just stabbed his wife – he wants the police to come and get him." She jabbed at the keys that would dial in again. "He sounds weird – really out of it. I think he's telling the truth."

"I've got a woman who says her husband's gone blue and won't wake up." I heard this in my periphery. I was still trying to connect Charlotte with someone – anyone, I'd have taken the coastguard at that point – but those words lodged in my mind. Husband's gone blue. Like the little boy on my last call.

"Daddy?" The little girl's voice sounded in my ear. "Where's Mummy?"

Then a man's voice came through quietly in the background. "Mummy's sleeping."

The hairs on my arms rose at the strangeness of his voice, as if everything was a big joke but only he was in on it. I made my voice light. "Charlotte, put Daddy on the line." Perhaps I could talk him down. Maybe, it might give Charlotte a chance to get out of there.

But the man's creepy voice got closer, as if he was only inches from the receiver. "Put the phone down, baby."

"Wait!" I shouted into the phone, "Charlotte! Let me speak to Daddy – tell him it's very important."

The line went dead.

Ignoring the other calls clamouring to be answered with their relentless *ding-ding* sound, I checked the number and started dialling, even though calling back was against protocol – I was supposed to hand it off to the police. But there were no police.

No answer.

"It's your fault, you fucking bitches!"

All of us girls on the monitor bank looked over at Joel in shock. He was standing in the middle of the carpeted walkway and pointing at us, his face an unhealthy-looking dark red.

He was an easy-going guy, balding, in his fifties, wearing chinos and a short-sleeved checked shirt. I'd never heard him swear, or raise his voice, even if I'd messed up a call he'd be like, *don't worry, it happens, go make a cup of tea and take a break*. It was almost funny to see him there, pointing, his eyes wide, his nose streaming.

But what he did next was not funny. He went to the woman nearest him, a student with a trendy haircut and thick-rimmed glasses, and he grabbed her head. Then he smashed it on the desk. She hadn't the chance to struggle, and our shock was so great that we just sat there, not quite believing what we saw. She lay unmoving, face down on the desk, but that didn't stop Joel from digging his fingers into her hair once more, bringing her limp head off the desk and driving it again onto the blood-spattered workspace.

Then we reacted. You'd think there'd be screaming, but no. Just a silent agreement as we all lunged at Joel, tearing him off the girl.

"We need to call down to Security," said one of the girls.

But when I looked over at the door to the office, Security had already arrived.

And they were infected too.

Evie

It was late and Mum looked exhausted.

Plus, her story was far more visceral than I'd anticipated.

I don't know what I thought she'd lived through in the first wave, but the lessons at school are removed, depersonalised. I thought Artemis would be as horrified at the things my mum was saying as I was. But he looked mesmerised. His tea had gone stone cold, forgotten.

"What happened?" he said. "The security people were men, right? How did you escape?"

Mum looked gaunt in the low light. I cut in before she could answer. "Let's leave it for tonight. We can finish another time."

"But I just wanted to know." Artemis's hands balled up on the table. "Did the women with you get out? What happened to the boss man, Joel? What is a fucking bitch?"

Mum sighed. "I'm tired, Artemis. Tomorrow – I'll finish it tomorrow, after dinner. You wouldn't want me getting overtired, would you? Not after I've been feeling so much better."

"No, Lois." Artemis visibly swallowed his disappointment, and then, "Would you like a hand upstairs?"

"That would be lovely – thank you. Then you can come down and help Evie clean up the kitchen. It would be nice for Evie to have some company in the evening for a change." She grinned and I felt my cheeks get warm.

When Artemis came back from helping Mum, I was busy cleaning up the kitchen.

"Can I help?" He mumbled, half-heartedly picking up a dirty bowl and holding it out to me, unsure as to what he should do with it.

"Put it in the sink to soak – I'll worry about it in the morning." He did as he was told and, in doing so, leaned in close to me. His pale green shirt, too tight across the shoulders and too short in the arms, brushed my shoulder. I noticed how stubble was beginning to appear on his wrists. I resisted the urge to run my fingers over the bristly hairs and dried my hands on a tea-towel.

"We should turn in." My voice was a little too high.

Artemis didn't move. "Is Mae coming home?" He caught my eye as he said it, suggesting that the question was not just a request for information. It was a declaration, an intention.

I felt pulled towards the safety of my bedroom upstairs, our bedroom, mine and Mae's. But also rooted to the spot, in the corner of that small kitchen, next to the gently rising steam of a sink of soiled dishes. I shook my head. She's working in the Citadel – won't be back until late tonight.

Artemis's eyes held mine, and I saw something in them that I hadn't seen in a long time. Longing. It was as if his need called to my own, a feeling that had been lingering under the surface.

"I want to... to kiss you," he whispered. But he didn't move. Whether he was making it harder for me on purpose, or if he really couldn't initiate the kiss, I didn't know. But the hard catch in his voice was enough. I stepped in and raised my face. He dropped his to mine. It was chaste to begin with, a breath, nothing more. His lips touched mine, a delicate brush, and we stayed there for a moment, poised on the precipice. Even then I could have broken away – said it was a mark of affection, an act of goodnight, nothing more. Instead, I raised myself on my toes and pushed harder into his kiss. As I did, I wondered if this was something he'd done before – with men at the facility or women in the visitation programme. Was I pushing him too far? But then he dragged me closer, enveloping me in his arms and his strange earthy scent, like warm leather.

His touch left me in no doubt how much he wanted me, and I returned his searching desire with my own. I thought perhaps that our embrace might be cold and awkward, that it might purge any further thoughts of him in my bed. But it was the opposite. It was hot and desperate and honest, and it filled my mind with more visions, more desires. He led me into the sitting room, where the fire glowed amber, and pulled me down on the rug. Lying down like this, I was able to explore him, unbutton his shirt, watch as he left it in a pile on the rug.

"Have you been to a visitation?" he asked, his voice rough. "Do you know what's like?"

I shook my head. "No. You?"

He nodded. "A few." He eased my jumper over my head. "I'll show you."

Tony

Snow died that night. Poor, massive, soft Snow. Sam came into the kitchen carrying Tess and told us. Molly was stoking the fire. She replaced the poker and when she turned to face us, I could see that she'd started to cry. Immediately, she rubbed the tears away with her podgy red hands, leaving a smear of soot on her cheek. "I'll take her to bed," she said gently lifting Tess from Sam's arms.

"You should go to bed too, Tony." Melanie said, her face etched with misery. She didn't meet my eye when she spoke.

I could sense that something had changed, that somehow it involved me, and I didn't know if it would change back.

Over the next few days Tess was inconsolable. Layton did everything he could to cheer her up, making birds out of paper, laying bowlfuls of blackberries from the garden at her feet like a sacred offering, trying to entice her into a game of hide and seek. But nothing worked, and I saw the light in the little boy's smile flicker and dim. Everyone was subdued. Eloise was always out, and when she'd come home late in the evening, she'd grab some food and take it to her room – sometimes she didn't come back until after I'd gone to bed. I was sad that she didn't seem to want to spend time with me anymore.

Then, one evening when the rest of the family were downstairs listening to the news on the radio, Eloise sidled into my room. To begin with, I stayed downstairs and listened to the radio with everyone – I enjoyed listening to what was going on, local events, news from the Citadel, how the MWA male fostering programme was going, reports from outside the Union. The world, it seemed, was a large, complex place. But after Snow's death, I didn't feel welcome downstairs. There was a shift in the atmosphere when I entered the room. I don't know if Molly and the others felt it, whether they meant to make me feel uncomfortable, but there was less laughter, Sam stopped teasing me. The quiet made me uncomfortable.

Therefore, I'd snuck off to bed early, pleased to have the small room to myself for a little while. It was cold, as I wasn't sure if I was allowed to set the fire myself – Eloise and Melanie were allowed, Layton and Tess were not so I wasn't sure where I fitted in the hierarchy. I snuggled down under a heap of blankets just as the door squeaked open.

"Hi," whispered Eloise from the door. "Are you asleep?"

I wriggled my way out from under the pile. "No, I was reading." I held up a battered copy of *Charlotte's Web*.

She relaxed a little and smiled back. "Can I show you something? Something I've been working on? It does mean going outside, not far. Just a few minutes' walk."

It was dark outside and the very last thing I wanted was to leave my warm den and go walking about in the cold. But on the other hand, I didn't want to disappoint Eloise, not again. "Are you sure we should be wandering about in the dark? There are crazy people out there."

Eloise sighed. "It's still on our grounds, Tony. We can take a rifle if it makes you feel better." There was a note of annoyance in her voice but then it softened. "Actually, I could do with your help."

Motivated by the idea that Eloise needed me, I dragged myself from the warmth of the covers and was up and fully dressed in a few minutes. Downstairs, I could hear the rest of the family in the sitting room, voices from the radio punctuated by Sam's deep laugh and Molly's higher pitched giggles. We put on coats and boots and Eloise grabbed one of the three rifles lined up by the door.

"Shouldn't we tell them where we're going?" I asked, eyeing the gun.

Eloise's gaze flicked towards the living room. "No, it's fine. We won't be long."

My gut told me in no uncertain terms that we should definitely tell them we were going out into a cold and somewhat stormy night, but instead I followed Eloise in silence. At least she had a gun.

We passed the barn and Snow's pen, empty now, and hiked along the side of the nearest field towards the line of trees at the end. Eloise had mentioned something about a few minutes, but it felt like a lot longer until we finally reached the trees. Then, to my horror she led us into the woods.

Trees are beautiful in the day. The first time I stood under a tree, I marvelled at how high their branches stretched, craning my neck to see the top. But, at night, trees change. They become hulking creatures, looming from nothing, rustling with displeasure and offering refuge to unknown animals. The eeriness of the darkness was not helped by the noises – chirrups and yelps, the occasional shriek coming from the canopy above – it all made my heart pound. Cold sweat pooled on my back as every moment I expected something to reach for me from the shadows. Tree roots tripped me constantly, whilst low branches poked at my face. "Eloise," I called, struggling to keep up. "Can we go home. I don't like this. I've… I've changed my mind."

"Not far now," she said, without slowing or turning back to check on me. The rifle bumped along on her shoulder, supported by a strap.

A terrifying thought occurred to me. What if Eloise was *not* okay at being rebuffed? What if she was luring me into the woods to take some terrible revenge? Tying me up perhaps and leaving me to the mercy of whatever beasts roamed here? Or shooting me with the rifle and blaming it on a stranger! I hung back a bit, navigating the tripping roots and keeping a wary distance between me and Eloise, despite the fact that she had the only torch and without its protection I was basically adrift in the darkness. Just as I was about to insist we turn back, something appeared from the trees before us, a building.

"Here." She waited for me to catch up and handed me the torch and the gun whilst she rummaged around in her pocket, pulling out a long iron key. As we approached, I could see it was a small stone cottage, squatting in the middle of the trees. A shiver ran through me as I remembered Mary telling us fairy stories in the rec-room back at the facility. Cottages in woods usually spelled doom for someone. The door was thick and wooden and opened with an ominous squeak.

Eloise leaned in and clicked a switch on the wall, causing a number of strip-lights to flicker into life. "Come on, shut the door. It's freezing out there."

The inside was one long, low room. It was surprisingly warm, and a strong earthy smell hung in the air. Around the edge sat shelves containing strangely shaped glass tubes, bulbous containers, vials, tongs, measuring cups and various oddly shaped devices of unknown purpose. In the middle of the room stood a long table strewn with more weird apparatus, brightly coloured potions, small plastic dishes and piles of printed paper, many with *WINCHESTER – Knowledge is wisdom* in bold letters across the top. At the far end of the table was a large cloth-covered box.

I stared slack-jawed about me. "What *is* this place?"

Eloise dumped the gun in the corner and fiddled with a switch connected to a black rectangle. The rectangle glowed red, and the room became even warmer. "This is my lab. I told you about my research in phylogenetics and genomics. Well, that involves a lot of experimentation. Until I can get a proper place at Winchester, this is where I work. It used to be where we kept spare grain and feed, until we extended the barn."

"I thought you just read books and wrote reports. Does Molly know?" Moving slowly round the room, I tried to take it all in. Pinned on the wall were diagrams. It took a few moments before I realised that the diagrams were all of men, naked men, without skin so that body parts were visible and neatly labelled: *aorta, lung, pulmonary artery, rib*. I found myself clutching my own chest, disgusted and fascinated by the idea that these lumps of flesh and bone sat just beneath my skin.

"Sam knows." She'd picked up a notebook and was scribbling something in pencil. "It costs a lot to keep the temperature correct, so I couldn't keep it a secret from everyone. And Melanie, but she won't tell."

A troop of tiny bottles, each the size of my thumb and containing a silvery liquid, stood to attention in a wooden box. Picking one up, I held it up to the light, marvelling at how it seemed to absorb the light and glow from within. "Is this the stuff you sold to the woman behind the Old Dray?"

"Don't touch that, Tony!"

Immediately I replaced the bottle. "I'm sorry. I'm sorry." I wiped my hand on my cloak.

Eloise came over to me, still clutching her notebook, and picked up the bottle. "It's a synthetic drug. Some women like to inhale it. It's like having a vivid dream whilst being awake. I make it from the same toxin you find in the nests of the moths."

Living in a waking dream sounded horrendous, as did messing around with moth nests. "What effect would the drug have on me?"

She shook the little vial, making the liquid swirl and bubble. "I don't know, Tony. I really don't. On an unvaccinated man, inhaling this concentration would probably be fatal. But with the vaccine... paralysis, damage to the brain, perhaps." She put the vial back with the others and pushed them to the back of the shelf. "Let's not find out."

I left the toxic bottles and followed her around to the far end of the table.

I passed a line of what looked like tomato plants. This was

the source of the earthy herb-like smell. "What are these?" I asked running my fingers over the spiky fronds.

Eloise smiled. "That's a special ingredient for Sam's cigarettes. Payment, I suppose, for the lab. But this is what I actually wanted to show you, Tony." She stopped by the large cube and, with a flourish, removed the cover. Underneath sat a large clear plastic box. Inside, disturbed, no doubt, by the sudden appearance of the outside world, a small army of moths fluttered and fought, beating their wings on the clear plastic. I took a step back and faced Eloise, who was smiling as if she'd just revealed a pile of raisin cookies.

I didn't know what to say, although Eloise seemed to be waiting for a response. "Goodness," I managed weakly. "So many... moths."

She placed the cover onto the table and leaned over the box, peering inside with a look on her face that bordered on delight. "They're beautiful, aren't they?"

We stood there for a few moments as she admired her hoard, before she opened her notebook and scribbled something inside. It was then that I realised that the wall behind her was covered in frames of dead moths, of all colours and sizes, pinned wings outstretched, all labelled in tiny meticulous script. I shuddered. "Why do you have cages of moths, Eloise? What I really wanted to ask was: *what does all this have to do with me? Why am I here?* My bad feeling had returned, and I wondered if it wasn't safer in the outside darkness after all.

"Yes... sorry, Tony." She dragged her eyes away from her notebook and back to me. "How much do you know about genomics and entomological selective breeding?"

I returned her enthusiastic look with a blank one of my own.

"No, of course, okay – in layperson's terms then. These..." She gestured to the box where the moths had settled on an assortment of sticks and leaves and were staring out at us. "These are common *Oxytenis Aeger* moths, Plague moths. These are the moths that appeared forty-three years ago, at least, their ancestors did – they had some evolutionary advantages in that they were able to mate with other species, and they were toxic to predators at the time. But you probably know this from school."

I shrugged.

"Oh, well, it doesn't matter. What matters is that it is their hairs, and those of their larvae… caterpillars, that are poisonous and because there were so many of them, the insecticides at the time just weren't enough.

I nodded patiently, although I really wanted to go back to the farmhouse.

"In the 1950s some scientists began working on breeding self-limiting insects to deal with agricultural pests, that is to say, selectively breeding insects that would mate with invasive species and then render the female offspring infertile."

I must have looked confused because her voice slowed down.

"Unwanted moths ate all the cabbages. The scientist's made special boy moths who had babies with lots of girl moths. The babies couldn't have any more babies. No more moths eating cabbages."

"So, these moths can't have babies?" I pointed to the cage.

She shook her head. "I was just using it as an example. I'm using the same principle, but I'm trying to engineer a moth that *isn't* toxic. One that also has a shorter breeding cycle than *Oxytenis Aeger*. If I could get these things right, then we could one day eradicate *Oxytenis Aeger* completely."

I frowned. "But we have the vaccination, now. The moths are no longer dangerous." I looked over at the plastic cube, to the rows of shining eyes. As horrible as they were, I need not fear them. "Why would we need" – I waved my hand at her notebook – "engine breeding or whatever?"

Eloise went quiet, so quiet that I thought I'd upset her. I quickly tried to make it right. "Although what you've done is *very* impressive. All this equipment and the moths and such. You obviously belong at a place like Winchester…" I trailed off.

"Tony, why do you think that you are only given the vaccine every month?" Her voice was quiet, sad even.

I shrugged. "I guess it's something to do with the chemicals. Or testing, or something to do with men's bodies?"

Eloise looked away. "No. It's so that the government can control you."

I almost laughed, but one look at her face told me that she was completely serious. "Why would they want to do that?"

"Before the infestation, before the moths, the world was very different. Men sometimes hurt women. Many of those in charge of rules were men. More than women. They made decisions that… that meant women couldn't have the same rights as men. It's complicated and many strong women fought hard to convince these men that women should have equal rights and freedoms, but it wasn't equal, Tony. Not by a long way."

That was the sort of nonsense the apple seller in the market had been talking about. I looked in Eloise in disbelief. The sort of world she described, a world where men were not only in charge, but *bullied* women, was unthinkable. "But, how could men do that, I mean, who made them think it was… okay?"

Eloise placed her notebook down and looked me straight in the eye. "They had the power, Tony. They decided it was okay."

"Were all men like that?"

She gave me a thoughtful look. "I don't think so. It's difficult to get accurate accounts. Much of the literature from before has been removed or adapted. The books and plays you read with Mary. They were not the originals."

I felt tears well up in my eyes but didn't know who I was sad for. The women of before? The men being controlled now? I looked over at the box of moths and they stared back at me, now silent and still. Imprisoned. Controlled. I turned to face Eloise. "Your research – how long will it take you to make the safe moths?"

Eloise smiled, but again, there was a sadness in her eyes. "I'm only at the theory stage, Tony. It could take years to breed an invasive non-toxic *safe* moth. We have to check that there are no unforeseen side effects. What if we created a moth that was safe for men, but it turned out it caused birth defects, or killed all natural pollinators. That's why I need to go to Winchester and do more research."

I nodded. "What do you need me for?"

She pulled out a small box from a drawer. Opening it she revealed a syringe and a small vial. "I need a particular enzyme to continue the editing, one contained in the vaccine. I need your blood."

It wasn't until I reached the edge of the woods, trundling along in the dark behind Eloise, her clutching a big pile of books, notes and journals, whilst I clutched a cotton pad to my arm, that I worked up the courage to say what was on my mind. The wind rushed through the dark trees, and I felt the words whipped away from me as I spoke. "Eloise, what if men *should* be controlled. What if letting us out of the facilities is the wrong thing to do and we end up hurting women?" I was shivering through my words.

She stopped and turned to me. The torch light swung round in my face, blinding me for a moment. She must have slipped off her cloak, as she was wrapping it round my shoulders. I leaned into its warmth. "No one should be kept in a cage, Tony." She took my hand and led me home.

XX104

When the chain finally gave out, the door crashed into the wall with so much force it shook the windows. Dad stood in the doorway clutching a fire extinguisher.

I stood in front of the door to the bedroom where I'd left Bella. "Dad?"

He didn't look like my dad, not the laid-back man I loved.

His face was twisted into a snarl and was flushed red. Sweat beaded on his forehead. "Dad?" I repeated. "What's wrong?"

"What's wrong?" He dropped the fire extinguisher on the floor and the thud made my heartbeat even faster. "You didn't let me in!" He took a few steps towards me.

"I wanted to wait till Mum got here. She said –"

"She said! She said!" His voice was high and mocking. "I bet I know what she said!" He was spitting as he spoke, and although he was looking straight at me, I felt he wasn't really seeing me. "She said I was weak, that I was unreasonable – lazy. Let me ask you this. What are you all for? Bella? Miranda? Your mother? What are any of you actually... for?"

"I don't understand." I was trying to keep the tears out of my voice as I placed my back against the door to the bedroom. This wasn't my dad. This was someone... something else.

A monster.

"Dad?" The door behind me opened, and Bella's face appeared from the gloom, tear-stained and pale. "S... stop shouting."

"Come here, BabyBells." His voice had changed again. It was sticky and cloying. "Give Daddy a hug."

But Bella didn't move. She could tell as well as I could that this was not her dad.

"I said. Come. Here. Bella."

"Get behind me, Bells. It's okay." I tucked her behind me and towards the door at my back. "Mum'll be here soon."

"I SAID!" His scream made us both jump. "COME HERE BELLA. NOW DO WHAT I SAY!" He lunged for my little sister, who slid out from behind me and ran behind the sofa, keeping it between her and Dad. "Stop fucking around, you little brat."

I grabbed him. "Leave her alone. Dad. Stop it. You're scaring her."

She was crying, sobbing loudly.

"Get off," Dad hissed at me, then did something he'd never done before. He slapped me hard across the face. There was a moment of numb shock before the pain hit like an aching fire spreading across my cheek. He grinned and raised his hand again, this time in a fist. "That's what you need. A lesson."

I backed away from him, aware that Bella now had her back pressed up against the door to the balcony. She'd stopped sobbing and was making panicked hiccupping noises.

Then a noise, just behind Bella, made me and Dad look in that direction. Bella turned. I recognised the noise from earlier. A bird thumping on the glass, then two more large birds, black and white, Magpies. Dad moved to the door and looked into the skies. He put his head right to the glass pane and watched as more birds plummeted towards the ground. When they hit the balcony, they bounced a little, like a parody of splashing raindrops. The shadowy street seven stories below must have been littered with them.

Dad's face creased into a frown. He looked at his clenched hand and then at the birds, falling like small meteors. Then he looked at Bella.

"No!" I forced my legs to move towards him despite the fear pulsing through me and the pain still blazing in my cheek. "Leave her alone." I grabbed his arm and tried to pull him away.

But he didn't move closer to Bella. He yanked his arm from my grasp and opened the doors to the balcony, stepping out into the falling flock of birds. Then he turned to me. His gaze was not confused now. Just sad. "I love you, sweetheart. Look after Bells and your mum – I'm sorry about Miranda and Jorge." He was my dad. The man with whom I'd fought monsters in the forest. The man whose shoulders I clung to on the way home, muddy and tired. I felt a sudden urge to go to him and allow him to wrap me in his arms. But I just stood there breathing hard, feeling the tears cool on my hot cheek.

His next move was firm and purposeful. He didn't hesitate, didn't look back at me or Bella. He placed his hands on the railing, brought his legs up sideways, and in one fluid movement, leapt over the railing and was gone.

Bella lunged towards the railings, but I held her back and slammed the balcony door shut. I was breathing heavily. My hands shook as I fumbled with my phone, trying Mum's number.

My mind repeated the same three words as the phone rang and rang: Dad-is-gone-Dad-is-gone-Dad-is-gone.

Over and over – no reply.

CHAPTER 13

Evie

Afterwards, Artemis and I dressed quickly, fumbling like teenagers in the dim light of the fire.

"Is it okay? Are you okay?" His face was so earnest, so focused, as if everything in the world depended on my answer.

"It's great," I said, and smiled. He smiled back although his eyes remained unsure. I couldn't quite bring myself to remember the act itself, it was all too new and strange. A buzzing coursed through me, and I couldn't tell if it was happiness or shame – or a strange mixture of both.

He looked to the door. "I should go to bed." It was a half statement, half question.

I opened my mouth, wondering how to say the thing I didn't want to say.

"Before Mae comes home and finds us like this."

I closed my mouth. He knew.

Then he kissed me once more, soft and chaste, and even the brief touch of his lips had me wanting to pull him towards me. But it was after nine and, as unlikely as it was, Mae might have left the Citadel early.

Before he left the sitting room, he turned in the doorway. "It's going to be fine," he said, "We're going to be fine."

Although I knew that he had no way of knowing whether

it would be fine, no way of making this less complicated, I felt myself relax a fraction. "Goodnight, Artemis."

I lay down on the sofa in front of the dying fire, watching the embers glow and bank. As a child, I would watch the fire before bed and imagine that the hearth contained a molten landscape, one where tiny fire creatures lived in the caves and crevices created by the wood. I kidded myself that I could see them scurrying around their blazing world, collecting the ash for food and bedding. I pulled up a blanket and closed my eyes, concentrating on nothing but the warm glow on my face.

"It's *unforgivable!* You should be ashamed." Mae's voice crashed through the house.

I shivered as I woke, the fire died in the night. Outside it was just beginning to get light, the pale sun reflecting on the ice that clung to the windows.

My heart rate spiked – she knew about me and Artemis. *She knew!*

I shot from my burrow on the sofa and through to the kitchen.

Mae stood, dressed and ready for work by the table. She must have arrived late and not woken me. Across the table lay the innards of the toaster in neat little piles around what may have once been the main hub of the machine. And peering over the table in his nightshirt and an old cardigan was Daniel, his upturned face a perfect disc of despair.

"How am I supposed to make toast? What possessed you to UNSCREW it?"

"L–Lois said, she t–told me..."

"Don't make things up, Daniel." Mae was leaning over him, her arms trembled as she leaned on the table. "Only wicked children, make up stories. Who's going to pay to get this fixed? Because it's not you, is it?"

"Mae." I gently clasped her wrist and pulled her away. "He's scared."

"Look what he's done!" She gestured to the piles of filaments and wires carefully laid out on the table. "What sort of delinquent tears apart a toaster?"

"Mae! Stop. He didn't mean any harm."

"Well who's going to put it back together? You?"

I knew the look on her face, the hard line of her jaw and the shine in her eyes suggesting that the whole world was against her, that she alone carried the weight of reason on her back. Then she sighed and shook her head. "You're out of your depth, Evie. I don't think you're cut out for this. They need discipline and boundaries." Then she pointed at the table. "I'll sort this out later – don't make it any worse."

"You'll be late for work," I muttered, not looking her in the eye.

She nodded and then patted me on the arm. "I need to talk to you this evening – things need to change," she shot back, before grabbing her coat and heading for the door.

I wanted to say that I didn't know how long the funeral would last, that I might be back late, but she'd already gone. There was a long pause, as if Daniel and I were waiting for her to come back, both of us wondering if we were allowed to breathe.

Then Daniel gave a defeated look which broke my heart in two. "I'm sorry."

I gathered him up in my arms, allowing him to wrap his scrawny legs around me and marvelling at how warm he was despite the chill in the kitchen. "No, Lois said you could. It's fine."

He took a shuddering breath and leaned his head on my shoulder. We sat there for a minute or so, until he began to fidget. I released him and watched him scramble back to his seat, as I sat in the chair opposite.

"She told me to wait for her and that we'd do it together. But I woke up really early, and everyone was still asleep, and I just thought I'd have a *look* at the toaster, but then I saw I could unscrew the panels on the bottom with a butter knife, and then… and then… I just kept going." It was the most words he'd ever said at once in my hearing, and as he spoke, his eyes scanned the table, the different coils, wires, boards, the metal housing. "It's *amazing* the way it all fits together and how these levers, look" – he demonstrated by pulling down a set of sprung levers on the hub – "see how these levers make the claws grab the bread?" Again, he demonstrated the mechanism, pulling the lever down, breathing fast in his excitement. Suddenly a thought seemed to strike him, and his face fell. He looked at me in horror. "Are you going to send me back, Evie? Because of Mae, and because I didn't wait for Lois before starting this?" He gestured to the table. His forehead was lined with worry, too much worry.

I looked him firmly in the eye. "No, Daniel." I'm not going to send you back. I want you to stay here for as long as possible. You belong here."

He gave one solemn nod, as if my words were the ultimate authority, then turned back to his toaster, the fear in his expression replaced with keen interest. I suddenly wanted to cry. To be believed and trusted so completely – I wasn't expecting the wave of fear and joy that his response delivered. Fear that I couldn't live up to such confidence, joy that I was to be allowed to try. I swallowed hard and looked out of the kitchen window. The sun was trying it's best and had managed to melt some of the grass frost.

"That's it, young man. A little more on the left." Mum's voice came from the stairs. She was being escorted down by Artemis. I saw his shoulders first hunched over, his arms gently supporting Mum as she made her way downwards. Then his face appeared, stoic, pensive. The hairs on my arms stood up. Visions of last night flooded through my mind, things I hadn't allowed myself to think about. Flesh and warmth and the rumbling groan that had shaken Artemis as he climaxed.

"What's for breakfast?" said Mum as Artemis lowered her

into the chair nearest to the stairs. "Oh, goodness me, Daniel has been busy. Porridge then?"

I dragged my eyes away from Artemis. "Porridge, yes."

Daniel began explaining the mechanism to my mother, picking up pieces and handing them to her as she squinted at them from close range.

"You've managed to find the element assembly centre, well done! You are a clever chap. Next, we'll have you work on the vacuum cleaner."

Daniel squirmed in his seat in happiness. "Shouldn't we put the toaster back together, first?"

"We certainly should. After breakfast, Artemis can fetch my tools from the shed. That will make the whole process easier."

"What kind of tools?" Daniel's excitement was palpable.

Artemis brushed passed me and handed me the milk. "Good morning." His voice was both shy and warm. As I took the milk, he brushed my hand with his fingers.

"Morning," I replied, smiling.

Tony

Mary saved my life many times. She taught me to read, not the stupid laminated scrolls, but poetry. She sat with me after Logan was infected and taken away, despite the fact I wanted to die. I shouted at her and told her many times to leave me alone. But she didn't report me for it. She just came back the next day with a cake or some nice cheese. I don't know much about mothers, or at least I didn't until I went to live with Molly and Sam, but I like to think that Mary was my mother. And now we were going to say goodbye for the last time.

It was the day of the funeral, and I was waiting for Evelyn to arrive and take me to the ceremony. Layton was with me, kicking stones through the dirt.

"Where's Tess?" I asked.

He didn't look up but gave the stone by his foot a sharp whack. "Doing the cows."

"Why aren't you helping?" Apart from when Tess went to school, I hadn't seen them apart since we'd arrived.

He rubbed his eyes hard with the heel of his hand. "She doesn't want me there. She thinks I killed Snow."

"What! Why would she think that?"

"She thinks that if I hadn't come, he'd still be alive, which is the same as killing him."

I sighed and searched for something to say that might make the boy feel better. He was usually so cheerful, just seeing him with his head bowed and his eyes rimmed in red was heartbreaking. "She's hurting, now. Because of Snow. But she'll come around. She knows it wasn't really your fault."

He sniffed and didn't answer, just kicked another stone.

Since Snow had been poisoned by the mystery letter-writer, the mood in the house had been muted. Molly was short with everyone, snapping at Layton for wearing his muddy shoes indoors, and mumbling about the price of butter at breakfast.

Sam had become angry over the missing rifle. "You can't go leaving guns about the place, Eloise, especially now." He nodded at me, which I took to mean, there were people that wanted to shoot me.

"Sorry, I must have left it at the croft. I'll get it later."

"What are you two whispering about?" snapped Molly, returning to the kitchen and wiping her hands on a tea towel.

"Nothing, love," said Sam quickly.

Last night's dinner had been virtually silent after that. "We'll need another dray. I'll go to the market at Chichester, Saturday," said Sam halfway through the grim silence.

At which point Tess had burst into tears and slammed down her spoon on the table. "It won't be Snow, though, will it?" she sobbed, before running upstairs and slamming the door to her room.

Layton had gone to follow her, his face stricken in grief, but Sam stopped him. "Leave her be for now. Finish your stew."

That was the other thing about last night's dinner. The stew had contained chicken. I was horrified. The idea of eating something I'd been feeding, something I'd given a name, made me ill. Then, when I couldn't finish the food, Molly got angry. "There're people who'd give anything to have chicken for tea, and on a weeknight, too! You're just so ungrateful, Tony. You don't know how good you have it."

"Molly, love –" Sam tried, but she wouldn't be stopped.

"You come here, and you eat – you eat a lot. I can hardly keep up. And some women in the village... well, I don't think you realise, it's been very difficult. You can bloody well eat your food and thank me for it. I never heard such nonsense. You sound like one of those city women. Not wanting chicken, indeed!"

Mortified, I tried nibbling on a bit more of the chewy meat.

I could usually count on Eloise to stick up for me, but recently she'd been absent – probably at the laboratory working on her mutant moths.

Eventually, when Molly had deemed I'd eaten enough, I went to bed, but couldn't sleep. I wanted to go back to the facility. I even considered finding some way back on my own, begging them to let me in. Isla would be pleased to see me, I guess. But I could just imagine Daisy's voice. *You've made your bed now, Tony. Time to sleep in it.* That was one of her favourite phrases.

I must have drifted off because I was woken up this morning to find Eloise sitting on my bed beside me. I looked over and Layton had already gone down to breakfast.

"I've made good progress, Tony. Because of the enzymes in your blood, I was able to get further than I ever have before. I've still some way to go, but it's looking really promising." Her smile made her face glow with happiness, although I noticed that her eyes were rimmed in red suggesting a long night at the laboratory.

I smiled back. "That's great, Eloise. You're the cleverest person I have ever met. Winchester will be beating down the door to have you."

She blushed deep down to her roots at my words and her grin widened.

Then I remembered Molly's anger the night before. "Do you know why Molly and Sam are angry with me? Is it just because I eat too much?"

"They're getting some pushback from people in the village. Someone is spreading rumours about the quality of our produce. Only a small minority, but it's costing us. Then there was all the stuff with Snow and the incident at Chesterford."

"What incident?" I was putting on my pants and dungarees.

Eloise looked down at her trousers and rubbed at a small stain. "Some woman blew up the village hall. One of these XXs. Killed a bunch of participants. Even killed a couple of the kids."

I thought back to my journey here with Artemis, the women with XX on their tee shirts and their shouting and catcalling. "Why don't they want us here? Why would they blow people up? Boys? Is it because of the way men were before? Keeping power for themselves?"

"I guess. It's dollies mostly, you know, women from before. They're afraid of what might happen. They don't realise that a lot of what made men like that before has gone."

I had a vague collection of Mary using this term about herself. A dolly is a woman who wanted to go back to the way things were. But she'd also said that there were many things she didn't miss. I'd thought about it a lot since my trip to the woods, the ideas swirling and merging in my mind, making me queasy. "But, if women have the power now, isn't keeping it just the same as when the men had control?"

"It's very similar," Eloise replied, but there was a look in her eyes I couldn't identify. Something pensive.

After breakfast, Eloise had left towards the woods, giving

me a wink as she went, and Molly had given me some newer clothes to wear. A pair of black trousers, a dark blue shirt, and a knitted jumper. I thought of telling Molly that I preferred skirts, but she still wore the grimace from the night before, so I took my smart clothes without complaint. Both the shirt and the trousers were tight.

Also, I was cold, despite the jumper. I was about to go back inside and ask Molly if she had an extra coat, when the car arrived. A reclaim, patched and of differing colours, but the body was not too badly rusted. Daniel jumped out and ran towards Layton. The two boys hugged, and I was glad that he'd have someone to play with. Molly stood by the door and waved to Evie, who waved back from the driver's seat. She looked pale.

I was surprised to see Artemis. I thought it was just going to be me and Evie. I got in the back beside him. "Hi, Evie. Artemis. How's it going?"

Artemis shrugged and looked out of the window. "Good… I mean fine. Nothing new. You know how it is." He spoke quickly and there was an odd defensiveness about his tone. It was difficult to tell in the car's darkness, but I thought I saw him blush.

Evie

As I drove to the funeral, my mind flicked between two narratives. First, part of me was convinced that the whole incident was inconsequential, an experiment, part of the programme, a fumble, something almost too silly to tell Mae about. And if I told her, then it'd be an offhand comment, a joke even.

You'll never guess what happened…

The other story contained words like affair, betrayal, and a whisper of deviance. That story, I could not tell Mae. But lots of women did it, didn't they? The visitation programmes were popular, for good reason it seemed. It wasn't as if I was a freak. We'd both wanted to – there was no harm done. *But would you have done it if Mae had been at home?* I buried the thought and concentrated on the road.

The men were quiet in the back, Artemis avoiding Tony's attempts at conversation. This was not suspicious – Artemis was always taciturn when it came to other men, especially Tony. But I found myself silently begging him to be friendlier. Every silence, every short answer, felt like an admission of guilt. I couldn't bear the idea that Tony might suspect. I was being stupid, of course. No one was that observant. Even so, it was an uncomfortable journey. But then Tony told us about Molly's dray and offered me something else to worry about.

"Are you sure?" I asked. "That it was deliberate, and he didn't just eat something bad in the field?"

"Yeah, there was a note. Something about men being a poison and telling them to send me back." There was an anger in Tony's voice I'd not noticed before.

We neared the wrought-iron gates to the crematorium. Law Abidance officers lined the drive, holding back a crowd of women holding placards. "What's going on now...?" I mumbled as I slowed down to drive through the space cleared by the officers.

Tony answered from the back. "The XXs – the women who don't want us here. They were at the entrance to the facility when we left, although not this many."

I looked in the mirror and caught Artemis's eye. He looked tense, placing his hand on the back of my seat. I wanted to reach back and touch it, but with Tony there, that would have been impossible. "It's fine," I said. "The LA has it under control." And they did – just. The women holding the boards were being held back from the road. But I could still read some of the signs. NO ONE ASKED ME! In red paint, dripping like blood as it had dried. Y – DO WE NEED THEM BACK? and

VACCINATION=REGRESSION XX! And those women looked furious. Something struck the side of the car, a rock perhaps, and I sped up as we neared the gates.

"What a lot of fuss," said Tony, crossing his arms. "Women are so... mean."

"Not all women, Tony," replied Artemis, quietly.

"Well, you've changed your tune," snapped back Tony, as we pulled into the parking area.

The crematorium was squat, red brick, architecturally sturdy. Nothing romantic or ornate. It had a slightly pitched roof – and a large chimney, of course. There was a pale square on the front above the door that may have borne some religious motif from the time before.

A few women chatted in little knots of twos and threes outside. We were early and stood in the weak sunshine at the entrance, attracting a few sideways looks from bystanders. They'd dressed Tony in trousers and a shirt that were obviously too small for him. His face was smooth. Molly, it seemed, was keeping his face shaved, although his hair was now a stubbly dark shadow on his head. Artemis was wearing a pair of my trousers, a little voluminous in the hips, but at least they reached his ankles, and a large navy sweater knitted by Mum. His facial hair had grown over the last few weeks, and his hair too. It made him look older. A memory surged into my mind. The feel of his bristled cheek on mine, the warmth of his hand as he placed it on the nape of my neck and pulled me towards him by the fire. His naked flesh, so hard as I touched it, so little give to his skin compared with Mae's.

"Tony! Artemis!" I jumped at the cry of a blonde woman marching over to us.

"Oh – hi, Daisy," replied Tony. There was a sudden change in both men as she approached. A deflation.

She turned to me. "Hi! I'm head sister at the facility where these two" – she gave an exaggerated wink – "reprobates lived before they were vaxxed." She held out her hand and offered me a tight smile. "So, boys, behaving yourselves, I hope? Doing everything you're told?"

I took her outstretched hand; aware the boys were uncomfortable.

"Yes," answered Tony. "I think so. Is Isla here?"

"No, she wanted to but one of us had to stay on E block, make sure the men didn't get up to mischief, so it was decided she should stay."

Tony's face fell. "That's a pity. I thought I might see her again."

"I'll tell her you were asking about her," said Daisy with another tight smile.

Artemis stayed quiet but stood a little closer to Tony and pressed his wrist against the back of the other man's hand.

Daisy continued brightly, oblivious to the men's discomfort. "MWA delegate Freya Curtis is leading the service. She asked me to describe Mary to her, which I was happy to do. Although I may have played down Mary's more eccentric qualities. Did you know Curtis was a Waterloo survivor? It may be a bit old-fashioned, but I love hearing those stories. What an example she is. A true heroine of the Union."

I was about to say that we should go in and sit, thus saving the boys from a woman they both obviously detested, when a car pulled up outside the entrance, grey and newly manufactured. From it came two large Law Abidance officers and two men, one in his forties, with curly brown hair and clear blue eyes, the other a little younger, blondish hair, blue eyes and impossibly handsome. A young woman stepped out next, hair pulled back into a fringeless ponytail and shadow moons under each eye. She straightened down her navy dress and then took the hand of each man and walked past us into the crematorium. The officers walked alongside, scanning the area. One looked at me, then at the men, and gave me a quick nod before following the others inside.

"I wondered if they'd let him come," said Daisy in a nasally half-whisper.

"Who?" I replied.

"Mary's son." As she said the word, she couldn't hide the distaste in her voice. "I heard they're holding him, and the other man she rescued from Jen Harding's place, in a safe house in the Citadel." She leaned in. "Death threats from the double Xs, apparently."

So that was Nathan. The man Mary sacrificed her other son to save. Yes – the eyes were the same. "And the girl?" I remember Mary telling me about the story of that night, as she lay in her hospital bed, unable to sleep – or too frightened to dream. Although, sometimes her memory failed, she forgot where she was in the story, and occasionally her story had changed – she'd smashed the windows to let in the moths – she'd shot Jen Harting with a benzo gun. So, it was difficult to know what was true and what was the musing of an addled mind.

"I would guess that's Sophia Matzo. Jen's assistant. She turned on Jen at the trial – the prosecution's star witness, although there's still some mystery about why she turned, and about her relationship with one of the men they kept hidden there. Look – there he is, the good-looking one with sandy hair and blue eyes. Mary rescued him too. He used to be at our facility, until he started a riot – before my time, mind." Her tone suggested that there would be no riots on her watch. "We thought he'd become infected. But it turned out that he'd been sent to the Harting compound in Surrey. Lomand? Logan? Something like that. I think you knew him, didn't you, Tony?"

XX104

It was getting light outside. I'd tried Mum's mobile every half hour but just got a weird busy tone. I'd tried 999 as well but got a hold message.

I was on the sofa. Bella, asleep beside me, groaned and whimpered every few minutes, her small head turning on my lap until I brushed her hair and murmured to her, and she calmed down. Every time I drifted towards sleep, the sight of Dad's face as he said goodbye yanked me back into wakefulness. *I'm sorry about Miranda and Jorge*. I couldn't think about it – what those words meant.

I froze as I heard footsteps at the front door, and Bella groaned again. I gently lifted her head and shuffled along before replacing it with a cushion.

"Hello?" I whispered. "Who is it?"

"It's Mum. Are you okay?" She was out of breath. "The roads are gridlocked. I left the car in Battersea and had to run –"

I stood up and threw myself into her arms. "Mum –" I couldn't help it as the tears streamed down my cheeks. "I was so scared."

"Sweetheart, I know, I know… shhhhh… It's going to be alright. We need to get to the train station and out of the city and then – my god, what happened to your eye?"

She'd pulled back and was staring at me in horror. I put my hand up to my aching cheek. "Dad…" The correct words refused to form *jumped – he jumped! He was sick. He wanted to hurt Bella. Then he was okay again, but then… then he jumped.* I hadn't slept, and everything was jumbled. The side of my face he'd struck was tight and tender, my eye sore and swelling.

"Is he still here?" Mum looked about the room. "Did he hurt Bella?"

"No. I don't…" The tears came again, so strong I just had to allow them to take me. My voice was lost to a barrage of sobs.

"He jumped off the balcony." Bella was sitting up. She looked calm, her voice flat. "He jumped off to be with the birds. Can I watch Aladdin again?"

Mum went pale as milk. "The balcony? He's dead?"

I nodded. Still crying.

"Stay here." She opened the doors to the balcony and leaned over the edge.

I could tell by the horrified look on her face that he was down there. I hadn't mustered the courage to check. "I tried to call 999, but I couldn't get through." The crying had made my throat sore, so my voice came out as a croak. "I tried... but –"

"It's okay. It's okay." Mum held me by the shoulders and looked into my eyes. "You did fine."

"I'm hungry." Bella's tone still had that odd flat quality. "Can I have Chocopops? Miranda got them for me."

Mum and I exchanged a worried glance.

"How are you feeling, Bella?" asked Mum, going over to the sofa.

She shrugged. "I'm fine. I just want breakfast."

Mum paused. I thought she'd say something else, but she just smiled. "Sure. Go get yourself a bowl. We need to leave soon if we want to catch the right train."

Bella slid off the sofa and padded into the kitchen in search of cereal.

"Where are we going?" I asked.

"Nanny Beth's. If we're going into some kind of lockdown, I want to be away from the city."

Nanny Beth, Mum's aunt, lived with her girlfriend on the outskirts of Totnes in Devon. Hippy shops and new-age, vegan cafes, we'd been to visit a few times. One Christmas we'd had a mushroom nut roast instead of turkey. Dad hadn't been impressed. *Dad* – I pictured him like the crows I'd seen earlier, lying on his back, head twisted back at an impossible angle, his hands forever clenched in a fist.

Mum switched on the TV. The morning news was full of confusion and speculation. Some reports saying it was a type of coronavirus, one that affected the brain. Some said it was a bioweapon, released by Russia or China in response to 'unfriendly' economic sanctions. Some said it only affected men – other reports suggested women were also affected but in far fewer numbers. Brain misfunctions, allergies, terrorism, natural phenomena, outbreaks of violence. Even the newsreaders had lost their usual professional confidence – they kept looking from side to side as if wanting a conclusive report to arrive on the teleprompter.

What should the public do? This question was repeated over and over again, as was the follow-up question: *Where is the Prime Minister? What is the official word from Downing Street?*

"... It is vital that the public stay indoors until we can ascertain the root cause of these events... Stay indoors!"

Bella came in clutching a bowl of cereal. "Are we going to stay here?" she asked, slurping down the browning milk. "Like the man on the TV says?"

"No, we need to get a train to Nanny Beth's," replied Mum.

"Cool. Pancakes." Bella was fond of Nanny Beth's speciality breakfasts.

"Finish up then." Mum started throwing our stuff in our bags. "Where's Bella's other trainer?"

Suddenly, I didn't want to go. "They said to stay indoors. Maybe we should stay here."

"No." Mum's voice was firm. "London is not the place to be in something like this. Come on. Shoes on. We may have to walk for a bit."

Bella drank down the last of her cereal. "I don't want to walk. I want to stay here and watch Aladdin."

"No arguments." Mum's voice was light as if she'd just asked us to tidy our rooms. "Shoes on. Coats on." But there was an edge to it. Bella and I knew not to argue.

Reports are coming in that the Prime Minister is due to brief the public at 9.30 this morn – Mum switched off the TV and threw the remote on the sofa. "If we catch the nine o'clock from Waterloo, we'll be in Totnes, eating pancakes, by teatime."

Should I have fought harder to stay? Should I have listened to my instinct, which was telling me not to go?

Waterloo, the biggest massacre of the first wave.

My mother, my little sister and I, were headed right into the middle of it.

Tony

Logan.

Logan?

It wasn't his long hair, or his smart dark suit that I didn't recognise – it was the fact that he'd been infected, and therefore could not possibly be walking towards me. They told me he was dead. And I believed what I was told. And my life and my future and everything I cared about died with him. I thought I might fall. I felt Artemis's arm next to mine, strong and reassuring.

Logan – *my Logan!* – walked from the car towards the entrance of the crematorium, holding onto the arm of a woman with dark hair. He saw me and he paused, the look of shock on his face a mirror of my own. "Logan?" Did I say it out loud? I think I did, although my heart was beating so hard and so fast that I couldn't hear anything other than the blood coursing in my veins.

The woman he was with paused and gave him a puzzled look. When he turned to the woman and smiled, I knew it was a fake smile. His *charm smile,* I used to call it. Something he used on carers when he wanted to get something by them.

"Are you okay?" asked his companion.

"I'm fine," he replied, glancing down then offering a quick glance at me. There was a warning in that look – *don't say anything.*

My mind was reeling. *Logan-Logan-Logan-alive!-alive!-alive!* I wanted to cry.

Artemis led me to our places in the crematorium, ushered me onto the hard wooden bench. I craned my neck looking for Logan, finding him at the back, next to the dark-haired woman, her hand casually on his leg. Her other hand held Nathan's, Mary's son. She saw me looking and didn't smile. I looked away.

I tried to concentrate on what was happening, but the words blurred and drifted, drowned out by one wonderful, thought;

Logan was alive and he was here. But I would have to wait. He would find me and explain. He would have a plan. He always had a plan. So, I took in my surroundings, and waited for Logan to tell me what to do.

There were about thirty people in the small hall, all but four of us women. It occurred to me that none of these women knew Mary, not really. Her nurse, Evie, more than most, but even she only knew Mary at the end, when she was frail and confused. I was closest to Mary, but I had to sit and listen to people I didn't know, many of whom Mary didn't know. Freya Curtis, the woman from the MWA, talked about Mary's sacrifices, hard work, and discipline. That wasn't the Mary I knew. She told stories, funny stories about talking rabbits. Freya Curtis also thanked Daisy for describing Mary as a serious, quiet person. Always the professional. Daisy – Mary *hated* Daisy! I glanced at Artemis, who sat next to me on the hard wooden bench. I was looking for an ally for my indignation, but his face was unreadable as usual. I could feel my jaw tighten. Mary would hate this.

I looked round at Logan again as Freya Curtis wittered on about the battle at Waterloo. Logan wouldn't meet my gaze, staring fixedly ahead. Her words filled the hall, how women like Mary were stepping up and shepherding the Union through the difficult time of adjustment. As she said those words, *difficult time of adjustment*, she paused. I turned to the front to see that she was staring straight at me, and I felt all eyes in the hall turn to me and Artemis. A song began to play on some speaker attached to the walls. Words about storms and walking and golden skies. The wooden box rolled towards the curtains.

Suddenly I couldn't stand being in this hall with these women. And the idea that I was in the same space as Logan and unable to touch him or talk to him made me want to be sick.

As I stood up, I could hear muttering rise from those around me.

Evie leaned over Artemis and grabbed my sleeve. "What are you doing?" she whispered. "It's not finished."

I thought I was going to speak, to tell these people that this was not who Mary was, and that it was her kindness they should talk about, and her humour. I wanted to point at Logan and say that the man I loved was back from the dead and for some reason, I wasn't allowed to speak to him. I felt tears well up and I opened my mouth. But the look of panic on Logan's face made me close it without uttering a word.

I walked out. I walked past the wooden benches and the upturned startled faces. I walked past Logan but didn't look at him. Opening the door, I stepped out into the bright sunshine.

The doors swung closed behind me and I leaned on the wall of the building. A feeling of foolishness welling up inside. What was I doing? Should I go back in? I showed myself up in front of everyone.

Stand still and breath for a moment, Tony. Give yourself some space. It was Mary's voice, not a ghost or anything, but an echo, of one of those long nights where she'd stayed with me, when she dragged me through another night when I didn't want to live. I did what her memory told me to do and took three deep breaths, closing my eyes, feeling the sunlight on my face. Real, outdoor sunlight, a breeze, the sound of birds.

I heard the doors open beside me and opened my eyes. I expected to be met by an angry Evie, but it was Logan. He was as handsome as he'd ever been. Older, tired looking, now with an abundance of blonde hair instead of shaved stubble. But even after four years, still my Logan.

I threw myself into his arms. "They told me... that... you were dead." I was sobbing.

He held me and let me cry. "I know, baby. Shhh, I know."

Finally, my tears abated enough for me to take a long wobbly breath and stand back. I held onto his arms, in case he drifted away, like the dreams I'd had of this moment.

"How?" I asked. It seemed as good a question as any as I used my sleeve to wipe a mixture of snot and tears from my face.

"It's a long story," he replied. "I don't think we have much time." His voice was sad, rather than urgent. He looked at the door and I followed his gaze. "I was taken from the facility, from you, to a secret place and given the vaccine, but I escaped. And now, Sophia and I live in a big house, a long way from anywhere..." He trailed off.

I took a deep, shuddering breath. "Sophia? The woman with dark hair?"

He nodded and his gaze shifted towards the crematorium.

"Have you told her, about me. I mean you should let her down easy but, now I have the vaccine we can..."

He shook his head. I didn't recognise his voice, thick and rough. "I don't know what she'll do if I say I want to leave. I think she might stop giving me the vaccine. She's never said it outright but if I do something she doesn't like – want to be on my own, for example – she says things, like *don't wander off too far, we might forget to give you your dose*." He hung his head. "I'm always so scared, Tony. Sometimes I think she might send me back, to a place like the one I escaped from. When I think about it, I wish... I wish maybe I would get infected and become a Blue. It would be over then."

I ran my hand over his back, trying to tamp down the anger in my chest. This wasn't like Logan at all. Logan was the strongest man I knew. He was clever and kind and always positive – *always*. But pain was etched deeply into new lines on his face. Then I thought of what Eloise had said, about the monthly vaccine and how it was set up to control us. Perhaps this Sophia woman was using the vaccine in this way. "What did they do to you, at the secret place?" I asked softly, wiping away a tear from his cheek. "What type of place was it?"

His eyes closed and he sagged into me. "I can't go back," he whispered.

We stood there for a long moment before Logan pulled away. "Don't worry about me, Tony. I'll be okay."

I frowned. "It's me, Logan. It's Tony. You can't pretend –"

But he'd turned and was pointing towards an oily black smudge that had just landed on the wall of the crematorium by my shoulder. "It's the first I've seen," he said. "Since we've been out. Since the night I escaped." His voice had changed too, as if he'd shoved the pain somewhere deep.

I looked sideways at the fat moth. It was huge, its hairy legs clinging to the rough brick as its black eyes regarded us coldly. Even knowing that I was immune to its toxin, I still wanted to move away. Decades of being told that they represent death and madness still sat keenly in my mind.

"You'd do best to forget about me, Tony," Logan said in a not-quite-cheerful voice. "Carry on with the foster programme, keep your head down. Ensure that the next generation of men are accepted. One day people like you and me can make it on our own, but not yet. There's no place for us here." And then he did something astonishing. He reached over and brushed at the moth, touching it, sending it flapping into the sky.

I watched it flutter off, skittering about in the breeze, higher and higher until it was just a tiny speck. Anger gripped me. Anger at his words and his lack of heart. Who'd hurt him this much? How could Logan, brave fearless Logan, be so afraid? And he wanted me to be afraid, too! No, I thought. I'd been scared my whole life. Trapped inside, behaving myself, keeping my head down. "Logan, there might be another way. The girl I'm staying with, she's really clever and she's doing something with genies and gnomes. One day you won't need the vaccine, and…"

But he wasn't listening. He was looking behind me, towards the gates, as four women ran towards us, dressed in XX tee shirts, fury on their faces.

He pushed ahead of me, and murmured, "Get inside!"

Just as something heavy and sharp struck the side of my head.

CHAPTER 14

XX104

Although there had been minor outbreaks in the UK over the preceding two days, it was Waterloo that was this country's ground zero. We learn at school that the moths can lay in trees and burrows, in houses – in sheds if they must – but their favourite habitat is the damp moulding darkness of the underground. Underneath Waterloo lies a network of abandoned caverns and arches. A paradise for the moths that first summer, full of the marshy spores that the caterpillars prefer – although the moth's favourite meal, we've since discovered, is the membrane of the human eye. And they ate their fill in that first infestation.

We pushed our way into the station. A crowd of at least a hundred stood looking up at the departure boards, many holding baggage, hastily stuffed carrier bags bulging with clothes, toys, nappies. The early birds fleeing the city. There was a background hum of soft murmurs and people muttering into their phones: *I'll try to change at Reading… In the hospital… didn't wake up! Doctor says some kind of infection…*

There was also something else which clung to the periphery of my awareness. Sneezes and sniffs, rising into the air like audible punctuation. People – men – wiping their noses on tissues as they made their way through the crowd, dragging their families behind them. I noticed one man, in a smart dark suit, standing at the edge of the crowd, staring blankly ahead. His nose was running, but he didn't seem bothered. He stood still and there was something in that stare that I recognised. A confusion I'd seen the night before.

Mum struggled through the tightly packed space. I followed, breaking away from the suited man's cold stare. Over her shoulder she said, "Just need to check the platform."

The journey from Dad's had taken about an hour on foot and Bella had complained every step of the way. In the end, I carried her on my back as Mum took all the bags in one hand and tapped on her phone with the other. Then she called Nanny Beth. I heard little of the conversation, Bella was whining in my ear, telling me how tired she was, but I caught two words from my mother's whispered side of the conversation: "*Broken neck.*" I'd decided by this point that the only way to deal with everything, Dad, Kari, everything, was to lock it away somewhere deep. Don't look at it, no matter what. At least until we were safe in Devon. I could think about it then. So when Mum asked me if I was okay, I nodded. "Fine."

"I want to get down!" Bella wriggled about on my back, poking her bony knees into my side. "Beans, let me down!"

I lowered her to the floor, thankful for the relief. "Hold on to my hand, tight, okay?"

"Platform four," said Mum, pointing to the end of the row of gates. "But not for half an hour."

"I'm *thirsty.*" Bella tugged on Mum's jacket. "Can I have some chocolate milk? Or some sweets?"

I could tell that Mum just wanted to get to the gate and wait there, but her eyes flicked back to the M&S food court. She sighed. "We should probably get some supplies. Sandwiches and some water, perhaps."

"And some smarties?"

Mum looked into Bella's dark-ringed eyes. "Sure, okay. Smarties."

The three of us made our way over to the food court, and I wrestled Bella past the displays of cakes and biscuits, picking up a tube of smarties and some sandwiches. I also snuck a packet of jammy dodgers into Mum's basket along with water and some bananas.

There was hardly anyone in the shop. The woman ahead of us at the till was trying to pay for a couple of bottles of water with her phone, but it kept declining. "I'm sorry," she kept saying to the man behind the counter, "I don't know why this is happening. I'm so sorry."

Mum stepped in. That was the thing I remember most about my mother. She always tried to help. It was part of her – looking after people. "It's fine," she said, "let me get these for you."

"Thank you!" The woman stood back and allowed Mum space at the till. "If you give me your number, I can pay you back. As soon as all this is over and –"

"It's fine, don't give it another thought," replied Mum, scanning our supplies. "I'm sure it's just a glitch in the system. Too many people using the payment service."

"What's the man doing?" Bella's eyes were wide, as she clutched onto my leg. She spoke so quietly I didn't hear her the first time.

"What's that, baby?" I bent down so my face was closer to hers.

She didn't reply but pointed to the man behind the till who was swiping at his face as if trying to rid himself of a plague of invisible insects. Then he began to make a strange high-pitched noise, like a strangled scream. We all looked at him. "My head!" Tears streamed down his cheeks as he spoke.

Mum pushed the woman with the water away. "Get back. He needs help."

"Is it a fit?" replied the woman, standing back.

"I don't like it," whispered Bella. "We need to go now."

Mum stepped closer to the man who was now clutching his

short mousy hair and shaking his head from side to side. "Sir, are you –"

Then chaos broke over the station like a summer thunderstorm. Sporadic screams rose in every direction as the infection reached the men's brains in grisly unison. Some fell to their knees clutching their chests, struggling to breathe. Later they'd be marked out as Blues – those whom the infection killed outright. But it wasn't the Blues who decimated the population those first few days, who reduced women from around thirty-five million to just over twenty-four million. It was the Manics, those that survived the initial infection and then went on to rape, murder, and terrorise.

I've heard some reports recently, research from those born into the safety of after, that it wasn't all men. That the infection was milder in some men, depending on hormone levels and brain physiology. That we were led to believe that it was black and white when the science doesn't back this up. Well, I don't remember the mild cases. And to me, at seventeen, clutching my little sister's hand at Waterloo, listening to the screams grow louder and louder – all the men were infected.

The air was thick with that smell, the infected smell, like nail polish remover. It coated my tongue, making me gag.

"Mum?" The fear on her face made me freeze.

Then her expression changed as if making an internal decision. "Keep Bella behind you."

"What –?"

The young man from behind the counter lunged at the woman holding two water bottles. She gave a small cry as if offended rather than afraid, but then both she and the young man fell to the floor.

"Get... off!" she gasped.

I thrust Bella behind me and watched as my mum tried to drag the young man from the woman. He raised his hands to her face and pressed his thumbs into her eyes. She squealed and beat at him with the palms of her hand, grabbing at his ear and pulling so hard I thought she might tear it clean off. He didn't seem to notice. My mum put her arm around his neck and prised him off her.

"Whore!" he screamed. "You're all whores!"

She held him from behind as his skinny legs scraped along the floor.

Whilst this was happening, the roar of panic from outside was growing. A group of women, twenty, maybe more, came running into the store.

"The men, they're just hitting people for no reason." The woman speaking was in her fifties, dressed in walking trousers and an anorak. She saw Mum struggling with the man and stepped in, bending his arm up and around his back.

Another woman, her hair half up, half down as if someone had grabbed at her bun, was breathing hard. "My husband. He was fine and then…"

The man in my mum's arms collapsed suddenly and began to sob. "My head. My fucking head. I don't know what's going on."

Mum looked around at the women in the store. "Pull down the shutters."

No one moved.

I still clutched Bella's hand in mine.

"Someone, pull down the shutters!" Mum shouted, still struggling to hold on to the till assistant.

A woman in a pale work suit and cream high heels dropped her expensive-looking bag to the floor and began fumbling with the shutters above the door. "Is there a button, or do you just pull them down? Oomph!"

A man from outside punched her in the stomach. She collapsed onto the floor and lay there panting, winded.

"Oh god," said a woman to my right. "Oh god, Oh god."

I felt Bella's small hand squeeze mine and a small voice come from where she was standing. "It's just like Dad."

It was just like Dad.

I looked out the doorway, past the woman in the cream suit,

lying on the floor, and the man standing over her. There were men standing, staring at us. Women, some covered in blood, crawling along the floor, and trying to get away. Other women, unmoving on the ground, women's bodies lying with limbs bent at impossible angles, a small clump of flesh connected to a ponytail – sequined scrunchy glinting in the sunlight filtering down from the windows high above.

"Beans?" Bella whispered as the men moved towards us.

A button, a button. There had to be a button, right? That was how the shutters worked? I scanned the wall for anything that looked like it might operate the mechanism.

"Here!" The woman with the rainbow bracelet jumped on the switch on the wall.

With a clank, the metal barriers straightened out from above towards the floor, but far too slowly. I caught the eye of one man outside – the man in the suit from earlier. He smiled. He knew that we were trapping ourselves here and that in just a few steps, he and his friends could duck under the shutters and be in here with us. A woman standing next to me wearing a white tee shirt and red jeans was looking around her frantically. "My daughter. She was right here. Wait! I need to –"

The shutters clanked to a stop as a something large and black, a hardcase suitcase, was jammed to one side, making the machinery whirr and then stop.

The man in the suit crouched down so I could see his face in the ten or so inches below the shutters. He let out a low wolf whistle and began to crawl inside.

Evie

Freya Curtis was still speaking when pandemonium seized the crematorium.

Minutes earlier, Tony had got up in the middle of the service and left. A few women raised their eyebrows, but then we all turned back to the front, where the MWA delegate continued her sermon on duty and responsibility. Artemis was about to get up and follow, he looked around but then stopped and settled back down next to me.

I looked at him quizzically. "Logan – Tony's... friend," he said as an explanation. "I'll leave them to it."

Artemis's kindness warmed me. He came across as curt most of the time, but when it came to Tony, to Mum and especially to Daniel, he was patient – loving, even. I found my mind slipping back to the evening before, touching the back of my neck with my palm in the place he'd touched when he pulled me in, thinking about his weight pressing on me as he laid me down. Then I sat up straight, remembering where I was. I looked over to the opposite bank of wooden benches and saw the girl who'd entered with the two men, Sophia, looking at the door. Then she looked at me and my gaze fell to the floor. There were whispers about her and the two men. Would there be whispers about me if word got out about me and Artemis?

Freya read out a letter from the Prime Minister of the Union. She apologised on the PM's behalf, as she'd wanted to be here herself, but there was some kind of emergency diplomatic issue with the Australians that had to be attended to. You could tell by her drawn out tone and the way she bobbed about on the balls of her feet that Curtis was fizzing with reflected importance, subtly suggesting that the PM had confided in her regarding affairs of state.

The PM's letter said the same sort of things about Mary as before, but this also included phrases like 'brave patriot' and 'duty to the Union'. There was something off about Freya Curtis, something about her actions, her voice, the way she paused and sighed, and gestured. It all seemed staged and overdone. An overly polished performance. I wasn't buying it.

We all turned as the doors crashed open. Curtis stopped speaking, as Logan dragged a bleeding Tony through the door.

Things happened all at once.

Artemis and I jumped up and made for Tony, stumbling over the other women still sitting in our row. The window behind us smashed, launching a wave of glass shards in our direction. I felt one catch me on the hand, a pinch like a bee sting. Framed by the now gaping window, a mob of women ran past and around the back of the building.

"His head," gasped Logan. "What do we do?"

There was another crash, louder this time, as another window broke right behind Logan. I looked down at a small shard of glass which had embedded itself in the back of my hand. A group of LA officers ran past and outside in pursuit of the mob.

"Logan!" Sophia picked her way over the glass, holding the arm of Nathan, and grabbed Logan. He looked like he was about to shake her off, as he stared down at a dazed and bleeding Tony.

Artemis looked up at him. "Don't worry, Logan, I'll make sure he's okay."

"We have to keep you safe," Sophia said as she pulled him towards the exit. Through the door, I watched as she and one other bodyguard ushered both men into a grey car that had just pulled at the steps. They sped off towards the exit. A few women in the XX tee shirts chased the car down the drive and threw more stones, but it disappeared into the distance unscathed. I could see Law Abidance officers rounding up protesters, dragging them to the ground and cuffing their arms behind their backs.

Ignoring the pain in my hand, I got to work. Tony had a nasty gash on the side of his head and blood was dripping in long splashes onto the shoulder of his jumper. He was semi-conscious. Awake but unfocussed. "We touched a moth," he murmured. "We shouldn't have done it... Logan?"

"Tony, are you hurting?" I grabbed a hankie from my pocket, wishing I had something to disinfect it with, holding it against the wound on his temple. It wasn't too bad, but there was no telling if his brain was okay. He was obviously concussed.

I gave Tony a quick pinch on the ear.

"OW! What was that for?" To my relief, his eyes were focussing on me.

"I'm checking your reactions, Tony."

He looked around. "What's happening?"

Artemis answered. "Some women threw stones at you."

Women were standing by windows, peeping out and muttering to each other. Freya Curtis stood at the front, waving her arms. "Keep calm, everyone. The LA officers outside will have the situation under control. Keep away from the windows. Please! Stay away from the windows."

But her pleas fell on deaf ears… *blew up the hall in Chesterford… dangerous women… Something should be done!*

"What can I do?" asked Artemis. "To help?"

"Here, put your hands on the hankie. That's right. Keep it there – firmer. Good." I pulled my hand away and let Artemis tend to Tony for a moment.

Outside, I could see a group of LA officers, in their blue and red uniforms, jogging towards the building. "See!" cried Freya. "The whole of the LA will be here soon. No need to worry." She crossed the floor towards the door. "It was just a few dissenters." But her voice was strained.

"Oh dear, Tony. That looks bad." Daisy loomed over us. "Nasty business, this. Some women just don't know when to stop." She reached down and patted Tony on the arm. "I bet you miss the facility, huh? We looked after you there."

"I don't." Tony brushed Daisy's hand away and fixed her with a fierce stare. "I don't miss it, Daisy, and I certainly don't miss most of the staff – especially you!" His voice was low and angry.

"Well, really, Tony!" replied Daisy, standing up again and peering down at the bleeding man. "With an attitude like that, is it any wonder that the XXs are concerned? I may not agree with their methods, but I can understand their sentiment. After all we've done for you. Honestly." She turned to me as if I was supposed to reprimand him as if he were a naughty child and I was responsible for his behaviour. "I was right to choose Tony and Artemis for the programme. Since they've been gone, we have had far fewer *incidents*. I'm only sorry that you now have to deal with their rudeness."

I cleared my throat. "The XXs are a bunch of crazies, and their misanthropic ramblings are silly and old-fashioned. If you share their views, Daisy, then I don't think you should work with men at all."

Daisy's face went a dull pink. Then her eyes narrowed, and she looked at Tony, then Artemis, and back to me. "I've seen your kind before," she said in a low, mean voice. "I doubt it's Tony. He was never that keen on women. Artemis then. Yes, you're just like that Sophia girl."

I didn't answer. I could sense Artemis tensing up.

"It's written all over your face, girl –"

"Sorry to butt in." An LA officer stood next to us. "We need to get the men out of here. The situation is under control. The women in question have been arrested. But to be on the safe side, we think it's best not to linger. Would you mind?" She gestured outside to where a group of uniformed women stood together. "We'll escort you to your car."

"No, I don't mind at all." I glanced at Daisy and was met with a look of pure venom.

"Could you give us a lift back to the village?" A voice came from behind us. It was Freya. She pointed to Anita. "Anita's wife, Dr Rosya, was due to pick us up, but she'd been delayed. I'm staying in a house near Borne Copse. My car's there. I can drive Anita home."

"Of course," I replied, helping Tony to his feet. He seemed steady enough. "It's on our way." The broken glass crunched under our feet as we walked.

"You're hurt," said Artemis, reaching for my hand.

I snatched it away. "Leave it. It's nothing." My face grew hot as I guided Tony out, following the LA officer towards the car. Artemis, Freya and Anita trailed behind.

As we neared the car, one of the LA officers turned to her colleague. "What a waste of resources," she said under her breath, but loud enough that both Tony and Artemis could hear. "It was a lot simpler when they were all locked up."

XX104

In school, as you will remember, if you are over a certain age, you will have been taught about the massacre at Waterloo. Those smudged old printouts on manual presses, the ones that left dark ink on your hands and under your nails. The grainy pictures of the aftermath. Some photos from the actual day, syphoned from mobile phones and replicated. Not the worst pictures. Not the ones showing much detail. Plans and diagrams of how the women barricaded themselves in, where they fought, who died, and a list of the dead. How they were killed. If there was evidence of rape.

Rape. A word we hear seldom these days. Some of us are still coerced into bed by less than truthful partners. We make mistakes, are lied to, told we're loved. Even now, relationships rarely have completely even power dynamics.

But held down and sexually penetrated, assaulted? These are things, along with the Waterloo massacre, that are no longer taught in schools. Now children learn consent, along with Union, trade routes to Australia, and breakthroughs in genetic engineering. For most women under the age of thirty, rape is a metaphor, something to describe an atrocity in general terms. The rape of the oceans, for example.

But on that warm day in July, four decades ago, the violence in the air was not a metaphor. It was visceral and petrifying. They say that thirty-eight women fought off a hoard of a thousand men. That the women embodied the spirit of the New Union. Their names are read out and carved into the cenotaph in London, a city once so vital, now deserted. And the survivors, most in their sixties and seventies now, go round the country and talk about what happened. Only, people have stopped caring. The groups of listeners at the town halls have become smaller and smaller. New voices have sprung up, talking of reintegrating men, speaking of cures and a brave new world, a world of plurality and diversity. Few women make the river-born pilgrimage to the entrance of that crumbling station and lay their gifts on the stone steps anymore.

Predominantly, it was the men that raped and murdered, in the infestation and before. A conveniently forgotten truth in the face of such modernity. We live in a world where men are safely locked away, a world where that day, that terrifying day, could never happen. We live in relative freedom, and the younger women forget this with their liberal hand-wringing and their voices calling for us to *save* the men, *look after* the men, *protect* the men. If I could show them what I saw, just one moment of the hours I spent in that cold stone tomb, listening to women's screams, hearing the jeers and cheering of the men, smelling the blood, they would not be so quick to forgive and forget.

The men jammed the shutters on their way down so that a few at a time could wriggle under. The women in the store were packed together. I was in the centre of the group, clinging onto Bella with a few other children and teenagers – one woman, in her early thirties, clutched a toddler to her chest. She thrust the child at me. "This is Freya. Keep her safe." I took her as the woman kissed her on the forehead, lingering a moment to sweep a dark curl behind the child's ear and whispering, "I love you, sweetheart," before standing alongside my mother, facing the entrance. There had been no discussion, no organisation, just an automatic formation where the older women had positioned themselves in front of us.

The men began to crawl under the shutters, but we had the advantage. My mother led the charge. *Don't let them get up! Keep them on the floor!* The cry gave the women permission. Actions that, minutes earlier would have been inconceivable, became necessary. Tin cans, broken shelving, glass bottles. The women grabbed anything they could find. I watched as the lady in the anorak stabbed a man in the eye with a short metal pole, part of a refrigeration cabinet. She did it in silence, with the expression of someone unblocking a drain. Freya's mother stood in a widening pool of blood and rained down blows on a blonde man who was almost through the doors, he was already sitting up. In her hand was a jar of something, jam or chutney, perhaps. On the third blow, it smashed, and a slick tide of red gloop covered the already gory scene.

Another middle-aged woman, armed with a tin and a bottle, was about to strike an older man whose face had just appeared under the shutters. "John?" The tin fell from her hand. "John, what's happening? Are you okay?" The man reached up his hand as if to caress the woman, then grabbed her hair, dragging her towards his face. She screamed as his teeth sunk into her cheek and a torrent of red stream dripped down her face and neck. She wrestled herself away, her face a bloody mask, and struck him on the temple with the bottle so that it smashed in her hand. She was just left holding the shattered neck, slashing at him, blinded by her own blood.

The carnage went on, but the shop was not breached. So many bleeding, dying men blocked the floor that it was impossible for any others to come through. The infected dead and wounded formed a kind of barrier, offering a moment's heaving respite.

We turned in unison at a new noise… *swish, swish.* The men began disappearing back under the shutters, dragged back leaving behind thick strips of bloody floor.

"They're making space! They're coming again!" Mum shouted.

I clutched Bella's hand tightly in mine as Freya wriggled in my other arm.

More snarling men's faces appeared under the shutters. Tins and shopping baskets rained down on them, women kicked, punched, bit and gouged, and they brought down the attackers.

The onslaught slowed and then stopped. My mother got on her knees about a few feet away from the shutters and lowered her face to the floor. "I can't see them."

We looked at each other. Women covered in gristle and clumps of flesh. Scarlet footprints and skid marks decorated the white tiles on the floor. Was it over? Had they gone?

A high-pitched scream split the air outside the store. A young girl's scream. Then *"Mummy! Muuuuummmyyyy!"*

A woman, the one with the red jeans, pushed her way through from the back. "It's Poppy – POPPY!" The woman ran to the shutters and began to scramble under. "Poppy! I'm coming!"

She was half-way under when the rest of her disappeared as she was dragged to the other side by an unseen force. "Poppy, *baby*. It's going to be okay."

The next five minutes were excruciating. Bella burrowed into my side like a tick, so close I could feel her sobs through my jeans. The toddler in my arms buried her face into my neck, hot and slick with tears. We all stood and listened as Poppy and her mother were torn apart, the mother's screams falling silent, as the little girl's rose in pitch. She never once stopped calling for her mother. No one in our group could look at each other as the little girl's screams ground on. I made Bella put her hands over her ears until it was over.

Then more snarling faces appeared under the shutters – worse, five or so pairs of hands started wrenching the shutters up. It began to move upwards in small rough jerks.

The woman in the anorak grabbed me. "You need to hide. There's a storeroom at the back of the shop. Take the kids."

Mum nodded. "Barricade the door. Understand?" turning to face the oncoming hoard before I could answer. I grabbed

Bella's hand and shifted Freya's weight onto my hip, peering into the darkness. Then I shepherded the rest of the children into the storeroom. One of them, a girl with black hair and dark eyes, tried to hold on to her mother's leg.

"Go on, sweetheart," said her mother. We won't be long and then we'll come and find you." The mother peeled the sobbing girl from her. "Please, Hattie. Be a good girl. I love you, sweet pea." The mother had tears streaming down her cheeks as she pulled the girl away from her.

I bent down so my face was level with Hattie's. "Mum will only be a little while. I promise." How I managed a reassuring smile in that moment, when the world was crashing down around us, I will never know.

Bella took the little girl's hand. "Don't worry, Beans will look after us," she said, looking up at me with complete confidence.

The little girl sniffed. "Beans is a weird name."

"That's not her real name," replied Bella as I led them to the storeroom door. "Her real name's Anita – Anita Beans." Then, at the little girl's blank look, "And-eat-her-beans. It's a joke."

Tony

The car moved towards the exit with me squashed into the back, next to Artemis and Anita, the door handle digging into my thigh every time we went over a bump. The women had gone – the ones with the placards. I still pressed the soggy hankie to the side of my head even though the bleeding had stopped. Crowds of Law Abidance officers milled about, eight or nine cars sat parked on a nearby bank of grass, all of them white and embossed with a logo – cupped hands holding a red rose. Logan was alive. But now he was gone, whisked away by his... carer? Lover? Whoever she was, he was afraid of her.

"They must have called every officer within fifty miles," said

Freya. "Head office is going to need a full report, Anita. This won't look good for the programme. It will set us back a bit. The next phase of the programme may need to be delayed. No more men vaccinated for a while."

We trundled past the sea of uniformed women. "Why?" I asked. "It wasn't men throwing rocks. Why are we being punished?"

"Should we take him to the hospital?" said Freya, twisting around in the front seat and looking back at me. "Those awful women. I hope the LA deal with them harshly. I'm going to explain things to the MWA and the Prime Minister. I'll see if we can get extra security."

"I don't think that will be necessary." Anita sat with her arms crossed tightly across her chest on the other side of Artemis. I suspected that she too was feeling the uncomfortable lack of space.

Evie spoke whilst driving, navigating a rash of potholes in the road. "I'll speak to Molly about it when we drop him off. I could take him to A&E after I get you home. This car's not due back until tomorrow."

I didn't like the idea of going to the hospital. I suspected it would be very much like the facility – sterile and strict. "I'm feeling much better," I said. "The bleeding stopped ages ago."

"It was a beautiful service," said Freya, ignoring me. "I never met Mary, but Prime Minister Philips spoke highly of her."

I wanted to argue about the service, that it hadn't even occurred to them to invite her son to speak, or me, for that matter. I opened my mouth to speak, but Artemis nudged me, and I knew what he was saying. *Leave it.*

Well, he'd changed his tune. He also seemed anxious. Less aloof. I wondered if I offered him the same option that he'd offered me on that first day – to run away and keep running – would he take me up on it now? And another thing, his gaze was never far from Evie. Like a compass finding north, it would back drift to her every time he wasn't directly talking to someone else. A sinking suspicion took root. *Oh, Artemis. What have you done?*

The car slowed to a crawl. "These roads are terrible," said Evie. "At this rate, it'll be dark before we get back to the village."

"It's hard to get enough people to work on the repair crews," replied Freya. "Long hours, poor recompense, little in the way of advancement. It was thought, when the men's integration programme becomes more established, that construction might be a possible avenue of employment for them. In the time before the infestation, men dominated such industries, so we know they're capable of it. They'd need supervision by someone qualified, but what a wonderful way for them to give back to a society that has protected them all these years, eh?"

Neither I nor Artemis replied.

"Who's that?" said Evie, looking out of the side window. "It looks like someone lying down on the bank."

"Keep driving," replied Anita. She was sitting up stiffly, holding on to the door handle, scanning the road and surrounding trees.

"Let's just check she's okay." Evie pulled over to the side of the road, about thirty meters from the figure, and opened the door. "Hello? Is everything okay?"

The person on the ground remained still. Evie got out of the car and moved closer.

"Is she okay?" shouted Freya from the passenger seat.

Anita was still clutching the door handle, her knuckles blanched white. "We should get back to the house." Her voice seemed a higher than before, strained.

A sick feeling settled in my stomach. And I could smell something, a sharp tang, like vinegar. My mouth inexplicably filled with saliva.

"Can you smell that?" asked Artemis. "Like the bleach they used to clean the ovens at the facility?"

I didn't reply.

Evie reached the figure on the bank and knelt down. Her head turned to us, and she shouted over. "It's a man. From one of the facilities, I... I think he's dead. There're blue veins around his face."

"Come back to the car, Evie!" Artemis called from the back seat. He leaned over and tried to move Anita's hand, to open the door to get out of the car. At first, she wouldn't budge and then she relented, climbing out and allowing Artemis to exit. He jogged over to Evie who was still checking the man on the ground for signs of life.

Anita, standing by the driver's side, was holding a metal object and pointing it at Freya. It was bigger than a benzo gun but in a similar shape, with a longer, spout-shaped end. "Okay, change of plan. Freya. Get out of the car."

"What are you talking about, Anita?" said Freya frowning at the object in Anita's hand. "What is this?"

"It's a gun, Freya – as I'm sure you know, growing up in the compounds. And I'm sure you know what it does if I pull the trigger?" Anita's forefinger wiggled over a small lever at the front, and she pointed the spout towards Freya. "Get out of the car, Freya. You too, Tony."

Freya slowly slid from the seat and stood on the road, only a pace away from Anita. "What on earth...?"

"Tony! Out!"

I scrambled out of my seat, trying to keep the car between me and Anita.

"You tried to look a bit older with the suits and the hair, Freya. But no one who lived through Waterloo would ever condone what you're doing. Someone who *actually* remembers it would never consider bringing men back to our lives. But you don't remember it, do you? Do you really? That is to say, you didn't see it."

Freya paled. "I... My mother survived Waterloo. I was there."

Anita took a step closer to the driver's seat. "Yes, Josephine was one of the only women to make it through. She fought alongside my mother, alongside many other brave women, and none of us would have got through it without her bravery. And this is how you repay her – by betraying everything she protected you for? Does she agree with this?"

Freya looked away. "She died, eight years ago." Then her voice regained some of its usual authority "What's this all about, Anita? What in heaven's name has gotten into you? Put the gun away."

Evie and Artemis appeared on the other side of the car. "What's going on?" asked Evie.

But Anita ignored her and just raised the gun higher, so it was pointed to Freya's face. "If she were alive, she'd have told you what a stupid idea this whole thing is. She'd have begged you to stop. She would have told you about the horror that was happening outside whilst we huddled in a storeroom, you too young to remember anything."

"We? What do you mean? You weren't there, Anita. Your name's not on the list."

"Oh, I was there, holding you. I remember how the lights went off and our phones couldn't connect. How I kept you and those children alive for hours whilst men raved and raped and murdered around us. You don't remember, Freya, how, you cried, and I nearly had to… That I thought the men might hear you and come back. You don't remember the children's screams, or how towards the end we only had two cans of coke left and no idea how long we'd been in there or how long we were going to have to stay. You were too young, Freya. A child of this world. You have no memory of what men can be like. Infected or not. But tonight, you're about to find out."

"Look, Anita," replied Freya, shaking her head in disbelief, "you've obviously been under a lot of pressure recently. You didn't tell anyone you were at Waterloo, and you should have said something. But this cloak and dagger act is a bit too much don't you think? Now, give me the gun."

"Step back, Freya. You don't understand anything. This is

bigger than just Waterloo. Tonight, the Union is going to be reminded of what a danger men are. Get back!"

Freya reached for the gun, grabbing Anita's hand and dragging it downwards. "I don't, for a moment, think you intend to –"

The shot echoed off the trees and Freya bent over, clutching her stomach.

Anita looked down at the gun in her hand as Freya slumped to the road. Then she raised it and pointed it at me. "You don't have a clue what I'm capable of. It ends here." I thought she was going to shoot me. I thought that it ends here meant me. But instead, she slipped back into the car still holding the gun. The car jerked then sped up, bumping over a hole and swerving, before speeding down the road and out of sight.

Evie

I knelt down and turned Freya Curtis onto her back, just as all life drifted from her eyes.

"Is she going to be okay?" asked Tony in a small voice.

I shook my head. "She's gone."

Artemis's hand appeared on my shoulder, a warm comforting weight. "What do you think happened. Why did Anita hurt Freya?"

I looked from Freya to the dead man on the grass a little way away and tried not to let the shock show in my voice. "I don't know, but I think these two are connected somehow. Anita said something about tonight... about finding out about men." I stood up. Both men looked at me expectantly, waiting for answers. "I think she's part of the XXs, and that this" – I pointed to Freya and the man – "and the protest at the crematorium, is part of the same plan. We need to call the LA."

Artemis looked around. "Were in the middle of nowhere."

As a nurse, I saw death every week from disease and old

age. But murder? Violence? even car crashes were rare. I had
to think. I don't know why there was a dead Blue on the
side of the road, but I suspected that was also part of this and
whatever the XXs had planned. We needed safety. "The house
Freya was staying in is a couple of miles up the road. She'll
have a phone." I sounded far more confident than I felt. "We
can call the LA and then try and get in contact with Molly. Let's
go. Single file."

"Are we just going to leave her here?" Artemis pointed to
Freya's body.

"We'll let the LA know where to find her. Come on now, it's
getting dark."

Until now, the XXs had been a threat, but a marginal
one. Even at the funeral today, it just seemed like a group
of misguided dollies, spreading misinformation and trading
conspiracy theories. But to smuggle a man, maybe more than
one, out of a facility required planning, organisation, inside
help. I looked around at the trees, which by now had merged
into one shadowy mass.

How many men had they smuggled out?

XX104

The rest is history as they say. Me, Bella, Freya's mother –
Josephine – and a handful of others were rescued from
Waterloo station on the second day of the infestation. Those
of us barricaded in the storeroom survived on cola and
crisps – we went to the loo in a bucket. A few others in the
main station survived too. When the soldiers came for us, I
didn't want to let them in, I wanted to wait a while. *Don't
let anyone in*, my mother had said. *Not even a woman*. But
eventually they broke down the door, pushed past the crates
of cleaning supplies I'd piled in the way and collected us.

"It's rough out there," said one of the soldiers, a young

woman only a few years older than me. "You might want to close your eyes and let me lead you."

"I'll be okay," I said. "Bella you should –" But she was already looking around, blinking in the glaring light of the station, clutching my hand in a vice-like grip.

The smell was incredible, festering death, worse even than the latrine of the storeroom we'd just left. I gagged as I turned my head from side to side, trying to filter out what I was seeing, interested only in the navy shirt of a midwife's uniform. But it was Bella who saw her first. She squeezed my hand tighter. "There," she said.

My mother was partly covered in a blanket, lying on her belly with her head and one arm uncovered. Her brown curly hair was matted and greasy-looking, and her arms were covered in deep scratches. I broke from the soldier and moved towards her, still clutching an exhausted Freya to my shoulder.

"I'm sorry," she said, catching my arm as I tried to go over to my mother's body. "I need to get you into the trucks."

But Bella would not be swayed. "Mum!" She evaded the soldier, running around scattered blanketed lumps, like strange sandcastles. "Mum?"

She was about to bend down when the soldier picked her up. "No," the soldier said firmly.

Bella had been quiet in the storeroom, worried when the other children made a noise. But now she screamed, as if all the panic and fear of those dark hours had bubbled to the surface. "MUM! Let me see her! MUM!"

I didn't know what to do. Perhaps seeing Mum would have given her some closure, perhaps things would have turned out differently. Or maybe the damage was already done and the countdown in her little heart had begun. It doesn't make any difference all these years later, I guess.

"Freya?" To our left, a woman was being treated by an army medic, I recognised her as Freya's mother. "FREYA!"

"It's okay, she's okay." I placed the young child beside her mother. Later I would discover that the woman's name was Josephine. She would become one of the Waterloo survivors – those who travelled the length of the Union talking about their experience. The little girl scrabbled into Josephine's arms and the woman grimaced in pain, but still held her child close.

"Thank you," she whispered to me, tears in her voice. "For keeping her safe."

I nodded and turned away. I didn't just turn away from Josephine and the body of my mother, I turned away from Waterloo. I didn't give my name to the soldier with the clipboard. Later we told everyone we were the other side of London when it happened, hiding in our father's flat. Few people asked, anyway – it wasn't the polite thing to do.

From London, we were taken to an army barracks, first in Aldershot and then in Gosport. People, younger women, often ask if I knew about the way the men were treated in the first few weeks, how so many were left to die. I didn't – I stayed in the barracks with Bella, working with the comms team. But had I known, I wouldn't have cared. They could all fry.

Everyone was nice to me and Bella, especially when they found out that we'd been at Waterloo. Bella said very little. She never left my side. Even when I went to the bathroom she'd come and wait at the door. I could tell she was counting the seconds until she heard the flush and I reappeared.

The first winter was tough; everyone who was there will tell you that. No electricity for large stretches, little food or medicine, bodies, grief, trauma. But the spring was slightly easier, the summer more so.

By the second year, I thought it was going to be okay. We moved to a compound near Milton Keynes. Bella started to seem a little more confident. She went to the makeshift school whilst I worked as a radio engineer on the compound's internal station.

She didn't make friends, always hovering on the edges of any group, wincing at the children's cries and yells, but her nightmares became less frequent. She no longer came to me in the night, clambering down from her top bunk to wrap her shaking arms around me. I thought that she'd get through it – she was by no means the only one struggling. She refused to go to the groups, sit in a circle with other children of her age and share her feelings. *"What's the point?"* she'd say. *"Why think about it on purpose?"*

Perhaps I should have insisted she go? Maybe it would have helped.

Then one time, I found her sitting by the compound fence staring up at the barbed wire. Something was caught on the razor wire, a plastic bag, sliced into ribbons and dancing in the breeze like a party streamer. She was crying.

"Hey, Bells," I whispered, sitting on the grass next to her and running my arm around her shoulders. My arms were tanned, strong from all the work, fixing speakers, running cables, connecting up generators. She was pale, thin. How had I failed to notice how thin she'd become?

She looked at me, her big brown eyes so similar to Mum's. "What if they come back?"

I nearly said, "Who?" but realised just in time. "They won't," I replied. "They're dead or locked away by now."

"But what if they escape and come back for us?"

I pulled her closer to me. "I won't let them, Bells. I swear it."

She turned away, looking back at the caught bag, its torn tendrils reaching out into the clear sky, and didn't reply.

Tony

The lack of light was playing with my mind. The moon threw dancing shadows onto the grass verge. Every ruffled leaf, each snapped twig, made me spin and look into the trees, my heart pumping and sweat breaking fresh on my shoulders and back. I hated being outside in the dark. I followed Evie with my head down, trusting Artemis not to crash into the back of me when I slowed to navigate the way.

"Tony, I need to talk to you," Artemis's whisper came out of the darkness behind me.

I didn't answer him. I just wanted to get somewhere safe.

"Something happened, with Evie. And now, I don't know what to do."

Again I kept silent, putting one foot in front of the other, half walking, half jogging through the long damp grass.

"Tony, Tony!" Artemis was not about to let it lie. He jogged up, so he was alongside me on the narrow verge.

"Evie said single file," I hissed.

"We slept together," he whispered. "Like at a visitation, but different. Better... But now I don't know what she's thinking. She seems... unhappy."

I walked slower, looking up at him, aware that Evie was now a little way ahead. Part of me wanted to point out that we were abandoned in the middle of nowhere, possibly in the vicinity of violent Manics, and he should worry less about sex and more about surviving the night. But his young face, half hidden in the darkness, was clouded in misery and I relented. "If she had sex with you, she probably likes you, Artemis."

"You think so?" His eyes lit up with hope. "Because I like her very much. If she was in danger, I'd want to help her. Like back there, if Anita had pointed the gun at Evie, I would have stepped in. Even if it meant hurting Anita."

It was against everything we'd been taught in the prep house and in the facility. Violence against women, against the very people upon whom our lives depended, was the very worst crime imaginable. It was unnatural. "I think she could protect herself, Artemis."

"Yes, but what about Freya Curtis?" replied Artemis, quietly.

I was so caught up in Artemis's words and their horrifying

implications, I didn't realise Evie had stopped. Artemis had to grab me to prevent me from walking into her.

The three of us huddled together at the foot of a tall tree. "Freya's house is just up ahead. I'll look around, see if it's safe."

"I'll come with you." Artemis's voice was firm.

"Fine." Although Evie's tone suggested annoyance.

"I'm not staying here on my own." I peered into the darkness, expecting at any moment a something to jump out at me.

Evie sighed. "Okay. Both of you keep close and be quiet."

We crossed to the other side of the road and stopped at the foot of a tall hedge with prickly spindly limbs springing up into the darkness, then swooping down to head height. As I shuffled along beside it, the spikes caught on my sweater, so I had to stop and untangle myself. It was then, when the cool air shifted, that the smell from before drifted around me.

"Artemis?" I hissed.

"I smell it," came a whispered reply from the dark.

We caught up with Evie and came upon a gravelled driveway leading from the road. On the drive sat a smart grey car. A newish looking kind. Behind it loomed a two-story house, its thatched roof catching the moonlight. No light shone from the windows. The smell was stronger – much stronger than earlier. It was a solid thing in my mouth and my nose. My eyes watered, making it even harder to see.

"Try not to make any sound," whispered Evie. "Stick to the grassy edge around the driveway."

We tiptoed around the drive towards the house, then followed a muddy path leading around the back. I tripped over some kind of hard edge and stifled a yell, nearly falling. Artemis caught me and we all stopped, listening hard. My toe throbbed in my shoe.

"Careful!" breathed Evie, as we stood in the quiet night – just the rustling and fall of leaves in the breeze.

We reached the kitchen door and Evie peered inside, cupping her hands around her eyes to block out any light.

"Anything?" asked Artemis, urgently.

"It's too dark," replied Evie. She tried the door and found it locked. Bending down, she picked up a large stone. She removed her cardigan and wrapped the stone in it, then holding the bundle, broke the window. The connection made a soft *woomf* followed by a tinkling crack. Evie leaned through the broken glass and opened the door from the other side. She raised her hand, signalling us to stop, before disappearing into the dark house. Artemis waited for a couple of seconds, then followed.

There was a crash inside, obscenely loud in the still evening, making every one of my nerves light up. The door swung open. Artemis stood in the centre of a small kitchen, surrounded by shards of broken crockery. We all looked at each other – waiting for something to happen, for the heavy footsteps of the infected, for the room to fill with snarling, spitting faces. But there was nothing. No noise. After about ten seconds, Evie spoke. "I think we're alright."

"Sorry," said Artemis. "The tray was on the edge of the counter."

Evie flipped on the lights, blinding my dark-adjusted eyes. "I'll find a phone. Stay here," she gave Artemis an arched look. "I'll call if I need you."

Artemis nodded. "Sorry." But she'd already disappeared further into the dark house. He picked up bits of crockery from the floor, miserably adding the shattered pieces back onto the tray. "Stupid, clumsy…" he muttered.

I gave him a pat on the shoulder. "It's okay. She wasn't very angry."

He stood up suddenly. "I'm going to the garden for some fresh air."

"I don't think you should. Evie said to wait here. She specifically told you to stay –"

"I'm going anyway," Artemis said, as he passed me and stepped outside.

I dithered for a moment, torn between doing what I was told and checking that Artemis was okay. Eventually, I followed.

"The smell – it's coming from the garden."

Artemis was right. Out here, the vinegary tang was so much stronger. "We should wait for Evie," I said, following him down the path at the side of the house. "Tell her about the smell and –" But Artemis was already in the back garden.

There was something about the smell that attracted me. I felt that if I didn't follow it, then something awful would happen to me. It's hard to explain the pull. All I know is that it didn't feel like much of a choice, and I think Artemis felt it, too. We walked to the end of the garden. At the bottom was a huge pile of what I assumed was covered wood. We had a pile similar at the farm.

The heap loomed out of the dark. The smell was stronger, and I knew that something in that pile was the source of the smell.

"Let's go get Evie," I said, trailing after Artemis.

He didn't stop, didn't turn around. Just moved onwards, towards the dark shape.

I should have gone back to the house.

But I didn't.

CHAPTER 15

Tony

The medicinal tang was so heavy in the air it felt like a struggle to breathe. It was making me dizzy. But I couldn't focus on that. Artemis approached the pile and stopped.

I leaned in and looked over his shoulder. "What is it? What are the shapes?" Then in a fainter voice. "What are they, Artemis?"

It was not wood. I understood, that is to say, my brain half recognised what I was seeing. But I couldn't process the horror. Something soft and doughy? Pillows, maybe, dumped carelessly. As my head swam, I felt a heaviness seep into my limbs.

"What is it?" I didn't want to move, and I had a sudden feeling of sharp dread. "What are they?" I asked in a hushed voice, more to myself than Artemis. I squinted in the dark, trying to get a good look without going any closer. The medicinal smell was stronger, and I put my hand up to my mouth.

Artemis was shaking. I touched his arm and he flinched, his skin cold and wet with sweat. "Something is crawling – in the dark," he whispered. "Something's moving."

"Come away," I replied, trying to prise his arm towards me, but he held fast, staring into the abyss. As I spoke, the moon appeared from behind a cloud and the pile was bathed in light. For a moment we both saw the full horror. Iridescent moths –

thousands of them, feeding. It took a moment for my mind to decipher what I was seeing, what it was that the moths were feeding on – limbs and flesh and skin and eyes. Then, disturbed by our intrusion, that dark blanket lifted and broke apart into a thousand pieces, every fragment streaming towards us. There wasn't time to run. The two of us turned away and covered ourselves, and each other, as best we could. I felt Artemis's arm around my shoulders as I squashed my face into the grass, the swarm brushing our backs as it took to the sky.

Moments later, they were gone. I unwrapped my arms from my head and stood. "Artemis?" But Artemis was already on his feet, moving towards the pile.

"They're dead," he said, almost in wonder. "The men, they're all dead."

Without the blanket of moths, you could make out the details of the piles of bodies littering the shed. The shorn heads, the grey robes, the blue veins around mouths and down necks.

"We should go." My voice was coarse and torn, but I still stood there, holding onto Artemis's arm. Both of us rooted to the spot for seconds, stretching into minutes.

Then, something happened that shocked us both from our terror. The pile moved. An arm reached out of the slaughter, stretching towards us. We both took a step back and I turned to run. But Artemis held onto me. "Listen, he said in a low voice. "Can you hear?"

I listened, and in the direction of the arm I heard a faint cry that came from the depths of the pile. Soft but clear. "Please…" it said. "*Please.*"

Artemis approached the pile and clutched the arm, pulling a man clear. As he did so, a cascade of bluish arms and slack torsos toppled to the ground. He dragged the moaning man free and as he did so, one of the other bodies rolled to my feet with a thud and lay there gaping sightlessly at the moon. There were dark patches around his mouth, snaking out in veiny lines, disappearing into the collar of his robe.

"It's so cold." The man in Artemis's arms was in his thirties, pale except for a few faint blotches around his mouth. But his eyes, blinking at us through tears, were clear in the semi-light. "They thought I was dead. I couldn't do anything." He was shivering hard.

"Shhh. Let's get you into the kitchen. It's warmer."

We picked our way over the fallen bodies, and the man looked down at the dead men on the floor. "Oh... Oh..." His breathing quickened.

"Wait, Artemis," I said. "What if he's lying? What if he's a Manic? They can pretend – or he might be in a lucid phase."

Artemis didn't stop gently leading the man towards the house. "Then we can deal with him. He's just one man. Tony, help me get him to the house."

I stood where I was for a moment, feeling a kind of paralysis, whether it was the horror of the bodies, or the overpowering smell, I didn't know. I took hold of the man. He was small of build and light. We half carried, half dragged him, one on each side, arms wrapped around his waist, towards the house.

Evie

A fire had died in the grate, but the sitting room was still warm. The room contained Freya's possessions, her files on the side table, some papers from the MWA, a small radio, a blanket on the sofa, draped in such a way that it seemed she was about to come back to it at any moment. But she wasn't. She was dead, murdered by Anita, who must have been working for the XXs all along. *But why?* What makes a woman turn against her friends, her neighbours, like that? I tried not to think of Freya's closing eyes, as her life seeped from the bullet wound in her stomach. It was shocking how quickly she died, how swiftly the bullet had torn through her organs and purged her of so much blood. Just moments.

I slapped down the cradle button on the phone in rapid clicks. Then tried the LA again. I tried the local number and the Union emergency number, punching the number into the large buttons.

Just the engaged tone, long pips like one syllable in morse code repeated over and over.

I tried again.

I clung to the handset with both hands. Hung up and redialled a third time.

Every time, in the past, when I'd had to call the LA – when my mum had a fall and needed an ambulance – the time Mae had had too much to drink, and I thought she might actually hurt me – they'd answered on the second ring.

I tried home. Needing to know Mum was okay. *Beep... beep... beep.* Finally, I tried Molly's farmhouse. But all I got was the engaged tone bleating at me. Mae sometimes talked about 'old infrastructures' and 'too much pull on the line'. But what would be causing so many calls at the same time?

I hadn't heard Tony and Artemis for a while, so I replaced the handset and went into the kitchen. They weren't there, and the door was half open. Dammit. I didn't want them going outside. It wasn't safe. I was about to step out into the darkness when Artemis and Tony half fell through the door towards me. They were dragging with them a stranger, a man, and my adrenaline went into overdrive. "What are you doing? Fuck, is he infected?" I stepped back and my back collided painfully with the counter.

As they lowered the man into a spindly kitchen chair, he clutched the edges of the seat as if afraid he might fall.

"Artemis found him in a pile of... he was outside." Tony's voice was uneven, and he was shivering hard.

"Artemis, you shouldn't have brought him in. He's got to go –"

But Artemis wasn't listening to me. He crouched on the floor, so his face was below the man's. "What's your name?"

"H–Hugo."

"And how did you get here?"

Hugo sat unmoving for a couple of seconds, then his face creased, and he uttered a string of heaving sobs.

Artemis and I looked at each over the head of the sobbing man. I frowned but didn't insist he leave. I looked around for a weapon in case he became Manic, noting the knife block on the side.

"It's okay, friend," Artemis said, patting Hugo awkwardly on the back, then turned to me. "We found men, all dead from infection. Their mouths were blue, there were moths... feeding and –"

"How many men?" I glanced out of the window and towards the garden.

"Fifty, maybe."

Fifty dead men, all Blues. The implications clarified in my mind.

Artemis said what I was thinking. "Only half died. That's right, isn't it? Half die and half go Manic – if this was just half, then..."

"The rest are out there." My voice shook.

"Anita," said Tony. "When she left us, she suggested that that she'd done something terrible – is this what she meant?"

My mind raced, and thoughts sparked off in different directions. How did they get so many out at once? "What happened, Hugo?" I took a small step towards the stranger on the chair. "How did you end up here?"

He was still crying, his sobs becoming less frequent. Finally, he was able to speak. "After the f–f–filter breach at the facility, the women told us we'd be safe. They gave us the vaccine." He jerked his left arm towards us as if showing us. "Then took us on a bus. It was only until they could find us foster homes, they said –" He stopped as a fresh set of sobs coursed through him. "B–b–but everyone got sick. When it started, they told us it was just a side effect of the vaccine. But then..." His sobs were quieter now, like painful breaths. "It was h–h–horrible. Some men turned; they started attacking us. Men I'd known all my life kicking and spitting and falling on us, saying we were different – that we didn't *smell* right. But women came in with benzos and took them away. Then, everyone around me started to die – they just went to sleep and never woke up. I was so scared to fall asleep. Me and Sadio, we tried to stay awake. But in the end, I was so tired. Then I woke up in the barn and Sadio was dead, and the moths, they were –" He couldn't finish the sentence, as another painful clutch of sobs wracked his chest.

Tony looked at me, pale under the harsh kitchen light. "Didn't the vaccine work?"

"They didn't give them the vaccine." I said, trying to keep the anger out of my voice. "They must have given these men dummy injections."

Hugo was crying so hard that I didn't even know if he'd heard what I said.

Artemis looked at me. "Why isn't he dead? He's a man, and he's been infected. He has the blue rash. How is this possible?"

I shrugged. "It's not my specialist area, but there has been some research on levels of immunity. Genetics, sex, hormones. People like to think it's clear cut, but it's a messy business. There were anecdotal accounts of men showing immunity in the first wave, although the chaos masked the true number. When things settled down, I suspect that anyone who looked like a man, whether or not they were showing symptoms, were treated as infected."

"Okay," Tony cut in, "but is he likely to turn Manic?" We all looked at the man in the chair.

He looked up at us with wide eyes. "Will I? I don't want to go to a sanatorium. Please."

He was right to be afraid of the sanatoriums, the places you went if you became infected. Despite what the carers at the facilities said, they were terrible places. "I don't know."

I leaned over Hugo and scanned the blue marks on his face. "The blue marks on your face are fading. Perhaps you have enough immunity even without the vaccine. But as I say, this is not my area of medicine."

"We should tie him to the chair just in case." Tony paced the kitchen, eyeing Hugo with suspicion.

Artemis let out a hissing breath. "No, he'll be fine. He's just been through – we're not tying him up."

I could see Tony wanted to argue, but there was something in Artemis's stare, a hardness, that I'd not seen before. "I think Artemis is right," I replied. "We just need to keep an eye on him." And then to Hugo, "Tell us if you start to feel anything abnormal, especially if you're feeling angry, okay?"

He nodded. "I will."

Artemis turned to me. "Did you get through to the LA? The MWA?"

I shook my head. "I think the network's down." And then, "Hang on." I returned to the kitchen with a small reclaimed old MW wind up, switching it on to the Union's official channel.

After a little tuning, Prime Minister Jade Philips's measured tone addressed us through the tinny speakers:

"This is an official broadcast from the Government of the Union of Britain. There has been at least one facility breach in the Southeast of the country. Infected men have been reported near the villages of Chesterford, Churt, Blackriver, Bordon and Petersfield. If you live within twenty miles of this area, please stay inside your homes. Do not leave your homes for any reason until you are told it is safe to do so. If you are approached by a man, assume he is infected, leave his vicinity if you can. Otherwise, use any force necessary to protect yourself. Remember, some of the infected have moments of lucidity – this does not mean it is safe to be near them. Infected Manics are highly dangerous. Do not leave your house unless it is unsafe to remain. The Government of the Union and the LA are working to bring the situation under control, and we expect to update you in the next few hours."

The message was on repeat.

"We should we stay here," said Tony. There was a note of relief in the way he stood, a sagging of the shoulders.

Artemis looked at me from over Hugo's shoulder. "What about Lois. And Daniel."

I nodded. I didn't like the idea of Mae looking after my mother and although Molly and Sam would look after Daniel, I needed to be with him. "We need the car outside."

"But the radio said –" Tony's face fell, obviously disappointed at the proposed change to the plan.

"What about Layton, Molly, Sam, Eloise?" replied Artemis. "Don't you want to check they're okay?"

Tony sighed. "Yes – but I don't know how much help I'll be. Or even if they'd want me there."

I suspected things had become a bit strained at Molly's place. She'd told me about the gossip in town, rumours spread about rotten produce, and how they were struggling to manage on the additional rations. There was some stress about Eloise's university application. Poor Tony, it seemed, was caught up in the middle of it. "It's okay, Tony. Molly and Sam will want to know you're okay – bring Hugo. Artemis, check it's clear outside. We'll pick up Mum and go over to the farm. Stay there till this all passes."

I started rifling through kitchen drawers, looking for the keys to the car.

Anita

Some people can compartmentalise horror or bury it deep like a murderer buries evidence. Some talk about trauma, endlessly raking over every detail, describing every negative emotion out of existence. I worked. I threw myself into the comms detail I was assigned, spending my evenings studying every electrical engineering book I could lay my hands on. It helped, I guess, to keep busy. But Bella was still young. I'd ask her how she was feeling, after lessons in the food hall, and she would pause, a spoon halfway to her mouth, and say *not bad*. And I would hear, *I'm good*. So, I would leave it and carry on trying to survive, working, being part of the Union's great new birth.

We did okay. After two years, we moved on from the compound to one of the villages that had been marked as a new community. We cleared brambles and scrubbed out mouldering fridges, reported bodies the blue crew had missed the first time round. I helped set up the first electricity grids, local ones repurposing domestic solar panels and wind turbines. Much of the energy was syphoned off to power the air conditioning in a new prep house – a home for new-born uninfected boys. At nineteen, I received a letter that offered incentives to contribute – more land to cultivate, more tokens for trade. *It is the duty of the brave women of the Union, women such as yourself, to ensure that our hard-fought survival has purpose... Aside from our sisters in Australia, we have received no other signs of significant populations and must concede that we are one of only two surviving societies with a working government. It is important that we look forward and remake ourselves into a modern peaceful world. Contribution and repopulation is the only way...*

"What happens when you contribute?" asked Bella at lunch one day, a few years after we'd moved into our two-bedroom house on a newish estate near Bordon. It was so uncommon for her to speak by then that I hardly recognised her deeper thirteen year-old's voice.

I wasn't prepared for such a question. I cleared my throat twice before answering. "You get men's sperm put inside you and it fertilises your egg. Then you grow a baby. If it's a girl, you look after her yourself, and if it's a boy, he becomes a contribution. He goes to the prep house."

She replaced her spoon in the leek and potato soup. "Do you have be close to the men for your egg to get fertilised? Are the men with the sperm infected?" There was a crack in her voice as she spoke, and she crossed her arms across her chest.

"Yes, they are, but you don't have to, you know... be with them like that. You don't have to have sex with them. A nurse will bring the sperm from one of the men and do it for you. You just need to be in the same building." The ins and outs of insemination is studied from a young age these days. New techniques, genetic engineering and insemination techniques, girls grow up knowing exactly how and when they expect to procreate. But back then, we were just finding our way.

"Some women do, though, don't they? Some have sex with them?" said Bella, staring at her cooling soup.

It was true, some women did – they said it increased the chances of conception. But what a terrible notion – having an infected man tied up whilst you... I picked up our bowls and moved into the kitchen, pouring Bella's soup back into the pot for later. "Don't think about it," I said, coming back into the dining area. "There's some crumble left over from last night. I could heat it up with a bit of cream if you like –"

"I don't want you to do it." She wound herself up in her cardigan, pulling it around her body, constricting herself. "I don't want you to get pregnant or contribute. Something could happen, they could escape whilst you're in there. Then you wouldn't come home, and I'd be on my own..." She didn't cry, but the tears were in her eyes, frozen there almost. She gulped in some air and continued. "Or we'd have a baby, a soft and cute baby, and we'd love her and then one day they'd escape and come for her and she'd... she'd disappear." It was the most she'd said in one go for months and it came out in a painful whoosh.

I ran to her. "Bells, Bells, I won't! I wasn't going to anyway. Plenty of women are volunteering. The world will have enough babies without me." I felt her push herself into my arms.

I'd never told her what happened to Miranda and Jorgie. I checked the records about a year after the first wave, as most

people did, looking for relatives. I suspected Jorgie would have
been infected, but Miranda? Their bodies were found in Dad's
car in the hospital car park. Just one line next to Miranda on
cause of death: *Suffocated with a blanket.* And by Jorgie's name:
Infected – dehydration. How long had Jorgie suffered in the car,
lying next to his dead mother?

So, I never contributed, neither of us did. She left her lessons
at eighteen and began to drift, moving around small holdings
and farms, working the land in sowing and harvesting seasons,
spending the rest of her time hitching around villages – never
ones near prep houses, facilities or sanatoriums.

She found a new drug, a liquid synthesised from the caterpillar's
cocoons. *Ghia, Drift, Fliss, Lepwing, Moonshift* – it went by many
names. I'd get reports from women in the village about what
they'd heard of her stumbling in and out of pubs and in and out
of beds, some reports delivered with sympathy, some with relish.
These gossiping women became the only way to keep track of
her. When I hadn't heard anything for a while, I'd go looking.
When I found her, she was always in a worse state, skinny, pale,
sores on her hands and face, yellow circles around her eyes,
cracked skin around her lips. I'd take her home and clean her up
as best I could, but it wasn't long before she slipped away again,
usually at night, or when I was at work. She disappeared for
weeks, months, eventually years went by without her contacting
me. I thought about her every day. I travelled to the Citadel; by
then it had become a vast town, inhabited by thousands. I asked
around, showed people a sketch I'd had done – nothing.

She reappeared a few years ago, just turned up at my house.
Pearl was working late, and I came home to find Bella sitting
on the garden wall, waiting. She looked well – calm, clean.

There was some sobbing – on my part – she held onto me,
stoically absorbing my tears. Then I was angry, shouting at
her and shaking her by the shoulders. But finally, we sat in
the living room, clutching tea, staring at each other. She sat
up straight with her ankles crossed, her jacket folded neatly

on her lap. She'd put on some weight and looked strong. In her forties, she had the bearing of an older woman. But her eyes were clear. Her face had the same impassive blankness I remembered.

"Where have you been?"

She half smiled. "Scotland. There's a commune. I've been there for the last four years."

I nodded but let the silence stretch. I wanted to know more but didn't want to blast her with questions. "It looks like it's done you good," I said eventually.

"They found me when I was in a really dark place and they…" She tapped her finger on the side of the cup. "Sorry, I should have called you before I came."

I said nothing.

She bit her lip. "Can I use your phone? I want to tell them I'm okay."

"Sure."

She made the call in the other room. I listened, of course, but she was mumbling so I could only make out a few words. *A few days… my sister… It'll be fine.*

She came back in the room and picked up her tea. "They worry about me," she said with a half grimace.

Let them worry, I thought. I've had to worry about you for most of my life.

She told me about the place she was living. It sounded weird. There seemed to be an obsession with cleanliness, meditation, and lots of group meetings. I sensed a whiff of cultishness about the whole thing. But when I asked her if she was happy there, she smiled. A real smile, something I hadn't seen since she was little. "I am," she replied. "You must come and visit – see for yourself. You'd love it up there."

I could have been kinder; I should have said that I'd think about it. All she wanted was to show me her home, but there was still some anger in me, lurking beneath the surface. "I don't think so, Bella," I said, a little sharper than I intended.

"I have a job, a wife. I can't get all the way to Scotland, even for a holiday. How would I even get there?"

She looked crestfallen. "You're right, Beans. I should have thought about that."

I felt a lump rise in my chest at the sound of my old nickname. I suddenly understood how Bella must have abdicated it all, all the pain and stress, all the fear – now she had nothing to do but live on a commune and grow vegetables. And that was a good thing, after everything she'd been through. I wanted to tell her I understood, but she was already standing up to go.

"Stay!" I said, jumping to my feet. "Meet Pearl, she'll be back from work soon. I could make us all some dinner and then –"

But she was already putting on her jacket. "Next time," she said. "I'll come down again, I promise." She snaked her arms around me and gave me a squeeze. "I really am sorry, Beans. For everything."

I sighed. "It's Okay. Really." Then, when she pulled away, "Can you call me when you get back? Just to let me know you're okay?"

She frowned. "The community phone is only used in absolute emergencies – but I can write letters."

I walked her to the bus stop, and I waved her off. It was as if a weight had lifted from my chest. Things were going to be alright, I thought.

Finally.

CHAPTER 16

Tony

Cars, I thought as we sped towards Evie's house, are miraculous things, possibly the most impressive things I'd seen since leaving the facility. I particularly liked the feeling of protection, of being inside and knowing nothing can catch you. Unless it was another car, I suppose. But even then, you'd still be in a metal bubble, safe. I felt this way right up until we bounced across a large branch. It looked like half a tree had fallen across the road, and Evie struggled to keep control, swerving around it and making the seatbelt cut painfully into my neck. She kept us on the road by sharply turning the wheel from right to left and cursing heavily. After a few breathless moments she straightened up and kept driving. I reconsidered my view on the safety of cars.

"You two alright in the back?" called Artemis from the front seat.

I looked at Hugo, who was holding the armrest in a death grip. "You need to breathe." I said, weakly.

"I'm okay. I'm okay," Hugo gasped. "Just, I thought we might crash into something and… die."

"Bloody branch. Sorry." Evie didn't sound sorry. She sounded shaken.

When we pulled up to Evie's house it was dark. She leapt

from the car and ran to the house. Artemis shot after her without hesitation. Hugo and I sat for a moment in the darkness.

"Should we follow them?" Hugo asked, peering into the darkness beyond the window. His voice suggested that the very last thing he wanted to do was get out of the car.

I sighed and unclipped my seatbelt. "I guess so."

But before I had the door half open Artemis came out of the house holding an old woman in his arms. He moved to the front passenger door as he leaned down, gently placing the woman in the seat. "Make sure you put your seat belt on, Lois." Then he gave a half smile before closing the door.

"Don't be bossing me around, young man," said the woman, even though Artemis was no longer within earshot, having gone back to stand with Evie. But she strapped herself in all the same.

I was about to use my politest voice and introduce myself when I heard raised voices a little way from the car. Panic surged through me as I assumed the Manics had found us. I was flooded by images of being dragged from the car along with Hugo, and this old woman, and being torn apart by a hoard of infected men. But the shouts were Evie arguing with another woman. The woman turned on Artemis, who was standing nearby, and began shouting at him. Artemis said nothing but looked angrier than I'd ever seen him, frowning with his mouth drawn up into a tight line. *Oh, dammit Artemis, look what you've done!*

"Who's that?" asked Hugo pointing to the shouting woman with Evie.

I was about to reply that I didn't know, when the old lady spoke. "That's Mae, Evie's wife." The nasally way she said *Mae* suggested that she did not like Evie's wife at all.

Mae took a step towards Artemis, shouting something that sounded like *disgusting*, pointing to the car. Artemis hesitated. Mae shouted it again, louder this time.

Evie turned and said something to Artemis who grimaced before moving towards the car and opening my door. "Move over," he snapped. As I did so, he slid into my vacated seat, so I was squashed in between him and Hugo. I tried to wriggle away; Artemis was emitting heat like a bread oven. He slammed the door behind him making me and Hugo jump. The women outside had stopped shouting and Mae was talking urgently to Evie, as she took her wife's hands in hers, and seemed to be asking something important.

"You're hurting me," whispered Hugo from my other side. "I need some more room." There was a long silence inside the car as the two women continued to argue outside. "What are they arguing about?" Hugo asked.

No one answered, although I had a fairly good idea.

"Are you okay, Lois?" Artemis asked the old woman.

She smiled. "I am, sweet boy. Have you heard from Daniel?"

Artemis shook his head. "We couldn't get through to the farmhouse. We're going there now."

"They'll be fine. Sam and Molly won't let anything happen to him."

Evie got in the car. She was breathing heavily. "I can't believe it," she gasped, her voice full of anger and tears. "I can't believe she'd even suggest that. And I can't believe that she thought I'd agree!"

Lois patted her on the arm. "It's okay, pet. Let's go and find Daniel. That's what matters now."

Evie nodded and wiped her eyes with the back of her wrist, looking behind her towards the house. I followed her gaze. Mae was standing by the door, arms wrapped around her body, a look of fury on her face. I looked from Artemis to Evie then out to the seething form of Mae.

Oh, Artemis.

Dear Beans,

Thanks for the letters, and sorry I haven't written in such a long time. Back at the community, time feels different. You lose whole weeks, months. Time wanders. This spring, I'm in charge of maintaining the machinery, and I also work with the bees. There's always so much to do. How is Pearl? I've got some close friends here, but we don't marry each other. The elders think that ownership like that fosters jealousy. Some of the girls don't like this, but I find it a relief. I think I'd find it hard to belong to one person like that. But I'm glad you've got someone. How's work? Are you still working on radio broadcasts? I bet you're ace at making it work perfectly. I haven't listened to it as we don't have it here. I'd like to – one day.

There are some children here in the community, some born here, some arrive with parents. They're kind of raised by everyone. It's nice that I get to be a small part of their childhood. They have a proper childhood, not like mine, not one of fear (I know you tried your best, Beans. Please don't feel bad. I'm happy now, it wasn't your fault – you know that, right?) We don't talk about the time before, here. It's forbidden. When you join the community, you promise to accept rebirth. The elders tell you that this is how it is now and that is all that matters. The past is dead. I try to remember this, but sometimes at night… Well, I still don't sleep all that much.

There's been something worrying me for a few weeks, and I wondered if you've heard anything about it. One of the new arrivals here used to be part of the MWA, she worked for Jen Harting. Whilst we were both on kitchen duty a few nights ago, she told me a story about a special place she used to visit in the countryside. She said that it was like the community but that there were men there. I was horrified. I thought she meant the infected, but she said that the men had been given some kind of vaccine so that they could go outside. I don't want to believe it, Beans. I don't know what to believe. Every time I think about it, I start to shake. I told one of the elders what I heard, and she said that the woman was lying, that there was no vaccine (the woman was asked to leave soon after). But what if there is? I can feel my heart beating faster just writing about it. Will you find out for me? If I leave the community again, they may not let me back in – but I can't stop thinking about it.

Anyway, sorry to ask. And sorry that I've been so bad at writing *letters. Don't send your next letter straight to the community, send it to the address at the top of this letter. The elders read all the letters before they give them out. Jasmine's a vet who lives offsite. She's agreed to bring any letters with her when she next comes to check the animals.*

Love, Bells xxx

Dear Bella,

Don't worry about not writing. I called and spoke to someone at the community a few months ago, just to check if you were okay. They were a little bit stand-offish at first, but they told me that you were still there and that you were fine. Things here are fine. Pearl is obsessed with her research, something about hamsters, and I'm still working at the Union official radio station. We're trying to implement an outreach programme into parts of Europe – bringing some semblance of civilisation to the pockets still surviving out there. But that's a dangerous project. It will mean a group going out to mainland Europe. Not something I'm volunteering for, as you can imagine.

I've not heard anything about a vaccine – I even asked my comms manager, who has a friend on the Council, but she'd heard nothing either. She thought the idea quite ludicrous. Perhaps the woman who told you this was trying to impress you – curry favour as the new girl?

Look, it's a little worrying, Bells, that you have to do so much sneaking about regarding the letters. What are the elders scared of? You know you can always come here, yes? I'd love it, and I'm sure Pearl would be thrilled. Anyway, let me know how it's going – via 'vet-mail'.

Love you always,

Beans xxx

When the story broke about Mary Langham, Jen Harting and the existence of the vaccine, I'd heard nothing up until that point, not even a rumour. I called the community in a panic, but they wouldn't let me speak to Bella. I left my number. Then I sat down and wrote a letter, redrafting it about a hundred times. I reiterated what they said on the radio – that the vaccine was one hundred per cent effective. That there was no risk to the population. But as I wrote the words I could hear Bella's panicked replies, her panting breaths, and I could picture the wild fear in her eyes. They're coming back. Men. They are coming out of the facilities where they'd been sequestered for four decades, and they'll be here in the streets, on buses, at schools and in cafes. Even to me, the idea seems absurd. Why, after all this time, would the Union want to change things? The effectiveness of the vaccine aside, why bring them back?

I heard nothing from Bella. No call, no letter for a month. I checked the post every morning. I started making plans to go up there and called the community and begged to be allowed to speak to her.

Eventually I got through. "She's not here anymore. She left a while ago."

"Where did she go?"

"We don't know." A pause. "She'd been smuggling information into the community – we had to ask her to leave."

It was a week later I got a knock on the door. By that time, I'd contacted all of the LA departments in the country, giving a description, asking them to contact me if they found anything. I thought it was her, and I rushed to the door. It was a young LA officer. She was softly spoken and introduced herself as a trained psychologist and part of the counselling arm of the force.

Her words drifted in and out like a poorly tuned frequency – Annabel Swift... B&B... Leeds... landlady... locked door... Called LA... vial of Fliss... overdose...

Did everything they could.

I felt Pearl's arms around me, lowering me to the sofa. A blanket that appeared. The weight of it seemed immense. Murmurs from the LA officer to Pearl, about *keeping an eye* and *sweet tea*. And something about a note. Then the LA officer said something that I remember as clear as day. "I've seen this a lot in the last few weeks – women of a certain age who lived through the first wave.

This whole vaccine thing has had some serious consequences."
Then the voice dimmed as Pearl led her from the room.

Dear Beans,

I should have come to you, I know. I couldn't stop thinking about the vaccine, and I ended up in a pub. The drinking was just to calm my nerves. But it did something else. It gave me courage. I'm so exhausted trying to pretend I don't feel like this. I'm afraid all the time. If you knew how I felt, you'd understand. Don't be sad, Beans. By the time you read this, I won't be frightened anymore. I won't wake up screaming. I won't have to see Dad's face as he jumps from a balcony, or a woman's yellow dress as it disappears under a train. I'll be asleep. Properly, for the first time in forever. I'll be with Mum.

I Love you, Big Sis. I'm so sorry.

Bella

Evie

The road was getting narrower. I concentrated on getting my breathing under control and staying alert. The roads around here were notoriously bad – pot holes, overgrown verges. Eastor's roads were low down on the Council's priority list. Another reason that Mae had flung at me on numerous occasions under the banner reasons-we-should-move-to-the-Citadel. I tried not to think about Mae, and about the things she'd just said to me, the things we'd said to each other. By clutching the steering wheel really tightly, I could stop the shaking in my hands. But what was it that was making them shake? Anger? Fear? Shame?

Do you know what people will say when they find out about your thing with Artemis? People at work? They'll laugh, Evie. At me and at you. You think I'll be able to get the promotion I need when this comes out? All that stuff with those pictures in the drawer. You didn't think I knew? Pathetic!

I clutched the wheel even tighter. And narrowly missed a pothole in the road, making everyone in the car gasp. "Sorry," I mumbled.

"Slow down a bit, love," said Mum, sitting next to me. "It's dark and these roads are in an awful state."

I slowed down and tried to concentrate on the road, but Mae's words kept coming back to me. She'd changed tack, becoming conciliatory and lowering her voice as she eyed the car: *If we leave right now – If we take that car and go to the Citadel, leave the men here, then I'll forgive you. We could start over. Take Lois, even. Find her a place in the Citadel. I love you, Evie. Don't throw it all away for nothing.* That was the truth of it right there – Tony, Artemis, even Daniel meant nothing to her. She wanted me to leave them here whilst Manics were roaming around. *I've sorted a place for us to stay – that's why I've been gone so much lately. I wanted to surprise you – to have it ready. You could drive us there, Evie! We could just go.*

Poor, harmless, helpless Daniel. She knew him, lived with him. How could she suggest we leave him? How could she have thought it was okay? *Molly can look after him, and she could take in Artemis. I'm sure she'd like the extra tokens.*

Stay inside, I'd told her. *Turn off the lights and lock the door. Goodbye Mae.*

And that was how my marriage ended.

We were nearing Molly's farmhouse; I could see it up on the hill. The lights were on, which was a good sign. Just let Daniel be okay – Daniel and Layton and Molly and Sam and the girls.

I don't know whether it was because I was distracted, still angry about Mae, or afraid for what I might find at the farmhouse, but the object in the road came out of nowhere. Blocking the whole road, sitting, just round a sharp bend so it was invisible right up until the last moment. Luckily, I was not going that fast. I screeched to a halt, and we all lurched forward skidding and stopping inches from the dark mound.

One of the men in the back screamed, and then there was silence.

"Mum! Are you okay, Mum?" I took a deep breath, turning to Mum and forcing myself to stay calm.

She coughed. "I think so, Evie."

"Everyone else?" I demanded, trying to unbuckle myself and turning round to face the back. "Artemis? Can you hear me?"

"I'm alright," replied Artemis.

"I think Hugo's dead!" This from a panicked-sounding Tony.

"I'm not dead. I just have my eyes closed."

"Oh, it's okay Evie, he's okay," said Tony. "Why's there an old car in the middle of the road?"

That was exactly what I was wondering. We'd been down this road only a few days ago – this car had not been here then. It was an old, reclaimed van of some kind, mottled with rust blotches. There was no one in the cab. Had it been left there by someone? In which case, why was it at an angle, blocking the whole road? I felt a ripple of anxiety run over my shoulders.

"I'll carry Lois," replied Artemis. "It's not that far, just up the hill."

"No. Stay in the car," said Tony.

Artemis had already opened the door next to my mother. "Careful, Lois. That's right, put your arm around me." He unbuckled the belt and then lifted her out gently.

"So kind, Artemis. You really are a good boy."

"Wait," I said as I undid my own belt and wriggled up. A few moments later, Tony came to my door. I stepped out, glad my legs didn't dissolve into jelly. The three men all stood and looked at me. My mother lay curled up in Artemis's arms.

"Why is the car like that?" asked Tony, echoing my own thoughts. "Why is it at an angle blocking the whole road?"

Artemis shrugged, still holding my mother. "Maybe it broke down? Come on, let's go."

"Yes, but," I replied, "It feels like it was put there – Hugo, what's wrong?"

Hugo was looking around frantically; he was shaking and had gone a deathly shade of pale. "Can you smell it?" he said in a wild voice. "That awful smell. I know that smell."

Tony took a deep sniff and looked at Artemis, fear on his face.

"What is it? What can you smell?"

It was Artemis who answered, clutching my mother tighter and turning towards the farmhouse. "The infected! They're close!"

CHAPTER 17

Anita

It was on the verge of dusk and my part of the plan was complete. A massive contingent of Law Abidance had attended the violent protest at the crematorium, and everything else was in place. The chaos that would ensue was sure to make the Council rethink the vaccine programme. They were being pressured on all sides at the moment, and it just took one Council member to demur for the project to be pulled. There were complaints from the Law Abidance Association, the Education Department was complaining about not having the resources nor the expertise to teach boys. I also knew that XX02's rich benefactor was financing opposition in other ways too, flyers appearing on buses, adverts pinned to notice boards, warning about the dangers of men. The ranks of the XXs were swelling, and the Council couldn't ignore the dissenters forever.

It hadn't been my intention to shoot Freya Curtis. I hadn't even fired a gun for nearly forty years, not since my training at the compound. But when she came for me, I'd reacted. I didn't wait to see what damage the bullet caused. For weeks I'd had to listen to her nonsense – lived through Waterloo, indeed! Her *mother* had been a hero, I can attest to that. I wouldn't have got through those dark hours without her, but Freya... You must *remember* it to have lived through it. You don't get points for generational bravery, despite her name being carved on the cenotaph.

Getting the men out was the hardest bit. One of the ward sisters at a facility near Pullborough was a member, XX117 – an *ardent* believer. She managed to recruit a couple more women, a cleaner and a carer. I don't know if the newer recruits really knew what they were getting themselves into – or how this all would end. But she must have talked a good talk because between the three of them, they managed to smuggle out a whole wing – over one hundred men. They did it at night, making sure that they were the only ones on duty and then giving the men dummy injections – just to keep them quiet. Then they just marched them to a couple of waiting coaches outside the gates. Coaches provided by the deep pockets of whoever XX02 was working for.

When anyone asked, they were to say that they were part of the Council's fostering programme. I was able to get some headed paperwork to them that looked authentic enough. They put the men on a bus then we all waited to see who'd turn. The Blues were no use to us. I gave them directions to a barn at the house where Freya was staying – a nice little reminder for her of what she was a part of – and a coach was sent to dump them there. The other men, the infected, were benzoed and left to wake up in various places around Eastor.

I'd sent Pearl to the Citadel for the week – suggesting a few days visiting friends from medical school. And now, all I had to do was make it back to HQ for a debrief. We'd need to lay low for a while. Pearl would come round. XX02 had said that her benefactor had connections in Australia and that we'd be safe there. It would be good to have a change. A fresh start – no risk of men.

Eastor's roads were narrow and winding, but in a few miles I'd be on the main road. Anyhow, this was a reclaim, a fairly sturdy one at that. The men would have woken up by now, the infected, so I needed to keep an eye out for them. But what could they do? I was in a car, they were not. Worst case scenario, I could just plough a few down. Soon I'd be out of the area, and then I wouldn't have to worry. We only left them as far as Stevenage, although the Council didn't know that. We told the Council that we'd left men all over the south. It'll take hours, days even, for the LA to round them all up – added to the fact that XX agents at the crematorium had taken advantage of the chaos to disable many of the LA's fleet of cars earlier. What carnage would the men wreak? Enough, I hope. Enough to dissuade the Council of using the vaccine. I know there'll be casualties, but as XX02 said, there always are in war. This will ensure fewer casualties in the long run.

I worried about Pearl. She might not understand – she hadn't been born when the first wave hit. But she'd seen what happened to Bella. I'd tell her about Waterloo – something I'd never done before. She loved me; I knew she did. She'd forgive me.

XX02 would be pleased. I might even meet her mysterious backer. It was as I was contemplating this, that I was forced to slam on the brakes, narrowly missing a huge pile of logs strewn in the road. The pile looked like it had been built on purpose, constructed rather than chaotic. Shit. *The men would have woken up by now.* I put the car into reverse and looked over my shoulder. A massive log now stretched across the narrow road twenty or so feet behind me. That hadn't been there a moment ago.

I fumbled around for my gun on the passenger seat and checked the chamber. It was nearly full. XX02 had smiled when she'd given it to me. "This is it soldier – this is the last battle."

I locked the doors and felt safer. *What could they do against a gun?*

Just then, the first rock smashed into the windscreen.

Tony

I could smell it too. The acrid tang that made my mouth water and mind buzz. They were near. "What should we do?" I looked around in the darkness. "Should we get back in the car? Try to find another route to the farmhouse?" I wanted to get back into the car. Despite my recent experiences swerving all over the place, the well-sealed, warm bubble seemed the safest place to be right now.

Evie looked from us to the car and then up to the farmhouse on the hill. "I don't know of another road up there."

"Then we go – now!" Artemis, clutching Lois in his arms, strode along the path that led up the hill. "Daniel's up there."

Evie gave the car one last look and went after Artemis, who'd managed to go a surprisingly long way, weighed down as he was. I turned to follow.

"Wait, Tony!" It was Hugo. "I don't think we should go out there. We could wait in the car, at least until it's light. Lock the doors. We'd be safe."

Hugo made a good argument, and every fibre in my being longed to crawl back into the car. It was really dark, clouds covering the moon, and freezing cold. My jumper was proving wholly inadequate out in this wilderness. The small square windows on the hill were the only source of light in the whole area. I thought of Molly's warm kitchen, of Layton and Eloise and Sam crowded around the table – eating dinner, perhaps. I glanced down the road behind us, beyond the now dark and silent car, and thought I saw a movement. "Come on," I said to Hugo. "It won't take long." I jogged after Evie and Artemis.

I was about ten paces away when I heard Hugo call out to me again. "Tony, I can't see."

Gritting my teeth, I and turned around to find Hugo groping his way along the brambly verge. I was about to shout out to him, to tell him to get a move on, when I noticed a shadow appear in the road behind him. Then another and another. "Ohhh Huuuugoooo," whispered one shadow, and Hugo stopped still, shocked.

"Hugo! Run!" I cried out. "Come on, Hugo. As fast as you can."

"Gordon, is that you?" Hugo turned around and faced the shadows. There were seven or eight of them now. "Gordon? Kyle?"

"Hugo!" I whispered, but it was too late. The nearest shadow jumped on Hugo and knocked him to the ground, sitting on top of him and pinning him down. I looked desperately for Evie or Artemis, but they'd both run ahead. "Oh, no. Oh no," I whispered to myself, caught between wanting to help Hugo and wanting to run away as fast as I could.

The man on top of Hugo began to slap him, meaty slaps with the flat of his hand, and the men around cheered as each one fell. "You're not one of us," he said as each slap fell. "You're soft and scared – I can smell it on you. "You're different."

"Gordon? Stop. What are you doing? It's me, Hugo. We're friends. We… we played together in the prep house. We even spent recreation time together. Remember? It's me, look, It's Hugo." His voice had taken on the whine of desperation.

"It'ss mee It'ss Hugoo," said the man on top of him in a high mocking wail. Then he bunched up his hands into a brutal ball and hit Hugo with his knuckles. "HUGOOO, HUGOOO, HUGOOO."

Hugo couldn't do anything but sob, and I desperately wanted it to all stop. But I was afraid. Seven men and just me. What could I do? Despite my fear, I took a step towards them.

Then one man took something out of his robe and pointed it at Hugo's head. I recognised it from earlier. It was the same thing that Anita had pointed at Freya Curtis in the car. *A gun.*

"This makes a great noise, Huuugooooo. Do you want to hear it?"

"No, Gordon. Pleassse. Ssstop." Hugo's words were mumbled, like he was gargling.

The man looked at the cowering heap lying before him. Then he turned to the men standing around. "Who wants to see Hugo's brains?"

The other men shouted their responses: *Me! I want to see his brains, let's see them, do it, Gordon.*

Then a very tall man stepped forward from the group and grabbed the gun from Gordon. "No. I'll do it. Last time, with the women in the car, you missed the head."

Gordon tried to grab the gun back, but the other man was taller and held it high. "Give it to me! Kyle. I had it first."

The taller man was already bending down, pointing it at Hugo's forehead. "This is how you do it, Gordon. You have to stand close."

The sound when it came was incredible, like a hundred heavy doors all slamming at once, like a physical thing pushing through the air. And it sounded so close, like it was happening inside my ears. I was too late to put my hands over my ears and so I caught the full force. It was that noise which made me move. I didn't decide anything; I just acted. A part of me, a deep fearful part, knew that I didn't want to be anywhere near that noise or what made that noise, or what that noise had done to Hugo. I ran. I knew I should be ashamed of leaving Hugo, but I ran, nevertheless.

I didn't look back. Keeping to the hedge, I groped my way through the darkness, convinced that the men would have heard my retreat, and followed on. I could see the farmhouse ahead, only one field away. I ran with every measure of force I possessed, struggling in the dark to find the path.

Evie

Artemis jogged up the hill with my mother in his arms, his thick legs pounding the ground, as I followed behind. I was expecting an arm to reach for us from the tall grass at the side of the road, or a shape to launch itself upon us. But none came. By the time we reached the porch of the farmhouse, my breath was being torn from my lungs in shuddering gasps. Artemis, too, was heaving. Mum was light – I knew. I'd often carried her to the bathroom when she'd not been having a good day – her bones having been eaten away, no fat clinging to her frame. But we'd run fast, uphill.

"I'd like to stand now, Artemis," she croaked. "Put me down for a moment."

He gingerly lowered her to the ground, and she straightened out her nightgown.

I knocked on the door, still trying to get my breathing under control. Nothing. I tried the door, but it was locked. I knocked again. Artemis and I shared a nervous look. On the third try, Sam's face appeared at the small window. I nearly fainted with relief.

The door opened. Sam looked over our shoulders. "Where's Tony? Is he with you?"

I looked around and saw Artemis do the same, an expression of worry etched onto his brow. "I thought he was behind us. Him and another man, Hugo."

I noticed the rifle in Sam's hand. I was about to ask if they'd seen any Manics, but Sam made a shushing gesture and ushered us inside.

"Evie!" a small body threw himself at me, nearly toppling me over. I picked up Daniel and squeezed him tightly. "Oh, baby." I gave him a kiss on his head and rubbed my cheek over his stubbly hair. "It's okay, I'm here."

"I was scared. I kept asking Molly when you'd come and she just kept saying, not yet. She wanted me to go to bed with Layton and Tess, but I wanted to wait for you." His earnest little face stared into mine, "I knew you'd come."

My heart swelled with love for him. I gave him another squeeze and fought down tears. "Always. I'll always come for you."

"Get in, now, near the fire. You look half frozen." Molly rose from the table and came towards us, flapping her hands and shepherding us towards the fire in the corner of the large kitchen. "Lois let's get you sat down. As Mum shuffled past the kitchen table, I noticed two more rifles and a pile of little cylinders. Bullets I assumed.

"Thank you, Molly. That's kind of you." Mum lowered herself onto a chair, pulled up to the fire and visibly sagged.

Eloise, get some blankets. Melanie, grab some extra chairs from the snug and bring them through. Eloise! Did you hear what I said?"

But the girl was heading past us and towards the door. "You said Tony was following. Where is he? He should be here by now, right?" Her voice was sharp with fear.

Artemis spoke up. "Yeah, I thought they were following right behind."

"We need to find him." The young girl looked around at us all. "We need to make sure he's okay."

Sam and Molly shared a glance. Molly replied. "It's dangerous out there at the moment. You heard what they said on the radio. I think –"

"Radio be dammed." Eloise grabbed a cloak from a hook on the door. "I'm going. The Manics are probably nowhere near us. He's just got lost in the dark."

"I'll come with you," said Artemis. "You're right, we can't leave Tony out there."

"Wait," I said. "There are Manics about – lots of them. The XXs planned this. In fact," I paused, wondering how to say it. Finally, I just blurted it out. "Anita is one. She killed Freya Curtis."

Molly gasped. "Anita? She'd never, I mean, I've known her for years."

Sam's mouth set into an angry line. "You just never know, Molly."

"There are at least fifty Manics out there," I carried on. "And there was a car blocking the road. It looked like it had been put there on purpose."

"But Manics can't do that, can they?" This from Molly's other daughter, Melanie. "I thought when they were infected, they became stupid. They can't set traps."

Sam replied. "They can. In the first wave, they did it a lot. Sometimes they used family members to lure women from their safe hiding places. They can work together."

"I don't care," replied Eloise. "If there are Manics out there, then even more reason to get Tony safe." She looked from Molly to Sam and then back to Molly. "You promised to look after him. To treat him as family. She dragged the cloak around her shoulders and started towards the door.

"Wait." Sam moved the rifle from one hand to the other, then picked up some small cylinders that were on the table. "I'll go, Eloise. You stay here and wait with the others."

"I'm coming with you," said Eloise. "You shouldn't go alone."

"No," said Molly, flatly. "And Sammy, I don't want you taking any risks."

Sam cupped her face. "I'll be careful, Pet. I've a gun and plenty of shot. They're unarmed. They won't get anywhere near me. Stay here – whatever happens, stay here – and shoot any Manic that comes near. Even if they're lucid. Shoot 'em, Molly. Don't hesitate." Molly gave a half sob and nodded, a strand of her curly hair falling over her face. Sam gently took the curl and pushed it behind her ear. "I'll be fine." Then, turning to Eloise, "I'll find him. I promise."

Anita

The problem with the infected in the first wave, was that they were not afraid of guns. Whatever weird chemical affects their brain, it takes away their ability to fear for their own lives. Back then, it was possible for the army to gain control because men failed to protect themselves. They'd just run towards the gunfire, believing that they were impervious to it. The problem I had is that these men didn't know what a gun was. Rocks smashed through the windscreen and men jammed the wheels up with logs, so I couldn't drive the car. I pointed the gun at the men, screamed for them to stop, and they laughed at me.

Then I shot one, right between the eyes, one of the older ones. The shot made a tiny hole in his forehead but blew off most of the back of his skull, covering the surrounding men – a crowd of at least ten –in their friend's brains. A silence fell upon us as the men, dripping in flesh and bits of bone, stood wondering at what had happened. The shot man fell to the ground.

A cheer went up, like when someone scores at a football game. Then the rocks and logs showered down upon me again.

There were more men than bullets, and they were going to break into the car in a matter of minutes. *Shit*. This wasn't how it was supposed to happen. I wanted to do my part for the movement, but I wasn't like XX67 at Chesterford. I didn't want to *die* for it. I wanted to see my wife and make a new life, protected against this kind of violence. XX02 had promised me escape. *Courtesy of our benefactor*, she'd said, *for your loyalty*.

One man was on the bonnet and leaning in towards me. I aimed carefully and fired. The man slid from the bonnet and slumped to the floor. Another cheer. But while my attention had been on what was in front of me, two men had been levering open the back window. A hand grasped my wrist from the back seat and wrestled the gun from my hand. "I want it," the man hissed.

He wrenched it free, then pointed it at my seat. "I watched you do it – squeeze it, like this, yes?"

The blast in the car was appallingly loud, and I felt my seat jerk forward as something hit my thigh. I wiped my hand along my leg, then held it up in the dark. Blood, my blood.

I looked over my shoulder, feeling myself shake. The noise had shocked the men in the back of the car. They were cowered in the back seat, hands over their ears. The gun was in the back footwall, out of reach. I didn't even know if I could move my leg. A deep, cold ache pulsed from my thigh to my ankle.

The door next to me screeched open as a hand reached in and dragged me from the car. This was it, I thought. The memories of women at Waterloo filled my mind, blood, biting, tearing, the crack of bone. What happened to Mum was about to happen to me. I tumbled onto the road, crying out at the sharp increase of pain in my leg. I looked up, trying to channel her bravery.

But the men weren't looking at me.

"Where is it?"

"I want it."

"Give it to me! I want to squeeze it."

They were scrambling about in the car, crawling over and pulling each other away so they could find space for themselves. I took my chance, hoping to God that my leg would support me. I climbed to my feet and swallowed down the pain, then lurched away from the car. I didn't look back, even when I heard another shot behind me. When I saw a break in the hedge, I forced my way through, ignoring the scraping brambles and sharp branches on my face and hands.

I don't know how long I stumbled on, through fields and over hard, frosted mud. I looked up and there was a light on a hill. Molly's place. But I couldn't go there. If Evie had got in contact, they'd know about me shooting Freya. The blood had soaked into my trousers and the fabric slapped against my wound. The pain was coming in sick waves and my head was spinning. I should stop and staunch the wound. It wasn't bleeding heavily, but I was still losing more blood than I could spare. *Sit for a moment, rest.* I kept going, worried that if I sat down, I might never get up again. I found myself in a gathering of trees. *Maybe the men won't find me,* I thought as

I leaned against a tree looking up at the stars, shaking with cold. Another thought, a far more unwelcome one, presented itself to me. I sagged into the embrace of the tree, looking up at the night sky, at the stars, thinking about what led me here. Something fluttered around my face. A feather? And then another, and another. I brushed them away, but as my hand fell, they came back. Moths. Not an eclipse, but more than I'd expect to see this time of year. Was I to die of exposure to moth toxins, when there were men in this very village completely vaccinated against it? The irony.

The moths' toxin was starting to have an effect on me. I could feel the tell-tale itch in the back of my throat, a heaviness in all my limbs, not just my leg. But I forced myself to start moving again.

Deeper into the woods.

CHAPTER 18

Evie

Artemis had his arms around me, and I didn't care who was watching or what they thought. We sat in a corner of the kitchen on an old sofa, as Molly handed out buttered toast. I wasn't hungry but I accepted the toast anyway and nibbled at the edge. Next to us on the sofa lay Daniel, curled up asleep, his head on my lap. My fingers rested on his cheek, and I drew strength from the even rise and fall of his breathing against my arm.

A knock on the door made us all jump. Me, Molly, Mum, Eloise, Melanie and Artemis, we all looked at each other, not knowing what to do. Was it Sam returning with Tony? Or a hoard of crazed savages? Molly picked up a rifle and walked to the door, peering out into the night beyond. A look of relief flashed on her face, and she opened the door beckoning in Tony. But her expression was quickly replaced by one of concern as she looked beyond us into the dark. "Is Sam with you?"

Tony shook his head. I didn't see him. I couldn't find the path, so I had to come through the bushes. He held up his bleeding hands and there was a long gash on his face. Eloise hugged him. "Oh, I was worried. Evie said you were just behind them, what happened?"

"Where's Hugo?" asked Artemis.

Tony burst into tears. "I wanted... to help him... but there were so many..."

Eloise held him whilst he sobbed. "Shhh. It's okay Tony. It's okay."

Artemis uncurled his arm from around me and stood up so that the space he left felt cool and empty. "What happened?"

When he'd calmed down, Tony was able to tell us about Hugo, and how he was set upon by Manics. The brutality of it was chilling and I was glad Daniel was asleep, unable to hear Tony's description.

"... and then they sh–shot him in the head with a gun."

"Where did they get a gun?" asked Eloise, her eyes wide.

"I don't kn–know."

Melanie brought over a med kit and started cleaning Tony's wound on his face, dabbing at the cut and pouring ointment from a bottle onto the cloth. "Keep still," she said gently. "It will sting a tiny bit. There you go, all done."

Tony sniffed. "Thanks." Then in a small voice, "I thought you hated me,"

Melanie rolled her eyes. "Don't be daft, Tony. Sisters are supposed to be mean. You'll get used to it."

Tony gave another sniff, but her words seemed to calm him down.

Molly paced the room, pausing now and then to look from the kitchen door to the kitchen window.

"Should I go and find Sam?" said Tony. He peered out into the darkness, wearing an expression of equal parts worry and fear.

"No, we're to all stay here," replied Molly, adding more wood to the fire so it blazed high. "It won't do anyone any good if we all wander away in different directions." Even as she spoke, I got the impression that Molly herself was itching to take the rifle and storm out into the night in pursuit of Sam.

"What can I do?" asked Artemis.

"Go check on Layton and Tess," said Molly. "And take up some more wood to the fire. Damn it, what's taking Sam so long?"

We all sat quietly for a few moments. I kept my eyes on the stairs, waiting for Artemis to reappear. I didn't want to be like this – so *needy*, but I felt that every moment I wasn't with him, was a moment wasted. I had no idea how the future might unfold for us, but I couldn't imagine being without Artemis or Daniel. But for that to happen, we needed to get through this night.

Artemis came down the stairs and caught my gaze but didn't return my smile. "The kids are fine. They're sleeping." He seemed agitated and ran his hand over his nose and eyes.

"Are you okay?" I asked as he declined to sit next to me, instead moving to the window by the sink and peering out.

"Yeah. Just uptight, I guess." He turned to Tony who was still sitting at the table, nursing his wounded hand.

Tony gave a small nod.

I was about to ask them about it when Artemis turned to Lois. "Tell us about the infected. Everything you know."

"I hardly think now's the time," I said, "for more horror stories."

"On the contrary," replied my mother. "I can't think of a better time. If there was ever a place my experience had any value at all, it's here. She gave me a hard stare. "Afterall, without Sam here, I'm the only one who knows what's out there." She nodded to the window. "There are things I learned the first time around we may find useful." Then she frowned, and she closed her eyes, her withered hands clutched tightly together. She didn't say anything for a long moment, and I thought she might have forgotten what she was about to say. But when she started to speak, her voice was strong and firm. "Manics crave power. They want you to run. They like it when you're scared. Those security guards at the exchange, the ones who I told you about. They didn't kill us – not straight away. They wanted to play with us, me and the two other women with me. They chased us round the office, laughing and shouting to each other, trying to cut us off as we scrambled, terrified, around islands of computers, office chairs and photocopiers. Every time I thought I could make it to the doors, one of the infected guards, red faced with exertion and excitement, would lunge at me, forcing me to retreat into the maze of office furniture.

"We got separated, me and the other women. Then I looked around and there was only me. The others had been caught in this wretched game of tag. That's what saved me. The infected like to be near each other, something about a hormone they secrete. Like bees or ants. When the other two girls were caught, the ones pursuing me left off and joined the larger group. They forced the women into the middle of the office, surrounded by the men – five, six maybe, closing in on their prey. They grappled them to the ground. I couldn't see clearly as they were behind some desks, but I could see enough. And I could hear the struggling women cry out under the weight of the men. I saw the men reaching greedily for them, clothes ripped and flung around like soft entrails. I stood listening to the grunting and the cheers, and the screams, and bile rose in my throat, hearing those women scream, and cry and beg for mercy that never came.

"Then I ran. Out of the office, down eight flights of stairs clutching onto the plastic rail, terrified each time I turned a corner that I'd run into one of them. But I didn't. Whatever men were left alive in the building, they'd all already gone to the ninth floor, following whatever hormone trail they emit. I tried not to think what those poor women were enduring, women like Jean, with her neat hair and her soft voice, who an hour before had been fielding calls and telling us about her latest holiday.

"I made it out into the breaking dawn, stopping to catch my breath, but only for a second. There was some kind of ornamental tree in a pot, a pair of them flanking the entrance to the office block, and in my peripheral vision the bush looked as if it was moving, shimmering in the early morning light. I stared, unsure of what I was seeing, unable to stop myself from taking a step towards it. The bush was covered in webbing. At first, I thought it was a spider's web, but it was more like grey cotton wool. And under strands something was moving, fighting its way through the mesh. Then it emerged. Brown and large, iridescent, as if its wings had been dipped in petrol, it burst from its soft cage and fluttered out into the summer sky. Then another and another, emerging into the new day, pushing their way into the sunshine.

"Just then, a man, young and rangy in jeans and a hoodie, came running along the street in front of the office. He stopped before me, staring at me with wild, glassy eyes. 'Hello,' he said, almost shyly. But I could see the way his eyes dragged over me. 'Hello,' he said again, a little louder this time.

"I sidled back, knowing beyond any doubt that if I ran, he'd chase me down. He was fit, fast-looking, wearing trainers versus my mules. I didn't like my chances. But he was facing me with an obvious and keen interest, so I readied myself to sprint. Then he turned and saw the bush, with its straggly cotton wool fibres. It was like a starving man at a feast. He rushed over and dipped his hands into the mesh, pulling it off the leaves and rubbing it between his fingers. An expression of pure rapture spread over his face. I didn't stop to see what happened; I ran down the street towards home. But I couldn't get rid of the remnants of that smell, nor the weird look of joy on the young man's face, nor the cries of the women I'd left on the ninth floor."

My mother stopped talking and placed her hands on her face, pushing into her eyes with her palms as if trying to hold back a vision. The room fell to silence.

"I can smell it," blurted out Tony. "The men's smell. It makes us —" He looked at Artemis, who was staring at the floor. "It makes me feel weird, it... it..." Tony was blushing furiously. "Calls to me..."

I looked at Artemis. "Is this true?"

He nodded. "I feel it more when we're near to… to them, the infected. It was strong near where we found Hugo."

"Why didn't you tell me?" An uneasiness crept over me, as I sat on the sofa staring up at Artemis.

He looked at me with big, sad eyes. "I didn't want you to look at me like you're looking at me now – like a freak."

We stared at each other for a moment in silence. The whole room, Molly, Melanie, my mother, looked away. I could feel the pity rising from them towards me as shame snaked its way through my blood. My feelings must have been plastered all over my face, because Artemis turned away from me with a look of undisguised pain on his face. "I'm going to check the windows and doors again," he mumbled, and left the kitchen.

I didn't move, didn't get up and go after him. Instead, it was Tony that rose from the table and followed. "I'll give you a hand," he said as Artemis climbed the stairs.

My mind swam with the implications of this new revelation, and I was grateful that no one spoke for a few minutes as I tried to work out what it all might mean. A man I had feelings for – one I'd slept with – had been keeping secrets from me. What else hadn't he told me? Was the vaccine even working properly? Was he going to turn round and do the horrible things my mother had described? But it wasn't about the secret he'd kept, not really. It was that I could suddenly see him as one of them – that he and Tony, and even little Daniel, were members of a strange tribe, forever different – other.

Eloise sat on the sofa next to me. "The smell is a kind of pheromone, it's present in the cocoons of the moths, but also in the sweat of the infected men. It's how they know… who's one of them and who isn't."

"And is Artemis one of them? If it's affecting him so much, does that mean the vaccine is wearing off?" I felt fear radiate through me at the thought.

"I… I don't think so. I think it's just some residual effects of the toxin. But Artemis is lucid and calm. There's no signs of infection."

Daniel squirmed on my lap. "What's that smell?" he asked as he raised his head, eyes bleary, sleep lines etched onto his little face.

My heart jumped, and I pulled him up into a sitting position. "What smell?" I demanded, trying to keep the fear out of my voice.

"It's like..."

Could he smell it too? Despite Eloise's assessment, my chest felt heavy with panic. I couldn't stand the idea of Daniel, my little Daniel, writhing and snarling and trying to hurt me.

"It's like burning. Smoke?"

I sniffed, and so did Molly, standing by the door.

"He's right," said Molly. "I can smell it too."

There was a crash from upstairs and then yelling.

Molly was running up the stairs, but Artemis and Tony were already coming down, pulling Layton right behind.

"There are men outside. Infected." Tony's voice was loud and urgent. He held Layton's hand, who was staring around with wide eyes. "And they've set fire to the house."

"They're smoking us out!" said Melanie, looking at the fireplace and covering her mouth with the edge of her shirt. "They've blocked the chimney."

Grey smoke had now billowed from the fireplace. It filled the room in moments, making it hard to see. More smoke came rolling down from upstairs, clinging to the ceiling and upper walls like coiling spirits.

"Can we unblock it?" I asked, jumping from the sofa and holding onto Daniel. "Shall we put the fire out?"

"It's too late," Melanie croaked. "It will just increase the smoke. We have to leave."

"Artemis, get Mum. Make for the barn." I tried to shout but couldn't, my throat raw and my eyes stinging. "I'll bring Daniel." It was hard to get even these few words out. The scrape of smoke made me gag. I grabbed a coughing Daniel and hoisted him into my arms before groping my way to the door. As I passed the sideboard, I spied the rifle and grabbed it. "Try not to breathe in, baby," I murmured, as I found the door and began struggling with the lock.

Tony

I'd been looking down from my bedroom window, patting Artemis on the back as he sobbed quietly. "It'll be fine," I said. "The vaccine is working. You're not sick."

"But you feel it, right?" Artemis whispered through his sobs. "When you're near them." He turned to face me, his eyes red and sore looking. "And it's getting worse."

I frowned. It wasn't getting worse for me. If anything, I think the second time I smelled it, when Hugo was attacked, it wasn't as bad. But I didn't say that.

Artemis gazed out of the window. "I can feel it right now. I'm heartbroken at the way Evie looked at me – but also, I feel torn. Like I'm missing out on something – like my place is with them."

"Who?" I asked.

He turned to me, fear bright in his eyes. "The infected."

I didn't like the sound of this – I hadn't felt the same at all. A tingling in my limbs, perhaps, a kind of mild sadness – but not this. I looked down at Layton, asleep in his bed by the window, and I suddenly felt afraid.

A shout outside the window made us both peer out. There, in the dim light of the farmhouse courtyard, was a crowd of at least twelve men staring back up at us. One of them, the tallest one there, held a gun in his hand, pointing it straight at our window. The men below didn't do or say anything but then a noise sounded above us, coming from the roof. *Thump, thump, thump.*

"There's someone up there," whispered Artemis.

"Why would they be crawling around the roof?"

Artemis coughed. The room was filling with smoke from the fireplace, long trails of it curling into the room and rising. Layton woke as I grabbed him from his bed. He squirmed in panic. "What's happening, Tony?"

I moved towards the door, dragging Layton behind me, but Artemis just stood there staring at the men outside, a strange far-away look on his face.

"We need to go," I snapped. "Something's happening to the fire." I pointed at the fireplace, now spewing dark smoke, hoping the panic in my voice might jolt Artemis from whatever stupor had overtaken him. "Come on."

I couldn't wait any longer and dragged Layton out onto the landing and down the stairs. It wasn't until I was halfway down that I realised with relief that Artemis was behind me.

Molly pushed past us on the way to the landing upstairs.

Layton turned as she went. "Tess," he gasped. "We need to get Tess."

I ignored his cries, leading him downstairs and to the door. I needed to get Layton out and safe. "Molly will bring Tess." I whispered.

Evie was struggling with the door, trying to hold Daniel in one arm and pull the heavy lock with the other.

I stopped her. "We need to go out the back door. The men are out there."

Her eyes were red, sore and streaming. Daniel and Layton were both coughing and gasping, and it was impossible to see any further than a few meters. Upstairs, Molly was crying out for Tess.

The four of us, Evie, Daniel, Layton and me, groped our way out of the room and down the hallway to the back door. I unbolted the door and opened it a crack. Two men. Just two. They stared right at me and smiled that horrible wide moist grin that all the infected seem to share. I froze. I couldn't fight them. I didn't know how.

Evie spoke in a low, urgent tone. "When I say so, take Layton and Daniel and run to the barn and hide the best you can." She opened the door a little further and raised the rifle. "RUN!"

I grabbed Daniel's and Layton's hands and pulled them over the muddy driveway between us and the barn. Behind, I could hear two loud bangs which seemed to echo off the very sky itself. Then the slapping of someone's feet on the mud. I turned, readying myself to protect the boys if it was a Manic following, but it was Evie, her eyes wide and her face pale. We reached the barn panting and wheezing and I ushered the boys to the back. Layton crouched down behind a pile of sacks and Daniel cowered next to him.

Evie's hands shook, and she clicked open the rifle "Empty," she said. Then she snapped it closed.

"Are the Manics dead?" I whispered, so the boys couldn't hear.

She nodded. "I think so. Yes – I shot them and they…" She took in a shuddering breath.

Then someone else entered the barn, the silhouette of a man with someone in his arms. Evie raised the unloaded rifle and pointed it at the figure. I spied a shovel leaning against the rough wall, but before I could grab it, Artemis's voice sounded rough in the darkness. "I'm sorry, Evie. Your mum told me to."

I couldn't work out what he was talking about. Then Evie put the rifle down and went over to him.

"What? I told you to get Mum –"

The small figure in Artemis's arms coughed.

Artemis lowered the figure to a bed of straw. Layton bounded over and kissed her. "Tess! Oh, Tess."

The little girl sat up and wiped her mouth. "Where's Molly? Where's Sam?"

Evie made for the door. "Mum's still in the farmhouse."

Artemis looked distraught. "I'll go back, I'll get her. You stay here."

He turned to go but Evie grabbed his arm. They stood there

for a moment looking at each other. "I don't want anything to happen to you," whispered Evie.

Artemis looked to the house, smoke streaming out of the door, and then back to Evie. "I'll only be a minute. We can't leave Lois."

He darted out – away from Evie and out the door of the barn. Evie tried to keep hold of him, but he shook her off. "Artemis!"

I stared after him from just inside the door. The area outside the barn was no longer clear. The noise must have alerted the other Manics. A group of six men were now standing between us and the farmhouse, staring down at the two shot men on the ground. If Artemis could keep to the shadows, the Manics might not notice him. He was only a little way from the farmhouse when, round the corner of the house, came the tallest Manic; the one with the gun. He held it up and pointed it straight at Artemis.

"Hello," he said. Then shot him in the head.

CHAPTER 19

Evie

I nearly cried out. It was only the thought of Daniel and Layton, the need to protect them, that made me swallow down my shock. Artemis crumpled to the ground as the other men cheered and ran to his lifeless body, kicking at it and examining the wound. I felt my stomach lurch and my mind go blank, refusing to consider what I'd just seen. Someone wrapped their arms around me and stopped me from falling.

"They shot him," I managed to choke out.

Tony gripped me. I could feel him shaking.

"What happened?" whispered Daniel from behind me. "Who did they shoot?"

Tony and I looked at each other for a moment, a brief and silent agreement passing between us.

"No one," Tony whispered, and ushered Daniel back into the barn. "Tess" – he looked down at the little girl – "I know you're very good at playing hiding-seek."

Tess shrugged and looked towards the door. "Where's Molly? And my sisters?"

Tony shot me a quick glance.

"They're coming soon," I said. "But until they get here you need to find a really good hiding place. Somewhere no one will find you."

Tess thought for a moment. "Snow's stall." She looked back over her shoulder. "There's a big cupboard below the window, where we put old tack. I go there when I want to be alone."

"Good," said Tony, "show me."

He shepherded Tess and the two boys to the back of the barn. I stayed by the door and watched the yard. I tried not to think about the lifeless figure on the ground, now abandoned by the Manics, who were clowning around, pushing each other and laughing. One tried to get the gun from the one who shot Artemis, but he held it up over his head, laughing as the other fought to reach it.

"Give it to me, Kyle. I just want to look at it."

"Then take it from me." Suddenly, as if sensing he was being watched, Kyle stopped teasing the other man and looked straight at the barn. The rifle I'd used to shoot the two men earlier was empty and lay discarded on the muddy floor. I didn't bring any bullets, and if I had I wouldn't know how to load them. I looked around for any kind of weapon as Kyle took a few steps towards the barn.

I found an old shovel leaning against a wall and picked it up. "Tony!" I hissed towards the back of the barn. But there was no reply.

Then Kyle stopped and turned to face the house. Three more Manics rounded the corner in a kind of procession. To my horror they each held a woman. Molly was covered in mud, her dress torn and a long bloody gash on her arm. Eloise, her left eye swollen and purple, was being led by a rope around her neck, her hands tied behind her back. And finally, two men were trying to drag Melanie, who was fighting like a cornered rat, and raining down blows on the Manics, screaming at them to let her family go. More Manics appeared, and the crowd around the women swelled to at least fifteen.

Kyle grinned and clapped at the women's arrival. "This will be fun!" The other Manics, all dressed in grey gowns and sandals, gathered round in a half circle looking like an overexcited choir. Some of their silk tunics were stained red.

Molly sobbed. "Please. Let them go. They're just children."

Which only made Kyle laugh. "They're women. And that means they're made for us." He grabbed Eloise by the hair and dragged her onto the ground.

I looked over my shoulder into the barn and Tony stood watching all this, his eyes wide and his mouth open.

I clutched the shovel. "We need to do something," I whispered. "They're going to hurt them, kill them, if we don't..."

But Tony had already turned around and was heading deeper into the barn. He opened the window to the barn and swung his leg over the sill.

"Tony! You can't run away. We need you."

He gave me one last look, filled with fear and sadness, then shifted out of the window and disappeared into the darkness. I heard a soft humpf as he landed on the grass outside. Then nothing.

"Where did he go?" Layton's head was sticking out of the cupboard above.

"You need to get back in, Layton. Hide, remember?"

The little boy nodded and closed the cupboard door.

Where did he go?

I returned to the barn door and peered out, just as the leader of the Manics gave Eloise a sharp kick to the leg causing her to collapse to her knees. "Who wants to play with this one?"

All the Manics laughed.

Tony

Alone, cold, blind. Three feelings I'd never experienced whilst in the comfort of the facility. But now all three accompanied me on my journey through the woods. I knew I was heading in the right direction, downhill with the back of the farmhouse receding behind me. But as soon as I entered the trees, my sense of direction became blurred. The thing is, you don't need a sense of direction when you've lived all your life in a cage.

Although cages have their upsides. If I was still in a cage, I wouldn't have had to watch someone kill Artemis. I wouldn't have seen Eloise cower at the hands of an infected man, or Molly beg for the lives of her daughters. Even Melanie. As the men pulled her forward, I wanted to grab their stinking hands and tear them from her. Sisters – apparently, you want to risk your life for them, even though they're mean to you *most of the time*.

Risk my life – was I really going to do this? Artemis's words near the graveyard on our first day came back to me, as yet another branch flicked me in the eye. *We could just keep going...* But even as I thought it, I knew I couldn't. Layton, Tess, these were my family.

I'd been out here too long. I'd missed it, surely? But then in front of me and to the left, nestled like a toad in the shadows, there it was. I had to be quick. In, out. Get back to the farmhouse – hope that they hadn't killed anyone... *anyone else.*

I expected the door to be locked, so I moved to the window, readying myself to break the dusty glass. But there was no glass to break.

Someone had already smashed it, even going so far as to clear the shards from the frame. Who? A Manic? Someone looking for the serum? I tried to see into the room, but it was too dark. The bad feeling in my stomach doubled. I took a deep sniff. The Manics' scent was there but faintly. It could just be the caged moths. I stood listening for a sign, a clue, but heard nothing except the rustling of wings in plastic cages. *Hurry, the others are counting on you!* With a deep breath, I launched myself through the broken window, banging into a shelf the other side and tumbling to the floor.

I pulled myself to my feet using the large table and felt my way around the room. My fingers hovered over a selection of alien objects, test tubes, circular plastic dishes, half-filled jars, before finally resting on what I was searching for. *Success!* I grabbed what I needed and thrust them into my pockets. This would work. I was going to be a hero, like in Mary's stories.

"Stay where you are."

I leapt around to face the corner, the direction from where the voice had come. A shadow sat slumped on a wooden chair, her leg supported on a small stool.

She raised a rifle and pointed it at me. "What did you just put in your pocket, Tony?"

Evie

Molly was on her knees sobbing, her hair in her face. Kyle had shifted his attention from Eloise to Melanie, pulling up her shirt to expose her breasts and laughing as she tried to hold it down.

"Stop it," begged Molly. "Just let her go!"

Melanie was crouched down on the ground dressed in nothing but her underwear now, having been forcibly stripped by Kyle to the cheers of the others. She wasn't crying. Her mouth clenched in a bitter line and her eyes were hard with rage. "Fuck off!" she snarled as Kyle ran his hand over her back as if he was petting an animal. His hand paused before he hit her on the side of the head, making her fall flat on the ground. Then he jumped on her and began bunching up his robe. "I'm going to give you a free hetero-recreational visit. Aren't you the lucky one?"

Every instinct in me was to help her, but I'd risk alerting the Manics to the position of the hiding children. I could only watch as Kyle dug his fingers into the elastic of Melanie's underwear, using his other hand to keep the struggling girl still.

To one side lay Artemis, unmoving. The back of his head

was a mess of darkness and blood, but his face was as strong and pale as ever, his jaw pressed on the ground and his arm reaching forward as if trying to crawl towards the Manics. But there was no last-minute rescue for him. His eyes, forever open, stared blindly as the horror unfolded. Empty. Gone.

A blast rang out, and I thought for one horrifying moment that Kyle had shot Melanie. But the leader of the Manics stopped his assault and looked down at his left shoulder. Blood. He looked around; fury etched onto his face. Another shot, this one taking out the Manic to the left of Kyle, the young man's chest gaping through ragged grey silk as he fell to his knees. Then heavy footsteps in the dark, before Sam launched at Kyle. Confusion and chaos spread over the Manics. Some raced over to watch the fight, jeering and screaming as each punch found its mark. A few Manics scrambled for the gun that Kyle had dropped as Sam attacked. Melanie was on her feet in moments and helping her mother free her bonds as Eloise dragged the rope from around her neck.

I opened the door of the barn and frantically waved them in. All three ran to the barn, but Molly stopped in the doorway. "Sam," she cried.

Staring back and leaning over the prone form of Sam, was Kyle, bloodied and bruised.

He was staring right at us.

Tony

Anita. The woman sitting in the corner was pale and unhealthy-looking. What little light there was in the room reflected from the dark red patch on her trouser leg. The barrel of Eloise's gun bobbed in the air as if she was struggling to hold it still. "Sit down, Tony."

"I… I have to go." I shuffled towards the window, but she made an ominous locking sound with the gun.

"They taught us about lots of weapons at the compound after the infestation. This is an old hunting rifle. Heavy, only two rounds, but powerful. It will tear you apart before you move another inch."

I stopped and held up my hands. "I really need to go, Anita. Please."

"What did you put in your pocket?"

I didn't want to say anything. But she was a woman, and a lifetime of conditioning is hard to shake. "Drift, the liquid Eloise makes."

Her eyes narrowed and she looked around the room. "This place is a drug lab?" A bitterness edged her voice.

I nodded and looked at the floor.

"What do you want it for, the drift?"

I considered lying but couldn't think of anything believable. "I want to stop the Manics. I want to save my family." The words came out in a desperate whisper. Every moment I stood here, the Manics could be hurting, killing someone back at the farm.

Anita gave a small cold laugh. "Family," she spat out. "They only took you in, Tony, for the tokens. You should have seen their application. Extra rations, more education funding, arable land, whatever this is." She gestured to the lab. "When the government chuck you and Layton back inside the facilities, those women won't give you a second thought."

"I don't care," I said, trying not to let her words hurt me. "I care about them. That's what matters."

Anita shifted on her chair and a flash of pain crossed her face. The gun wavered in her hand. "I can't let you go, Tony. I don't know what you're planning to do, but tonight needs to play out."

I raised my gaze to hers for the first time. "Why?"

She shook her head as if very tired. "It's not you, Tony. If all the men were like you then we might have a chance. But there will always be men who will want to control us, rape us, kill us. She sighed. "I don't want that world, Tony. You wouldn't understand."

I didn't agree. Artemis was controlling and angry in the beginning, but he changed, and he never wanted to rape or kill anyone. Men didn't have to be the monsters she described. And if we worked together, we could stop it. But she was not going to listen, and I was running out of time. "Tess, Daniel, Layton." They're all at the farmhouse – surrounded by Manics. If I don't get back, they'll be slaughtered.

Anita looked away. "There are always casualties, Tony."

"But children!"

She didn't answer.

"I'm going," I said, my voice sounding far braver than I felt.

"Don't, Tony."

I took another step towards the window.

"This is your final warning." She raised the gun to her eye.

I took another step, forcing my heavy legs to move.

Her finger made a clicking noise on the gun.

Get down, Tony! Was it my voice in my mind, or Mary's? I ducked behind the table just as the gun went off. Above me something on the table shattered, something plastic. A fluttering filled the room like an angry cloud. Anita cried out in the dark, as I flung myself out of the broken window and ran into the woods.

Evie

I slammed the door to the barn but there was no lock. A moment later the door burst inwards, and Kyle stood in the doorway, surrounded by Manics. I still held the shovel, Molly had found a rake, Eloise and Melanie clutched old pieces of wood. We backed off towards Snow's stall, ready to protect the children.

Molly and I exchanged glances. She gave me a grim nod.

This was it.

The first Manic came at Molly and she swung the rake, tearing into the flesh just below his jaw. Another man cried out as Eloise smashed the wood into his temple. Kyle ran at me, grinning. I aimed low, sweeping the sharp end of the shovel across his bare ankles with all my strength. He went down and I felt a spike of intense joy as his expression changed from one of glee to one of pain. Then he kicked me hard in the leg and I felt it give way under me, toppling me to the ground and knocking the air from my lungs. I could see that four men now surrounded Melanie and Eloise, one snatched the wood from Melanie's hands and grabbed the young girl's hair. Eloise smashed the wood into the stomach of the Manic holding her sister. Molly was fighting off three men, still holding her rake but her left eye was bloody and swollen and she was heaving with the effort of fighting on three sides.

"Evie!" It was Daniel's voice, crying out from somewhere behind me. "They've found us, Evie."

I tried to get up, but Kyle knelt on my back. "Bring the children here".

"No!" I squirmed, trying to get up, but fixed to the spot.

One of the children screamed, Tess, I think. "Get off me!"

I tried again to get up, digging my nails into Kyle's wounded ankle, but he wouldn't budge. A swift blow to the side of my temple made me fall to the ground.

Another Manic came into the barn, this one with his face and head wrapped in a sweater. He marched to the centre of the barn and fumbled in his pocket, drawing out some small bottles before ripping off the tops and dousing any manic who was within a short radius of him. Including Kyle. A strong astringent smell filled the barn, so strong that it made my eyes water and my head swim. My limbs felt heavy and filled with a molten warmth, a soft ache seized my muscles. I fought the numbing bliss, crawling, trying to ready myself for the next attack from Kyle. But it didn't arrive. *Daniel... where was Daniel...?*

Tony

Lie at my mercy all mine enemies!

It was a good quote. Mary would have been proud. But, because my face was covered by a sweater, no one heard it. If I was about to die or go mad, at least my last words should be good.

Nothing happened for a few seconds as the liquid soaked into the tall Manic's grey robe. He looked down at me with a puzzled expression but didn't move. I wondered if the serum was working. What if I'd picked up the wrong bottles? But then I felt it, a heaviness in my limbs and a warmth snaking through my mind. I tried to hold my breath as I fell to the ground. There was pain somewhere – my chest, maybe? But it didn't matter. I was dimly aware of what was going on around me. A strange quiet, so different from the chaos of a moment ago. Only heavy breathing. Then the coughing started. All around me, Manics, bent double, hacking and spluttering. One grabbed me, the tall leader. *"Make it stop!"* he wheezed, his eyes wide and rimmed in red. But then he released me, rolling onto his back, pinkish froth dribbling from his mouth. Would this happen to me? I didn't care. The Manics were dying. I could just sleep here and never wake up. I'd done what I had to do.

Layton, Daniel and Tess were over by Snow's stall. "Layton... *Run!"* I managed to choke out. But it cost me. I had to breathe in deep to shout and another wave of pain coursed through my chest. I was done, then. My story had reached its end.

You can't stay here.

I thought for a moment it was Mary's voice.

We have to go.

"Shhh, Mary. It's time to sleep now."

Someone grabbed my arm and pulled me to my feet. "Tony, come on." It wasn't Mary, it was Eloise. She had her sleeve over her mouth, making it hard to understand what she was saying. "You need to take off the shirt. Quickly. It's covered in Drift."

Her face was coming in and out of focus as she ripped off my shirt. "I want to rest."

"Stand," she ordered.

"I can't," I replied, but realised she probably couldn't hear me over the sweater. I tried to take it off.

"No! keep it on."

I swayed on my feet. My legs were going numb.

"Melanie! Help!"

Two set of arms supported me as I was dragged out into the cool night air.

I looked up into the sky, tinged with dawn.

Moths – just a small swarm, dancing through the trees.

EPILOGUE

Evie

I visit Daniel in the prep house every Thursday. He waits for me in a small room by the entrance. A carer stays with us and eyes me warily as we sit in silence. Daniel's initial shyness has returned.

I miss his grin.

I wanted Daniel to be allowed out to come to my mother's funeral, but the prep house manager said no. We can't spare the staff to accompany him, was her reply. I tried to point out that I'd be fine to accompany him, that I'd been doing it for weeks. But she wouldn't budge. She gave me a dismissive look and I know what it meant. She was saying that I didn't look after him, that he was in danger from the very first moment he was under my care.

"How's Layton?" I ask. Molly had wanted me to find out for her. Molly's whole family was under investigation for drug offenses. Apparently when they picked up the XX agent, Anita Swift, they discovered a Drift lab. Eloise lost her coveted place at Winchester. Molly and Sam have been stripped of their extra land and may not be able to stay at the farm.

The little boy looks at the uniformed carer sitting in the corner. The young woman gives an almost imperceptible shake of the head and Daniel shrugs and remains silent.

At first, I thought when the furore had died down and the truth had been picked out of mess of that awful night, Daniel would be returned to me. But when details of the murders came to light the next day, public resentment grew, and grew fast. Not just Freya Curtis's murder, those who'd crossed paths with the infected that night. Eleven murders in total – two children and nine adults, including my mother. The court case was upcoming, but it was being held in a closed court, unavailable to the public. This was stoking the flames of conspiracy theories and accusations – that the Council hadn't thought the programme through in the first place, that the LA hadn't acted fast enough, that there were members of the XX in the government. Misconceptions, rumours, and wild assertions abounded. The state radio tried to calm things down, offering detailed information of the safety of the programme and highlighting the treasonous actions of the XXs, especially Anita Swift, but the people were rattled. The Union felt it was losing control.

So, all men returned to facilities. Daniel remains in the sterile confines of the prep house, His vaccine will have worn off by now. And I sit here in this small uncomfortable chair in this bleakly claustrophobic room, with the smell of disinfectant making me nauseous, whilst a boy whom I think of as my son stares at me in silence.

"I brought you some honey-cake," I say, rummaging in my bag – a bag that has already been searched on my way in. Again, he looks at the carer but this time she nods.

He opens the wax-paper wrapping slowly and carefully, so different from the way he'd fall in his food in the kitchen back home. He picks at the edges of the cake and places a few crumbs in his mouth. There's no joy in it. I suddenly find it so painful to be here, to watch his pale little face munch on cake as he tries to avoid my gaze. I should go. I shouldn't put him through this. But then, what's waiting for me at home? Don't get me wrong. I'm relieved Mae's gone. She collected her stuff a few days after Daniel was taken away and returned to the Citadel. I was at work. There was no note, no last words, just a large space in the wardrobe and a few gaps around the house – the radio, her papers, the reading glasses she left on the coffee table. She left the keys on the kitchen table, next to the half-assembled toaster.

I haven't cleared out Mum's room yet. I'm so tired all of the time. Molly offered to help. She's been my rock, making sure I'm eating, keeping my mind off... everything. I go over to the farm most nights and talk, drink tea. Without her I don't know what I'd have done. I don't go near the barn, though. I can't even look in that direction when I pass by on the way to the house.

Daniel looks at the door, only a furtive glance, but it's all I need to know. He wants to be as far away from this room and from me as possible. Cake or no cake.

It was me who had to tell him about Artemis. Not the details, of course. Not how the bullet penetrated Artemis's skull and cut through his frontal lobe before exiting via his occipital lobe whilst smashing his cerebellum to pieces. How he was dead in moments. As a nurse, I find the swiftness of the death comforting. But I had to deliver the news – Artemis was not coming to see him. The deaths of the men that night – sixty-eight in all, including the Blues in the heap behind the Curtis house – were not reported. And over thirty infected Manics were rounded up later the next day. It was only because I had an old nursing-school friend who worked for the LA that I got the info.

"I have to go," I say, picking up my bag and standing.

The carer nods. "Daniel, we need to get you scrubbed down before you can be with the other boys, in case of threads. Finish your cake."

He sighs and stuffs the cake down. For a moment, with his mouth crammed with food, he reminds me of what he was like before and I smile. He doesn't smile. He turns to the door. But then he turns back. "I miss Artemis," he says, and the words feel like a sharp kick.

"Me too," I say and for a moment, just a moment, my hand lingers over my belly, before I force it away. I shoot a quick look at the carer but to my relief, she's not looking at me.

"I'll see you in a week, baby."

Daniel pauses and I wonder if he is going to ask me not to come. He takes a deep, sad breath. "Okay, next week." The carer leads him away.

I rise from the seat and choke down another wave of nausea. As I leave the prep house, out into a bitter January morning, I touch my still flat stomach once more and think the same thing I've thought every day for the past month.

Please, please be a girl.

Tony

I'm a hero!

That's what the LA officer who picked us up on the road outside the farmhouse said. Apparently, anyway. I was unconscious by that time. I have no recollection of being brought here to the hospital. I woke up after three days in a coma, unable to move my legs.

When I woke up, Sam was in the bed next to me. He leaned over, with a bandaged face and his arm in plaster. It was difficult to make out his words, muffled as they were by cotton wool and dressings, but they sounded something like, "Ye did good lad."

I beamed.

It took another week before I regained feeling in my legs. The doctors were very pleased with me. They say I should get feeling back within a few weeks, although because most of their experience is with women's physiology, they can't be sure of anything. Molly, Eloise, and Melanie have visited me three times. The last time, Molly brought me a basket of apple muffins which I fell upon. My appetite has fully returned and the food here is not that great. Melanie laughed at my enthusiasm, poking me in the stomach and telling me I was getting fat. Then she laughed again when I put my half-eaten second muffin back in the basket. I know that this is Melanie's way of showing affection, and I'm working on being grateful. Apparently, she and Eloise carried me half a mile before the LA finally found us.

When Molly and Melanie were with Sam, I asked Eloise about Layton and the prep house.

"He's not doing well. He misses Tess and the farm."

"And the Council won't change their mind about the vaccination programme?" As soon as my legs got better, they were planning to send me back to the facility.

She shook her head. "Big mistake in the first place, they say. Needed more safeguards."

Things on the outside had been so difficult, so confusing, but I knew that after a few weeks at the facility I'd be standing at the viewing room window, pressing my nose to the glass, desperate to be able to smell the cold hard ground and feel the wind on my face. And it killed me that somewhere out there Logan was having the vaccine held over him by Sophia, unable to make his own choices. It was all too unfair.

"Eloise?" I lowered my voice.

"Yes, Tony?"

"The moths in the cabin, the ones that escaped when Anita shot the glass, will they do what we talked about? Will they make baby moths that aren't toxic?"

Eloise shot a glance at Sam and the others, who were deep in conversation, then looked around the ward to see if anyone was nearby before lowering her voice. "You can't tell anyone about that, Tony. If the Council find out I'll be in so much trouble, more than I'm in now."

"Yes but, they might though, right? The moths?"

Eloise leaned in close, so close that I could smell the farm on her clothes, the grass and the earthy vegetables. "A lot of my research was just theory. Their offspring would have to survive the winter. And then" – she checked again to see if anyone could overhear – "then there's the risk of adaptations, dangerous side effects... unforeseen mutations. If I've made even a small miscalculation, and those caterpillars survive to the eclipse and breed, the toxin of that new generation could have whole new set of properties, and the ramifications could be –"

"But there's a chance?"

There was a complicated look in her eyes, part pity, part fear. Her voice was almost inaudible. "Yes, Tony. There's a chance."

I took her hand in mine and squeezed it. "Thanks."

All I needed was the hope that one day, Layton could go back to the farm. That I would get out of the facility, that I could find Logan and rescue him from whatever dungeon Sophia was holding him prisoner.

That together we could build a new world, one where men like us are safe.

Anita

For the last seven months, I've shared a room with six women. None are from the XXs. They wouldn't put us in the same room. I am officially a terrorist.

Pearl left me. She sent a letter at the beginning explaining that she understood I was under a lot of strain because of Bella's suicide, but she couldn't excuse the things I'd been accused of. At first, she didn't believe them, but then she was shown evidence, testimony by Evelyn Levi and Molly Coombs.

The LA found me unconscious in the hut in the woods and later pieced together what happened from the accounts of others. The vaccination programme was suspended. The men and boys were all sent back to the facilities and preps. My mission was a success and I'm glad of it, whatever happens to me. There's a generation of women out there who owe their safety and peace of mind to me. There's been a suggestion of banishment, that I be sent over to mainland Europe, to face starvation, lawlessness, and disease. All this after a trial, of course. The Council have to be seen to be doing the correct thing.

The Council said that if I told them about the organisation, radio XX, people I worked with, the ones funding the operation, that I could get my sentence reduced. Ten years in a re-education camp. I've resisted. Mostly because I don't know the answers to the questions. But the little information I knew, I kept to myself. Why?

I believe XX02 will come for me. The organisation has deep pockets, and it looks after its own. That's what XX02 said. Every day I look out for a sign, a note or a message, something to tell me it's time. I listen to the news on the radio, when they let me, searching for something that proves they are still active. I've heard nothing yet. Tonight, it was all about an invasive new moth species that has scientists all hot and bothered.

But I wait. I keep my faith. They will come for me.

For I was the woman who saved their world.

ACKNOWLEDGMENTS

When I sent my self-published book, *Moths*, out into the wild in 2021, I had no idea that my weird venture into post-apocalyptic dystopian fiction would find such a happy home. Since then, I've sold more copies than I ever dreamed, had many lovely and supportive comments on Amazon and Goodreads, and received many emails of encouragement via, Twitter, Instagram, Facebook and my website.

To all those readers who expressed a desire to read the sequel by preordering *Toxxic* after its initial release – I apologise. I promised you *Toxxic* in August 2021, when I was still a self-published author. The pre-orders on Amazon were substantial, and I was excited to release *Toxxic* and share the next chapter with everyone. However, my career took a turn. I found a wonderful agent who then signed me up with an awesome publisher. Great for me! Not so much for those hoping to read *Toxxic* in the summer of 2021. The editing and proofing process has been much more diligent, marketing campaigns have been formulated and scheduled, cover and marketing artwork have been perused by a committee of people who, unlike me, know a thing or two about such things.

I think it's safe to say that this book is a vast improvement to the one that I was due to publish two years ago, and so, if you were one of those early adopters, I hope you can forgive the wait and thank you so much for your patience and support.

A big thank you to the writing crew, Flo, Emma, Hannah

and Kari for your constant support and Emily and Celina for beta reading and offering me a steer in the early stages.

To my boys, Alex and Jude, thank you for quietly fending for yourselves when the "mum's writing" sign is sellotaped to the snug door. And to my husband, James, whose ongoing support for my storytelling is both steadfast and unnervingly enthusiastic.

Also, a huge thanks to the Angry Robot editorial team, Eleanor and Gemma for nudging, corralling, finessing and occasionally kicking the story into shape – you are superstars. And the marketing team, Caroline, Amy and Des – thank you for creating a whirlwind of excitement. You guys are the best.

Finally, a massive thank you to Liza and Kiya for their tireless agenting on my behalf. Liza was one of the first to read Toxxic and we worked on it together. Without her initial input, I don't know if I would have mustered the confidence to send this baby out into the world.

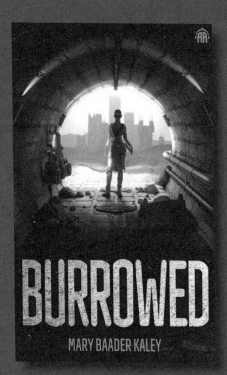

CHAPTER 1
Horrific Thing to Say

Ghosts roam the shadows of our Sublery's walls. Or, at least, that's what some of the younger sublings claim. I don't normally see them – the withering souls reaching from the shadows – but today I do. My mind tells me they're not real, but the icy tendrils of fear reaching through me scream otherwise.

My nurserymaid snaps my travel skirt in the air, sending enormous shadows cascading down the slate walls of the underground room. Even the ceiling lights flicker as if to complain from the sudden breeze as I shiver in my underslip. *They're not real, they're not real,* I chant silently to myself, even as these shadowy ghosts and flames reach for me one last time to claim me as their own before I can leave this place. As nursery lore tells it, they're the spirits of deceased children wailing in the crematorium, screaming for the lives they don't get to live, and cursing the rest of us who remained healthy enough not to die. We believe they want to steal life from the surviving children, not realizing that once a life is separated from a soul it cannot be used by anyone else. Robbing a life only creates another dead child, and the cycle starts again, much like the plague that sent sublings underground in the first place.

"Stop your whining," Na'rm Anetta says as she snaps the skirt again.

I flinch, but neither she nor the ghosts can spook me much longer. I'm leaving today, I remind myself over and over. I take my deepest breath.

"May I wear a cap?" I try to smooth my wispy hair, but

my goggle straps get in the way, and it sticks out in confused directions.

A scowl grows on my nurserymaid's face. "Hats are only for boys, and only because they have no hair," she says to the beat of her up-and-down skirt snapping, and then holds it out for me to step into. She'd taken the hem up and adjusted the waist so that it falls exactly at midcalf-length.

Across the room, another nurserymaid sings a melody while brushing her subling's long, white hair. I begin to hum with her but she's singing at a slower pace, and the usually comforting song now has a hymn-like lilt to it. The subling girl wipes tears from her cheeks, her voice crackling as she tries to sing along for the last time. I'm sad for her, but she'll be okay at the burrows. She's a good size, has never been to the infirmary for longer than a week, and she doesn't wear goggles.

"Pay attention." Na'rm Anetta holds out a starched blouse. Her gaze bounces across the room and back to me. "I don't suppose we'll miss each other as they will."

I straighten my body like she's taught me – as if a giant Omnit is pulling me up by the roots of my hair. "I will always be grateful to you for your dedication in raising me to my seventh year," I say perfunctorily, as I hand her my good-bye gift. The traditional hand-painted bead will be her first ever memento, so I used the finest brush to paint a design that the artmaid *oooh*ed over – she said it reminded her of a mist of water frozen in the air.

My na'rm isn't moved by my masterpiece, though, and drops the bead onto the wheeled dressing cart. It falls with a tinny clank next to the brush that we don't need.

On the other side of the room, my roommate's na'rm kisses the simply striped bead she's been given and strings it onto her necklace – which now has two beads – before replacing it around her neck. The two of them weep, embracing as if they could never be separated by something as slight as Sublery Graduation.

I tilt my head at my na'rm and blink really hard, testing if tears will sprout from my eyes. I'm too excited, though; glad we're leaving a month early. After Common Good sent word that they're clearing all subs from this region, it forced my graduating class to pack for the burrows that much sooner. I was the only one who clapped when the Grand Na'rm announced the news.

"Maybe we'll miss each other in smaller ways," I say to my na'rm, trying to be as grateful as a non-wicked subling should be. But that's the difference between us – she's allowed to tell when I misbehave, but I cannot help her see her own temper. "You're a wonderful seamstress," I add.

Na'rm Anetta's eyes sour, as if everything about me has grown blurry. It's the face she makes most when she looks at me – like she's pretending I'm not really there, like I'm a child-ghost on the wall. She bumps into the dressing cart, and the bead begins to roll. I point as it nears the edge, but then it slows to a stop.

"Don't stare at me like that, subling!" She smacks my hand and sighs. "I never did connect with you. *Give it a few months*, they said. *How can I raise her if I can't see her eyes?* I implored. Somebody had to, though, and I was that unfortunate somebody." She hands me the satchel packed with my book. "Hear me this one last time, girl. Do not allow your temper to slither out of that wicked mouth of yours."

I swallow the redhot words at the tip of my tongue because *unpleasant sentiment isn't to be tolerated*. My thick goggles hide my rage. Besides, I've only pointed out her blunders to help her do better with her next subling, not for the purpose of being wicked. Not the sole purpose, anyway.

"Your medera will not allow you the same cheekiness I have endured all these years. My full report includes pointers on how to manage you."

My face prickles as if she slapped me. "Report?" Sublery Graduation is my chance to start fresh. "You didn't say I'm cheeky–"

"I've relayed the pertinent facts." She steps back to inspect me. "It's up to Medera Gelia Cayan to gauge the degree of your wickedness."

"No." I rub the sweat from my palms into my new skirt. "Fix it, please. Or at the least tell her I'm a model learner, and I coach the younger sublings to read."

"Your medera already has the report, not that I would revise one word." She steps back as if she's completely done with me. Her hand moves in a half-flutter-half-wave as she spins the wheeled table around to walk off. "Good health, girl." Her pleated skirt rustles about in awkward swishes as if it's fighting to free itself from her.

"I do *not* wish you good health!" I call back, tightening my fists. "*You* are wicked."

The other maid gasps, covering her subling's ears.

Na'rm Anetta flies around and stands above me in an instant, yanking my satchel. "Give me the book."

"No!" It's the memento I chose, the one thing that I'm allowed to bring with me – she can't take it back. "I will report you to Common Good." I have no idea if my threat carries any weight, but if our government is serious about their pledge for the good of common people like me, then they might be interested to hear about Na'rm Anetta.

Her face twists as I struggle, but she manages to strong-arm the bag away.

I jump for it as she slaps my hands again.

She rips the book out of the bag and throws the empty satchel at my feet. "This belongs to the Sublery." Her voice turns growly. "You were supposed to choose something of *mine* to take with you, you impudent, shameful child!"

"Anetta!" The other na'rm calls.

Na'rm Anetta's head snaps to her fellow maid, and then she straightens her back. She tosses my book to the floor: *The Chronicles of Narnia*. "Take it then," she growls. "We'll probably leave the paged books behind when the Sublery transfers to its new location, anyway. And they've all but promised me that my new subling will be normal, thank all that is good." She fixes the cuffs of her blouse and scuttles off.

I slump onto the floor even though my skirt will wrinkle, which will reflect poorly on Na'rm Anetta. But now I want it to wrinkle, so I crumple chunks of my skirt into my fists. I press lightly at first, but nothing happens. So, I squeeze my fists as hard as I can, grinning at the star-shaped creases I make. Something small and hard pokes into my thigh against the cold tile. Sweeping my hand under my leg, I pull out the bead – the one my na'rm should have strung onto her necklace. Something she should have worn to her dying breath, disdained and discarded.

"Come, child," the other nurserymaid stops near me, her subling's arms wrapped around her waist. "Walk with us to the transport tunnel."

"She hated me," I say as I hold up my bead. Perhaps she even wished me dead. My ears begin to ring as the lights flicker around me; the children of the shadows laugh at me from the walls. Their ghostly voices cackle all about me, and I want to flee. The shadows shift around with the flickering, and I'm sure the dead children begin reaching out with their ashy arms to steal my life.

I cover my head and scream.

"Okay, child! It's okay!"

I hiccup to a stop as the ringing ceases. It's the other nurserymaid who has picked me up, not a charred phantom. She holds me tight. Perhaps she got to me just in time.

The walls return to their gloomy slate color – I check each one to be sure. I don't have to squeeze my eyes or blink hard. The tears fall and fall, catching in a pool inside my goggles.

I am alone.

Hundreds of seven-year-old sublings from the region crowd together at the check-in line by the transport tunnel. All of the girls wear the same blouse and skirt, and all have various shades of albino-light hair grown to the standard shoulder-length. The hatted boys wear pants made with the same tweed material as our skirts, and collared shirts to match our blouses. We make up an army of tiny soldiers, marching off to fulfill our civic duty – to learn as much as possible so that we may embark on a sustainable trade when we graduate from the Burrows at the age of twenty. Or die trying.

The din of children shuffling and buzzing about calms me; I'm able to stay camouflaged in the center of it all. I scan the floor, hoping to discover an errant cap to cover my short, nonstandard hair. The Grand Na'rm told me not to worry, that it would grow by the time I graduated the Sublery. It didn't.

"What's wrong with you?" asks a tall boy with sunken eyes, four people in front of me in the queue. He carries a gallon-sized cage with a mouse in his left hand, and his right arm must be broken as it's covered with a wire-mesh cast.

There are many things wrong with me. Where shall I start? I'm forever unloved. My new medera must certainly already hate me because of the report from my na'rm. I can't possibly blend in because of my goggles and patchy hair. People will always detest me, and maybe I deserve it because I'm wicked whenever I'm angry, and I'm prone to anger whenever someone points out how I'm different. Like now. Always.

Before I can figure out how to respond, a transport tech spins him the other way, mumbling, "You're next."

I flatten the wrinkles in my skirt with my hands. All the other sublings probably know the difference between red and purple and green – no one else wears goggles, and they all have a favorite color.

When it's my turn, a travel tech scans my finger and then reads my identification number from his tablet. A machine begins to hum and whine, inscribing my data onto a shiny bracelet. "Terminal six. Your magnetran leaves in twenty minutes." He affixes the band onto my wrist and hands me a white fabric travelmask to go over my nose and mouth. "Good health."

I'm pushed forward and away. Finding my way to terminal six, I soon discover the perfect spot – just behind a wooden crate with giant letters spelling out *CAUTION*.

The boy with the broken arm and the caged mouse stares at me from the front of the terminal. I tighten my fingers around my satchel as he snakes his way through the crowd of children, edging closer. When he makes it to my side I pretend not to notice, studying the new scuff in my bootstrap. I do notice him, of course. His giant shadow could swallow me whole. *You're this size because you didn't grow when you were supposed to*, Na'rm Anetta exclaimed a year ago.

The boy's eyes continue to scour over me, so I inch my right foot to the side, and then my left, hoping I can shrink further behind the crate.

"You're a curious case," he says a little too loudly, and a few siblings turn our way. He'd never have survived Na'rm Anetta. "It's okay. I'm a scientist." He holds up his mouse as if it proves his claim. "Genetics are surely at the bottom of your – err – uncommon features." He doesn't seem to know when to stop talking.

My cheeks flame and I close my eyes. *He isn't here, he isn't here, he isn't here.*

He jabs two fingers from his casted arm like a sword into my ribs, singing, "*Touché!*"

"Ow!"

He laughs and lunges like he'll do it again, so I jump.

"I'm just playing. You're old enough for the Burrows, then?"

Without lifting my head, I hold up my bracelet. "Seven point seven years old."

He checks his own wristband, which only lists his date of birth. Seven point nine years if he wants to know, but he doesn't ask. Instead, he smiles like I've divulged the secrets of the universe.

"Ah – intelligence on top of your odd features. That's why you've been sent to Cayan. I'll bet someone messed with your genetic coding. You've barely any hair." He reaches out and flicks a tuft on top of my head.

"Clearly I have some if you can touch it. Please don't."

A girl I've never met turns around, and my muscles tense, ready for her to join in. But instead, she glares at him. "You're a rude, miserable subling. Leave her be." The rims of her eyelids are swollen, and her hair shines like silk. Her nurserymaid probably sang a lullaby too slowly before walking her to the travel tunnel.

"You've got to admit she's an interesting specimen with those glasses." He touches his cleft chin. "I'd bet she's nearly blind."

Wickedness fires up inside me, and I move away from the shelter of the crate. "These aren't glasses, you bumbling chunk of flesh!"

"Okay." He makes the peace-sign with his hand. At first, I think he's apologizing and say nothing. But he continues, "It's an experiment. How many fingers am I holding up?"

As the heat rises to my cheeks, I know without a doubt that I hate-hate-*hate* scientists. I shove him as hard as I can.

He grabs my arm and raises his mouse up high in the air. "Woah, a fast temper, too. You must be more careful before someone breaks."

The girl beside us lets out a screech and karate-chops me free from his grip. I lose my balance from the force of it and topple to the ground. My palms slap onto the cold marble floor. Our commotion has drawn the attention of all the children in our terminal. I want to stay down – to never get up, at least not until everyone stops watching.

A whack resonates over my head, and I pull my shoulders in.

When I finally look up, the girl is standing nose-to-nose with the boy, who is now rubbing his cheek. She presses her fingers into his chest, even though she's a few inches shorter than he is. "Mind your manners, lest you want someone to mind them for you. Is this how your nurserymaid taught you?" Her eyes shimmer like fire, and he shrinks away from her.

For a moment, I consider doing the same.

But she reaches down and yanks me from the ground. Lacing her arm in mine, she holds her head high and walks me to the edge of the platform near the metal grate. "I despise hateful people." She motions to my satchel. "What did you bring?"

"It's the book my na'rm wouldn't allow me to read while I was at the Sublery. She said it would inspire my mischievous side. I plan to read it on the magnetran." I rub my stinging palms together. "He's half right, though. I'm blinded by light, but I can see perfectly fine with these goggles because they block most of the rays. Except I can't make out colors – just white, black, and lots of gray."

She checks my hands, and rubs them for me, keeping one arm wrapped in mine. "It's okay. He's not worth an ounce of his own fuss."

I crane my neck to search for him, but thankfully, he's disappeared into the crowd.

"I'm scheduled on the next tran to the Cayan Burrow," the girl says, showing me the data on her bracelet. She's a month older than I am.

"Why?" I examine her up and down. She's grown to a good height, her hair falls to her shoulders, with no signs of sickness or ailment whatsoever. "I don't see anything wrong with you."

She drops my arm. "That's because there *is* nothing wrong with me." Her voice falls flat as one of her eyebrows arches high on her forehead. I've insulted her without even trying to, but I refuse to give up on having a friend.

"I'm going there, too," I whisper, grabbing the tube of emergency serum hanging from a chain on my neck, hidden under my blouse. "My na'rm said that Cayan is the poorest of all the burrows and only the sickliest, most disabled children go there. She said even with a full-time medtech, a good portion of Cayan burrowlings die before they graduate."

The girl gasps. "What a horrific thing to say. *My* na'rm said only the kindliest and most intelligent children go there. As in, off-the-charts intelligent." She blinks quickly, like it's settled.

Could Na'rm Anetta have lied to me?

The girl puts her arm in mine again and smiles. She's connecting with me – she doesn't mind the goggles. Even if it turns out I'm not good enough for Medera Gelia, this girl will be with me at Cayan. I smile so hard the muscles in my face hurt from the abnormal stretching, and it makes me want to giggle.

A bell clangs and the lights flicker, warning us to step behind the line. The flash reflects off a chain around the girl's neck, causing a sharp glare. I press my lids shut as a stabbing pain hits in the center of my eyes. The sharpness moves to the center of my head, and I keep them shut until the flickering stops. My new friend's neckchain mirrors mine, which means she has fatal allergies too. I tighten my grip on her arm. For her, I will pretend that the Cayan Burrow is packed with the most promising, intelligent children. After today, it will have at least two.

"I hear we're allowed to name ourselves once we know our calling," she says. "Medera Gelia Cayan may be old with hundreds of hairbeads, but I think that makes her all the cleverer, don't you?"

I nod as if I already knew these things.

Our magnetran blasts its way into the station underneath the grated edge of the platform, and the warm gust makes our bell-shaped skirts fan out. My friend's eyelids flutter and she buries her head into my shoulder. Her hair whips about, stinging my cheeks and forehead, and I can't remember ever being so content.

"My na'rm said that I'd save the world someday," she shouts over the squealing of the magnetran brakes while she pulls her travelmask over her mouth and nose. "I'm glad you'll be there to save it with me."

For more great title recommendations, check out the Angry Robot website and social channels

www.angryrobotbooks.com
@angryrobotbooks

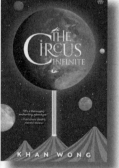